FLASH OF DEATH

BY
CINDY DEES

MILLS & BOON

First published in Great Britain 2013
by Mills & Boon, an imprint of Harlequin (UK) Limited,
Eton House, 18-24 Paradise Road, Richmond, Surrey TW9 1SR

© Cynthia Dees 2012

ISBN: 978 0 263 90345 4
ebook ISBN: 978 1 472 00694 3

46-0213

Harlequin (UK) policy is to use papers that are natural, renewable and recyclable products and made from wood grown in sustainable forests. The logging and manufacturing processes conform to the legal environmental regulations of the country of origin.

Printed and bound in Spain
by Blackprint CPI, Barcelona

Cindy Dees started flying airplanes while sitting in her dad's lap at the age of three and got a pilot's license before she got a driver's license. At age fifteen, she dropped out of high school and left the horse farm in Michigan where she grew up to attend the University of Michigan. After earning a degree in Russian and East European studies, she joined the US Air Force and became the youngest female pilot in its history. She flew supersonic jets, VIP airlift and the C-5 Galaxy, the world's largest airplane. During her military career, she traveled to forty countries on five continents, was detained by the KGB and East German secret police, got shot at, flew in the first Gulf War and amassed a lifetime's worth of war stories.

Her hobbies include medieval re-enacting, professional Middle Eastern dancing and Japanese gardening.

This RITA® Award-winning author's first book was published in 2002 and since then she has published more than twenty-five bestselling and award-winning novels. She loves to hear from readers and can be contacted at www.cindydees.com.

Kathy, you keep me sane even when I accept insane deadlines. Thanks for everything. You're the best!

Chapter 1

Chloe Jordan knew one thing: the combination of turning thirty and being one of the only single women at her little sister's wedding was thoroughly depressing—expensive-chocolate-and-cheap-wine-binge depressing. The hell of it was that she, as the maid of honor, emphasis on *maid, old* maid, had an ironclad obligation to be the life of the party. No matter how much she loved her little sis, this night officially sucked.

A chorus of spoons knocking on glasses startled her out of her momentary slip into melancholy. Shouts of laughter went up as the groom laid a smoking-hot kiss on the bride. *Sheesh. Somebody throw a bucket of ice water on those two.*

Chloe checked her bitterness. Sunny'd had a really crappy run of luck and deserved all the happiness she could get. The lucky groom, Aiden, obviously loved Sunny fiercely. Next up on her personal hit parade of depressing events was bound to be playing indulgent auntie to their perfect children. Yippee.

The band resumed playing too loudly to talk over, and thankfully a mob of guests piled out of their seats, relieving her of any duty to go out onto a painfully empty dance floor and "get things started."

It didn't help her mood that she'd had a little too much champagne and was starting to feel a little weepy. Sunny was so beautiful and radiant, and she was so proud of her little sis. Chloe noticed from her seat jammed in the corner that it had started raining outside.

One of the groomsmen got the bright idea to light up a cigar, and furthermore, to pass out cigars to all the other groomsmen. A cloud of noxious blue smoke enveloped her. Her stomach roiled ominously.

Enough was enough. She took her queasy stomach and crazy mood swings and fled the reception in search of fresh air. She burst out of the private club that was one of Denver's most exclusive addresses and inhaled deeply. But even the rain wouldn't give her a break and the skies opened up without warning. Her hotel was right across the street and she ran for it, racing down the club's wide steps. Streetlights glittered off the wet pavement as she dashed between cars.

She never saw it coming.

A big, dark SUV accelerated toward her out of nowhere, its engine growling hungrily as it shot forward. Its headlights were blinding and she stared into them in shock.

The impact was incredible, knocking her completely off her feet and sending her flying through space splayed out on her back. Something powerful wrapped around her torso, yanking her in a midair one-eighty so she landed on her stomach. She slammed into something…

…and didn't die horribly. Whatever she'd smashed into

had definitely been hard but not nearly as unyielding as concrete. Her breath was knocked clean out of her, though, and she gasped frantically to no avail. Disoriented, she stared down at the man lying beneath her. Had she been thrown into him and knocked him down?

An engine revved and tires squealed behind her. She looked up in time to see a black, shiny, wet SUV disappear around a corner at a high speed.

She'd nearly died. And the man lying so still beneath her had probably saved her life by breaking her fall. Had she *killed* him? All of a sudden, she was able to breathe again. She sucked in a sobbing breath and rolled off of the man.

"Are you okay?" she asked urgently.

His eyes blinked open, and silver eyes stared up at her, laser-intense. Eyes she recognized. Ohmigosh. He was one of Aiden's groomsmen. Trenton something. Hollings. That was it. She'd heard some of the other guys call him Trent.

"I'll live," he rasped. "You?"

"I'm fine. You broke my fall. I'm so sorry—"

He cut her off. "No need to apologize. Who was in that car?"

"I don't know. I didn't see anything, and then those headlights were coming at me. I guess the SUV hit me and sent me flying into you."

"Actually," he murmured, sitting up carefully, his dark hair tousled and sexy, "I'm the only thing that hit you. I knocked you out of the car's way at the last second. Had that SUV hit you, something that heavy moving that fast would have killed you instantly."

She stared, stunned anew. He really *had* saved her life. For a man who'd just been knocked flat by a human-sized flying object, he popped to his feet with a speed and grace that shocked her. A hand materialized in front of her eyes.

It was big and tanned and calloused in stark contrast to the pristinely starched white cuff and onyx cufflink above it.

She took his hand and floated to her feet.

"Are you sure you're all right?" he asked, his voice deep. Rough with concern.

She looked down at her red silk gown ruefully. The side seam had torn from the hem almost all the way to her hip. Her slender leg was entirely exposed. "I'm fine. But I can't say the same for my dress."

He looked down critically. "I like it better like this. A woman with legs like yours should show them off."

Her startled gaze lifted to his, and he smiled at her. But not just any smile, rather a sizzling hot one that promised a long night of steamy seduction if she was interested. She about fell off her three-inch stilettos in shock. Trenton Hollings was flirting with her? The hottest groomsman out of a whole batch of ridiculously hot men? No way.

He offered her his forearm, and she looped her hand around it in minor shock. The hard muscles beneath the soft Italian wool contracted sharply. "Ready to try crossing the street again?" he murmured.

"I swear, I looked both ways. I never saw that car coming. One second the street was clear, and the next, there it was, running me down."

Trent nodded, frowning. "I believe you." His frown deepened as they stepped gingerly back out into the wide boulevard. They managed to cross to the other side of the street without incident, although her escort did pause as they reached the far curb to take a long look back over his shoulder at the scene of her near miss.

"What's on your mind?" she asked cautiously.

Her words seemed to jolt him out of his reverie and he gave himself a little shake. "Getting you up to your room in one piece and cleaned up is on my mind."

She looked down at herself in alarm. Just how bad did she look? As if it mattered. She was darned lucky just to be alive, for goodness' sake. They stepped into a hotel elevator, and in the small, enclosed space, her tall escort dwarfed her. She was not short herself at five foot seven, plus three inches of heels, but he still had several inches on her. He was muscular without being thick. His shoulders filled out his tuxedo nicely, and well-defined biceps flexed within his sleeves. No wonder the impact of him slamming into her had knocked her halfway across the street.

"Do you save women from being run down a lot?" she asked to fill the silence.

His mouth twitched in humor. "Not often."

"What do you do when you're not doing that?"

He shrugged. "I'm a bum."

She blinked, startled. "You clean up pretty well for a bum."

A full-fledged grin flashed her way, all but knocking her off her feet again. Nobody got teeth that perfect and white without expensive orthodontic work. And that tuxedo was no rental monkey suit. It was cashmere with Italian lines exquisitely tailored to his athletic physique. Not to mention Sunny'd told her how wealthy and successful all of Aiden's groomsmen were, not so subtly hinting that Chloe should pick one and go for the gusto. The guys had all gone to college together, apparently. Frat brothers, in fact. And most of them worked with billionaire Jeff Winston at Winston Enterprises. Bum. Right.

"Tell me another lie," she murmured.

"You're ugly and not the slightest bit sexy."

Her gaze snapped to his. "Excuse me?"

"You asked for a lie."

Before she could think up a snappy comeback the elevator door opened and he reached an arm out to hold it open. His free hand came to rest lightly in the middle of her back as he shepherded her out. She felt surrounded by him, and it was the strangest sensation. Maybe it was because she was with men so rarely, or maybe it was because he was so freaking hot, but either way, her breath shortened disconcertingly.

As she exited the elevator, her heel caught in the door's track and stuck momentarily, pitching her off balance. Instantly, Trent's strong hand was on her elbow, steadying her. "I'm such a klutz," she mumbled.

"Good thing for you I'm not," he replied wryly.

She started down the hallway toward the snazzy suite Aiden had insisted on paying for. Chloe wasn't penniless anymore, but she surely wouldn't have wasted so much money on an extravagant hotel room that, outside of sleeping and showering, she'd spent about five minutes awake in each day.

She glanced sidelong at Trent. "Are you one of those athletic people who always manage to land on their feet and make the rest of us mere mortals look silly?"

He shrugged modestly.

She sighed. "That's what I thought." As she fumbled with her room's key card, he lifted it from her shaking fingers. Wow. That near miss with the SUV must have rattled her worse than she'd realized.

"Let me get that." He reached past her to open the door and then did a strange thing. He put a restraining hand on her arm. "Wait here."

She frowned as he disappeared into the dark suite. He was back in a minute, flipping on light switches as he came. What was that all about?

"What are you standing out here for?" he asked.

"You told me to—" She broke off as she caught the

glint of humor in his silver eyes. Dry sense of humor this guy had.

She followed him into the suite.

"When did you get into town?" he asked as he moved over to the picture windows and inexplicably pulled the blinds closed on a magnificent view of Denver's night lights glittering in the rain.

"Three days ago."

His brows flickered. "And you haven't had time to unpack?"

She glanced around the suite, startled. "I am unpacked. Clothes in the closet, toothbrush in the bathroom."

"Jeez. The room doesn't even look occupied. Are you always this...neat?"

"Well, yes." There was nothing wrong with order. It made life infinitely easier. She could always lay hands on exactly what she wanted when she wanted it.

"And what do you do for a living, Chloe?"

She winced at his question. She'd give anything to do something exotic and sexy that would impress this man. But she was who she was. She sighed and answered reluctantly, "I'm a forensic accountant."

"What does that mean? You do dead people's taxes?"

She smiled. "No. It means I take apart companies' books and find the discrepancies they may or may not be trying to hide."

"You're some sort of auditor, then?"

"Not exactly. Forensic accountants are used mostly in criminal investigations to find the money trail."

"Who do you work for?" Trent asked.

"I'm a freelance consultant at the moment."

"Sounds...interesting."

She laughed. "About as interesting as watching grass

grow, right? Actually, I find the work fascinating. But I don't expect other people to get it."

He wandered around the suite examining every detail, and although she enjoyed the view of him from so many angles, she was eventually prompted to ask, "Are you always so restless?"

"Hmm, what? Oh. Yes."

"And what do you do for a living?"

"Nothing."

She frowned. "How do you support yourself, then?"

He stopped roaming and turned to face her in surprise. "You mean you can't smell the trust fund at a hundred yards? I thought all women could do that."

"Sorry. Not me." Trust fund, huh? Big enough that he didn't have to work at all? Must be nice.

He resumed roaming, poking around behind the bar. "Aha!" he crowed. He turned around with a bottle of whiskey in hand. She recognized the label vaguely as an expensive single-malt variety.

"So, how do you fill your time if you don't work?" she asked curiously. She'd put in sixty- and eighty-hour weeks for so long, juggling bookkeeping jobs and school while she got her accounting degree and master's in forensic accounting she couldn't imagine doing anything else.

He set two shot glasses side by side on the wet bar and poured generous shots of amber liquid into each. He looked up at her and grinned. "I play for a living."

Play? She couldn't ever remember a time when she'd done that. Maybe when her folks were still alive. But even then, her hippie parents had been such flakes about money that she'd ended up taking over the family finances before she'd turned ten. She'd always been more of an adult than anyone else in the Jordan clan. And when her parents died in a boating accident halfway around the world from her and Sunny, orphaning them at ages thirteen and ten respectively, she'd grown up for real. Fast.

Trent thrust a shot glass at her and, startled out of her grim thoughts, she took it.

"Drink up. You need it."

She frowned down at the whiskey.

"You had a bad shock and your nerves are fried. Think of it as medicine," he coaxed.

Mentally holding her nose, she lifted the shot glass and tossed down the shot of whiskey in a single gulp. Fire exploded in her throat and roared down into her belly. She coughed and swore as tears streamed down her face. Trent, the cad, laughed as she mopped at her eyes.

He neatly downed his own shot and went back to the bar for refills. When he came back with another shot glass for her, she waved it off.

"Second time, it goes down as smooth as silk. I promise."

She snorted. "That's because every nerve in my digestive track is incinerated at the moment."

He smiled winningly. "Exactly."

"I shouldn't. I've already had too much champagne—" she started.

He cut her off gently. "Don't overthink it. Just trust me. You need this."

She *did* have a tendency to talk herself out of everything fun in life. And she was safely in her hotel room with a man her sister swore was a great guy. That pleasant, warm feeling spreading outward from her belly button really was very nice, too. She took the second shot and slammed it back before she could change her mind.

This time it made her feel light-headed. A little silly, even. Just what the doctor ordered.

"Another?" Trent asked.

"Are you trying to get me drunk, sir?"

He grinned unrepentantly. "I am."

"Why?" she blurted. Whoops. She hadn't meant to say that out loud, but it just slipped out all by itself.

He answered, "You've looked uptight all day long."

"I am not uptight!"

"Honey, if you were wound too much tighter, you'd snap in two."

Okay, she was starting to feel a little dizzy. But nice dizzy. Like she wanted to throw her arms out and dance to the sensation.

"Why don't we get you out of those shoes?" Trent murmured, guiding her over to the edge of her bed and sitting her down on it. He knelt at her feet, sliding his big hand down the back of her calf with sensual leisure. "I never have been able to understand why women wear these things. They look blasted uncomfortable."

He tossed one red shoe over his shoulder and she giggled as she wiggled her toes. "But heels make our legs look so nice," she explained earnestly.

"You don't need any help to make your legs look great," he announced as the other red stiletto went flying.

She stood up and hiked up her torn skirt enough to reach under it. It occurred to her in a distant corner of her mind that she would never, under normal circumstances, do something as intimate as take off her hose in front of a man like this. She stated, "Now if you want to know what's really uncomfortable and stupid in women's fashion, it's panty hose."

She started to peel hers down, but then warm, strong hands were there, pushing her fingers aside.

"Let me get those for you." His hands were a warm slide down her thighs, leaving a trail of wanton destruction in their wake. As her legs positively wobbled, she grabbed his shoulders to steady herself. She lifted first one foot and then the other so he could remove her hose.

"I say we outlaw panty hose," he declared as hers went flying over his shoulder.

She laughed gaily. "I second the motion."

"Turn around," he instructed.

She did so and was startled to feel her gown's long zipper sliding down. Cool air caressed her back. Warm hands kneaded her shoulders and she let her head fall forward with a groan of pleasure. His clever fingers went right to the massive knot that perennially twisted at the base of her neck.

"Are you always this tense?" he asked. His voice was smooth and deep and warmed her from the outside the same way the whiskey warmed her from the inside.

"Pretty much," she answered honestly.

"Do you need me to do something about it?"

He already was. The knot was unraveling beneath his fingers like magic. And then his clever plan dawned on her. She craned her head around to look at him over her shoulder. "Are you seducing me?"

"Would you like me to?"

"Well, duh. You're a complete hunk. But me? What would a guy like you see in a girl like me?"

He laughed softly. "Have you looked at yourself in a mirror? You're a knockout. Not too many women can pull off sophisticated and pure-as-the-driven-snow in the same look." He ticked off her additional attributes with his fingers against the side of her neck. "You make me laugh. And you're smart or you wouldn't be a forensic accountant. And you have a kind heart or you wouldn't have suffered through your sister's wedding with a smile on your face all day."

"I didn't suffer—"

"Sure you did. Anyone who really looked at you could see it in your eyes. The way I hear it, you practically raised her. She's your only family and she's starting a new life with someone else. No matter how much you love her, that has to hurt. Has to make you feel all alone in the world."

What a perceptive man to have noticed. And he must have a pretty kind heart himself to be here comforting her like this. "You're right, of course," she murmured. As the truth of his words sank in, a knife of grief and loss stabbed at her heart. She'd faced terrible loss in her life, agonizing loneliness. But this was right up there. *Oh, Sunny. I'm gonna miss you so much.* Tears sprang to her eyes.

She started to turn around to face Trent, but his big hands forestalled her. And then something warm and resilient moved against her neck where it joined her shoulder.

"You're not alone, tonight," he murmured against her skin.

Desperate need for that to be true had her leaning back toward him, her whole being reaching out toward the solace he offered. Just once in her life, she would love for someone to be strong for her, to take care of her. His hands moved slowly across her stomach, easing her back against him even more closely as if he was telling her to lean on him. But if his hands were there, what was that touching her neck?

His mouth! As realization dawned, a host of delicious sensations ripped through her, radiating outward from where his lips moved across her skin. Languor and lust rolled through her, making a beeline for her knees and threatening to collapse them. Whiskey, thy name is temptation.

Was she seriously going to do this? Trent Hollings? The bachelor every female at the wedding had been throwing herself at? Of course, he'd been the one to throw himself at her. Literally.

"Tell me again not to overthink this," she muttered.

He turned her around then, his hands unerringly finding every hairpin and tossing them aside. He plunged both hands into her thick, blond hair and pulled the French twist down around her shoulders in lush waves. Her hair was her secret pride, and she was glad he could see it like this. She never wore it down in her daily life. In her career field, she needed people to take her seriously and not treat her like some kind of sex kitten. But tonight, she was okay with that. If Trent Hollings thought she was hot, she was darned well not about to talk him out of it.

"Mmm. Better," he murmured. "I've been itching to do that all day."

"Really?"

He took her face in his big hands and tilted it up to his. "Really."

She tensed as his head lowered toward hers. He paused, his mouth inches from hers, and breathed, "Don't overthink this."

Right. Live in the moment. Go for it. *Carpe diem.* His lips touched hers and the platitudes fled in the face of this stunningly sexy man kissing her. His mouth was warm and smooth and confident, and in about ten seconds, he'd blasted past all her experience in kissing. His lips parted hers and his tongue tested her teeth. She gasped at the invasion and he took immediate advantage of it to taste her more deeply.

His arms tightened around her, lifting her against his big, warm body. A hand slid up her back to her head, cradling it in a large palm and drawing her even further into the kiss. And then he was kissing her with his whole body. Whether that was him moving against her or her

moving against him she couldn't tell and didn't care. Her
dress gaped open in the back and his hand burned her bare
flesh as it dipped inside the gown. She was shocked when
his hand slid down to cup her derriere and… Oh, God,
she'd forgotten she was wearing that silly thong Sunny'd
talked her into. Something about panty lines ruining the
lie of the gown.

He made a sound of surprised approval.

"What?" she blurted.

"I didn't peg you for a naughty-lingerie kind of girl."

Painfully aware of the drawer full of cotton granny
panties across the room, she didn't disabuse him of the
notion. For the first time all day, she was grateful for the
tiny scrap of spandex and lace nestled a little too intimately
in her nether regions. Trent's finger traced the thin line
of the thong downward and she groaned in pleasure and
embarrassment.

"You're overthinking," he warned laughingly. "Let go
and enjoy yourself."

Her knees did buckle then. He caught her up against
him with ease and kissed her with gusto until her knees
would bear her weight again. "Ahh, you're going to be a joy
to seduce. So artless. So natural. Such a nice young lady."

"Is that bad?" she asked, frowning up at two of him
swimming in her gaze. She did believe she was officially
buzzed.

"Not at all." His fingers slipped under the shoulders of
the lined gown with its built-in shelf bra. Which meant she
wasn't wearing a blessed thing under the gown. Except
that sexy little black thong, of course. He hooked the red
silk and slipped it off her shoulders, kissing her skin as it
was revealed. The gown whispered down her body to the
floor in a bloodred puddle and she shivered. Whether it

was the cool air on her skin or Trent's hot mouth on her skin that caused it, she couldn't say.

"You're magnificent, Chloe. How is it some man hasn't snatched you up and made you his?"

She blinked up at Trent as he straightened and shrugged off his tuxedo jacket. Nope, no padding in them there shoulders. His starched, white shirt clung to a physique that could make a girl weep with appreciation. Realizing belatedly that she was all but drooling at him, she answered, enunciating carefully so she wouldn't slur her words, "I'm too boring. And neat. Men hate neat."

Trent laughed as he stripped off his cummerbund and tossed it aside. "That's not how I hear it. Most men love a woman who'll pick up after them. When I settle down, I'll hire a butler to do the job. It'll save on resentment from the ladies in my life."

Ladies. Plural. Of course a man like him had scads of women chasing after him. "I'm just one more in a long string of conquests, aren't I?" she accused. Who knew whiskey brought out such a brutally honest streak in her?

He laughed lightly. "Never. You're one of a kind, Chloe Jordan."

At least he knew her full name. The way she heard it, that was an exception for most pick-up artists. For surely, this man was a master of the art. And yet, she couldn't bring herself to care as his hands slid over her ribs and cupped her breasts, lifting them and testing their weight. She wasn't all that stacked, although she'd always privately thought her breasts were rather nicely shaped. Trent seemed to think so, too, as his mouth captured one pert, rosy peak and sucked gently. Lightning bolts started at his mouth and spread outward through her body.

"Oh, my," she sighed. "That's lovely."

A strong arm swept behind her knees and she was

Flash of Death

tipped on her side all of a sudden as he picked her up and laid her on the bed. The down comforter gave beneath her weight, and the room spun lightly around her. And then Trent was there, stretched out beside her, propped up on one elbow, yanking the knot out of his bow tie with his free hand. Shirt studs went flying as he jerked his shirt free of his trousers and all but tore it off.

She reached up to help push the shirt off his shoulders and gaped as acres of tanned chest appeared before her eyes. "Yowza," she breathed.

He laughed heartily and she glared up at him. "Are you laughing at me?" she demanded.

"Yes, I am. It has been a while since I've gotten that sort of reaction out of a woman from taking off my shirt."

"Do you only date blind women?" she retorted.

He leaned close to kiss her lightly before answering, "No. Jaded ones. Like I said, you're one of a kind."

"Hey. I didn't fall off the pumpkin truck yesterday, you know. I live in San Francisco and work at a very up-scale address. Of course, I'm going to take that company down, but—"

He stopped her rambling with his mouth against hers. She wasn't sure how he got his trousers off or how the covers got thrown back, but in a moment, she was lying on her back on Egyptian cotton sheets with a thread count so high they felt like velvet against her skin, and Trent was stretched out in all his naked, unconcerned glory beside her.

"Please tell me you're a little bit drunk, too," she muttered.

He grinned, flashing that million-dollar smile at her again. "I'm drunk on you, baby."

She rolled her eyes and he laughed back at her. He really was incorrigible. But then the smile faded from his eyes, leaving them a dark, smoky gray that pierced through her whiskey-induced fog like high-beam headlights. All of a sudden, heat radiated from him. A promise of sex so steamy it would burn away all the fog and bring the night down around them.

Her breath caught on a gasp as, without breaking his gaze into her eyes, his hand traveled down the valley between her breasts, across the flat plane of her belly, and hooked inside the thong that was her only remaining defense. His fingers slid across soft flesh that was so sensitive she thought she was going to come apart this very second.

And then his fingers dipped lower, sliding across strangely swollen flesh that raged with lust in response to his touch. "Whoa!" she exclaimed.

He froze against her. "What's wrong?"

"Nothing's wrong!"

"Then why did you yell for me to stop?" he asked cautiously.

It took her whiskey-fuzzed brain a moment to sort that one out. Then she blurted, "Oh. I get it. No. I was reacting to how great that felt. You know. As in, whoa, that's awesome, dude."

He burst out laughing. "So you don't want me to stop?"

"No!"

"You have no idea how glad I am to hear that," he murmured. For a second time, the humor fled from his gaze, leaving behind a raw, sexual hunger in his eyes that completely undid her. Men never looked at her like that. And certainly not men like him.

He whisked the thong off her and it joined her other clothes somewhere across the room. And then he did that surrounding her thing again, all muscle and heat and impatient man. The room spun more wildly now. Where the whiskey stopped and the intoxication of this man making love to her took over, she couldn't rightly say. It was a heady cocktail, though.

His muscular thigh nudged hers apart and she tensed. He stared down at her as if waiting for her to say something.

"I'm overthinking again, aren't I?" she mumbled.

"Relax. Enjoy. Let go."

His voice was so darned seductive. It was so easy to sink into the pleasure of the moment, to lose herself in the whirling lights and giddy lust dancing around her and in her.

His other thigh joined the first one, and he levered her legs wide apart. This time she arched toward him with a soft cry of need. If she was going to do this, then by golly, she was really going to go for it. She flung caution to the wind and launched herself toward him. He caught her up against his shockingly hard body and kissed her deeply. And then he took her. There wasn't another word for it. He invaded boldly, filling her to the point of delicious discomfort, and then he made her his. Fast then slow, gently and then with driving force, he made love to her.

When she would have closed her eyes, embarrassed over how wantonly she was throwing herself at him, he wouldn't stand for it and made her open her eyes to look at him. When she would have shrunk away from the hoarse cries of pleasure torn from her own throat, he kissed her until she gave those cries to him. And when he drove her to release a second and even a third time, he ripped away any last vestiges of inhibition she might have clung to, with the sheer excess of pleasure he gave her.

Her entire being was raw and exposed to him. He played her body and soul like the master artist he was before he finally joined her in one last, shattering climax. It tore his name from her throat on a primal note she'd never sung before. It was, in a word, magnificent. And better yet, she wasn't alone.

He collapsed beside her on the now-damp sheets, breathing heavily. She rolled over and pushed up on his chest to stare down at him, and that was when the full broadside of the whiskey hit her. Dizzy and reckless, she retained just enough reason to know this was a once-in-a-lifetime opportunity for a girl like her. One not to be missed.

"If I let you rest a little, do you think we could do that again?" she asked.

A broad grin spread across his face.

She added hastily, "Well, not that exactly. There's something else I've always wanted to try…"

"Do tell. What does a nice girl like you think about alone in the deep of night?"

And in her whiskey-induced honesty, she told him. Every lurid, naughty detail of every lurid, naughty fantasy she'd ever had. By the time she was finished, his eyes blazed with desire and his body was obviously more than eager to play along.

"I don't think we can get to all of that tonight, Chloe, but we can definitely make a dent in your list." He rolled out of bed and fetched her discarded panty hose. With quick efficiency, he tied her wrists together and then to the headboard and knelt between her knees, his eyes burning with dark fire.

"Let's see just how far you're willing to go, my nice, normal little accountant."

Chapter 2

Trent slipped out of the hotel's delivery entrance in the last dark before dawn. He couldn't sleep anyway, and there was no sense humiliating Chloe by strolling out through the hotel lobby in his rumpled tuxedo for all the staff to see.

Normally, he would've spent the night in her bed and enjoyed a morning-after brunch with her, but he had a hunch that, after last night, she'd just as soon wake up alone. For one thing, she was going to have a hell of a hangover. And, if she was telling the truth and had never done any of the things they'd done together last night, he'd lay odds she was going to suffer a rather large dose of morning-after embarrassment. He hadn't been kidding when he called her a nice girl.

Who'd have guessed such a prim-and-proper lady would be such a wildcat after a few shots of whiskey? She'd pushed even a few of his sexual boundaries last night, and that was saying something. He'd spent most of his post-pubescent life enjoying the favors of beautiful women. But he'd never met one quite like Chloe Jordan, all sweet and virginal in public, and jaw-droppingly *not* virginal in private.

He crossed the street, stopping at the spot where the SUV had nearly run her down last night. As he'd thought. Not a skid mark in sight. That vehicle had *accelerated* toward her. Now why would anyone be out to hurt an uptight accountant who lived and worked half a continent away?

And more importantly, who would want to kill her?

Frowning, he returned to his own suite in the men's club where the wedding had been held. His family owned the apartment, and he used it when he was in town. As its dark wood, leather and Ralph Lauren décor surrounded him, he breathed in the easy, old-world elegance with guilty pleasure. Most of the time he shunned the trappings of his family's wealth. He was much more likely to be found in a shack on a beach, waxing a surfboard than lounging in high-end men's clubs. And frankly, he was more at ease in the shack. People were more real there. Had a better sense of what really mattered in life.

Being diagnosed with his illness in his second year of college had put everything in perspective for him. Life was too short to waste doing things or being around people who made him crazy.

But he had to admit, this condo's luxury was nice once in a while.

He took a six-jet steam shower to work out the worst of the kinks from last night's athletics with Chloe, and shaved and dressed quickly. Then he sat down at the walnut desk in the corner and made a phone call to Winston Ops.

It was the headquarters of a private, corporate intelligence network for all of the many Winston Enterprises companies around the world. The duty controller, a computer genius named Novak from somewhere in eastern Europe, took his call.

"Trent Hollings, here. I need you to run a quick background check for me on Chloe Jordan."

"Sunny's sister?" Novak asked, surprised.

"I think someone tried to kill her last night."

"Are you serious?" Novak exclaimed.

"As a heart attack."

The duty controller instantly shifted into all-business mode. "Got it. So, we're looking for enemies in her life." Trent heard clacking keys in the background as Novak typed furiously. "How was the wedding?"

"Great party," Trent answered. "Can't remember the last time I saw Aiden so happy. He's a lucky man."

"Maybe you should find yourself a nice girl and settle down, too."

He laughed. "Not me. I'll never slow down enough for any girl to catch me."

"When you least expect it, one's gonna come along and trip you all up, buddy."

Visions of a blonde accountant blowing his mind in bed flashed through his head. "Nah," Trent replied. "Not me. It's not like I can give any girl a life evenly faintly resembling normal." Hell, he couldn't even promise to give a girl children. With his inherited disorder, careful genetic counseling would be necessary to ensure that his condition—spinal muscular atrophy—wasn't passed on to his offspring.

"Okay, Trent. I've got a preliminary report on our girl. She's a certified public accountant. Just finished a master's degree in forensic accounting. Company called Paradeo filed a W-2 on her about six months ago. But they're an investment firm, not forensic accountants."

She'd said she was freelancing. And there'd been that reference to taking a company down. Must be investigating her employer for someone else. "Where's this Paradeo company headquartered?"

"San Francisco. No satellite offices. Anything else you need to know right away, Trent?"

"Do you see anything at a glance that could explain someone trying to run her down in a large SUV?"

"Other than some rich, pissed-off CEO she might have put in jail? Nope. You don't suppose it has anything to with Code X, do you?" Novak asked.

The controller's question made Trent's blood run cold. That was the one place he'd been mentally avoiding going this morning. He'd known it would give him exactly the headache he felt coming on. "I don't know. Keep digging and let's see what you come up with before we go there."

"Roger. I'm on it."

Trent paced the spacious room restlessly. He never had been able to sit still even before he'd accepted the experimental stem cell therapies that were both his miracle cure and the heart of the Code X project. Toss in a liberal dose of stress and worry now, and he could forget sitting down, let alone being still. He changed out of the clothes he'd donned only minutes before and into running gear. It was early enough that he should be able to stretch his legs a little without anyone seeing him.

He jogged down the stairs, too jumpy to wait for the elevator, and restrained himself until he'd cleared the lobby of the club. But when he hit the sidewalk, he couldn't contain the bursting energy any longer. He exploded into motion, sprinting down the street with strides that grew longer and faster with every step. In moments he was flying along at twenty-five miles per hour, the wind ripping through his hair and making his eyes water. God, it felt good.

Every time he ran like this, he remembered the early onset of his disease, the progressive muscle weakness, the loss of tendon strength, the continuous respiratory infections, the pain. And the fear. Not knowing what had been wrong with him was the worst of all as his body had literally wasted away before his eyes. It had taken over a year to get the diagnosis. SMA usually showed up in infants and small children, and it threw the doctors off when his case waited until adulthood to present itself.

A delivery truck backed out of an alley in front of him and he dodged around it with a lightning-fast move a professional football player would have envied.

He accelerated again, reveling in the flow of muscles and sinew and blood working in extraordinary harmony, his quick twitch muscles reacting completely off the charts for a normal human. But then, he wasn't normal at all. Not anymore. Not since Jeff Winston had called and suggested that there might be a radical cure for Trent's disease. It was highly experimental and had side effects, of course. He'd grabbed on to the lifeline his old friend had thrown him and never looked back. He was entirely and for the rest of his life a creature of Code X.

He ran for nearly an hour, slowing only when people began to emerge onto the streets and he risked someone seeing him race along at world-class sprinter speed for block after block.

He'd turned around to head back to the club when the cell phone in the breast pocket of his skin-tight running shirt vibrated. He slowed to a walk to take the call. It was his boss and friend, Jeff Winston.

"Hey, Jeff. What's up?"

"Couldn't you at least sound out of breath after tearing around like you do?" Jeff groused.

Thankfully, along with his quick twitch muscles had

come extraordinarily quick oxygen uptake. "Sorry, bro. I'll try to huff and puff a little. What can I do for you? It's early for you to be up, isn't it?"

"I need you here at the club ASAP. Take a cab."

"I can get there about as fast if I run."

"I don't need you drawing any attention to yourself just now," Jeff answered in clipped tones.

"What's going on?" Trent was alarmed. It was completely unlike Jeff to be this terse.

"When you get back."

Trent spotted a taxi stand and jogged to it at normal human speed, chafing at the slowness of the pace. He jumped into the first cab in line and gave the club's address. Had Novak uncovered something else about Chloe? Something that would explain her attempted murder? What on earth could it be?

The first thing Chloe became aware of was that her brain felt twice its normal size inside a skull that hadn't expanded one bit. Every beat of her heart sent throbbing pain through her head. As she swam slowly toward consciousness, she registered lying on her stomach among wildly tangled sheets and blankets, which was strange. Usually she was a quiet, neat sleeper who didn't disturb her bed much. And the rest of it registered. She was *naked*.

That startled her the rest of the way to full consciousness. She *never* slept in the buff. What if there was a fire and she had to race outside to safety? She rolled over onto her back and groaned as her entire body protested, sore. God, she felt like she'd been run over by a truck. Vague memory of that exact thing nearly happening tickled the edges of her fuzzy brain.

Memory of Trent came back to her. He'd been such a smooth operator, and she'd been so blessed eager to have him seduce her. Where was he now? Peeling one eyelid open, she groaned as sunlight creeping insidiously past the curtains pierced her skull like a sword. Agonizing pain exploded behind both eyes. No sign of Trent. He and his sexy tuxedo and bedroom eyes were gone. It was as if he'd never been here and knocked her world completely off its foundation.

The old hurt stabbed at her heart. Everybody always left her. Every time she took a chance on caring about someone, she ended up all alone. Her parents. Her foster families. Even Sunny. They all abandoned her sooner or later. An urge to cry nearly overcame her. Was it too much just to want a normal life? To find a nice man, settle down in a modest home, have a few kids and a dog, and be happy?

By way of an answer, her stomach gave a mighty, and threatening, heave. Moaning in pain, she forced herself upright and ran for the toilet. After duly worshipping at the throne of the porcelain god and emptying what little remained in her stomach from last night's binge, she felt a few inches further away from death. But that wasn't saying much. A shower sounded good, but the idea of listening to the pounding of water sent her back to bed showerless.

She couldn't remember the last time she'd had a hangover, and she'd never had one that even began to compare to this. Prepared to sleep for another, oh, decade, she crawled back into bed and threw an arm across her eyes.

A jangling noise that nearly split her skull in two made her swear and dive for her cell phone on the nightstand. "'Lo," she grumbled.

"Hey, sis! I missed you leaving the party last night."

Oh, God. Did Sunny have to sound so darned perky this morning? "Sorry. I drank a little too much champagne, and then some guys lit up cigars. The smoke made me nauseous, so I snuck out early."

"Rats. I was hoping some hot guy picked you up and took you back to his place."

Visions of the hot guy who'd knocked her off her feet, and then brought her back to her room and knocked her world completely out of orbit flashed into her mind.

Oh. My. God. Had she really asked him to… Had they really… She would never be able to look anyone from this wedding in the eye again… And she could never, ever, face *him* again… Mortification almost sent her back to the toilet a second time.

"Chloe? Are you still there?"

Her brain engaged belatedly. "Uhh, yeah. I'm here. Why are you calling me, anyway? Aren't you supposed to be on your honeymoon?"

"Aiden and I are at the airport. He won't tell me where we're going, but Jeff loaned us the Winston jet to get there. I just wanted to say goodbye. Aiden says I won't have phone service where we're headed."

"Wow. Sounds private and sexy. Have fun, eh?"

"It's my honeymoon and my hubby's a hottie. How can I not have fun?" Sunny retorted, laughing.

The cheerful sound nearly made Chloe's eyeballs fall right out of her head. She pressed a hand to them to hold them in. "Love you, baby sis."

"Love you, big sis."

Chloe groaned as she disconnected the call and turned her cell phone completely off. She prayed to sleep off the mother of all hangovers before she had to go back to San Francisco tomorrow. And then she prayed fervently that Trent Hollings would leave town today and go somewhere far, far away. Forever. There was no way she could ever look him in the eye after what they—what *she*—had done last night.

She took a solemn vow then and there never to touch

alcohol again as long as she lived. The idea of losing all her inhibitions like that again made her positively ill. Who'd have guessed a few shots of whiskey would turn her into such a slut?

Groaning in pain and embarrassment, she pulled the sheet up over her head and prayed for death. Or at least a long, long unconsciousness.

Trent burst into the conference room Jeff Winston had appropriated from the gentlemen's club to do business in while he was here for the wedding. Several of the other Code X operatives were there, complete with their own genetically engineered mutations, and they all looked worried.

"What the hell's going on?" he demanded without preamble.

Jeff answered, "Novak scared up some video from a traffic camera and ran the license plates of the SUV that tried to run down Chloe Jordan last night."

"And?"

"And it belongs to a corporation that doesn't exist."

Trent frowned. "Come again?"

"It's registered to a dummy company. Address is a P.O. box that doesn't exist, phone number is a fake and no company by that name is currently doing business in the United States. It's a cover for someone."

"Like who?" he asked his boss.

Jeff shrugged. "No idea. But it does lead me to believe it was no accident last night. Someone was out to hurt Chloe."

Trent replied grimly, "Wrong. Whoever gunned that SUV at her was out to *kill* her."

And that meant Code X had a problem. Chloe's sister had just married one of Code X's charter members—a guy who could hold his breath under water for over twelve minutes. And Chloe had spent the past two days in the company of the lot of them at various prewedding functions. How could her attempted murder *not* be aimed at the Code X team?

Trent suggested hopefully, "She said she's a forensic accountant. Maybe it was just a bit of revenge by an enemy she's made in her job."

"Possible," Jeff replied slowly. "If that's the case, we'll need a complete list of companies she has investigated." Trent watched as his boss pulled out his cell phone and dialed Chloe's cell phone number. As Jeff's frown deepened and he didn't speak into the device, Trent's apprehension grew.

Jeff put the phone down. "Her cell's turned off."

Trent winced. "She probably turned it off so schmucks like us wouldn't disturb her." She was *probably* sleeping off her hangover. But he wasn't about to share that little detail with the guys in this room. They would want to know how he knew that, and then they would inevitably draw the exactly correct conclusion. Frankly, it was none of their damned business how he and Chloe had spent the evening. Hell, even if he told them exactly what the two of them had done, these guys would never believe it. They would guffaw that quiet, controlled Chloe Jordan couldn't possibly be that wild.

Hah. Little did they know. He was a pretty adventurous guy in the sack, but that girl had made him blush a time or two last night. She was some woman.

"Maybe someone should go to her room and check on her," Jeff suggested, startling Trent out of recollections that were going to get him all hot and bothered very fast.

"Nah. I'm sure she's just sleeping. She was pretty wiped out last night."

"You walked her to her room and locked her inside sit?" Jeff asked.

"Yes. I searched her suite from top to bottom before I left. She clearly wasn't planning on going out again last night and was safe and sound when I left her."

Of course, she'd also been sexually sated and sleeping like the dead when he slipped out of her bed. She no doubt would need most of today to sleep off the booze and sex, though. A few of the things she'd asked for were going to leave her good and sore for a couple of days, but he'd been careful to do nothing she wouldn't recover from.

He wasn't sure he would recover anytime soon, though. How was any woman going to top that for him?

"Rather than bother her, couldn't we call her employer and ask for a list of companies she's investigated?" one of the twins, recent Code X additions with truly scary mental skills, suggested.

Trent shook his head. "She mentioned that she's a freelance consultant. I assume she contracts with law enforcement agencies or maybe banks. If we leave her a message, when she wakes up she can fire us a list of companies she has investigated." He desperately hoped his efforts to protect their little secret weren't rousing any suspicions.

Jeff nodded. "In the meantime, someone should keep an eye on her."

"As in surveillance?" Trent blurted, surprised. Damn. He'd been plotting ways to arrange a repeat of last night, but if the other guys were watching her around the clock, that was going to be hard to pull off. Unless he was the guy doing the surveillance...

"I'll keep an eye on her," he volunteered.

Jeff nodded. "I'll spell you when you need to sleep."

Speaking of which, it was about time for him to pop some sleeping pills and power down for a few hours. He might be able to go like the Energizer Bunny for days at a time, but when he crashed, he completely shut down. To that end, he commented, "I'm going to go catch a few zzz's now, so I'll be good to go tonight."

Jeff nodded. "I'll make a call to the concierge at her hotel. He can give us a heads-up if she leaves her room in the next few hours."

The powwow adjourned, and Trent headed for his own room. He showered again, popped his pills—a sleeping medication that would drop an elephant—and fell into bed. The soft sheets against his naked skin made him think of Chloe draped across him last night, and he fell asleep with a smile on his face.

Trent rolled over and glanced at the clock beside his bed. Six o'clock? Wow. He'd slept all day. Chloe'd tired him out more than he'd realized. Another side effect of his special abilities kicked in and his stomach growled loudly. He'd been known to burn in excess of twelve thousand calories a day when he was really active.

After ordering a steak, two baked potatoes, a large salad and a chocolate milkshake from room service, he moved over to his window to have a look across the street. Chloe's room was on the fourth floor, last one on the left. No light showed through the curtains. Given that Jeff had left no messages indicating that she'd left her room, she must still be sleeping off last night.

He probably shouldn't take satisfaction from that, but he couldn't help it. The idea of having made love to her until she had to sleep all day to recover made him smile. The last time he'd felt this kind of adolescent pride had been his first time with a girl when he was about sixteen.

A houseboy arrived with supper, and he pulled the wheeled cart over by the window to eat. His body eagerly absorbed the calories, and he eventually pushed back his empty plate in deep satisfaction. That should hold him for a few hours. He picked up a newspaper and browsed it while he kept an eye on Chloe's window.

Somewhere between the business and sports sections, her lights finally came on. Good thing. He was starting to get a little worried about her. About a half hour later, his cell phone rang. His pulse leaped as he dug the device out of his pocket. He was disappointed to see Jeff Winston's name on the phone.

"Hey, boss."

"Chloe just sent me a text. Turns out this Paradeo company is her first forensic accounting job. She says she's been hired to take a look at their books. Didn't say who hired her, so I assume she doesn't want to name her employer. We'll be in the conference room, researching Paradeo if you feel up to helping. You may have a long night tonight watching our girl, so don't feel like you have to come down."

"No problem. I slept and just finished eating. I'm on my way."

As the group researched Chloe's employer, nothing seemed out of the ordinary about it. Paradeo was a small-ish investment firm specializing in Central and South American markets. They reluctantly concluded that the Code X team might be forced to follow her and wait until another attempt was made on her life before they identified her attacker. Assuming there was one.

But Trent knew what he'd seen. That SUV had waited until she stepped into the street and then gone straight at her with the intent to seriously harm or kill her.

"Anybody know Chloe's travel schedule?" Jeff asked the room at large.

Novak's voice came across the speakerphone almost

immediately. "She's flying out of Denver Stapleton tomorrow morning. Arrives in San Francisco at 2:10 in the afternoon."

Jeff nodded. "We've got the manpower here to get her to Stapleton and onto that plane safely. Trent, if you want to go on ahead to California and get into position at the other end to take over watching her, that would be great."

He didn't like the idea of leaving her, even for a few hours. But what choice did he have? The odds were much greater that she'd be attacked at home rather than here where she was surrounded by Jeff and the rest of the Code X team.

Reluctantly, he packed his bags and headed for the late flight Novak arranged for him with Jeff's last warning ringing in his ears. "It would kill Sunny if anything happened to her sister. And you know what's on the line if this thing turns out to be aimed at Code X. I'm counting on you, Trent."

One thing he knew for sure. Chloe Jordan was not getting hurt on his watch.

Chapter 3

Chloe inhaled the seaweed and fish smell of San Francisco Bay, and grief that never grew less painful washed over her. The scent reminded her painfully of living on the boat with her family for that last year, before Mom and Dad had left her and Sunny behind and sailed to their deaths in the Indian Ocean to protest commercial fishing practices decades before it was cool to do so.

It had been a mistake to take a job in this town. Too many memories lurked here, waiting to ambush her. Too much loss. Too many ghosts. This was the last place she'd been happy, innocent, carefree. But all of that was long gone.

Not that Denver was destined to fare much better in her memory. Her experience there had been an embarrassing anomaly in too many ways to count.

In spite of it being in San Francisco, she was glad to get back to her regularly scheduled life. Her orderly, quiet, controlled life. No more whiskey, no more drunk hookups, and no more unleashed fantasies.

She took a taxi to her modest apartment in a relatively quiet corner of downtown. Stepping into the spartan elegance of her modern Asian-fusion flat, she soaked in the calm of it. She hit Play on her phone's voice messages while she set about unpacking her things.

"Chloe, Don. We need to talk. Call me."

Don Fratello was the FBI agent-in-charge of the secret investigation into Paradeo Inc., a firm that was suspected of being a money laundering operation for a Mexican drug cartel. Despite her inexperience in forensic work, Don had cut her a break and given her a shot at this gig, for which she would be eternally grateful to him. It was nigh unto impossible to get hired without experience, and until she got hired for some jobs she couldn't get any experience. This chance he'd given her was a huge deal and she wasn't about to blow it.

She was working as quickly as she could on the case, but the firm used the most complicated accounting system she'd ever seen—a possible sign that Paradeo was playing fast and loose with where its dollars came from and went.

She put a load of laundry into the tiny washing machine that was one of her flat's best selling points and picked up the phone. "Hey, Don. It's Chloe."

"Are you back in town yet?" he demanded without preamble. "How was the kid sister's wedding?" he added as an obvious afterthought.

"Great. She's safely married off, and I'm a free woman now." She'd meant the comment as a joke, but what Trent said about her being alone in the world came back in a flash. A hot knife of pain twisted in her gut. Damn him, anyway.

"There've been a few developments at Paradeo since you left."

Interested, she replied, "Do tell."

"A new guy's been brought in. Name's Miguel Herrera. Title's Chief of Security. He looks like a major thug to me. My contacts south of the border have heard rumors of the guy strong-arming various judges and political officials."

"Which means what? You want me to target him specifically because he's a big fish?"

"No!" the FBI agent replied sharply. "Steer clear of him. This man could be dangerous. As in you disappear and never come back if he figures out what you're up to."

She highly doubted it was as bad as all that. This was San Francisco, for goodness' sake. Not some lawless Mexican frontier town.

"This guy could be a drug cartel hit man. If that's the case, he won't hesitate to kill you or worse."

"What's worse than being killed?" she asked.

"Trust me. You don't want to find out. Just be careful, okay?"

"Okay. I'll be careful."

She'd accuse Don of being a nervous Nellie if he wasn't an experienced FBI field agent. But if he was that uptight about Herrera, she'd take his advice and stay away from Paradeo's new security chief.

She hung up the phone and resumed listening to her messages. There were the usual hang-ups from telemarketers, a request for gently used clothing items for some charity, and then another male voice began to speak in hushed tones.

"Chloe? It's me, Barry Lind, from Paradeo."

Barry? She looked up, surprised, at her telephone. What was he doing calling her? He was a bookkeeper and did basic data-entry work for the firm. He was very good at his job but not particularly social with his coworkers. Chloe considered him at best a casual acquaintance.

His tense voice continued, "I didn't know who else to call. Can we meet somewhere to talk? Outside of the office. Call me as soon as you get this message."

Bingo. This was exactly the sort of break her professors had told her to look for during an investigation. The statistics were shocking as to how often the break came from a low-level worker. They always knew all the dirt.

Eagerly, she dialed the number Barry had left for her. "Hi, it's Chloe. I just got back into town and got your message—"

He cut her off sharply. "Can't talk now. Julio's after work? Say six o'clock?"

"Uhh, sure. I'll be there." Wow. He really sounded nervous. Her stomach leaped in anticipation. He must have stumbled onto something big. Perfect. The faster she took down Paradeo, the faster she could get away from thugs like this Miguel Herrera guy.

She unpacked, shopped, finished her laundry, and generally put her life in order while she waited for six o'clock to roll around. Finally, it was time to go. The streets were crowded at this time of day as workers poured out of their offices and headed for home.

Barry was waiting for her when she got there. His sandy brown buzz cut was distinctive in the shadows. The guy was not ex-military, but at a glance, someone might mistake his short hair and beefy build for that of an ex-Marine. He looked past her nervously as she slipped into the booth, predictably a dark one in the back corner.

"Hey, Barry. How are you?"

"I've been better," he muttered without moving his lips, his gaze sliding away from her and over her right shoulder. Wow. He was acting really nervous.

She smiled broadly. "A word of advice. If you act like a criminal with a big secret, people will watch you more closely. Relax. Try to look natural. No one's going to walk up to the table and shoot us."

"That's what you think," he grumbled. His hands were planted on the table like it was going to fly away if he didn't hold it down.

She reached a sympathetic hand out to him and gave his icy fingers a squeeze. "Tell me what's on your mind."

"So, yesterday I was working late. With the end of the quarter coming up and you out of town, we were behind." She nodded her understanding. "Anyway, I took a break to go to the bathroom. Except the one on our floor was closed for cleaning. No problem. I went upstairs to use the john." A sheen of sweat broke out on his upper lip, and he paused to mop at it with a cocktail napkin.

"So there I am, sitting on the can doing my business, and these guys walk in. And they're talking, see. In Spanish. My wife's from Mexico, and I've learned it from her over the years. Anyway, these two guys are talking about needing to destroy records."

"What kinds of records?" she prompted while he paused to mop his face again and grimaced.

"Financial records from Paradeo. They said there was this new accountant poking around and they had to get rid of the paper trail." His gaze darted toward the door yet again. Man, this guy was tense. And the feeling was contagious.

If Paradeo's executives were onto her, she would never get the dirt on them. They'd erase everything from the company's computers and she'd never find a trace of anything. She asked, "Who were the executives? Did you recognize their voices?"

"I think one of them was the new guy. Herrerra. Oh.

You haven't heard about him, yet, have you? New Chief of Security. Supposed to be a real hard-ass."

Crud. The last thing she needed was a violent killer suspicious of her.

"What did you do?" she asked Barry belatedly.

"I waited till they left, then I went back to my desk and I copied every last financial record I could lay my hands on in the company's computers."

Chloe gaped. "Are you serious?"

"Yup." He reached into his jacket pocket then laid his palm flat on the table and slid it toward her. "Take this," he muttered ventriloquist style.

She laid her hand over his and as he withdrew his, she felt the oblong shape of a flash drive. She palmed it unobtrusively and stuck it in the pocket of her jeans. "What do you want me to do with these files?"

"You are the new accountant they were talking about, right?"

"I suppose so."

"Then poke around and see what you can find, eh?"

She blinked, startled at how directly this guy was telling her to uncover the dirt in his company. "What do you have against Paradeo?"

His gaze hardened. "My wife is Mexican, remember? I have heard of Miguel Herrera's associates. If Paradeo is mixed up with animals like that, then the company needs to go down."

"Fair enough. I'll take a look at these files and see what we've got." She finished the soda the waitress left her and tried to engage Barry in small talk for long enough that it wouldn't look suspicious if she got up and left. But the guy was so freaked-out he couldn't follow the thread of even the simplest conversation. Eventually, she gave up and signaled for the bill. And all the while, that flash drive was burning a hole in her pocket. She couldn't *wait* to see what it revealed.

Trent fidgeted in the produce market across from some dive called Julio's. Who was the guy Chloe was with? He gnashed his teeth as she reached out again and touched the guy's hand across the table. Was that her boyfriend? He looked pretty normal. Could no doubt give Chloe a white picket fence and 2.2 kids and a Volvo station wagon. All the things Trent could never give a woman. His gut twisted in something resembling jealousy but a hundred times more painful.

Since when did this particular green monster bite him in the butt? He never cared who women slept with besides him. He'd always figured what was okay for him was okay for the women he had sex with, too. And it wasn't like he was looking for a permanent relationship complete with all the trappings. But Chloe…she had managed to blow his mind sufficiently that he might consider pursuing an actual, exclusive relationship with a woman like her. Okay, with her specifically.

But as that bastard in the bar leaned across the table to murmur something intimate to Chloe, Trent tasted for the first time the bitter gall of having been a one-night stand when he wanted to be more.

Had she played him? Was *she* the accomplished pickup artist who'd conned him into giving the hot sex she wanted and then walked away without a backward glance? He was pretty sure he could hear women laughing uproariously on several continents at this very moment.

And to think he'd been plotting ways to romance her, to sweep her off her feet and into a relationship with him. All the while, she'd just been using him. Damn, she had that vulnerable and lonely act down to a fine science. He could not believe he'd fallen for it!

Fuming, he moved to another vantage point inside the small grocery store he was using for surveillance. In this day and age, a guy couldn't lurk in a dark alley for too long without someone calling the cops. No one wanted a terrorist hanging out on their block.

"You gonna buy something, mister, or are you just fondling the fruit?"

Trent glanced down at the tiny Korean woman glaring up at him like he was some kind of pervert. "Yeah, sure. I'm buying." He threw a few bananas, a bunch of grapes and a container of cut, fresh pineapple into a small basket and shoved them at the woman. He hated leaving the window, but he had no choice. And he could do without seeing the bastard kiss Chloe. The way the guy was leaning across the table, he was gonna lay a big wet one on her any second.

Trent threw a couple of bills on the counter and waited impatiently for the proprietor to ring up his sale and count out his change. Hurriedly, he grabbed the plastic bag and headed for the front of the store.

Dammit! Chloe and Lover Boy were no longer at their table. Trent bolted out the grocery's front door and looked up and down the street frantically. There. Pale, golden hair in a flawless French twist. Relief made him faintly nauseous as he hurried after Chloe. She was almost a block ahead of him.

Not that he had any trouble catching up. Even at a walk, his extraordinarily quick reflexes allowed him to cover a lot of ground fast without really seeming to. Chloe crossed a street, but a changing traffic light forced him to wait at the corner. She opened up a gap with him again. But he had gotten close enough to realize with a start that Lover Boy was not with her. Where had he gotten off to?

Trent didn't know whether to be more relieved that Chloe hadn't gone home with the guy or worried that she was out strolling around after dark by herself when someone wanted to kill her.

The light changed and he pushed through the thinning foot traffic until he was within about fifty feet of her. She walked another three blocks or so and never once checked behind her to see if anyone was following her. Someone had to have a serious conversation with her about situational awareness. Of course, she probably had no idea that she was in danger, let alone the target of a would-be assassin. Despite Jeff's decision not to alarm Chloe until they had proof someone was trying to kill her, Trent was going to have that talk with her. Soon.

Although how he was supposed to just call her and casually bring up the fact that she was in mortal danger, he had no idea. Hell, she probably wouldn't pick up the phone if she knew it was him. Not after the way she'd taken advantage of him in Denver.

He was irritated enough that his attention lagged. One second she was in front of him, and the next, she was gone. Startled, he darted to the spot she'd been standing in a few seconds before. Where did she go? He was at the mouth of a dark alley full of trash Dumpsters and piles of bulging garbage bags. Several apartment buildings were nearby and she could have ducked into any one of them. Her place was still a half-dozen blocks away...maybe she was rendezvousing with the eager schmuck from Julio's.

Trent heard a muffled noise behind him and leaped into the alley. He made out violent movement in the gloom and a female form being dragged deeper into the alley by a much larger male form. A flash of pale hair caught what little light trickled in from the street.

His muscles coiled and sprang so fast he barely managed to control the motion. He regained his balance and his fist shot past Chloe's head to smash into her attacker's face almost too quickly for his eye to see the movement.

The mugger grunted and shoved her hard into the brick wall beside him. She cried out and her knees crumpled, but Trent had no time for her, yet. He threw punches at lightning speed until the mugger started to draw a weapon in slow motion from the back of his waistband. It was ridiculously easy to knock the weapon out of the guy's hand with a fast chopping blow. The guy's mouth opened slowly and his arm cocked back at what seemed to be about one-tenth that of normal speed.

Trent brought his right knee up as fast and hard as he could and slammed it into the guy's crotch. The attacker grunted and doubled over right into Trent's best uppercut. The guy went down like a rock.

Trent spun toward Chloe. She was slowly sliding down the wall toward the ground. He reached out, grabbed her shoulders and dragged her upright. She let out a squeak of terror.

"Chloe. It's me, Trent. You're safe now. I've got you."

She sagged against him, taking huge, sobbing breaths. He held her for a moment, registering for the first time the stench of the alley.

"Honey, I need you to stand up on your own for a minute, okay?"

She nodded against his chest but made no move to step away from him. He pushed her gently back against the wall and knelt down to check on the status of the attacker. The guy was out cold. He looked about thirty and was dark-

haired and scruffy. Might be Hispanic, maybe Mediter-
ranean. Hard to tell in the dark.

Trent reached into the guy's back pocket and whipped
out the attacker's wallet. He pulled out his own cell phone
and took a quick picture of the guy's driver's license. Trent
put the I.D. back and stuffed the wallet back in the man's
pants. He searched the guy's pockets for anything else that
might be informative and found nothing. He did pick up
the attacker's .38 pistol, which had skidded a half-dozen
feet away, and tucked it in his sweatshirt's front pocket.
If they got lucky, the gun might tell the guys at Winston
Ops who this yahoo worked for.

"Is that really you?" Chloe asked tentatively. "You're
not a hallucination?"

"Yup, I'm me. In the flesh." She looked like hell
warmed over. "C'mon, Chloe. Let's get you home."

"The police…arrest him…report…"

"I'll take care of it," Trent answered smoothly. He
pitched his voice to calm and reassure her. The last thing
he needed was police snooping around and asking too
many questions. Besides, the beating he'd administered
to her would-be assailant was a more effective deterrent
than anything the cops could do. However, it also opened
Trent up to some questions by the police that he'd really
rather not answer. Like how he was so fast, and had dis-
armed the assailant so easily, and why he didn't have a
scratch on him.

"I didn't recognize you in those clothes," Chloe commented randomly.

He glanced down at his jeans riding low on his hips
and his University of Hawaii hoodie sweatshirt. This was
what he usually wore. "What's wrong with my clothes?"
he asked.

"Nothing. I've only seen you in a tux or—" She broke off.

Or naked. He grinned down at her. If she could think about sex after having just been assaulted, she was going to be just fine once she got over the initial shock.

They walked the rest of the way to her place in silence. He watched without comment as she let herself into her apartment. But when she reached for a light switch, he forestalled her. "Stay here," he murmured.

She nodded as he slipped into the darkness and took a quick look around her place. It was as tidy as her hotel room had been. Its spare, modern furnishings left little or no room for someone to hide, and his search was complete in under a minute.

"Okay, Chloe. It's safe. You can turn on the lights."

A row of recessed halogen lights went on in the snug kitchen that was open to the living room. He watched cautiously as she dumped her coat on a bar stool and unceremoniously started stripping off her outer clothes in front of him.

"Whoa, there. What are you doing?" he asked in alarm. She wasn't going to jump his bones here and now, was she?

"I stink. I can smell him on me," she muttered.

And then he noticed her hands were shaking and she was unnaturally pale. In fact, her entire body was trembling. He moved to her swiftly and wrapped her in his arms. She went stiff against him.

"It's okay, honey. I've got you. You're safe. I swear. You can let it go, now."

She might have been close to tears in the alley, but she didn't break down like he expected. Instead, she pushed against his chest and he turned her loose, surprised. Where was the funny, relaxed, adventurous woman from two nights ago? Surely she was locked inside Chloe somewhere.

"Turn your back," she ordered tightly.

He did so, frowning. He felt her move past him and head for the single bedroom that opened off the living room. The door closed with a thud and a lock snicked into place. She thought a lock would work against him, huh? He didn't disabuse her of the notion. All the guys at Code X learned how to pick nastier locks than her little bedroom door's as part of their extensive military-style training.

He sat down on her sofa to wait her out. He didn't buy for a minute that this tense, uptight woman was the real Chloe Jordan. She'd emerge eventually, and then they'd have that conversation about who might want to kill her.

Chloe scrubbed furiously at her skin under a scalding hot shower until it was red and felt raw. Whether she was trying to get rid of the feel of her attacker's arms or the feel of her rescuer's she couldn't say. Where in the heck had Trent Hollings come from, materializing out of nowhere to save her? He must have been following her. But why? Obviously, he was some kind of stalking creep. She couldn't believe he'd followed her from Denver all the way to San Francisco. Apparently his notion of playing for a living included terrorizing single women. Was he some kind of pervert?

An insidious thrill that he might have flown halfway across the country to see her again insinuated itself into the back of her brain. She tried to scrub it away, too, but failed.

After rinsing shampoo out of her hair for the third time, she gave up on getting any cleaner and stepped out of her shower. She felt horribly vulnerable being naked with Trent in the next room, and forewent her usual, meticulous drying and moisturizing ritual to hurry into clothes. She pulled on jeans and a bulky sweater that was the most concealing article of clothing she owned. She even put on socks and shoes. Anything to cover herself from *him*.

The humiliation of waking up stark naked in that hotel room and knowing he'd seen her—all of her—and done all those things to her, and that she had let him, was far too fresh in her mind.

She dried her hair and pushed it back from her face with a simple headband. In her efforts to delay facing him even further, she even applied a little makeup. Finally, when even her watch was strapped to her wrist and she couldn't think of a single thing more to do, she gathered the rest of her filthy clothing in her arms.

Oh, God. The flash drive. The mugger had groped her coat pockets—no doubt looking for her wallet. She didn't remember if the guy had reached into her pants pockets, though. She'd been too panicked to register such details.

Chloe reached frantically into the pocket of her jeans and felt a hard rectangle of plastic. Exhaling in relief, she tucked the drive into her underwear drawer. It wasn't the most original hiding place ever, but it would do until she could get rid of Trent Hollings and make a bunch of copies of the data files. And she wasn't giving him permission to go fishing through her lingerie anytime soon.

Steeling herself to face the devil, she opened her bedroom door and stepped into the living room. As she'd expected, he was still sprawled on her sofa, waiting. In that baggy sweatshirt and tennis shoes with his hair all tousled, he looked like an overgrown kid. She could barely believe he'd been the dark, dangerous lover of two nights ago.

"Feel better?" he asked neutrally.

"Yes, thank you," she answered equally neutrally. Lord, she barely recognized him like this with that tousled hair, sloppy clothes and dark stubble on his jaw. He looked nothing like the wealthy trust-fund playboy he apparently was. He reminded her of some surfer-dude, hippie throwback of her parents' days. Ugh. She much preferred him in an Italian designer tuxedo.

She bustled over to the closet by the front door that hid her washing machine and stuffed her smelly clothes into it. She doubted they would ever be wearable again, but getting that awful stench out of them felt therapeutic, at any rate.

Too nervous to be still, she moved into the kitchen and poured herself a big glass of water. Although it annoyed her to do it, she poured Trent one, as well. Just because he was a possible stalker didn't mean she could bring herself to be rude, particularly when he was behaving himself so well at the moment. It just wasn't in her nature. And that darned thrill in the back of her head kept doing backflips that he was here.

She set his water down on the glass coffee table in front of him. He picked it up and sipped at it without comment. At a loss for anything else to do, she sat down on the matching chair across from him. "Thank you for rescuing me…again," she started stiffly.

"My pleasure. But let's not make this a habit, eh?"

Her gaze snapped up to his. "Do you have reason to believe there will be more occasions in which I need saving?"

"Yes, actually. I do. And we need to talk about that."

She stared at him. "You think the SUV in Denver and that mugger are related? Wow. And I thought I was paranoid."

"You have an enemy, Chloe. And he or she could be rich and powerful. Given the frequency and violence of these attacks, that person is very angry at you."

She frowned. "But this is my first real gig as a forensic accountant. And I haven't found anything that could convict Paradeo's senior executives, yet."

"That doesn't negate the fact that you're the person who could uncover the evidence to put them in jail."

"If not me, someone else would do it."

"Still, you have no business strolling around a big city like this at night, alone, enemies or no enemies."

"What business is it of yours how I live my life, anyway? It's my life."

"True. But your sister loves you a great deal. She'd be devastated if anything happened to you."

That was a low blow, invoking her sister. "And why do you give a darn about Sunny's state of mind?" she snapped.

"Why *don't* you?" he shot back.

She recoiled, offended. "I think you should leave. Now."

"Sorry. I'm not done talking, and you really need to hear what I have to say," he retorted grimly.

She gauged the distance to the phone on her kitchen counter. She would never make it across the living room and get 911 dialed before he reached her. She'd seen his reflexes firsthand in the alley, and although she was pretty out of it after her head hit the wall, he had moved in a blur of speed.

He shoved a hand through his hair. A pang of memory, of the lust provoked by that hand on her body, speared through her. Fine. She admitted it. He was still as handsome as ever. And sexy, darn him. And his smile was still as charming when he said, "This conversation got off on the wrong foot. How about we start over?"

Her eyes narrowed skeptically, but she made no comment. He could talk all he wanted. It was his breath to waste.

"Sunny married my good friend and colleague, and that makes her family. Which, by extension, makes you family, too. If for no other reason than that, I would be concerned for your safety. Additionally, in spite of what you seem to think, I consider you and I to have a…connection…after Saturday night."

"Do not *ever* speak of that again," she gritted out from behind abruptly clenched teeth.

He frowned as if he'd like to argue the point with her, but then continued plowing through whatever twisted logic he was pursuing. "The fact remains that I am worried about your safety. And so is Jeff Winston. He asked me to keep an eye on you until we can figure out who's trying to—" he paused as if stopping himself from saying something too revealing "—who might be trying to harm you," he finished lamely.

"Harm me?" she exclaimed.

"You said yourself that the SUV in Denver came out of nowhere. I heard its engine gun. And there were no skid marks, Chloe. That vehicle was accelerating toward you."

She shrugged. "The driver probably didn't see me."

He leaned forward, his intense silver gaze altogether too sexy and distracting. "Then why didn't he stop or even slow down when he nearly hit you? I guarantee you, had I not knocked you out of the way, he would have hit you, and you would have died."

"Are you implying that the driver was trying to kill me?"

"I'm not implying anything. I'm telling you outright that's how it is." He leaned back once more in a casual sprawl across her sofa that left her abruptly short on oxygen. Did he have to be so blessed attractive?

"That's crazy," she declared forcefully.

He sighed. "I figured you'd feel that way. I was hoping not to have this conversation until I had solid proof. But that guy in the alley forced my hand."

"So you were planning to follow me around without my

knowledge and spy on me indefinitely while you gathered this hypothetical proof?"

Chagrin crossed his features, but then a cajoling twinkle in his eyes took over, making him look even more boyish than ever. "I'm not spying on you. Think of it as me providing security. Good thing, too. Who knows what that jerk in the alley would have done to you if I hadn't been there."

"I'd have gotten his hand off my mouth and screamed my head off, and someone would have come to the rescue."

Trent snorted. "That guy was a lot bigger and stronger than you. Don't kid yourself. He'd have done exactly what he wanted to with you long before the police could come to the rescue, no matter how fast they responded."

A chill chattered down her spine. Was Trent right? Had she really come that close to disaster? Surely not. She announced, "I don't buy your conspiracy theory. Muggings are an everyday occurrence in big cities. And as for that car in Denver, the driver had probably been drinking and didn't want to stick around in case I called the cops on him."

"You're determined not to believe me, aren't you?"

"Pretty much."

"I'm going to keep digging until I get the proof I need to convince you."

Crud! She really didn't need him following her around and tipping off Herrera and his cronies that something was odd about her. Trent would totally mess up her investigation if he persisted with this little delusion of his.

The first order of business was to get rid of him and his boyish smile and magnetic charm. The second was to call his boss and have a chat with the man. Jeff Winston struck her as eminently reasonable. He would call off this obsessive lackey. "Fine. Whatever. Please leave and don't bother me again."

"Bother you? I'm trying to save your life!"

"Whatever makes you feel like a hero. Just keep your distance from me or I'll call the police."

He opened his mouth. Shut it. Stood up. Took a single step toward the door, then turned to face her. "For the record, my being here has nothing whatsoever to do with Saturday night. I've had hot lays before and I've never followed any of them around to save them from their own misguided ignorance."

Her jaw dropped in outrage, but before she could gather herself to tell him in no uncertain terms what a giant jackass he was, he was out the door. Dang, that man could move fast.

So furious she nearly flung his glass of water across the room, she squeezed her fingers into fists until they hurt. How did Trent keep getting under her skin? Call her ignorant, would he? She definitely hated him. Passionately.

Yup, the man had passion down to a fine science. And as memory of the things he'd done with her flashed through her mind, she groaned with a different kind of passion. The man was as irritating as sand between her toes.

Not about to waste another minute on him, she picked up her phone and dialed Jeff Winston's number.

"Winston Ops. Go ahead."

"This is Chloe Jordan. I'd like to speak to Jeff Winston, please."

"One moment, please" the smooth female voice said, "while I check to see if he can take your call."

While she waited for the secretary or whoever it was to return to the line, she opened up the laptop on her counter and typed in Jeff Winston's name. She was till absorbing the shock of the long list of companies he and his grandfather owned and the total cash value it represented when the female voice returned. "One moment for Mr. Winston."

"Hi, Chloe. This is Jeff. Is everything okay?"

"Yes. Fine. Except I have a little problem with an employee of yours. This may sound strange, but I think he's stalking me."

"Are we talking about Trent Hollings?"

"Yes. Does he have a history of this sort of behavior?" she asked in relief.

Jeff laughed. "Hardly. Women chase him like crazy, but he never gives them the time of day."

"Well, he's following me."

"I know. I told him to."

"Excuse me?"

"Sunny is family now, and so are you. I sent Trent to keep an eye on you until we can figure out who might want to, umm, bother you."

"You mean kill me?" she retorted.

"I'm not sure I'd go that far," he demurred with patent insincerity. Jeff Winston obviously believed someone was out to kill her, too. She tuned back in to what he was saying.

"…wouldn't want to unduly alarm you, Chloe. But my people pulled footage from a traffic camera in Denver, and that SUV appeared to be targeting you specifically," he finished delicately.

"It was a fluke. Or the driver mistook me for his ex-wife, or he didn't see me. I don't know what Trent thinks he saw, but the man's delusional."

Jeff replied gently, "The vehicle idled with its engine running for nearly an hour in its parking spot. But the moment you exited the club, it pulled out into the street. It waited in place for you to start across. When you did, it accelerated directly at you. I hate to alarm you, but Trent wasn't mistaken."

She didn't know what to say to that.

"Look. He'll stay out of your way. I can put a full surveillance team on you if you'd like, but I thought you might be more comfortable having someone you know do the job. Plus, Trent will be a little more unobtrusive than a large team of operatives."

She swore mentally. An entire team of security men trailing her around was the *last* thing she needed. No way would Herrera miss something that obvious. And if this hypothetical security team was as ham-handed as Trent in its approach, it would surely succeed in wrecking her case and maybe getting her killed. Like it or not, Trent Hollings was the lesser of two evils.

"Really, Jeff. I don't need any protection. I'll be just fine." God, why couldn't her life ever be normal?

"With all due respect, Chloe, I'm not convinced. Tell you what. If Trent watches you for a couple of weeks and there are no more incidents, I'll pull him off the job and never bug you again."

It wasn't a great compromise, but it was better than nothing. And as long as Trent kept his distance, she supposed she could tolerate a few weeks of knowing he was watching her. Although the mere notion of him checking out her every move sent shivers through her. *Yeah, but what kind of shivers?* A little voice murmured in the back of her head.

Not *those* kind! she shouted back at herself. "Fine," she grumbled. "Two weeks. And then he's out of here."

"Deal. Pleasure doing business with you, Chloe."

Was that laughter in his voice? Why did she suddenly

feel like she'd played right into his hands? Nope, she didn't like Jeff Winston much more than his incredibly annoying employee.

Chapter 4

Chloe spent the remainder of the evening making multiple copies of all the files on Barry's flash drive. She burned them to a CD, saved them to her online file storage account and, most importantly, forwarded them to Don Fratello. He couldn't read even the simplest financial statement and would expect her to do the heavy lifting in analyzing the files, but this way the FBI had a backup copy. And their computers were super secure.

She took a cursory glance at the files, and it looked like Barry had grabbed a complete record of Paradeo's activities for the past several years. It would take days or even weeks to plow through all the information, but if there was a money trail buried in here, she would find it.

The physical stress of travel and the emotional stress of being attacked had exhausted her, though, and eager as she was to dig into Barry's files, she turned in early. Her professors always stressed that a case like this was a marathon, not a sprint. She had to pace herself if she wanted to stay sharp.

The next morning, she stumbled through her usual routine by rote, showering, dressing and eating breakfast with blessed normalcy. She kept a sharp eye peeled for Trent as she headed for work but never spotted him. She didn't know which was creepier: seeing him following her or not seeing him at all. At least he was keeping up Jeff's end of the bargain and staying out of her way. She made her way to Paradeo's offices on the fifth floor of a downtown office building and spent most of the morning digging through the minor crises that had piled up on her desk in her absence.

It was nearly 11:00 a.m. before she was able to make her way past Barry's cubicle without being obvious about it. She poked her head in to thank him for the gift and to give him a quick thumbs-up regarding the completeness of the content. But when she looked around the corner, he wasn't at his desk. His computer was turned off and no papers cluttered his desk. Which was strange, come to think of it. His desk was normally messy enough that she had to restrain an urge to straighten it.

She asked his supervisor in the cubby next door, "Have you seen Barry, today?"

"No. He didn't come in to work. And," the woman added tartly, "he didn't call me to tell me he was sick, either."

"Okay. I'll catch up with him tomorrow." Something didn't feel right in Chloe's gut. Barry hadn't been sick last night when she saw him. And now that the files were out of his possession, he had nothing to worry about. He should've been at work today and acting as if nothing was wrong. Trent's paranoia was contagious, darn him! Barry had probably spent the morning in bed sleeping off his stress or maybe a hangover.

At lunch, she left the office and bought herself a salad at the deli down the street. She called Barry's cell phone number to check on him, but got no answer. Her unease intensified. And speaking of which, where was her own personal ball and chain? She searched up and down the block for a tall, gorgeous physique in the crowd. No sign of Trent. But she swore she could feel his gaze on her. It was almost a physical caress in its intensity. No doubt about it, he was there even if she couldn't see him. If only he didn't make her skin tingle like that!

Aww, c'mon. Admit it, Self. You like knowing he's looking out for you.

That little voice in the back of her head could just go take a hike. She went back to work and threw herself into finishing her piece of the quarterly report, which took the rest of the day. At quitting time, she had about an hour's worth of work left to do on the thing and decided to stay late and finish it. Not to mention doing so would probably irritate the heck out of Trent.

The office emptied and the phones quit ringing. As silence settled around her, she focused intently on the columns of numbers on her computer screen. One more footnote to post on a one-time charge as required by law, and she'd be done.

"Chloe Jordan?" a heavy male voice said in her doorway.

She looked up at a man she'd never seen before. "Can I help you?"

"I'm Miguel Herrera. New Chief of Security."

She swore to herself. Way to go avoiding the guy who'd be most likely to stick around late and lock the place up. Dumb, dumb, dumb. Pasting on a polite smile, she moved around her desk to shake hands with him. He was about her height and powerful in build. His neck was thick and muscular, and she had no doubt that under his suit the rest of him was equally beefy. "Glad to have you here, sir. Now I'm not the newest kid on the block anymore."

Herrera smiled, but the expression never touched his cold, black eyes. She got the distinct feeling he was mentally calculating the best way to dissect her into Chihuahua-food-sized kibbles. "How much longer will you be here this evening, Miss Jordan?"

"I'm just finishing up the quarterly report. Two more minutes, tops."

Herrera gave her a long, assessing look like he was measuring the truth of her explanation, and she restrained an urge to squirm. "Next time you plan to stay late, tell me first," he finally growled.

"Of course." He left her office and she sagged in relief. The guy really did reek of contained violence. No wonder Don had warned her away from this guy. More eager than ever to get home and dig into Barry's files, she hurried through the last footnote, sent her data to Paradeo's Chief Financial Officer and headed home.

She didn't bother looking for Trent when she stepped out of her building. She was in too big a hurry to get away from Herrera's disturbing presence. When she had to walk past the alley where the man had jumped her the night before, she couldn't help herself. She swung wide of the dark gap, edging along the parked cars and hurrying her steps.

Thank goodness Trent had been there last night. As much as she might resent his intrusion into her life, who knew what that mugger really would've done to her? In a moment of brutal honesty, she allowed reluctantly that Trent probably hadn't deserved her generally rude response to him last night. It wasn't his fault she'd gotten drunk and found out the hard way what a floozy she was on whiskey. She was embarrassed, but that wasn't his problem.

Thankfully, she'd left a lamp on in her apartment this morning and didn't have to step into a dark space. She kicked off her high-heeled shoes gratefully. Visions of a red stiletto flying over a broad, sexy shoulder came unbidden to her mind.

Get out of my head! Echoes of rich male laughter were the only reply her mind offered up.

To drown the memory of Trent's voice urging her not to overthink, to let go and show him just how naughty she could be, she turned on the television. Local news blared as she moved into the kitchen to whip up dinner for herself. The act of chopping and stir-frying a wokful of cashew chicken calmed her.

She poured herself a glass of chardonnay and moved into the living room to relax while the rice steamed. The news anchor's voice caught her attention. "And in local news, accountant Barry Lind was found dead in his apartment this afternoon, the apparent victim of a robbery gone wrong…"

Her wineglass slipped from her fingers and crashed to the floor, shattering on the slate tiles.

Gut-twisting fear slammed into her harder than Trent Hollings had on that street in Denver. She collapsed on the couch, staring at the television in horror as it flashed a picture of Barry that looked a few years old and declared his death a tragic loss. The reporter moved on unconcernedly to the next story as if he hadn't just destroyed her world.

Her front door knob rattled and she scrambled to her feet in terror, stumbling on the edge of the area rug as she backed away from the door. A snick and the knob turned. Ohgod, ohgod.... Someone was breaking in. She was next to die—

She spun and ran for her bedroom. A hard, powerful arm snagged her around the waist from behind, yanking her back against a muscular body. She screamed and a big hand slapped across her mouth.

"Easy, Chloe. It's me. What the hell's going on? Why did you freak out like that?"

She nearly sobbed aloud in relief as Trent's deep voice rumbled in her ear. His hand lifted off her mouth. His body was big and warm and protective plastered against her back, and an urge to sink into him and let him take care of her came over her. But then anger erupted inside her. "You scared me to death!" she exclaimed.

He turned her in his arms, but infuriatingly didn't let her go. Or to be more accurate, she was glad he didn't turn her loose, and *that* made her furious with herself.

"Me?" Trent exclaimed. "You were completely terrified by something long before I got here. I saw you drop your wineglass and go as white as a sheet. That's when I hoofed it over here as fast as I could."

How had he seen her? She glanced over at her picture windows in chagrin. She'd always been claustrophobic and preferred to leave the blinds open to the city view.

"Chloe? What's going on?" he urged.

His question pulled her back to Barry's tragic fate. "He's dead," she mumbled as tears started to flow down her cheeks.

"Who?" Trent's voice was sharp now and his hands tightened on her shoulders.

"Barry. The guy I met for drinks last night."

"Your boyfriend?" Trent's voice changed tenor. "Oh, honey. I'm so sorry." He wrapped his arms around her and drew her against his big, comforting chest.

"He's not my boyfriend. He is…was…" her voice cracked "…an accountant where I work. He wanted to talk over a problem he was having at work."

"What kind of problem?"

Not the kind that she was prepared to discuss with anyone but Don. "Just some accounting stuff," she replied evasively.

"How did Barry die?" She couldn't fail to hear the charged anticipation in Trent's voice. He didn't seriously think Barry's death was related to her, did he?

"The news said he was murdered at home possibly confronting a robber."

Trent frowned, but didn't comment as he pulled out his cell phone and plastered it to his ear. While he waited for someone to come on the line, he used his free arm to guide her over to the sofa. He sank down onto it and pulled her down beside him, never removing his arm from around her. Whether she liked it or not, he held her practically lying across his chest.

In spite of how frustrated she was at having him shadowing her life, she had to admit his body heat and slow, steady heartbeat were both comforting and calming. What the heck. She gave up resisting his superior strength and relaxed against him, accepting the comfort he was offering. His hand stroked her hair absently. She would have purred like a contented cat if the man who'd stolen sensitive data and passed it to her hadn't just been killed.

"Jeff, it's Trent. Coworker of Chloe's was killed today. She met him for drinks last night to talk about work stuff and he was murdered in his home overnight."

She faintly heard Jeff's reply. "I'll send a full team right away."

"No!" she exclaimed, struggling to push upright on Trent's chest. "No team!"

"Honey, you're in grave danger," Trent replied soothingly. "We need the extra manpower to protect you."

"I can't have an entire security team trailing me around. It'll ruin everything!"

Trent answered whatever Jeff said with, "Nope. No idea what she's talking about. Yeah, I'll find out. We can't exactly force her to cooperate with us."

She stared at Trent in dismay and mouthed again, "No team!"

He frowned at her while he listened to Jeff. He said only, "Got it. I'll be in touch." And then he disconnected the call.

Trent stared down at the exasperating woman trapped against his chest. Single-handedly protecting her from killers was a tall order. And he *really* didn't want to see anything bad happen to her. He had plans for the two of them.

"Will you please explain to me why don't you want a team of highly trained field operatives to keep you alive, Chloe?"

"I can't."

"Can't or won't?"

"Same difference."

He sighed. "Look. I'm one of the good guys. I'm trying to help you, but you're making it damned hard to do."

"I don't need your help."

"I beg to differ. Twice now, someone has tried to harm or kill you, and your colleague, to whom you must have been one of the last people he spoke with, is dead. Wake up and smell the coffee. You're in real danger."

She stared at him a long time, her eyes as big and blue as the sky on a clear day. Emotions washed through her azure gaze, one after another. Distrust. Doubt. Frustration.

And finally, fear. Relief flowed through him. At last, she was getting past her denial enough to believe him.

But then she said, "I've been in rough situations before. I'll be okay."

"Not this time. Whoever's coming after you is violent and proficient."

"They can't be that proficient. I'm still alive."

"Because I've been around to save you," he snapped. And he'd succeeded in protecting her both times by the skin of his teeth. "Pretty soon, your would-be killer is going to start figuring me into the equation, and I won't be enough to keep you safe any more." His arm tightened protectively around her.

Her flash of defiance faded. "What am I supposed to do?"

"Let me help you. Let Jeff and a full-blown security team help you."

She was silent a long time. Finally, reluctantly, she said, "All right. But no team. Just you."

"I can't be everywhere at once. You'll be safer with a full security detail."

"I might be safer, but it would ruin my investigation. It's you or nobody."

He sensed that was her final offer. But he didn't like it. "What or who, exactly, are you investigating?"

Chagrin washed across her face. "I assume you followed me to work today and figured out which company I'm working for."

"I did," he answered evenly. "And where are you in your investigation with Paradeo?"

She hesitated, and then capitulated and spoke in a rush. "Barry gave me a flash drive with a bunch of financial information on it. That's why he wanted to meet me last night."

"Were they worth killing over?"

She stared at him, appalled. "You think that's why Barry was killed?"

He shrugged. "Hard to tell." He didn't want to suggest that mere contact with her could have been enough to cause a motivated killer to go after Barry. She would never get over the guilt of it.

"So how do we do this?" she asked.

An image of her naked and tied up beneath him flashed through his head. Startled, he shook it off and forced his mind to work. "I'm going to be glued to your side from now on. I'll figure out who's after you and, when the bastard shows himself, I'll catch him and turn him over to the authorities. Then you can resume your regularly scheduled life. In the meantime, you should take some time off work."

"I can't. The FBI has hired me to investigate Paradeo, and I have to see it through."

"Not if it's going to kill you."

She sighed. "A certain amount of risk is part of the job."

"Not this much risk," he retorted. "You've got Barry's files here at your place, don't you?"

"Well, yes."

"Then you can work on them at home."

"But it will raise suspicion if I suddenly disappear from Paradeo. And, I don't know if Barry got the entire goods on the company. If he didn't, I may still need access to the company's financial records. And that means keeping my job and the appearance of normalcy for a little longer."

He didn't like it one bit, but he could see her point. "I'm still staying glued to your side," he declared.

"You can't exactly sit beside my desk all day long without raising serious red flags with my superiors," she replied, alarmed.

Dammit, another good point. "No, but I can drop you off at work and pick you up, and I can watch you in your office from across the street."

She frowned. "I suppose I could live with that."

He wasn't giving her a choice in the matter, but he refrained from sharing that particular detail with her. She was finally letting down her guard with him, and he wasn't about to raise her hackles again unnecessarily.

"Where do you keep a broom?" he asked.

"Excuse me?"

"If you'll get a towel to mop up the wine, I'll sweep up the broken glass."

She fetched him a broom and dustpan. As she disappeared into her bedroom in search of a towel, he raced through cleaning up the glass. He was done by the time she got back.

"Man, you're fast," she commented. "How did you do that?"

He swore at himself mentally. He would have to be more careful not to give away his special ability. "It wasn't that big a job."

But her frown suggested she didn't entirely believe him. To distract her, he asked, "What's that delicious smell coming from your kitchen. Have you eaten yet?"

"It's cashew chicken. And, no, I haven't. Have you?"

He winced. "I should warn you. I'm pretty much always hungry."

"Good thing I made a big batch, then."

After a delicious supper, he called Winston Ops. "Hey, it's Trent. Has Jeff briefed you on the latest from here? Good. Can you get a hold of the police report and find out what their preliminary guess is as to how Barry died?"

He only had to wait a minute or so. How on earth Winston's people got access to the San Francisco police department's database so quickly, he hadn't the slightest idea. Frankly, he didn't want to know. The favors Jeff was able to call in on a moment's notice were scary.

Novak announced, "Death by strangulation with a metal wire. Looks like your guy was garroted."

Trent grimaced. That was the method of a professional killer. Quiet, fast and effective.

Novak added, "We I.D.ed the guy from the alley last night. Mexican national, crossed over into the U.S. as recently as a week ago. Rap sheet in Mexico a mile long. But all his arrests stopped about a year ago."

"Police bought off to leave him alone?" Trent bit out.

"Looks like it. If he's involved with one of the powerful drug cartels, they'd have the power to get the *Federalés* off his back. We're still working on which cartel he's hooked up with."

"Thanks. Keep me updated, will you?" He ended the call.

"Well?" Chloe demanded.

"Well what?"

"How did Barry die?"

"He appears to have been murdered." She didn't need to know all the gory details; she was already upset enough. "How about I do the dishes so you can take a peek at those files Barry gave you?"

She nodded and disappeared into her bedroom. When her kitchen sparkled, he dried his hands and strolled into her bedroom to check on her. She sat at her desk, concentrating fiercely on her laptop screen.

Her apartment had about as much personality as a wet sock. Odd how so passionate a woman was so restrained in expressing herself. Her bathroom was as bland and neat as the rest of her place. He opened her closet and wasn't surprised to find a row of boring suits. He checked over his shoulder to make sure she wasn't paying attention to him and opened her drawers one by one. Nothing. No sign of the woman he'd made love with in Denver. Her socks and panties were as practical and uninspired as everything else in this place. Clearly, Chloe Jordan needed whiskey soon and often to break out of this shell she'd locked herself inside.

He stretched out on her bed and read a newspaper for the next hour. Finally, she pushed her chair back and raised her arms over her head in a stretch. He rolled off the bed and moved behind her. Yup, that knot in her neck he'd felt in Denver was back. He dug his thumbs into it and smiled as she groaned her pleasure.

"Taking a break or finished for the evening?" he murmured.

"Just a break," she moaned, her head rolling forward.

"Have you got any whiskey?"

She stiffened beneath his hand. Whoops. There was the knot again. "Why?" she asked cautiously

"Because you need to loosen up. Bad."

She turned in her seat to face him. "Let's get one thing straight. You are here to protect me. Nothing more."

"I never agreed to that," he retorted.

"Then I'm making it a new condition. This is just business. Purely professional."

"Sorry. No deal."

For a moment, she looked like she was seriously considering going along with his implied indecent proposition. But then her expression closed and her gaze went hard. "Excuse me?" she said ominously.

"You heard me. I make no promises to keep our relationship platonic."

"We don't have a relationship!" she exclaimed.

"I'm sorry. Have you forgotten Saturday night? As I recall, we have one hell of a relationship."

Her cheeks turned red. "That was…an anomaly."

"You can call it whatever you want, honey. That was the hottest sex I've had with anyone in a long damned time. Maybe ever. And I plan to do it again with you."

Her jaw dropped. "Never."

"Is that a challenge?" he asked softly. If she knew him better, she'd recognize the note of danger in his voice. But apparently, she didn't know him that well, yet.

"No, Trent. It's a promise. I'll never do that again with you."

"Ahh, you shouldn't have said that. I never could walk away from a dare."

Chapter 5

Chloe stared up at Trent in dismay. One of his hands still rested lightly on her neck, and electric shocks zinged outward from his palm and straight to her core. The rational half of her mind was appalled at his declaration. But the other half of her mind was thrilled, darn it.

Reason kicked in again. She didn't know the first thing about this man. And establishing her career left no time for relationships. Not to mention he was so beautiful she would always feel like a second-class citizen around him. He would leave her eventually. Everyone did. She could do without the heartbreak. Most important of all, she was terrified by how he made her lose control.

Mmm. But that's the best part, her emotional self murmured.

No. It was not.

Wanna bet? her wanton self retorted. *Tell him about the*

bottle of whiskey in the liquor cabinet in the living room and see what happens.

She steeled herself for whatever assault he planned to launch against her resistance, but he surprised her by stepping away from her and saying only, "I'll let you get back to work."

Stunned, she watched his yummy back retreat into the living room. She definitely hadn't expected him to back off that easily. Was he not all that attracted to her in spite of his big talk of bedding her again?

Hurt at the notion, she turned her attention back to the financial data in front of her and resumed her analysis. Or she tried to. But every time she wrote down a new column of numbers she ended up staring at it and making no sense of it whatsoever. Instead she kept seeing Trent's glorious body looming above hers. His face tight with desire and his eyes dark with need that she had put there.

As she added up a list of numbers for the third time and came up with a third different total, she gave up and threw down her pen. She stormed out into the living room to confront the source of her distraction. "I can't get a darned thing done, and it's all your fault."

He looked up from the book he'd borrowed from her shelves. She noted vaguely that the self-avowed beach bum with no job was reading an advanced tome on economic theory. Did he actually understand it, or was he just trying to impress her?

"How can I make it better?" he asked mildly.

He could scratch the itch he'd planted in her head, darn it. She opened her mouth to make a snappy comeback. Closed it. No way was she going to admit she was attracted to him. It was a passing thing. He was a hot guy and basic biology dictated that she would react. It was nothing personal and nothing she planned to do anything about.

She stomped into the kitchen and made herself a mug of herbal tea. Belatedly, she offered, "Tea?"

"Only if it's decaf."

"Do you have trouble sleeping?" Rats. Her curiosity to know about this man slipped out before she could corral it.

He shrugged. "I usually have to take medication to go unconscious. And those drugs don't mix well with caffeine."

"The way I hear it, sleeping pills can be habit-forming."

"They are."

"Have you tried to kick them?"

He smiled but his eyes remained closed. Secretive. "I really can't sleep without help. It's a metabolism thing."

Which also explained his comment about being hungry all the time. She sipped her tea and let its smooth flavor soothe her.

"So what's your story?" Trent asked her.

The question surprised her. He actually wanted to know more about her than how she behaved when drunk?

"You've seen my life. Work. Accounting. My apartment."

He frowned. "Hobbies? Interests?"

"No time."

"Friends?"

"A few. We go out to dinner now and then."

"Boyfriend?"

"Again, no time."

"That's a lie."

His statement startled her. It also offended her a little. Maybe because he was partially right. Other people, including her sister, were fond of telling her she needed to make time for a relationship. She might just make time for a man like Trent Hollings—

Horrified, she broke off the train of thought. That man

was way out of her class. Not to mention he'd break her heart as sure as she was sitting here.

"Why don't you want a boyfriend, Chloe?"

He asked the question in a conversational tone, but she didn't miss the intensity underlying it. "I'm not gay, if that's what you're implying," she retorted.

He laughed. "I already had that one figured out. I was there Saturday, remember?"

She rolled her eyes at him. "I really wish you'd quit talking about that. It was…" She didn't know quite how to describe it.

"It was what?"

She scowled. "A one-time aberration." She couldn't quite bring herself to call it a mistake. But she did declare, "It will never happen again."

"I think you're about three shots of whiskey away from a repeat performance. And I also happen to think you wouldn't mind that so much. Furthermore, I think you need a repeat performance."

"And that's why I've sworn off drinking for good," she snapped.

"Are you telling me I've ruined you for all other men? Why, Chloe, I'm flattered."

Her scowl deepened while his grin widened. "What say we head for bed?" he suggested casually.

She bolted to her feet, alarmed. "This isn't going to work. You need to leave—"

He cut her off gently. "I don't sleep, remember? I was suggesting that you go to sleep while I keep an eye on things. Out here. In the living room."

"Oh." And didn't she just feel silly. She turned away from the glint of humor in his striking silver gaze and stalked into her bedroom.

She locked the door, but immediately, his voice floated

through the panel. "You might want to leave that unlocked. If I have to get in there in a hurry to protect you, I'd hate to have to break the thing down. Better if I can get in straight away."

Disgruntled, she unlocked the door without opening it. A faint chuckle was audible and she stuck her tongue out at him from behind the safety of the door. It felt weird taking off her clothes knowing he was just outside, and she raced into the T-shirt and sweatpants she usually slept in.

She pulled the covers up to her ears and squeezed her eyes shut, but nothing could close out the memory of his hands on her skin or the wanton things he'd done to her. Things she'd craved. Begged for, even. She pulled a pillow over her head and groaned beneath it. If only he'd just go away and leave her alone!

Or else come in here and do all of those things again that had set her blood on fire and made her feel truly alive for the first time in a very long time.

Trent sat in the dark, listening to Chloe toss and turn in her bed. Trouble sleeping, huh? Thinking about him and their night together, perchance? He smiled into the night. His plan to seduce the good Miss Jordan was proceeding very nicely. She'd been so distracted tonight she could hardly see straight. And her gaze had kept straying to his mouth, his chest, his hands. Remembering the feel of him, was she? Like any good predator, he was patient. She would come to him and beg for a repeat performance even if he had to pour whiskey down her throat to get her to admit she wanted him. He'd already discovered her liquor cabinet, and it happened to contain an unopened bottle of a decent single malt Scotch whiskey. Yes, indeed. The good Miss Jordan was going to be his. It was just a matter of time.

* * *

Chloe woke with a start to the sound of her shower running. She jolted upright and then remembered. Trent. The water turned off and she slid down under her covers hastily. The bathroom door opened and he stepped out in a cloud of steam wearing…oh, God…a towel. Slung casually around his hips and showing off intensely male abs and a heck of a nice tan. Lots and lots of nice tan.

"Did I wake you? Sorry," he murmured.

"My alarm clock was about to go off anyway," she mumbled.

"Any requests for breakfast?"

"I usually have a cup of coffee and a bagel."

"I need something more substantial. You get ready for work and I'll cook."

She stepped into her bathroom and stopped cold. His clothes were strewn on the floor, the bath mat soaking wet with his footprints in it. There were specks of shaving cream on the wall of her shower, the things on her counter misplaced. It was like a tornado had blown through her bathroom. Heck, through her life. And he wondered why she had no interest in dating. Hah.

She piled his clothes in the corner, scrubbed down her shower, and put her shampoo, shaving cream and toothpaste back in an orderly row from tallest to shortest. There. Order restored. She showered, vividly aware that Trent had just been in this very spot, naked, with hot water sluicing over his body the same as it was doing over hers. More heated than her shower could account for, she dried off, dressed and twisted her hair into its usual knot at the back of her head.

As she applied mascara, she became aware of the most amazing scent emanating from her kitchen. "What are you making?" she called out.

"Scrambled eggs and crêpes suzette."

"For breakfast? Isn't that a dessert?"

He called back, "Crêpes are skinny pancakes. Strawberry's a fruit and whipped cream is a dairy product. Sounds like breakfast food to me."

She smiled beneath the lip gloss applicator. She checked her appearance one last time and froze. Since when did she put this much care into getting ready for work? Since Trent Hollings blasted into her life. She stepped out into the main room.

"Hey, beautiful." He smiled. "Fresh batch of crêpes is up. I ate all the eggs. Sorry." He put a plate on the breakfast bar for her beside a glass of fresh-squeezed orange juice, and she slid onto a stool, stunned. Two perfect crêpes oozing sliced strawberries and nestled in a blanket of whipped cream sat on her plate. "My God, these look fabulous."

"I like to cook. Since I eat so much, it seemed like a reasonable skill to master."

She took a bite and groaned in delight.

Trent grinned in satisfaction. "I'm glad to see you allow yourself at least a little pleasure."

She looked up sharply. "I beg your pardon?"

"You seem bent on denying yourself any happiness in life."

"I am not."

"Had me fooled."

Her frown deepened.

"So you often have wild sex with men you barely know, then?" he asked with deceptive mildness.

"No," she blurted, "I don't. Ever. I wasn't kidding when I said you were an anomaly."

"In my experience," he commented reflectively as he rolled four more crêpes and placed them on a plate for himself, "Very little in life is random. There's a reason you chose me to let down your hair with. I wonder what it is."

Truth was, he was the only man who'd really seen her at that wedding. Most men looked right through her like she wasn't even there. And he'd been safe. She was never going to see him again. Ships passing in the night, and all. She snorted mentally. That sure hadn't worked out the way she'd expected.

Trent's plate was already nearly empty. "How do you do that?" she demanded.

"Do what?"

"You do everything so fast."

His gaze was abruptly guarded. "I guess I'm just efficient."

"I leave the room for a few seconds, and when I return you've done ten times as much as I expected."

"Maybe you're just lazy."

Were it not for the glint of humor in his eyes, she might have been offended. As it was, she laughed. He smiled back and her breath hitched. He was so handsome he was hard to look at sometimes. Under other circumstances, it would be very easy to fall for a man like him. Of course, a man like him would never fall for a girl like her for real. He might have enjoyed the hot sex, but he would never really care for her. They were too different.

"What?" Trent asked suddenly.

She frowned, confused.

"You got this strange look on your face just now. If I didn't know better, I'd call it wistful. What were you thinking?"

"How different you and I are."

"How's that?"

"Well, you're the original blue-blooded playboy. I come from the exact opposite," she answered.

"Tell me about it."

"Trust me. You don't want to hear about it."

"I wouldn't have asked if I didn't want to know."

No way was she spilling all the sordid details of her dysfunctional life in front of this perfect man. She leaned over the counter to set her plate in the sink. Retreating from the dangerous topic of conversation, she collected her laptop and briefcase from the bedroom.

And he did it again. By the time she got back, the dishes were done. Efficient, her foot. That man must move at supersonic speed to get things done like he did. He glanced up at her innocently. "Ready to go?"

She nodded, frowning, and waited just inside the door when he gestured for her to let him go first.

"Hall's clear," he announced.

The streets were jammed with cars and bicycles. She boarded her usual streetcar and Trent angled his body between her and the other commuters, but it pressed him against her from shoulder to knee. He ended up wrapping one arm around her and hanging on to the overhead bar with his free hand. On cue, her breath shortened and her pulse accelerated.

Of course, Trent didn't miss a thing and smirked down at her. Jerk. He knew exactly the effect he had on her. The streetcar swayed and rattled, throwing her against him. His arm tightened, steadying her and pressing her a little closer against his amazing physique.

She tried to hold herself upright, to put a millimeter or two between them, but it was a complete failure. The car lurched again and plastered her against him. The stupid streetcar was never going to get to her stop!

But finally, her office approached, and she was stunned to feel regret as Trent stepped away and ushered her down the steps and onto the street. However, he kept one arm possessively across her shoulders and her glued to his side.

They had to look strange, her in a gray pin-striped business suit with matching pumps and her hair in a perfect up-do, and him unshaven and in his sloppy sweatshirt. Still, many women, and even a few guys, threw her envious glances.

Warmth spread through her. It was nice having a hunk like Trent publicly stake a claim on her. She checked herself sharply. She knew better than to fall for him. Caring about anyone was a sure recipe for driving that person out of her life.

Trent insisted on walking her into her building and actually depositing her at her desk. The other women in the accounting department made no bones about their appreciation for her escort.

"Who's the gorgeous hunk, Chloe?"

"Wow. Introduce me to his brother, will you?"

Some of the women just muttered things like, "Hubba, hubba."

Trent took it all with good grace. He must be used to that sort of reaction. As he lifted her purse off her shoulder, she grumbled, "The minute you leave they're going to interrogate me. What am I supposed to tell them?"

"Stick to the truth as much as possible. Tell them we met at your sister's wedding and hooked up. I was so blown away I followed you back to California."

"Excuse me?" she blurted.

He grinned broadly. "They'll think it's unbearably romantic and eat it up. Trust me. I know women."

Her body tingled instantly in response. He did, indeed, know women. She would never forget how well.

"I'll be across the street watching you. If you need me, just wave and I'll be here in a flash."

Her prediction turned out to be true. She barely got any work done all morning as women kept poking their heads in her door to demand the scoop on the pretty man-toy. She did tell them she'd met Trent at Sunny's wedding, but she left out the bit about him being blown away and following her back to San Francisco.

Yet another shadow darkened her office door and she glanced up, irritated. Whoops. *Miguel Herrera.* Her entire body tensed. "Can I help you?" she finally remembered to ask.

"I hear you were friendly with Barry Lind."

Alarm bells clanged wildly in her head. "I knew him. I don't know that I'd describe him as a friend," she replied cautiously.

"Did you see him before he died?" Herrera asked, watching her with an intensity that missed nothing.

Trent's reminder to stick to the truth as much as possible came to mind. "Let's see. I saw him last Wednesday before I left for my sister's wedding at the progress meeting for the quarterly report. He seemed fine."

"You didn't see him after you got back?"

What did this guy know? And how was she supposed to explain that meeting in the bar? She hedged, "Yesterday was my first day back to work. And he wasn't here—" Her voice broke. "Do they know what happened, yet? Was it a robbery gone bad like the news said?"

"He was garroted. Murder. Head was damn near cut off," Herrera answered bluntly.

She gaped, genuinely appalled. "That's horrible." Tears came to her eyes at the thought of Barry dying like that. Was it her fault in some way? Had this man discovered Barry's copying of the files and killed him for it? Her gaze strayed to the window in distress.

Herrera stared at her hard enough that she had to stop

herself from squirming. He made her feel like a guilty kid caught with her hand in the cookie jar. "You sure you don't know anything that could shed some light on his murder?" he demanded.

Oh, God. He did know something. Why else would he be pushing her like this? Panic clawed at her rib cage from the inside, desperate to burst out and send her fleeing from this man who could very well be Barry's killer. She stammered something inane and prayed Herrera would put down her reaction to shock.

"Hey there, beautiful."

The security man whirled, his hand twitching toward his hip.

Trent. How did he know? One second she was wishing for him to rescue her, and practically the next, here he was. She smiled at him in abject relief as he strolled past Herrera, whose hand was inching away from his hip slowly. She leaned into Trent as he reached her side and kissed her cheek. His arm slipped around her shoulders.

"And who's this?" Trent asked.

She mumbled through the introductions, and Herrera left quickly. She started to express her relief, but Trent quickly pressed a finger against her lips.

"I know it's a bit early for lunch, Chloe, but I want to take you somewhere special. Can you leave now?"

"Uhh, yes. I guess. My part of the quarterly report was just approved."

"Great. Let's go."

They were settled in a cab before Trent turned to her, expression grim. "Who the hell was that guy, and why did he put that scared look on your face?"

"Miguel Herrera. New Chief of Security."

"He's a dangerous man."

"Good eye. He may be linked to a drug cartel."

"Hence the FBI's interest in your employer. Do they think the firm's laundering drug money?"

She threw an alarmed look at the back of the cabdriver's head. Trent caught the hint and changed subjects. "I'm taking you to my favorite place in town to eat."

"It looks like we're headed for the docks."

"We are."

Chloe winced. The waterfront was fraught with memories she'd rather not face. Not to mention it was a pretty rough section of town. Not a place she belonged. She wasn't reassured when the cab stopped at the back of a disreputable-looking fish market. Exactly the sort of place her parents would have loved. The old embarrassment poured through her as if she were nine again. Her folks had been free spirits with no regard for social convention or propriety. They'd called such notions authoritarian repression of the masses.

Trent helped her out of the cab and banged on an unmarked door. It opened to reveal what could only be termed a dive. The dark room was full of rough-looking men in rough clothes bellied up to a bar where a rough-looking guy served up cheap plastic baskets overflowing with batter-fried fish and chips.

She could hear Mom and Pop crowing in delight now…a gathering place for the Working Man. Yup, her parents would've smoked enough weed to lose what little common sense they had and barged right into a place like this.

Speaking of which, "Trent, should we be here?" she murmured under her breath. "We don't exactly fit in."

"You don't, maybe. Stick with me, and you'll be fine."

Not reassuring. Particularly when whistles and catcalls announced that everyone in the joint had noticed her.

"What is this place?" she muttered. "Some kind of biker bar?"

"Something like that," he answered cheerfully. He elbowed them a spot at the bar and yelled a hello down the bar to the proprietor, who bellowed back, referring to Trent by name.

"You're a regular, here?" she demanded under the din.

He shrugged. "I know a few people here and there."

How on earth did a guy who came from his kind of money even find a place like this?

Trent yelled for two lunch specials, which were served up almost immediately. The fish was hot and flaky, the fries thin and crispy, just the way she liked them. She reluctantly had to admit the food was delicious. But she had worked her tail off to get as far away from this side of the tracks as she could. She wanted middle-class suburbia. Ozzie and Harriet Nelson. The Brady Bunch.

Trent, surprisingly, seemed entirely at ease. She had to admit his size and general roughness of dress and shave weren't all that out of place. Gradually, she relaxed enough to finish her lunch.

Still, she breathed a sigh of relief as they stepped outside without any brawls breaking out. She hurried away from the wharf, eager to leave behind the blast from her past.

"You really are a bum, then?" she asked him.

He glanced over his shoulder at the fish bar. "I like places like that, if that's what you mean."

"Why?" she asked, shuddering.

"The people are real. Not trying to be something they're not." He looked at her in surprise. "Why don't you like a place like that? You said yourself the food's fantastic."

"My parents dragged me to places like that and worse. I've worked my whole adult life to leave that world behind and make a better life for myself."

"And a better life means what? More money? Fancy

clothes? Shiny, clean places and shiny, happy, *fake* people?"

She stopped and turned to face him. "You don't seriously mean to tell me you prefer that squalor to, say, the gentlemen's club in Denver!"

"I'd absolutely rather hang out with a bunch of fishermen in some rat hole than with a bunch of snooty, blue-blooded hypocrites in some fancy club."

He was crazy.

"Why do you have such an aversion to that sort of place?" Trent challenged. "Why do you love the trappings of wealth so much?"

"I have no interest in dredging up my past," she replied tightly.

They hiked a little while in silence as they approached a street that a brave cabbie might venture down. Thank goodness her heels were low and her pumps fit perfectly.

He spoke casually and his steps sped up a little, "I can always have Winston Ops run a full background check on you. They'll tell me exactly why you don't like working-class places and where your obsession with money comes from."

"You wouldn't," she exclaimed, appalled.

"Either you tell me, or I'll find out for myself." He was walking noticeably faster now.

"That's an invasion of privacy!"

"We pretty well blew up any notions of privacy between us in Denver. I figure that night gives me the right to know." He glanced around as if seeking a cab. But no yellow sedans were in sight.

"I wish that night had never happened."

Something pained passed through his crystalline gaze. He covered it up with a crooked smile, but she didn't buy it. "Aww, you don't mean that, baby."

"Yes, I do," she declared.

He turned with that breathtaking speed of his and swept her up against him. Before she could draw a breath his mouth closed over hers. His kiss was carnal. Knowing. He invaded her mouth with his tongue, his arm a vise that smashed her against him without any pretense of polite restraint. He knew her most private desires and fantasies, knew she craved being overpowered from time to time, and he didn't hesitate to remind her of it.

It was no use resisting him. He knew her too well. He exerted the same mastery over her body and senses that he had that fateful night, branding her his all over again. And she melted. Again. She'd asked for a man to take charge of her and take her to the moon, and he had. It was still there. All of it. The fiery attraction. The flare of mutual passion. The synergy that built between them until it incinerated her soul.

He let her go as abruptly as he'd kissed her. "No. You don't," he declared quietly.

Huh? Her fuddled mind reached back for the thread of conversation he'd scorched clean out of her mind. Oh. She'd said she wished that night had never happened. *Okay, fine,* she told herself bitterly. She didn't wish that. But she was never, ever, going to admit it to him.

Trent resumed walking, and she stumbled, trying to keep up with his long stride. "Slow down," she finally panted.

"Sorry. Can't. We're being followed. Hold my arm if that'll help."

She grabbed his elbow and let him half drag her along at a near run. She didn't see anyone behind them, and Trent muttered an order at her to quit looking.

Scared and desperately trying to distract herself, she picked up the thread of the conversation. "Sunny said you're from a—I believe her word was stupidly—*wealthy* family." His jaw tightened but he made no comment. She continued. "So tell me this. Why do you hate money so much?"

He stopped briefly at the first busy intersection they came to and made a production of adjusting her purse strap on her shoulder. She noticed him surreptitiously watching behind her while he was at it.

"Is he still there?" she asked between her teeth.

"Yup."

"Now what?" she asked nervously.

"We're going to run. Now."

"Huh?"

"Run."

Chapter 6

Chloe did her best to keep pace with Trent as he took off running, but it was a stretch. They careened around a corner and Trent darted out into the street, dragging her along, to hail a cab. He shoved her inside and bit out instructions to the cabbie. She was stunned when he slammed the door shut on her and took off running back the way they'd just come.

The cab started to move.

"Wait!" she cried out.

"The guy said to take care of you, lady."

"But he's in danger. We can't leave him behind!"

"He told me to get you out of here."

She looked out the rearview window and there was no sign of Trent. She had no clue where he'd darted off to. "Somebody was following us. I can't just abandon my friend. Would you at least circle the block once so we can check on him? You don't have to stop. *Please*."

The cabbie relented, and the taxi turned the corner. She stared in shock at the sight that met her. A man was fleeing from Trent. But what dropped her jaw was how *fast* Trent was catching up. He looked like a track star. On steroids. In fast-forward video. The guy Trent was chasing looked like he was running in slow motion by comparison.

"Whoa. That guy can move. He a professional athlete or something?" the driver exclaimed.

"Or something. Follow him, will you?" Chloe directed the driver.

The cabbie had to punch the gas pretty hard to catch up with Trent. The guy he was chasing veered around a corner and Trent disappeared as he darted around the corner, too. By the time the cab got to the intersection, both the fleeing tail and Trent were gone. The cabbie circled the block again, but Chloe didn't glimpse Trent or the man he was chasing.

"They must've ducked inside a building," the driver announced.

She leaned back against the cracked vinyl cushions, perplexed. How did Trent move so fast? If he was that amazing an athlete, why wasn't he a professional sports star? "Thanks for trying," she told the cabbie in defeat.

"Okey dokey, miss. I'm taking you home, now."

She fretted the entire ride back to her place. Was Trent all right? Why on earth was he chasing after that guy? What if Trent's quarry turned out to be one of the bad guys and he turned on Trent? She realized with a start that she'd wrung her hands until they were bright red. She jammed them under her thighs to keep them still.

She paid the cabbie, tipped him generously for his help, and hurried up to her apartment. Funny how exposed she felt without Trent around to look out for her. How had he managed to worm his way into her life in one lousy day? Although she supposed it was a day-and-a-half if she counted Denver.

She double-checked the locks on her apartment and wielded an umbrella like a sword as she searched her place for intruders. Satisfied that she was home alone, she took the unusual step of closing the blinds. Distracted, she called the office to let them know she'd be working from home this afternoon. She tried to look at Barry's financial files, but she had the focus of a gnat.

Where was Trent? Should she call the police? She didn't even have his cell phone number to call him and check on him. But Jeff Winston would have it. She raced to her phone and called Winston Ops.

"Novak here. Go."

"Hi. It's Chloe Jordan. I need to get in touch with Trent Hollings."

"Turn around and talk to him," Novak replied jokingly. Then more seriously, "Isn't he with you, ma'am?"

"No. He chased after some guy who was following us and sent me home alone. I don't know if he's all right. It's been nearly an hour since I last saw him."

"Stand by." Abruptly the operations man was all business.

She waited in an agony of impatience. Trent had to be okay. He just *had* to.

"I'm tracking his cell phone and it is on the move. That doesn't mean he's with the device, however. He's not answering at the moment. Protocol is to give him thirty minutes to respond before we call the police."

"Oh, God." Something had happened to him. She knew she shouldn't have left him!

"Don't worry, Miss Jordan. Trent's one of our most experienced operatives. He can take care of himself. I'm sure he's fine. I'll call you back as soon as I know something."

And in the meantime, the clock was ticking down on something being very, very wrong.

Trent leaned back, badly rattled, in the cab as it lurched in fits and starts across San Francisco's crowded, construction-filled streets. Now why would that guy kill himself rather than let Trent question him? He'd only shouted out one question—the obvious one—to the tail as the guy ran out of room in the warehouse and crouched defensively in the corner. *Who are you?*

The guy had shaken his head, muttered back at him in Spanish and then reached inside his jacket.

Trent had tensed and coiled his body to jump at full speed to avoid being shot, but instead the poor bastard had jammed the barrel of the gun in his mouth and blown his own brains out. Shock had, for once, literally frozen Trent into immobility. And the mess had been incredible. His guts twisted into an awful knot. Had he not chased the guy, he'd still be alive. But the dude had definitely been following him and Chloe. He seriously hadn't been planning to hurt the guy. He'd just wanted to know whom the tail worked for.

Trent had snapped pictures of the body from across the warehouse and hoped the resolution was high enough that the wizards at Winston Ops could do something with the images. Maybe they could identify the poor kid.

If he was lucky, he'd left no forensic evidence behind for the police to find. It wasn't that he minded talking to the authorities, but right now he really had to get back to Chloe to check on her. If he knew her, she was losing her mind.

What kind of organization put its employees under orders to kill themselves before allowing themselves to be questioned?

He hopped out of the cab a few blocks from Chloe's

place and hoofed it the rest of the way back. No sense leaving an easy trail for anyone to follow. He paused for a moment in front of her apartment door to mentally gird himself for the next looming crisis. He'd glimpsed her cab following him earlier as he ran at full speed. He hoped the angle had been such that Chloe didn't get a good look at just how fast he was moving, but he feared that hadn't been the case.

He never showed civilians his true abilities. It raised too many questions with highly classified and controversial answers. The dead man's incredulous last words echoed in his mind… "What are you? Some kind of monster?"

That was him. A twenty-first century Frankenstein monster. And on that grim note, he knocked on Chloe's door.

"Who's there?" a quavering voice asked through the panel.

"It's me. Trent."

The door flew open and a blonde, fast-moving object launched itself at him. He grunted as Chloe's weight slammed into him, and he used her momentum to spin them through the door. He kicked it shut with his foot while Chloe wrapped her arms around his neck and all but choked him. Damn, but he was glad to see her, too. He'd hated being away from her, even for that short time.

"Miss me?" he asked wryly.

"I was so scared. And you disappeared and we couldn't find you and I called Winston Ops and they couldn't get a hold of you and—"

He cut her off gently. "I was worried about you, too." He showed her how much by kissing her. And hoo baby, did she kiss him back. Recognition exploded across his brain. *Here she was.* The passionate, unrestrained, expressive woman had finally broken through.

Her hands moved across his chest frantically as if she were checking to make sure each and every rib was intact. Her fingers passed across his neck, his jaw, his cheekbones and through his hair.

"Really. I'm fine," he murmured against her mouth. Warmth unfolded inside him at the depth of her concern.

"Don't leave me again," she begged.

"Well, okay then." He laughed against her lips. Her hands went under his sweatshirt and she groaned in what sounded suspiciously like unbridled lust. She shoved the soft garment over his head as he guided her toward the sofa. He let her push him down onto it, amused at her urgency. She tugged at his waist, and his belt slithered free of its loops. Then her hands were on his zipper.

As much as he wanted this, he was an honorable man. He didn't take advantage of scared, vulnerable women. He caught her wrists and asked, "Are you sure about this?"

Her answer was to yank down his jeans and throw a leg across his hips. He'd take that as a yes.

It took every bit of his nimble hand speed to divest her of her clothes while she literally crawled all over him, kissing him and nipping at his flesh until he was nearly as frantic as she. What was it about this woman that drove him completely out of his mind? Was it the contrast between the conservative, uptight accountant persona she showed the world and this private, passionate part of herself she only shared with him? Whatever it was, she lit a fire in him like no other woman had.

She impaled herself on him eagerly, and rational thought fled in a groan as pleasure ripped from his throat. He surged up into her tight heat, gripping her hips and pulling her down to meet him. She leaned back as if she were a wild creature riding an untamed bronco. And he bucked beneath her just like one as she drove him completely out of his mind.

They rolled off the couch and crashed to the floor laughing, never breaking the furious rhythm of their lovemaking, pushing each other into oblivion and beyond. Her lust unleashed was a sight to behold as her entire body flushed, straining toward him. She keened her pleasure, throbbing around him so sweetly that she flung him over the edge, as well. He rolled over, pinning her beneath him, and continued to drive into her as his body recovered without pause and demanded yet more of her.

Chloe's eyes glazed over as she lost herself in him, shuddering again and again against him and around him until, with a shout, he joined her in spasms that rocked his entire body again.

They collapsed together in a boneless heap and let the floor's cold slate gradually quench the fire between them. Finally, with a groan, he rolled over onto his back and drew her on top of him. With his metabolism, he was rarely cold, but she'd begun to shiver. "Better?" he asked.

"Mmm. Much."

"Convinced I'm unharmed?"

"Mmm-hmm."

She sounded like a contented kitten on the verge of passing out. He smiled into her hair. She did have a knack for making a man feel like the king of the world.

A faint buzzing sound from nearby interrupted their lazy relaxation, and he reached for his wadded trousers. He dug out his cell phone. "Yes?"

"There you are," Novak said in relief. "I was about to send the cavalry after you. Chloe's frantic."

"I'm with her now. It's all good. But the guy I was chasing blew his brains out rather than tell me who he worked for."

Chloe tensed against him abruptly. He sat up dismayed as she climbed to her feet, snatched up her discarded clothes and fled for her bedroom.

"I've got a picture of the guy," he told Novak. "Not sure how good it is, but I'll send it to you. Maybe you can I.D. him and figure out who he worked for." They ended the call and he duly sent the image from his phone to Winston Ops.

And now for damage control. He sighed, climbed to his feet and headed for Chloe's room. He had no doubt she would retreat into her cold, cautious persona the same way she did after the first time they'd made love. How could he convince her she had nothing to be ashamed of? That her wild passion was something to be proud of?

As he stepped into her bedroom, she yanked an oversize pillow sham off her bed and held it in front of herself. He skipped mentioning that he had a great view of her entire naked backside in the mirror behind her.

"For God's sake, put on some clothes!" she screeched.

"Why? It's not like you haven't seen me in all my glory a few times, now."

"It's embarrassing!"

He grinned. "After the things we've done together? We just had hot monkey sex on your living room floor."

"You don't have to remind me," she snapped. She did, in fact, look completely mortified.

Yup. The prude was back. He perched a hip on her dresser and crossed his arms as she scurried around grabbing clothes and yanking them on. "Tell me something, Chloe. Why do you pull this hot-and-cold routine?"

She whirled to glare at him. "I'm never hot. At least whenever you're not around."

She spat the last bit at him as if it were a dire accusation. He grinned unrepentantly. "Good thing I'm going to be around for a while then, eh?"

"No! This sucks!"

He intercepted her as she rushed past him in an apparent search for shoes, snagging her around her slender waist and pulling her close.

"Let me go. And for God's sake, put some clothes on."

"Relax, Chloe. I'm not going to tie you up and ravish you…at least not unless you ask for it again."

Her face reddened. "You're really a jerk, you know that?"

He kissed the tip of her nose. "I have heard that before. But the past half hour tells me you don't really believe it."

"Oooh!" she ground out.

"When are you going to get over this irrational fear of your own sensuality? It's nothing to be ashamed of. You should be proud of your capacity for giving and receiving pleasure. Embrace it. Enjoy it."

"Never," she ground out.

"Why not?" He stared down at her, genuinely interested in her answer.

"I already told you. I don't come from the same background you do."

"Honey, women from every walk of life are equally capable of enjoying sex. Why are you so tense about it?"

"I just want a normal, boring, everyday life. Not a life like yours."

What the hell was so weird about his life? Okay, so he could run like the wind. And he never slept. And there was the money, of course… Dammit, his life *was* weird. He stated matter-of-factly, "Fine. If you won't tell me about yourself, I'll have Novak run a deep background check."

"No!"

He looked her in the eyes and saw genuine panic.

"I want to know, Chloe. If you won't tell me, I'll find out some other way. But I'm done with you giving me emotional whiplash. Since it's clear Denver was not, in fact, a one-time thing, I'm going to have to insist that you share at least a few of your secrets with me."

"Why?" she all but wailed.

"Because I want to know you. All of you. Not just your body. I want to know what you like. Don't like. What you think about. What makes you tick."

"But why?" she repeated.

"Because it's part of having a relationship. I happen to like you, Einstein."

She just stared. He couldn't tell if it was shock or sheer, frozen terror immobilizing her like that. Eventually she thawed enough to grumble, "Fine. Then tell me how it is you can run that fast. How is it you do everything so freakishly fast?"

She *had* seen him running. He turned her loose and shoved a hand through his hair. Now what the hell was he supposed to do? He had a serious security breach on his hands. Maybe if he played it cool she wouldn't realize just how incredible what she'd witnessed was. Panic squeezed him as he stared down at her, silently pleading for her to not to comprehend what she'd seen.

"That's what I thought. You want to know all my secrets, but you aren't about to give up any of yours," she stated.

He swore under his breath as he marched into the living room to retrieve his clothes and pull them on. They weren't his secrets to tell. But he couldn't even explain that much to Chloe. In spite of the earlier chase and the more recent vigorous sex, he really felt a need to work out. Adrenaline was surging through his veins demanding release. And that meant he needed to move. Faster than he could move in her living room. It was a calculated risk to leave her alone. But it would take a brazen killer to break into her place with the lights on and the target wide awake and able to fight back. And he'd be no good to her at all if he didn't burn off a little of this steam.

She was so damned frustrating. She claimed to want a normal relationship but balked at sharing even the most basic information about herself. It was as if she was so terrified of losing control that she had to hold all the cards between them to herself. What kind of normal was that?

Of course, the one thing he absolutely, positively couldn't ever give her was normal. Not with his health complications. He was probably stuck taking the stem cell therapies for the rest of his life. Unless, of course, he wanted to die a slow and horrible wasting death from spinal muscular atrophy. Not.

Hell, depending on how their genes matched up, they might or might not be able to have children. The good news was the recessive gene for SMA was reasonably rare.

And then there was his work. It had seemed like a waste to have these incredible physical abilities and not put them to good use helping mankind. He'd never guessed he would take such satisfaction in the work. He and his Code X colleagues were quietly making the world a better place.

However, the constant travel and no-notice crisis responses made a normal home life pretty much an impossibility. It would take a special woman to live with his whacky health issues and whackier lifestyle. Someone who embraced weird. Not a woman who craved "normal" worse than life itself.

He'd finally met a girl he could see himself settling down with for a long time, and he was *all* wrong for her. If this was God's idea of a joke, the big guy had a *lousy* sense of humor.

He announced from the living room, "I'm going out for a little while."

Chloe appeared in her bedroom door immediately, looking worried. "I thought you weren't going to leave me alone again."

What the hell? One second she was screeching at him to get away from her, and the next she was giving him this kicked-puppy look and begging him to stay? She officially made him crazy.

Reaching behind his waist, he pulled a .38 revolver out of its concealed holster and laid it on the coffee table. "Do you know how to use one of these?"

"Don Fratello said every woman should know how to handle a gun, and he made me take a weapons safety class," she answered.

"Who's Don Fratello?"

"The guy from the FBI who hired me. He's an agent in the financial crimes unit."

Trent didn't like the affectionate look that came into her eyes when she spoke of the guy, but at least she knew how to use a gun. He growled, "My friends Mr. Smith and Mr. Wesson will keep you company while I'm gone." He was so jumpy he could hardly control himself as he headed for the door. "I'll be back in an hour or two."

"You did it again," she accused. "How do you move that fast?"

"I just do." And with that lame excuse, he let himself out and pulled the door shut behind him. He waited until he heard the dead bolts thrown home and then raced for the stairwell. He needed a major run in the worst way right now.

Rather than risk drawing attention to himself by sprinting up and down San Francisco's crowded thoroughfares, he took a cab to an exclusive health club that had private workout rooms for rent by the hour.

He cranked the room's treadmill up to full speed, which wasn't anywhere near as fast as he could run, but it was better than nothing. He jogged along at fifteen miles per hour until the jittery feeling left his limbs. Lord, that woman messed him up.

He showered and dressed, then took a cab to the hotel room he'd been using to watch Chloe's apartment across the street. Quickly, he packed the gear and clothes he would need for the next few days, and fatigue abruptly began to drag at his body. That was how it was with him. He went ninety miles an hour until he hit the wall. And then he crashed like a big dog.

Forcing himself to keep moving, he stopped by a small grocery store and stocked up on food. And then he carried the entire armload of luggage and grocery bags down the street to Chloe's building.

She let him in as soon as he identified himself, although this homecoming completely lacked the same… enthusiasm…as last time.

"What's all that?" she asked cautiously.

"Clothes and surveillance gear. And food for the next day or two. Until we know who that guy was that followed us today, I don't want you to go outside."

"But my work—"

"You just caught the flu. And you can use the time to study Barry's files, right?"

She scowled but didn't argue. As he put away the food, she retreated into her bedroom and sat down in front of her laptop. It was clear she planned to immerse herself in the files and have nothing to do with him for a good long time. Which was just as well. He could hardly focus his eyes.

He moved over to her door and leaned against the frame. "Chloe, I need to sleep for a while."

"Fine. Take a nap."

"Uhh, that's not quite how it works with me. I'm going to take a sleeping pill and crash for the next several hours."

"Okay," she replied, distracted, already turning her attention to the columns of numbers in front of her.

She still didn't get it. "I'm going to sleep like the dead. Nothing you do will rouse me and don't bother trying. Keep that pistol close by and be prepared to defend yourself if someone breaks in."

That got her undivided attention. "You wouldn't wake up even if someone tried to kill me?" she asked in disbelief.

"Nope. When I go down, I go completely down."

"Several hours, you say?"

He shrugged. "I might sleep for as much as six hours. I haven't slept for a couple of days."

"A couple of days!" she exclaimed.

Rather than try to explain the unexplainable, he backed out her door and headed for his bags and his bottle of pills. He started as her voice came from directly behind him. "What are those? Superstrength Xanax?"

"Something like that." In point of fact, the medication was a custom blend of powerful sleeping medications and a surgical anesthesia drug. The doctors running the Code X program hadn't found any other remedy for his intractable insomnia so far.

He popped the pill dry and kicked off his shoes. Chloe came back with a blanket and a pillow for him as he stretched out on the couch. She handed them over, murmuring, "Sweet dreams."

He plumped the pillow under his head as the medication began to have its effect, and he gratefully sank into its embrace. He replied groggily, "If I dream about you, they will be."

As Trent passed out, Chloe retreated into her bedroom and breathed a sigh of relief. Facing him after today's epic mistake on her living room floor was one of the hardest things she'd ever done. It had been bad enough to have hot sex with the man when she was under the influence. But this time…this time she had no excuse at all. She'd jumped that man like a complete hussy, and she'd been stone-cold sober.

She laid her head down on her desk in humiliation and self-loathing. She was not that kind of woman! In the hippie, free-love world she'd spent her childhood exposed to, she'd seen plenty of people happy to jump in the sack with anybody who came along. She'd always promised herself she would be different. Modest and respectable. How did that old adage go? Square parents raised round children, and round parents raised square children? She was a square, darn it. She was *not* round!

Trent brought out a side of her she'd vowed never, ever to let gain control of her. She was not a captive of passion, was not following in her parents' disastrous footsteps! She would control her life, and she would *not* cave in to these base desires Trent roused in her.

No more slips. He was strictly hands-off from now on. But a sinking feeling in the pit of her stomach warned her the promise was going to be a lot harder to keep than it sounded.

She took a hot shower, attempting to scrub the feel of his hands and lips off her skin with the scratchiest loofah she owned. But it didn't work. Even after she'd toweled dry, she could feel him on her. It was like he'd branded a memory of his body on hers.

She had to draw a line with him and stand by it. If she didn't, she stood in real danger of losing control of her feelings, her desires…heck, her entire life! And that wouldn't do at all. She'd mapped out the life she wanted for herself, and it didn't include a high-speed surfing bum with no job and hot sex on his mind.

Girding herself to face the monstrous temptation that was Trent Hollings, she stepped out into her living room. He was out cold. As in she could pick up his hand and drop it across his stomach without disturbing him even a little.

Man, those sleeping pills of his were powerful. She scooped up the bottle and did a quick internet search of the chemicals and dosages listed on the label. Dang. One of these pills could drop ten men…and very possibly kill one man. How did his body tolerate them?

She poked around on the internet for information on insomnia. When that didn't yield anything helpful, she moved on to researching extraordinary human speed. A few articles talked about how world-class sprinters had better quick twitch reflexes than most other humans, but nothing she found could explain Trent's incredible speed.

The cab had been going well over twenty miles per hour as it pursued Trent. And he'd been pulling away from the vehicle. Which meant he was measurably one of the fastest human beings ever recorded.

Who *was* he? Or more accurately, *what* was he? If only Sunny were back from her honeymoon. Maybe she could shed some light on Trent's superhuman capabilities. After all, Sunny had been hanging out with Trent and his buddies for the past several months at the Winston compound.

Winston…hmm. That gave her an idea. She searched the internet for all of Winston's many subsidiary companies. One in particular caught her attention. Winston Computer Research, Ltd. was a small firm run by Jeff Winston personally. Trent was listed as an employee, as were all of the groomsmen in Sunny's wedding, including Chloe's new brother-in-law, Aiden McKay.

But what really made her sit up and stare was the list of other staff members. Over a dozen physicians and medical researchers were employed there. What did doctors have to do with computer research?

Using her temporary FBI access code, she poked into the bureau's records of Winston Computer Research, Ltd. and immediately ran into a firewall declaring the records she sought classified.

Was Jeff's company working with the government in some capacity? She glanced through her open door to the big man sloppily sprawled, unconscious, on her sofa. Was Trent involved with the government in some way? Was his speed the reason?

A shocking thought struck her. Or was his speed a *result* of working with the government?

She walked out into the living room and gave his foot an experimental nudge. He didn't react in any way. She turned on the television full blast. Nada. She added a radio and her stereo system to the din. Still no reaction. Frowning, she fetched a pair of pot lids from her kitchen and clanged them together directly over his head, succeeding only in making him roll over.

If she made much more noise, her neighbors were going to call the police. She turned everything off and sat down to stare at Trent sleeping away. She might as well take advantage of the opportunity to learn all she could about him.

Being careful not to disturb the contents, she searched his luggage and discovered an array of high-tech gear that looked like it would mostly be used in surveillance—

microphones, headsets, binoculars and various small electronic gadgets that looked suspiciously like bugs. But
nothing in his equipment or personal possessions suggested he was any sort of secret supersoldier.

She returned to the internet to see what it could tell her
about Trent's life. His family was, indeed, worth tens of
millions and he was, indeed, rumored to have a substantial trust fund. His acceptance to Stanford was notable; he
must have been a good high school student, and she knew
him to be highly intelligent. He'd won several local surfing
competitions during the first three years of an unremark-
able college career. But then he apparently dropped out of
school for a while. She found one reference on a surfing
website that noted he'd withdrawn from a big competition
due to his ongoing illness. The date placed it in the sum-
mer before his senior year of college.

An illness? What illness?

Her blood ran cold as another website gave it a name.
Spinal muscular atrophy. As she read a description of the
disease, she couldn't reconcile its debilitating effects with
the man sleeping in her living room. He was the picture
of health—and more.

She kept digging. Trent had spent the last several years
traveling competing in—and winning—major surfing
competitions. Clearly, his SMA had miraculously resolved
itself. Did that have anything to do with all those doctors
working at the "computer research" firm? An uneasy feeling nagged at her gut. She didn't see the connection, but
she could feel it there, just out of sight.

His statement that he played for a living appeared to
be mostly accurate, for he showed up as often in gossip
columns these days as the sports pages. Clearly, he never
lacked for female company. Which made his hookup with
her in Denver all the weirder. He'd had his choice of all

the single women at Sunny's wedding, yet he'd chosen her. As Chloe recalled, there had been plenty of good-looking women panting after him during the reception.

When he woke up, she'd have to ask him about it. If he could interrogate her about her personal life, she had no problem doing the same to him. Her internet sources exhausted and Trent still out cold, she resorted to looking at Barry's files.

Most of the records were boring and straightforward. However, after an hour or so, the very boring-ness of the files made her suspicious. As convoluted as the company's accounting methods were, there wasn't an error to be found anywhere. No company's records were this perfect.

She performed an online cross-check of a random set of receipts against the scanned originals of the invoices. Huh. The columns of pristine sales figures didn't exactly match up to the actual transactions. This must be how they were laundering money. The discrepancies weren't large, a few dollars here and there. Except it looked like money was disappearing from the accounts, not showing up in them. Laundered money would be flowing *into* legitimate accounts, not *out* of them.

A bloodhound on the scent, now, she dug deeper into the invoice files. She lost track of time and was startled to realize it had gotten dark outside when she finally looked up from her screen.

Trent had been asleep for nearly eight hours. Was something wrong with him? Should she try to wake him up? She moved into the living room to examine him. He was so still she laid an alarmed hand on his chest to see if he was still breathing.

Without warning, his hand shot up and grabbed her wrist in a movement so blindingly fast she barely saw it. She jumped, badly startled.

"What's wrong?" he bit out, sitting up so fast he nearly knocked her off her feet.

"Nothing's wrong. You've just been asleep a long time and I was checking on you."

"How long?" he rasped. His throat sounded dry.

"Eight hours."

He stared at her. "Eight? I never sleep that long."

"Well you just did."

"What have you done to me?" he demanded as he headed for the kitchen and poured himself a glass of water.

She watched, bemused, as he immediately set about broiling steak and boiling potatoes. The question wasn't what she'd done to him. It was what *he'd* done to *her*. No man had ever made her insides feel all quivery and uncertain like this.

Out of reflex, Chloe went on the offensive. "So, Trent. Tell me about the medical research you're involved with at Winston Computer Research. Doctor Gemma Jones is in charge of the program, I believe?"

The pan of boiling water slipped out of his hand and crashed to the floor, splashing scalding water all over her kitchen. And Trent jumped out of the way fast enough to avoid a single drop of it touching him. She had never, in all her life, seen another human being move that fast.

"You're not just fast. You're freakishly fast." Chloe surged to her feet. "Who are you?" she demanded.

He looked up at her grimly, his lips pressed stubbornly together.

"Or should I ask, *what* are you?"

Chapter 7

Trent knew in his gut that diverting probably wouldn't work, but still, he had to try. "I think we've been over that already. I'm a rich bum who goofs off and doesn't do anything more serious than surf big waves."

"And yet, you're on Jeff Winston's payroll. In fact, you're the man he chose to entrust my life to. Now why is that, Mr. Surfer Bum?"

Frustrated and cornered, he just stared at her, willing her to leave it alone. Of course, she didn't.

"Could it have something to do with that lightning-fast speed of yours? Tell me, Trent. Were you born with that speed? Or does this have something to do with your miracle cure of a supposedly incurable degenerative muscle disease?"

"You found out about my SMA, huh?"

"Why didn't you tell me about it?"

"It never came up in conversation. And I'm over it."

The next words out of his mouth came unbidden and he couldn't have stopped them if he tried. "Is there any history of spinal muscular atrophy in your family?"

"Not that I know of."

"Thank God." Their children would be okay. He'd still insist on genetic counseling to make sure she didn't carry a recessive gene for SMA, of course. But odds were it would have shown up at some point in her family tree if the gene was there.

She'd already circled back to the speed issue. "If you were that fast as a kid, your parents or coaches would have pushed you into sports. You'd be a superstar playing for the professional sports team of your choice or an Olympic track star."

In point of fact, if he used his skills to play any sport full out, he would probably rewrite the record books for it.

"That means," she continued relentlessly, "you came by this speed as an adult. Now how is that?"

He tried not to wince or give her any hint that she was on the right track, but it didn't slow her down. He mopped up the spilled water on the floor and started a new pot of potatoes.

"Then the self-avowed trust fund bum takes an actual job. And the job is with an obscure research company that, although it's supposedly a computer research firm, has a shocking number of physicians and medical researchers on staff. Why is that, do you suppose?"

He stared at her from the kitchen, doing his damnedest to hide his dismay. "You're the one on the logic roll. You tell me."

"You've had something done to you," she accused.

"Like what?" His voice might sound mild, but his guts were jumping all over the place. Most of it was panic that she'd somehow uncovered his secret, but a tiny part of him actually wanted her to figure it out. Sometimes it was damned hard having a secret like his and nobody to share it with. Sure, the gang at Winston Enterprises knew about the Code X research, but that wasn't the same as having someone personal—a friend, or confidante, or even a girlfriend—who knew how extraordinary he was.

He checked himself. *Extraordinary* might not be exactly the right word for it. *Strange. Bizarre. Weird.* All of those words applied to him and his colleagues. Each of the men and women in Code X had a different enhanced ability. Some were massively strong or could see for miles, while others could calculate complex math equations like a computer or swim like a fish. As for him—he was Fast. Capital *F*.

"I have no idea what they did to you," Chloe answered. "Maybe they dipped you in a vat of radioactive chemicals or hooked you up to machines or injected you with some bizarre cocktail of drugs. But you're definitely not normal."

He did wince then. She was right. He was not normal. But that didn't mean he could admit it to her. Mentally, he sighed. He knew what he had to do. He hated it, but sometimes the only decent defense was a good offense.

"Like you're one to talk," he retorted. "You act like a frigid virgin ninety-nine percent of the time, and then all of a sudden you turn into a totally different woman, uninhibited and unbelievably hot. Why is that, Chloe? Why are you so repressed? And where did you even learn to imagine some of the things you had me do to you in Denver? Not that I'm complaining, mind you. That was a night I'll never forget and one I'd like to duplicate. But what's the deal? You're like Jekyll and Hyde."

Yup. That distracted her. She reddened from hairline to neckline and spluttered in what looked like a combination of outrage and embarrassment. And guilt. She knew he was right. And he'd lay odds she knew the answers to his questions, too.

"C'mon, Chloe. What gives?"

"If I thought you actually gave half a darn about me, I might just tell you," she snapped. "But all you care about is yourself. Having a good time. Where the next party's going to be and how you're going to get the next chick into the sack with you."

So. It was brutal honesty time, was it? He could do that. And he was just frustrated enough to take the gloves off. "Since you seem to have knocked yourself out on the internet, researching me while I was asleep, when was the last time I showed up in a tabloid wearing a piece of blonde arm fluff?"

She frowned and didn't answer.

"I'll tell you when. Three summers ago. I gave up the partying and the women, cold turkey."

"Why?"

"Because Jeff Winston forced me to take a look at myself and my life. He asked me if I respected the man I had become, and I realized I didn't. With his help, I decided to make a change."

"How big a change?" Chloe challenged.

Damn. He should have known she'd be like a dog with a bone in its teeth and refuse to let go.

"A big change," he allowed. "I can neither confirm nor deny any of your speculation, but I will say the changes in my life have been dramatic."

"That's a word for it," she muttered.

"Okay, your turn," he announced. "Time for you to share something about yourself with me."

She squirmed uncomfortably, and he felt like a cad. He'd successfully avoided giving her any real information about his physical transformation and had now put her on the hot seat. It was a mean tactic. But what choice had she left him?

"When was the first time you ever had sex?" he challenged.

"That's damned personal," she snapped.

"Chicken to be honest with me?"

Her gaze narrowed. Yup, he'd pegged her as the type who wouldn't refuse a dare. She glared as she bit out, "High school."

"Did you like it?"

"No!" she blurted with enough vehemence to make him grin. "It was disgusting. And messy."

"So you've always been a neat freak?"

"Growing up, everything around me was so chaotic that I craved order. I'm not actually obsessive-compulsive like most people accuse me of being. I just want a modicum of calm. Structure. Predictability."

"And what made your childhood so chaotic?"

She sighed. "My parents were, in every clichéd sense of the word, hippies. They ran all over the world championing environmental causes. Sometimes they dragged me and my sister around after them. We had no steady school, let alone a steady home or steady income. We never knew where the next meal was coming from or if it would come. And yes, they were heavily into the whole free-love thing. Orgies were frequent events in my world."

Trent caught the tiny shiver of recollection that rippled through her. "And when they weren't dragging you along to orgies?" he asked.

"We got dumped with various friends and neighbors so they could protest." A note of bitterness crept into her voice. "Their causes were more important than their own children, apparently."

Ouch. That had to hurt. Particularly for a child who'd obviously craved family and security the way Chloe had.

She continued, "I was more of an adult than they were. I practically raised Sunny."

Which might explain why Sunny didn't seem to have the same hang-ups about family and security that Chloe did. Sunny'd had a big sister who provided stability and unconditional love. But there'd been no one to do the same for Chloe. His heart ached for the lonely, abandoned child she'd been.

Chloe shrugged. "When they were around, I stole loose change from my folks and used it to keep Sunny and me fed. They were as likely to spend their money on weed as food."

"How did they die?" he asked soberly.

"Their boat went down in the Indian Ocean. Maybe a storm. Maybe pirates, maybe their own sheer stupidity." She shrugged as if she didn't care, but he sensed the deep pain behind her words. She blamed them for leaving her alone to raise her kid sister. And frankly, he had to agree with her. He would hug her if he didn't think she'd shatter completely at his touch. As it was, he stayed where he was and let her talk.

Chloe went on more reflectively. "When they died, Sunny and I were separated and tossed in the foster-care system."

He prompted, "And how was that?"

She shrugged. "Some of the homes were okay. A few of them were as bad as anything you've ever heard about. Mostly it meant more chaos in my life. I tried to keep in touch with Sunny as best I could. To let her know I loved her and was there for her."

He glanced around her apartment, seeing it with different eyes. The sparse neatness of it, the calm colors and quiet décor all made perfect sense now. No wonder she craved "normal" so desperately.

"Then what happened?" he asked.

"I figured out that getting an education and a decent job were my best bet to get out of the chaos. I graduated from high school with honors, picked up a few scholarships, worked a string of crappy jobs and went to night school, and eventually became a CPA. I even clawed my way through a master's degree. And here I am. Finally in control of my life. At least until that SUV in Denver and you came along."

"Don't you ever want to let go of all this order a little?"

"Like how?"

"I don't know. Throw your dirty laundry on the floor or leave dishes in the sink overnight."

She laughed a little. "I'm not that anal. I leave the house dirty now and then."

"Show me. Do something messy. Right now."

Abruptly serious, she replied, "You're in my life. That's the messiest thing I've done in a long time."

Ahh. A revealing observation. She didn't do relationships because they were too chaotic for her. "Is that why you avoid sex?" he blurted.

"Excuse me?"

"Do you avoid sex because it involves a relationship, and you can't control one of those entirely?"

"Of course not." Her words sounded scornful, but her eyes looked thunderstruck.

Predictably, she retreated to her bedroom, and he let her. He sensed he'd just stomped on a very sensitive nerve and she needed time to recover. She went to bed without ever emerging, and he spent the long hours of the night aching to comfort the lost and forlorn little girl she'd been.

Chloe was all business the next morning. She seemed to

have decided overnight that she was going to plow through the Paradeo financial data in its entirety today. She barely spoke to him all morning and well into the afternoon. He put a sandwich down beside her computer and she didn't even look up from the numbers she was totaling on a legal pad. Her concentration while working was as intense as when she made love. Turned on by the ferocity of her focus, he nonetheless backed out of her room silently to let her work.

By mid-afternoon, she was pacing the apartment muttering to herself over the legal pad. And by dinnertime, she was making sounds of frustration that bordered on primal screams. That was when he intervened.

"Time for a break, baby."

"What? Huh?"

"You need to step away from it for a little while. Clear your head."

She frowned but did as he instructed and fetched walking shoes and her purse. It was a balmy evening and felt good to get outside and stretch his legs. Her apartment was too tiny a cage for his taste.

"You're just itching to take off and run full out, aren't you?" she asked.

He looked down at her in surprise. "Actually, I am. But I won't leave your side."

"What's it like to run that fast?"

"It's like…flying. It's amazing."

"Is whatever they did to you permanent?"

He shrugged. "No comment."

"Aw, c'mon. It's obvious the doctors at Winston did something to you. Nobody runs that fast."

"Keep your voice down," he bit out.

"So it's classified, then?" she persisted.

"Yes," he snapped. "Very."

She looked entirely too thoughtful at that admission for his comfort. But what choice did he have? He couldn't let her blab about it on a crowded street for anybody to over-hear. He led her into a park not far from her place and they walked briskly in silence.

Without warning, Chloe exclaimed, "I've got it!"

He jumped hard, startled—a downside of his superfast reflexes—and Chloe giggled at him. "I'm glad you find that funny," he growled. "What have you got?"

"A way to track the money at Paradeo. It's all about the money trail."

"What's all about the money trail?"

"Proving that they're laundering drug money. I've got to trace the money back to its illegal sources. The company will no doubt have covered its tracks by passing the money through a bunch of bank accounts. But instead of tracking the cash itself, I'm going to try tracking the transaction fees."

"The fees the banks charge for making a deposit or withdrawal?"

"Exactly. The amounts are negligible, but each bank will have a record of them somewhere. And because they're a standard and tiny fee, they shouldn't be pro-tected by much or any encryption. Let's get back to my place so I can check out my theory. If I'm right, Paradeo's CEO will be in jail by the end of the week."

He grinned and lengthened his stride to match hers as she hurried along the sidewalk. Her passion for her work was obvious. He was quickly coming to the conclusion that she was, by nature, a passionate person. Her obsession with bloodless and emotionless order couldn't possibly be her default state of existence. But how to convince her of that? Maybe he should just engineer unbridled sexual encounters with her until she admitted she enjoyed them.

The idea had real possibilities. He spent the rest of the walk back to her place pleasurably contemplating strategies for accomplishing just that.

Chloe stepped past Trent as he swept open her apartment door with a flourish and waved her inside. The guy did a darned credible Prince Charming imitation. She flipped on the light switch inside the door and froze in horror.

Her apartment was completely trashed. Furniture was overturned and its stuffing ripped out. All the books were pulled off the shelves, the drawers pulled out, emptied and thrown on the floor. Glass was broken everywhere and sparkled on the floor like fairy dust.

A strong arm went around her waist, yanking her back hard and spinning her out into the hall. Trent uttered a single, terse word. "Run."

Terrified, she sprinted for the elevator, but Trent yanked her into the stairwell beside the elevator instead.

"Who—" she started.

"Later," he bit out.

"Why—"

"Hush."

She focused on the steps flying beneath her feet as Trent dragged her at a breakneck pace down the stairs. Who would destroy her place like that? What had the intruder been looking for? A sense of having been violated began to creep up her spine. It invaded her stomach and she was nauseous by the time they burst out of the stairwell and into the building's lobby.

Trent screeched to a halt. "Walk now," he ordered under his breath. "Try to look normal. Don't draw attention to yourself."

She stared at him in shock. "What?"

"Smile. Look like nothing's wrong. We have to get out of here without anyone noticing anything out of the ordinary about us." He punctuated his order by smiling and nodding at her.

Eyes huge with fright, she flashed him a grimace that she prayed passed for a smile. His grip on her arm was painfully tight, but she didn't complain. She nodded at a neighbor and prayed she looked sort of normal, and then they stepped out into the street.

She expected Trent to take off running, but he didn't. He strolled a few blocks to a hotel with a taxi stand and slipped the bell captain some cash to hail a cab. She piled into the vehicle numbly. What had just happened? She felt violated and off balance. Visions of her entire life grotesquely torn apart swam through her brain. She felt... naked.

Trent bit out a destination and leaned back, wrapping an arm around her shoulders and dragging her close to his side. He seemed to understand the depth of her distress and offered silent comfort. His body was big and strong and solid against hers, and she leaned against him gratefully. As the immediate crisis passed, she began to shake. Tears welled up in her eyes.

"Not yet, baby," Trent muttered. "Hold it together a little longer."

He sounded awfully tense for a man who'd made a safe getaway. What was wrong now? She sniffed and did her best to be strong as fear gripped her once more. If Trent was wired, something was definitely wrong.

And then she noticed him glancing out the back window of the cab. She did the same and saw only a tangle of vehicles. "What's up?"

"We've got a tail," he replied.

"Which car?"

"The big silver SUV about five cars back."

She picked it out without much trouble. Uh-oh. That thing could hold six or eight bad guys, easy.

Trent murmured, "We're going to have to jump out and make a run for it."

She watched in dismay as he shoved a twenty-dollar bill through the slot in the Plexiglas divider between them and the driver. He told the guy, "We're going to get out fast when we get to our destination. This should cover the fare. Keep the change."

The cabbie grinned at the giant tip and nodded.

"Ready?" Trent asked tersely.

"What happens next?" she asked querulously.

"We're going to head for the most crowded place we can find and try to lose whoever follows us. If we get separated for some reason, meet me at the Millennium Health Club on Stockton Street. Engage a private workout room in the name of Chip Jones if I haven't done so already."

"Who's that?"

"I made the name up. But it's an average name. It won't raise an alarm if someone goes in there looking for us."

She nodded, but she had no intention of getting separated from him. The idea of being alone and pursued by whoever'd destroyed her home and maybe killed Barry made her want to throw up.

The rippling glass walls of the Moscone Center—a massive convention facility—came into sight ahead and Trent reached for his door handle. "Here we go. As soon as the cab stops at the next stoplight, we'll go."

The traffic came to a halt and Trent threw open the door. Staying low, he ducked out of the cab and pulled her out with him. The door slammed shut and he took off, weaving in and out across several lanes of traffic in a half-crouch. She raced to keep up as he dodged between cars.

She stumbled up onto the sidewalk and he jerked her upright, diving into a crowd of people streaming into the Moscone Center. "What's in here?" she panted.

"Lots of people," he replied tersely.

He threw money at a ticket window and shoved a lime green, plastic hospital-style bracelet at her. They hurried through the turnstiles and into what turned out to be a giant travel expo of some kind. Colorful booths displaying alluring destinations and hawkers shoving pamphlets at her momentarily overwhelmed Chloe's panic. But then Trent grabbed her hand and urged her to hurry.

She made the mistake of glancing back over her shoulder as he dived into the crowd. A half-dozen tough-looking men had just stepped out onto the expo floor. They huddled for a moment and then dispersed. And they looked intent on murder. She turned and raced after Trent as he walked through the crowd so quickly she had to break into a jog every few steps to keep up.

"Try to look happy," he gritted out.

Right. With thugs on their tail trying to kill them or worse. She would die if something happened to Trent. Particularly if it happened while he was trying to protect her.

Meanwhile, according to all the people shoving fliers at her, paradise awaited her in an all-inclusive package that included round-trip airfare and meals. She dodged tiki hut overhangs and bikini-clad models and concentrated on keeping up with Trent. He twisted and turned, ducking between booths and racing down the long rows, seeking the thickest crowds he could find. Chloe could discern no pattern to his movements, which she supposed was the point.

All of a sudden, they popped out of the crush of honeymooners and retirees. A sign pointing to the restrooms loomed before them. Trent swerved abruptly, though, and jumped through a pair of double doors marked Employees Only.

She followed fast and emerged into an enormous kitchen. Trent had already taken off running and she gathered herself to give chase. He was probably slowing down to give her a chance to keep up with him, but his idea of slow was a run-for-your-life sprint for her. In moments, she was gasping for air and her legs burned like fire.

Trent dived left between stainless-steel worktables, and she charged after him as he accelerated away from her yet again. He shocked her by bursting through another set of doors that led back out onto the expo floor. She'd assumed they were going to sneak out some back exit and try to lose their pursuers that way. But instead, he'd circled back toward them! What was he thinking?

Of course, maybe that was the point, too. Do the unexpected and throw the bad guys off their track. Regardless, she was grateful he'd at least slowed to a walk and was winding through garish exhibits once more.

The entrance they'd come in through was drawing near and she was starting to breathe a mental sigh of relief when a voice called out of the crowd without warning, "Trent? Trent Hollings? How the hell are you, dude?"

A deeply tanned guy wearing baggy swim trunks covered in neon palm trees materialized out of the crowd in front of them. "Man, I haven't seen you since the North Shore. Where'd you disappear to, old man? You comin' back to the beach or what? The waves are bitchin'. Big surge rolling into Malibu tomorrow night."

Trent skidded to an annoyed halt, glancing over his shoulder quickly. Chloe did the same, and her blood ran cold. She spotted two thugs closing in from directly behind them, and if she wasn't mistaken, that was another one off to their left talking urgently into a cell phone. Not good.

"Go," Trent grunted at her.

"But—"

"Go!"

Horrified, she watched as the surfer dude snagged Trent's arm and shouted into a portable microphone that one of surfing's great champions was here and for everyone to give a big hand to Trent Hollings.

Trent threw her one last grim look and jerked his chin toward the exit as a crowd of surfing fans swallowed him up. All of a sudden, she was alone. No matter that thousands of people pressed in on her, jostling her.

She looked back frantically and couldn't see any of their pursuers. But that didn't mean they weren't there. She walked toward the exit, panic nipping at her heels, her steps getting faster and faster until she finally broke into a run. To heck with blending in. She raced for the door as fast as her tired legs would carry her. Faces flashed past in a kaleidoscope of irritation and frowns as she bounced off bodies heedlessly in her flight.

All of a sudden, she burst outside. The relative calm of the street startled her. She dived into the traffic, ignoring the horns that blared at her. She frantically flagged down a cab heading the opposite direction and leaped into it, shouting at the driver, "Go, go!"

Startled, the cabbie hit the gas.

Crouching low in her seat, she watched her pursuers pile into the silver SUV from before. Where had it been loitering? As the convention center retreated in the rearview window, the SUV was still struggling to make an illegal U-turn to pursue her.

"Turn here," she ordered the driver. He screeched around the corner, getting into the spirit of the thing. "Turn again," she called.

They wove across downtown San Francisco for another

dozen blocks before she finally said, "Okay. I think we lost them. Take me to the Millennium Health Club, please."

"The one on Stockton?" he asked.

"That's the one."

"What's the hurry?"

"My ex-husband has a private eye stalking me, and it's making me nuts."

"I hear you. My ex is a crazy bitch…."

She tuned out the guy's diatribe about his family troubles and lawyers demanding alimony he didn't think he should have to pay. She was still breathing hard. Trent had really run her around back there. Thank goodness he'd had the foresight to set up a meeting place if they got separated.

They had to quit splitting up, though. She hated being alone like this, so exposed. Had she always been this vulnerable and just not realized it?

She ran her credit card through the cab's card reader and typed in a generous tip for the driver. As she hopped out of the cab, he called through the window, "You need me to stick around for a minute? Make sure you get inside without that guy spotting you?"

She smiled in gratitude at the driver's kindness. "Thanks. But I'll be fine, now."

The Millennium Health Club was housed in a newly refurbished high-rise that was all brushed nickel, frosted glass and high-tech gadgetry. A male model depicted on an electronic billboard spoke up as she walked past. "Hi, Chloe! How about a fizzy break from your day?"

She swerved away, startled. How did that thing know her name? It must use some sort of credit card or I.D. sensor as people walked past it. Still, it was creepy. She stepped into a glass elevator that turned out to have no buttons in it. Great. How did this thing work?

"Where can I take you?" a honey-smooth woman's voice purred.

"Millennium Health Club."

"Right away," the elevator intoned. The doors slid shut and she shot up a clear tube into the innards of the building. She was duly disgorged on the sixth floor with an admonition by the elevator to have a great workout. Wow. Double creepy.

A blessedly human girl with a perky voice and entirely too perky body welcomed her at the front counter.

"I'm here to meet Chip Jones," Chloe said. "Is he here, yet?" She highly doubted Trent had managed to peel away from that crowd of surfing fans and somehow beat her here, but she had to ask.

"Let me check." Perky girl scanned a flat-screen monitor quickly. "I'm sorry. He hasn't arrived, yet."

"Then I guess I'd like to rent a private workout room or whatever it's called. He should be joining me shortly."

"Are you a member here, ma'am?"

Crud. Now what was she supposed to do. "Uhh, no. I'm not. But Chip is."

"No problem. I'll just use Mr. Jones's member number. After you try our facilities, perhaps you'd like to consider joining. I'm sure Mr. Jones will give you a recommendation, and I'd be happy to go over our member services with you. Our facilities are soundproof, and use one-way glass to the outside. They're completely private...."

Chloe pasted on a fake smile and mumbled something incoherent as the girl finished her canned spiel, passed her a plastic key card and pointed down a hallway to her right. This place looked like an office, not a gym. She stepped into the designated workout room and stared at the array of weights, mats, mirrors and machines before her. A dozen people could work out in here and never get in each other's way!

While she waited for Trent, she strolled around the private room, examining the various computerized machines and trying to figure out what a few of them did. Bored, she swung a personal television around on its arm to face her. Idly, she stepped onto a treadmill and strolled along to the drone of an all-news channel.

She heard the door open quietly behind her. Thank God. Trent was finally here. She turned to smile a greeting at him…and screamed as four strange men burst into the room and charged her. She dived under the treadmill's hand rail and behind a stand of assorted dumbbells. Picking one up, she heaved it at the men, shouting for all she was worth for help. But the blasted soundproof walls undoubtedly had completely contained her cries for help. One man went left and another went right. She kicked and scratched and bit as they grabbed her, but she didn't stand a chance against them all. They bodily picked her up to subdue her.

Cautiously, one of the men released his grip on her and fetched several large towels from the heated rack in the corner. He wrapped her tightly in the thick terry cloth, effectively immobilizing her. He stuffed a wadded washcloth in her mouth for good measure. Furious and frightened, she glared at her captors.

"Here's how this is going to work," the towel guy said in a Hispanic accent. "We're going to walk out of here like we're all friends and everything's fine. If you so much as look at anyone wrong, we're going to kill the girl at the front counter and anyone else who tries to help you."

Horror roared through Chloe. These guys were going to murder innocent people on her account? That was *awful!*

"You got it?" he demanded.

She nodded, deflated. No way would she be responsible for someone else's life being taken. It was bad enough dealing with her guilt over Barry's death. And he'd taken those files entirely on his own with no prompting from her.

"Okay. We're gonna let you go now. But my guys all have guns. See?"

The other thugs obliged by flashing pistol butts under their sports coats.

"Not a peep out of you. Not one hint there's a problem," her captor warned as he reached for the door handle.

Chloe walked as slowly as she could out of the room and down the hall, hoping against hope that Trent would step out of the elevator and rescue her. But he didn't. The phalanx of armed men hustled her into the elevator.

"Going down?" the elevator asked pleasantly.

"Lobby," the leader growled.

"Si, señor. Tiene una tarde agradable."

How on earth did the elevator know to tell this guy to have a nice evening in Spanish? She risked commenting, "Even the elevator knows who you are. And so does my bodyguard. He's going to track you down and take you out if you don't turn me loose right now."

Her threat only made her captors laugh. So much for intimidating these guys. Her throat went dry when she contemplated what these men might do to her. All of a sudden, she understood all too well Don Fratello's comment that some things were worse than death. When they reached the street she was going to put up a fight whether these jerks liked it or not. But when they stepped out of the elevator, they didn't head for the lobby. Rather, they turned left and hustled her deeper into the building.

They used a dim, concrete stairwell that stood in marked contrast to the shiny modernity of the rest of the building, and she stumbled down the steps as someone shoved her from behind.

"I'm going to fall and break my neck if you push me again like that," she snapped over her shoulder. "And obviously your boss doesn't want me dead, or you guys would have shot me already."

Her captors scowled and one of them made a rude comment in Spanish about what a bitch she was. She didn't bother acknowledging that she'd understood him. The steel security door at the base of the stairs opened to reveal a grim underground parking garage. Nobody would hear her scream down here.

They had to pass between a row of parked cars, and she faked a stumble against a door handle in hopes of snagging her shirt and leaving behind a thread or something to indicate she'd been here.

Her plan worked a little better than she'd anticipated. Her entire shirt snagged on the handle, and when one of the thugs gave her a hard shove, the hem tore with a loud ripping sound. She steadied herself against the car's window, leaving what she hoped was a perfect handprint on the glass.

The leader, who was in front, growled something about hurrying up, and the guy behind her shoved her again. He could really quit doing that. It was starting to get on her nerves.

No surprise, she got shoved into the middle seat of the silver SUV and men squeezed in on either side of her. She was surprised, however, that they didn't seem to care if she saw where they were taking her. That couldn't be good. They must expect to kill her after they extracted whatever they wanted from her.

But when the SUV pulled to a stop in front of its destination a short time later, she abruptly understood. They'd taken her to Paradeo's offices. And that was when she broke out in a cold sweat.

Chapter 8

Trent was on the verge of doing violence to his surfing buddy by the time he managed to peel himself away from the crowd the guy'd blithely gathered around to hem him in.

He searched frantically for their pursuers. Were they lurking nearby waiting for him to make a move? But there was no sign of a single one of them. That answered that. This wasn't about him and Code X at all. As he'd suspected, these guys were purely after Chloe. He swore violently and his terror climbed another notch.

If she'd done as he ordered and run for it, she'd had enough of a head start that she should have been able to get outside and fade into the crowd. Maybe grab a taxi or duck into a store and hide. *If. Should. Maybe.* Dangerous words to hang a person's life and limb on. Particularly a woman he cared about greatly.

He didn't panic often, but he panicked now. She had to

be okay. The idea of her injured or worse made his chest feel like someone had blown a massive hole through it.

She was no doubt cooling her jets at the Millennium Club, bored out of her mind and wondering where the heck he was. He would join her there, and she was going to laugh her head off at him for worrying that she couldn't take care of herself.

He headed outside of the Moscone Center to hail a cab, and while he waved at taxis he dialed her cell phone. It rang three times, clicked, and then cut off. That was weird. Not only had she not answered, but it hadn't kicked over to voice mail. The hole in his chest expanded until it choked off his breathing. He dialed again, praying fervently that her wireless network had just dropped the call. This time, he got a message that the number he'd dialed was not available.

Swearing in a continuous stream, he jumped into a cab and bit out the address of the Millennium Club and urged the driver to hurry. He'd run, but the streets were still crowded, and, at all costs, he couldn't give away Code X by letting the public see his mad speed. Of course, telling a cabbie to hurry was like giving a crack addict a shot of adrenaline. The taxi ride turned into a death-defying stunt derby…and he didn't care in the least.

He raced past all the cool electronics in the health club's lobby and fretted impatiently as the elevator whisked him up to the sixth floor. Racing to the health club's front counter, he asked urgently, "Has Chip Jones arrived yet?"

The receptionist smiled. "A woman showed up asking for him a while ago. And then those other men came and she left with them."

It was all Trent could do not to dive across the counter and grab her shirt. "What men?" he demanded sharply.

The receptionist recoiled in alarm. "There were four of

them. In suits. She walked out with them like she knew them."

"Let me see the room she was in," he ordered. He was scaring the receptionist to death, but he had no time to play nice. Something was terribly wrong.

"Of course," the girl stammered. She led him down a hallway to a closed door and leaned down to swipe the master key card hanging from a lanyard around her neck. He barged past the girl into the room.

Empty. Damn! The hum of the treadmill running was the next thing he noticed. And then the dumbbells scattered on the floor. As if they'd been tossed willy-nilly. Crap. Had Chloe been trying to defend herself?

A pile of towels in the middle of the floor and a lone washcloth made no sense. He took another look at the washcloth. It was wadded up and looked damp. Like it had been shoved in someone's mouth. He swore more violently.

At least there wasn't any sign of blood. If her captors merely planned to kill her, here would have been as good a place as any. These rooms were soundproof, and had he not come along demanding entrance, this room would have been left undisturbed for the rest of the evening. This was a very discreet club.

Apparently, someone wanted to talk to her before she died. And that meant he had a window of time to find and rescue her. Possibly a very small one, but it was better than nothing.

"Did they head down in the elevator?" he asked the girl tersely.

"Uhh, yes. I guess so."

"How long ago?"

"A few minutes."

"Is there a parking garage under this building?" he yelled as he sprinted for the exit.

"Yes!" the girl called at his back.

No time for the elevator. He slammed his shoulder against the stairwell door and burst through it, taking entire flights of stairs in a single leap as he practically flew downward. There was a chance…a tiny one…that her captors hadn't left the building yet with her. He tore through the lobby and burst out onto the side street where the parking garage had to empty out. He looked left and right.

A silver SUV was stopped at a red light about a block away. Was it the same one that had been following them earlier? He glanced at the black maw of the parking garage. Should he head inside to check for Chloe or should he follow that SUV on the chance that it was her?

He had only a millisecond to make the decision. His gut said not to lose that SUV. He stretched his legs out into a full run, devouring the pavement with each stride as he tore toward the vehicle. The light turned green and it pulled away from him. No way was he losing it! He pushed for even greater speed, determined to catch the vehicle. It turned a corner, and he swerved after it, dodging pedestrians and ignoring the occasional squawk as he shoved past someone.

Despite his incredible speed, the SUV gradually pulled away from him. He began to suck for air, and then to gasp for it. His thighs burned like acid, and muscles pushed beyond all human limits finally began to cramp and fail.

Devastated, he searched the avenue ahead and could find no sign of his quarry. He glanced around to get his bearings. Maybe the police could pick up the trail. And that meant a quick call to Winston Ops to pull some strings with the San Francisco Police Department—

It dawned on him abruptly that he was only a block from the Paradeo office. And it was in the same direction the SUV had been heading. What were the odds?

He took off running again, this time at something resembling a normal human speed. It was the best his exhausted body could manage. And frankly, he was starting to feel a little light-headed. He must have burned through a gazillion calories with that mad dash across the city.

Five minutes brought him to the Paradeo building. *Be inside, Chloe. Be alive, baby.*

He burst into the lobby, which was deserted after business hours, and reluctantly admitted to himself that he'd better take the elevator up to Paradeo's floor. It was immensely frustrating to have his body give out on him like this. Normally, anything he could imagine, he could do. Did comic book heroes ever feel like this?

The elevator dinged open and he eased out to one side. The space yawning before him was dim. Only every tenth overhead light or so was lit. A cubicle farm stretched away from him, still and deserted. If thugs from Paradeo had grabbed her, they would take her someplace private and quiet to question her. His mind shied away from imagining them doing anything else to gentle Chloe.

He slid along the wall, hugging the shadows and gliding silently across the carpeted floors. All of Paradeo's offices were on this floor. They would probably take her someplace tucked away in the back of the building. Skirting the open cubicles, he passed a pair of conference rooms. A hallway narrowed before him and he slowed, easing toward the first closed door.

She had to be here. She just had to.

Chloe had seriously expected to wind up in some dank, dark alley or deserted warehouse, not in a perfectly normal-looking, antiseptic office in the very place where she worked. She'd assumed they would want to torture her to death in peace. Where no one would hear her screams. She tested the duct tape that secured her wrists to the arms of an office chair. Not a chance she was getting loose anytime soon.

She nodded in unsurprised recognition when Miguel Herrera stepped into the office. Of course he was behind her kidnapping.

"Miss Jordan."

She stared up at him. *What did he want from her?* The unspoken question vibrated angrily between them. What was so important that he had to treat her like a criminal and kidnap her?

"My employers want their money back, Miss Jordan." *Money? What on earth?* "What money?" she blurted.

"The money you stole from Paradeo."

"That I—" *Was this guy crazy?* She was looking for funny business Paradeo's executives were pulling, not doing the stealing herself! "I haven't stolen anything from Paradeo!"

Herrera sighed and perched on a corner of the desk in front of her. "We can do this the easy way or the hard way. But make no mistake. Before you walk out of here, you're going to tell me how you did it, where those funds are now, and how to transfer them back to Paradeo."

"Well, Mr. Herrera, that's going to be a bit difficult since I didn't take any money, I'm not hiding it anywhere and I cannot return what I didn't take."

"Make no mistake, Miss Jordan. I will not hesitate to turn the boys loose on you."

She glanced over involuntarily at the four big men, standing silent, eerily eager, in front of the window. A shudder passed through her. Never had any of her forensic accounting professors mentioned that she might find herself duct-taped to a chair with a roomful of thugs flexing their fists in anticipation of pummeling her senseless…

or much worse. This was a nightmare. Fear for her life coursed through her anew. The idea of suffering the kind of pain these men could so easily inflict on her turned her insides to water.

Trent hadn't been wrong, after all. She'd been an ignorant fool to believe she was safe from harm.

She looked Herrera directly in the eye and saw only hard determination. There would be no quarter granted from this man. The calming effect of finding herself in such a normal and familiar environment fell away as the true jeopardy of her situation sunk in.

Satisfaction gleamed in Herrera's black gaze as he loomed over her. "Talk to me, Chloe."

She closed her eyes for a moment to draw strength from within. "Mr. Herrera. I am telling you the God's honest truth. I have never taken a dime from this company."

"Hah! Do you need me to show you the records? The missing funds, a little bit here and there? And funny thing, all from accounts you have direct access to."

"How much money are we talking here?" she asked, curious in spite of her terror. Not to mention, if she kept the guy talking, it delayed the inevitable moment when he lost patience and turned the dogs loose on her.

"You tell me."

"I don't know. I didn't take it."

"How long have you been with this company?"

"What does that have to do with whether or not I took your missing money?" she blurted.

"Answer the question," he snapped. But he frowned at her, almost as if perplexed.

"Six months, give or take. How long has the money been going missing for?"

"About four months."

"If it's that recent, it should be reasonably easy to track down. It can't have gone too far," she replied reasonably.

"Where exactly has the money gone?" he repeated darkly. It didn't take a rocket scientist to see that this man didn't have a whole lot of patience, and what little he had was wearing out fast. She eyed his meaty fists warily. This was really going to hurt. How was it she could go so damned fast from feeling so strong and in control of her life to feeling so weak and completely *not* in control? Was the order she imposed on her world that thin a veneer?

Understanding exploded across her brain. She'd been deluding herself all along. Life had always been this scary and insecure, and she'd been lying to herself to think otherwise. She could no more force the world to conform to her needs any more than she could Trent. She felt adrift, at sea without a life jacket, totally at the mercy of the currents she floated upon. She had, without question, never been this terrified in her entire life.

Her voice shook as she stated with all the sincerity she could muster, "I have no idea where your funds have gone. You can ask me the question a hundred different ways, but my answer is always going to be the same… because it's the truth. I didn't take any money and I don't know where it is."

He leaned down close to her, his breath hot in her ear. Her skin crawled and she leaned away as far as her bound wrists would allow, but it wasn't far enough.

He followed, murmuring, "You think you can steal from me and mine and we won't make you pay? You think if we show weakness to our enemies they won't turn on us like rabid dogs? You think I'm gonna let you walk out of here alive? That I won't make you suffer until you scream and beg and sing like a canary?"

She shook her head, too terrified to make a sound. She'd

seen the news. Heard the stories of the atrocities the drug cartels inflicted on their victims.

"Imagine the worst thing you've ever heard my kind doing to an enemy. Multiply it by a hundred. A thousand. Before I'm done with you, little girl, you're going to be a front-page news headline that shocks the world. You have no idea how much suffering a human being is capable of. But I'm going to show you every last bit of pain your body can stand. And I'll just be getting warmed up."

Her knees were already shaking, but the rest of her joined in as adrenaline surged through her veins, screaming at her to run for her life.

"You'll try to scream, but I'll cut your tongue out. You'll gabble like an idiot and choke on your own blood. And no one will hear you. I'll skin you slowly, peeling the flesh back in strips to expose nerves you never knew you had. You think having your flesh burned to a blackened crisp and your muscles charred to the bone sounds bad? Oh, you'll find out for yourself. And I'll just be getting warmed up."

She was going to be sick. Her body twitched in horrified anticipation of the things he was describing, and her nerves tingled from head to foot, demanding that she run away. Begging for it. Sobbing for it.

"Did you know that the only pain in the human body you're not able to pass out to escape comes from the kidney? I'm going to stick needles in yours. The pain will be so exquisite you'll beg me to kill you. And there will be *no* escape. It'll go on and on and on until you literally go mad from the agony of it. And I'll still just be getting warmed up."

Oh, God. Kill her now.

"There are twenty-six bones in the human foot, twenty-eight if you count the sesamoids at the base of the big toe. I'm going to break them one by one with a hammer. You'll be a cripple for the rest of your life. And if you still haven't told me what I want to know, I'll do the same to all twenty-seven bones in your hands. One by one. I'll smash them into useless pulp. You'll be unable to perform even the simplest tasks for yourself. And then I'll start on your teeth. I'll break them in your jaw, and then I'll pull out the pieces one by one. And all the while, you won't be able to scream. Won't be able to escape it. And then we'll move on to the real torture. Things so horrible that even contemplating them will make you scream."

She realized that tears were running down her cheeks and that rattling sound was her teeth chattering in abject terror.

"Do you need a small demonstration, little girl?"

She shook her head violently in the negative, her throat muscles so convulsed with fear she couldn't make a sound.

He leaned down to murmur in her ear, "If you scream, maybe I won't kill you so soon. You hear me? Scream for me, little girl." Without warning, he ripped the duct tape off her left wrist.

And she did scream. At the tops of her lungs. Every hair on her forearm had been pulled out by the roots, and tiny droplets of blood sprinkled across her flesh where the tape had forcibly torn off the outer layers of her skin. Her wrist went from ghost white to brilliant scarlet as she stared at it. Her arm felt as if she'd laid it on a stove burner and left it there long after her body shouted at her to yank it away. Tears ran down her cheeks as the stinging intensified and insulted nerves roared their displeasure.

She became aware of a whimpering noise and realized with a start that it was coming from her. Herrera reached for her other wrist. Sounds began to pour out of her mouth in a steady, pleading stream. "Nononononoooo…"

* * *

Trent jolted into motion as Chloe screamed. Someone might as well have stabbed him, so sharp and visceral was his reaction to the thought that someone was hurting her. A powerful need to kill flowed through him, giving his limbs lightness and speed, his mind a hyperawareness, that even he'd never experienced before.

At least he knew she was in the building and approximately where she was. Given that there was no one out here acting as a lookout, he had to assume that all four of the guys who'd been chasing them in the Moscone Center were in that room with her. He couldn't take them all at once. He needed to draw one or two of them out and pick them off. He looked around and spotted a wood-backed chair behind a receptionist's station. Perfect.

Ducking down behind the station, he intentionally banged the hard, wooden slats into the desk. He didn't have long to wait. A door opened, and the sound of Chloe moaning floated out to him. Trent's gut tightened. *Hang on just a few more minutes, baby.*

After a cautious check of the darkened hallway, two men surged out like fire ants protecting their mound. He ducked to avoid being spotted. The good news was neither man had pulled a gun. Yet. He waited until they'd split up and were moving away from him before he pounced. The first man was a piece of cake. He never saw Trent coming. A fast chop to the back of the guy's head and the big man went down like a tree.

Small problem: trees don't fall silently. The second man whirled, and all chance of surprising him was blown. Trent took a wary step backward. Glanced over his shoulder as if contemplating fleeing. It was too easy. The thug bought Trent's head fake and attacked on the assumption that

Trent was scared stiff and planning to run rather than stand and fight.

Time seemed to slow. Trent watched the thug's mouth open on a silent yell, his legs pump in exaggerated slow motion, his hands come up like glacial claws creeping forward toward his prey.

Trent ducked under the slowly arcing fist with casual ease, his own hands coming up to pummel the guy's vulnerable face. The problem with thick, muscular targets was that body blows had little immediate effect on them. For a fast takedown, he went for the bridge of the nose. The temples. Eyes.

In a flurry that even his gaze struggled to follow, he slammed his fists into the attacker's face over and over. Streams of blood flew through the air like tiny red rainbows, and the thug's torso arced away from the assault. The guy fell heavily to his knees, then toppled over, face first.

The office door opened and three more men poured out into the hall. Not good. Trent might be fast, but his build ran to the lean side and he was of average strength. Three huge guys landing on him would effectively immobilize him no matter how fast he was when loose.

He turned to run, hopefully to lead the men away from Chloe and give her time to escape. The men scrambled to give chase, and as they careened around the corner, the one in the lead stumbled. He threw his arms wide, knocking his buddies off balance, as well. Flailing like a human windmill, the first guy staggered into the second, knocking him into the third.

Looking over his shoulder, Trent watched in shock and relief as all three men went down in a pile. He spun on a dime, raced back toward the swearing and shouting pile of men and hurdled them all. He skidded into the room Chloe was in, and she looked up in panic.

Her tear-stained face was terrified and he bit out, "Let's go."

"I can't," she wailed, clawing at her ankles.

He saw the problem immediately. Her left ankle was taped to the leg of a chair. It appeared she'd already torn loose the tape securing her right ankle. He snatched up a letter opener off the desk and stabbed at the half-torn tape. She grabbed the loose end, gritted her teeth, and gave it a yank. A sharp gasp and she was free.

He pulled her out of the chair and half out of the room in one mighty heave. She stumbled and righted herself as they raced out into the hall. Shouting and swearing erupted behind them as her kidnappers struggled to untangle themselves and gain their feet.

"Run for your life," Trent grunted.

Chloe took off in an impressive sprint, and he kept pace beside her using his excess capacity for speed to yank chairs into the aisle behind them and even to pull over a tall filing cabinet to block their pursuers' path. As it crashed to the floor, a cloud of flying paper filled the air behind them.

"Call the elevator," he ordered as he paused just shy of the elevator bank to pull out more furniture and create a pile of obstacles for the thugs to navigate. Pounding footsteps announced that they had untangled themselves and were giving chase.

An elevator dinged behind him as three big, angry shadows burst into view. "It's here. Hurry, Trent," Chloe called urgently.

He dived around the corner and into the elevator with her. She was already mashing the Close Door button frantically. Would those doors *never* move?

The footsteps grew louder. Finally, ever so slowly, the elevator doors began to slide shut. A shout went up in Spanish. Trent swore in a steady stream under his breath. They weren't going to make it out of here before the bad guys caught up with them. He braced himself to jump. If it came to it, he would throw himself out there and buy Chloe the few extra seconds she needed to escape. Whatever had been planned for her would end up being perpetrated upon him, but so be it. She *had* to get out of here alive.

The guy who'd stumbled before slid around the corner, and promptly slipped on a manila file folder. Yet again, his feet went out from under him and he neatly leg-tackled the thug who was just barreling around the corner behind him. Both men went down.

The doors were halfway closed now. Through the gap, Trent recognized with shock the face of the clumsy man. Miguel Herrera. The Chief of Security for Paradeo. He was personally involved with this kidnapping? What was so important about Chloe that a man in his position would risk himself directly? Why not pass the dirty work to low-level henchmen who would take the fall for it if they got caught?

The doors shut with a quiet whoosh, and the car started downward. Trent's taut body relaxed a tiny bit. Chloe took a sobbing breath and turned into him, burying her face against his chest. He wrapped his arms around her, panting. "Catch your breath, baby. We're not home free, yet."

She lifted her head to stare at him in dismay.

"We'll get a little head start because of the elevator, but you can be sure your kidnappers are running down the stairs this very moment. And they may have someone in the lobby waiting for us."

"What are we going to do?" she gasped.

"When the doors open, we're going to run out like a pair

of charging bulls. Plow right through anyone who stands in your way. When we hit the street, turn right. There's a big hotel about a block down and it'll have a taxi stand with plenty of cabs."

"Where do we meet if we get split up?" she asked fearfully.

"Go to the nearest police station and call Jeff Winston. But we're not going to get split up this time."

"Promise?" she asked as the elevator lurched gently to a stop.

"Promise." And then the doors slid open and it was time to run again.

No one was waiting for them in the lobby and they burst out onto the street together. Chloe veered right and ran beside him with the choppy strides of panic. She collapsed into a cab with him, hyperventilating. He gave an address to the driver and turned to her in concern.

"Did they hurt you? Are you all right?"

She nodded, unable to speak. Whether she was nodding to having been hurt or to being all right, he couldn't tell. He turned his attention to her more immediate crisis. "Hold your breath and try to count to three before you exhale. You need to build up more carbon dioxide in your blood to settle down your breathing."

It took her several tries to follow his instructions, but gradually, her breathing deepened from shallow pants to something vaguely resembling normal.

The cab approached the block where she lived and Chloe was recovered enough to ask in alarm, "What are you doing? We can't go back to my place. Herrera knows where I live!"

"We're not going to your place. We're going to mine."

She stared at him, uncomprehending.

Trent explained, "When I first got to San Francisco,

I rented a room in a bed-and-breakfast across the street from your apartment so I could watch you, remember? I've still got that room. And frankly, I doubt Herrera and his pals will look for us so close to your place. We need somewhere to crash until we can form a plan and get some backup into town."

She nodded wearily. He knew the feeling. The crash after a big adrenaline surge was a killer. And the idea of Chloe being hurt or killed by her kidnappers had definitely been a major adrenaline event for him. He was going to need to sleep fairly soon. But there was no way he could go down for the count until Chloe was safe.

He instructed the cabbie to let them out around the block from Chloe's apartment. No sense making her visible to Herrera's men if they were staking out her place. He ushered her out of the cab, tucking her protectively under his arm as he led her into the B&B. They went directly up to his room, and as he hung out the Do Not Disturb sign and double locked the door, she moved over to the window.

"Wow. You do have a great view of my place from here," she commented dryly.

He moved over beside her and gazed down into her living room. "Yup. I saw every move you made."

"That is so creepy."

He put his hands on her shoulders and tugged her back to lean against him. "I assure you, it was only for your safety. I would never have invaded your privacy like that unless it was a matter of life and death."

She sighed, a gentle nudge of her ribs against his chest. "I guess we've established that Herrera and his goons are out to do me serious harm?"

"I'd say so. How are your wrists and ankles? Your skin looks pretty mad."

She looked down at the red stripes across her fair skin.

They looked like scraped knees and burned like them, too. "I need to wash them and get some antibiotic cream on them."

But neither moved to treat her wounds. Instead, they stood still, leaning against one another, silently savoring the fact that they were alive. There would be time enough in a minute or two to get back to business. Right now, they needed to acknowledge that they'd survived a near miss with death.

"Thank you for coming after me," she murmured.

His hands tightened on her shoulders. Like it or not, this was no longer entirely business for him. Somewhere along the way his feelings for her had become personal. "I couldn't live with myself if anything happened to you, Chloe. I…care…about you." *A lot.*

More than he'd realized until he'd watched her running from her pursuers in the Moscone Center and he'd been helpless to protect her. More than he'd realized until he'd heard her scream and it had felt like his own heart getting ripped out. More than he'd realized until he'd been prepared to leap through the gap of those closing elevator doors and sacrifice himself to save her.

She shuddered in his arms, clearly in need of some serious reassurance. He drew her gently to the bed and sat down, leaning back against the headboard. She curled against him like a frightened baby animal seeking comfort. His heart literally ached for her.

"Tell me everything that happened," he said quietly.

She described the chase through the Moscone Center, her terror when Herrera's men grabbed her, the shock of realizing they were taking her to Paradeo's offices. He was not surprised by the sequence of events. But then she told him how Herrera demanded to know where Paradeo's money was.

"He thought *you* were embezzling from Paradeo?" Trent exclaimed.

"Weird, huh? Here I am trying to find how their money's being laundered and what's wrong with their books, and so are they."

"There's a thief inside the company," he breathed. Shock vibrated through him.

"But who would dare steal money from a dangerous drug cartel?" Chloe asked.

"Someone who doesn't know who they are, I suppose."

"Or someone who doesn't care," she added.

He froze beneath her. "Are you telling me you think some rival of the cartel behind Paradeo is making a move on it?" Good God. If there was about to be a drug turf war, he had to get Chloe out of town and far, far away from the violence about to erupt.

"I don't know if another cartel's moving in or not. But I know where to find the answer."

"Barry's files."

"Exactly. I need to finish my analysis. And fast. At least I know now why I kept finding anomalies I couldn't explain. I was looking at two financial crimes and not one. If we can find this thief before Herrera does, maybe the FBI can turn him or her into an informant. The thief could testify against Paradeo in return for some sort of plea deal or immunity from prosecution."

He didn't particularly relish the idea of racing Paradeo's violent security chief to identify whoever was brave enough to steal from a vicious and efficient drug cartel.

Chloe was speaking again, "But I need a computer and internet access to do it."

"Done." He leaned over and picked up the telephone. In a moment, the owner of the B and B had agreed to send up a laptop computer and a laser printer within the hour.

"How did you get the owner of this place to do that for you?" she asked curiously as he hung up.

He frowned. "Why wouldn't he?"

"Because you could steal the thing and rip him off."

He shrugged. "I told him to buy me new equipment and charge it to my room bill."

"You charged a *computer* to room service?" she asked incredulously.

"Better living through trust-fund-assisted convenience," he remarked dryly.

"No kidding," she grumbled.

"Is my having money a deal breaker?" he asked soberly.

"Depends on the deal," she replied cautiously.

Now there was the sixty-four-thousand-dollar question. What deal, indeed?

Chapter 9

She slept that night, and Trent slept the next day while she worked. Herrera had mentioned small amounts taken from many accounts she had access to, and now that Chloe knew what she was looking for, the work went more quickly. She was able to pick out the trail of the laundering from the trail of the embezzling more easily. If someone was taking money from Paradeo, the thief was doing it very well and leaving practically no traces.

As the day wore on, though, something else began to dawn on Chloe. Herrera hadn't been wrong. The missing funds all came from accounts she was directly responsible for. If she didn't know better, she'd say *she* was the thief. Alarm started to vibrate low in her gut, gradually growing in volume and intensity as the afternoon wore on.

Who else in the company had access to the same accounts she did? She poked around but no one else had exactly the same financial footprint as hers. Paradeo was a highly compartmentalized company, and no matter how hard she searched, she couldn't find anyone else with access to all of her accounts. Not good. Not good at all.

Trent woke and immediately asked that food be brought up to them, but she ignored the plate he set down beside her. Eventually, he actually took her by the shoulders and turned her away from the computer. "You need to take a break, Chloe. Eat. Drink some water. Stretch your muscles a little."

Now that he mentioned it, her stomach was growling and her throat did feel rough with thirst. It didn't help that her alarm had grown into panic clawing at the back of her throat.

"Any progress?" he asked as she picked up a sandwich and commenced eating.

She winced. "I'm on the trail of something. I've identified a number of tampered-with transactions, and now that I've seen what accounts the thief is targeting and how he or she is disguising the thefts, I should be able to spot more fishy transactions quickly. Once I do that, I ought to be able to give you an idea of how much money has been stolen."

"When will you know who's taking it?"

"Honestly, it looks like I'm the only person with access to all the accounts the thief stole from. I may have a hard time finding someone else to add to the suspect list." She blurted, "I've got to solve this or else I could be in serious trouble."

"Are you being framed?"

She stared at him in dismay. It was entirely possible. But who could be setting her up?

"You'll figure it out," he said encouragingly. But his smile didn't reach his beautiful gaze. Instead, worried crinkles formed at the corners of his eyes. Worry that she shared in spades.

"The FBI will crack this thing as soon as they look at the files I sent them, and they'll come looking for me. They could knock on that door at any minute," she admitted, giving voice to her greatest fear. Urgency tightened her entire body into a tense mass of jangling nerves. She was running out of time. "I didn't sign up for this, Trent. I'm just a lousy accountant doing what I was hired to do, darn it."

He snorted. "Just an accountant a major drug cartel is trying to kill. Clearly, you're more important and more knowledgeable than you seem to think."

"I don't see how. Anyone with the most rudimentary forensic accounting training could do what I'm doing."

Trent tilted his head, his gaze surprised. "Seriously?"

She nodded, depressed.

"Why did the FBI hire you specifically, then, to investigate this firm? Do you have some particular expertise in this kind of company?"

"Honestly, I have no idea why Don hired me. I'm fresh out of school with nary a job credit on my résumé. I was shocked—and wildly grateful—when he hired me. Maybe no one else was available to move to San Francisco on short notice."

Trent stared at her thoughtfully. "That is weird. You've been out of school, what, seven months? So this Fratello guy hired you straight out of college, as in—ink still wet on your diploma?"

She stared, shocked. How did Trent know so much about her? Horror flowed through her in a muddy torrent. "Did you have Novak do that deep background check on me, after all?"

"No. Your graduation date showed up in the superficial

search Winston Ops performed on you right after the attack in Denver. We were purely trying to figure out why
someone might want to kill you. We weren't trying to pry
into your life."

Oh, God. She didn't want to know what else they'd
uncovered on her. Thank God she didn't have an arrest
record or any outstanding parking tickets! "You sure do
your research, don't you?" she managed to grumble past
the dry tuna lodged in her throat.

A sudden, sharp longing swept over her. If only she
were more to Trent than just a job. What was wrong with
her that no one was interested in her as a woman? Clearly
she was unlovable and managing somehow to convey that
to every eligible bachelor she encountered.

"It's my past, isn't it?" she blurted.

Trent stared blankly. "Excuse me?"

"That's why no one ever loves me. There's some key
lesson I failed to learn, some deep flaw in me because I
got so little love in my childhood, isn't there?"

He was in front of her almost too fast to see. "What are
you talking about?" he demanded.

"I'm talking about me. About why nobody loves me."

"From what I saw in Denver, your sister seems devoted
to you. I'm sure you've got plenty of friends who care
deeply about you."

She was shocked to feel tears well up in her eyes. Good
grief, what was that all about? She was never this weepy
and hormonal. "I'm sorry. I guess the stress of all this is
getting to me. Just ignore me."

"No, I'm not going to ignore you. Talk to me."

She wasn't used to anyone getting this pushy with her
and her impulse was to run and hide. But she knew how
fast Trent was. No way would she reach the bathroom and
get the door locked before he blocked it open. Instead, she

sighed and retreated into her work. "I've got to get back to the computer."

"After we talk about this. What makes you think you're unlovable?"

"Oh, I don't know. The empirical evidence of no one actually loving me, ever?"

"Are we talking about you wanting a long-term relationship with a man?" he asked carefully. Lord, he sounded like he thought her head was going to start spinning around in circles or demons would leap out of the top of her skull.

"I'm not crazy," she announced.

"Okay. I believe you. You're not crazy," he replied evenly. He didn't look like he was lying, thank goodness.

"Is it too much to ask for me to find someone who likes me a little?"

"I like you a lot," he answered promptly.

"I'm talking about romantically. As in a real relationship," she snapped.

His answer came more slowly this time. "So am I."

She stared at him, stunned. "You are not."

"Yes, I am." He looked as stunned as she must look.

"Are not."

"Are you seriously going to argue with me for telling you that I like you and am interested in pursuing a romantic relationship with you?" he demanded.

"I guess I am. Particularly since I don't think you mean it."

He snorted. "And there's your answer. If you kick to the curb every guy who shows the slightest interest in you, you're going to have a hell of time getting this relationship you say you crave."

He might as well have slugged her in the stomach. Was he right? Was she pushing away anyone who cared about her? So. She was broken, after all. It *was* all her fault.

Deflated, she pulled the laptop in front of her once more. But the focus had gone out of her search. She struggled to see patterns that had been crystal-clear to her a half hour ago. It was no use. She was done for the night.

"I'm going to bed," she announced.

He sighed. "Okay. I'll stand watch until you wake up."

She glared at him. "You need more than that three-hour nap you took earlier."

"Actually, I don't. That'll keep me going a couple days."

"It's my life. I'd say it's my call."

He raised a skeptical eyebrow. "And how are you planning to force me to sleep if I don't want to?"

She pursed her lips. She might not be able to force him, but she'd bet she could tire him out enough to go to sleep on his own. As soon as she thought about sex with him, a craving to be with him, to turn herself over to him, to lose herself in him ripped through her. Was she really that needy? Or was she just more messed up in the head than she'd ever realized? She desperately wanted to escape the fear and uncertainty swirling through her and just to feel safe for once.

It dawned on her belatedly that Trent was watching her far too alertly. He looked like a tiger on the hunt. A sudden need to be his prey, to let him stalk her and conquer her made her knees weak. Did she dare?

It was crazy to even contemplate. He would break her heart as sure as she was standing here. He'd love her and leave her without a backward glance.

So, then, the trick was not to get emotionally involved with him, her inner sex kitten argued persuasively. Right. No problem. Enjoy the sex. Embrace the raw pleasure. Escape reality for a little while. And then walk away, herself. She could do that, right?

Doubt wriggled like a parasite deep within her mind,

a disgusting, dark secret she shied away from in horror. She was not her parents' child, was not ruled by passion or her emotions! She *could* walk away from Trent, darn it. She was in control of her world. Of her emotions. Of her life. No man would ever change that!

A desperate need to prove it to herself, to shut up that niggling doubt eating at her soul, buried itself in her gut. She had to do this. To show herself once and for all that no man would ever have the power to destroy her or her world.

Recklessness coursed through her, and she rode the wave, rising to her feet and walking resolutely to the mini-refrigerator. It was stocked with tiny bottles of various liquors just like a regular hotel.

Trent pushed away from the doorway where he leaned, watching her cautiously. His eyes blazed, but his body was taut with something more akin to caution. Tonight was her night. No matter what they did together, no matter what he made her feel, she would remain in total control of herself. She was the master of her mind, her body, and her traitorous feelings. He had no power over her, and she was going to prove it to both of them.

She pulled out a mini-bottle of whiskey, but Trent was there in a flash, lifting it out of her hands. He announced grimly, "If you have to drink in order to make love with me, you're going to give me a serious complex."

She stared at him in open challenge. "Don't you think you can handle me when I cut loose? What's the matter? Afraid of where I'll go with you?"

His gaze burned as hot and turbulent as the core of a volcano. "I'm not afraid of you, Chloe. I can take anything you can dish out and more."

She seriously doubted that.

But his stark observation cut through all the noise in her head, leaving behind only her determination to do this. Once and for all, she was going to purge her fear of the chaos a man would bring to her life. But could she be that brave, sexy woman that she'd been in Denver on her own? Only one way to find out.

"What do you want, Chloe?" His voice was a silken sword, so smooth and sharp it cut her to ribbons before she even realized it had touched her skin.

"I want to show you—" she corrected herself "—to show me, once and for all, that I am in control of my life."

He tilted his head, staring at her quizzically, obviously turning over her declaration in his mind. "No one's always in control, Chloe."

She shook her head in denial, and he continued, ignoring her.

"Life is messy whether you like it or not. Take you, for example. You need love in the worst way, but you're hell-bent on holding anyone who might give you that love at arm's length. You're so afraid of being hurt or rejected that you can't let yourself take the chance."

Hah! Doing this was the riskiest thing she'd ever contemplated! "You're wrong—" she started. But he swooped in and pressed his fingers against her lips, forcibly stilling them.

"Don't play with fire, unless you're willing to get burned, Chloe."

"What is that supposed to mean?" she snapped.

"It means that if you plan to seduce me in some sort of twisted power play, you'd better be prepared to lose."

She heard the words, but no meaning registered on her mind. She clung to her denial, to her determination, to her desperate need to restore order in her universe. She might not be able to stop bad guys from chasing her or trying to kill her or framing her for a crime she didn't commit. She might not be able to keep them from trashing her apartment and slashing her clothes. But by golly, she could control this. Trent would not get inside her heart or her head. She could have the wildest, hottest sex with him either of them could imagine, and it would…not…touch…her.

Her gaze narrowed. "Give it your best shot, Trent Hollings."

Chapter 10

Trent took a mental deep breath. This was it. Either he broke through all her barriers tonight, or odds were she'd never let anyone get close enough to try it again. Ever. And she was too vital and sensual a woman to let that happen to. She might not know it, yet, but she needed him to break down her walls. Hell, she needed him to smash them to dust.

He considered her for a moment longer. *And he knew exactly how he was going to do it.*

He reached slowly for the hem of her shirt and stripped it over her head. Her bra was cut low and had flirty lace trim. As his gaze dropped to the view, her hands started up to cover her cleavage.

"Ah, ah, ah," he murmured warningly.

Her hands snapped back down abruptly, fisting at her sides. Resolution darkened her gaze. What the hell was he doing? He was no fan of sex as a form of emotional combat. Of course, she was in for a surprise when he changed up the rules of engagement for this particular battle. She thought it was a fight against him, but actually, it would be pitched war against herself.

He reached for the zipper of her jeans, and she sucked in a sharp breath. He pushed the denim down over the sweet curve of her hip, and he saw the source of her chagrin. A smile split his face. "She still wears thongs, does she? I'm so proud of you."

Chloe scowled back at him. "It was small and easy to grab fast."

Right. As if he bought that lame excuse. But if she still needed her excuses to explain away her entirely normal and natural urge to feel a little sexy, he would let her have them…for now.

He lifted each of her feet in turn to ease her shoes and socks off. Since he offered her no help with her balance, she ended up having to grab his shoulder to steady herself while he massaged the arches of her slender feet. One of his goals tonight was to get her to touch him of her own free will—often and intimately, in fact.

Her right foot still cradled in his palm, he looked up at her. "If anything we do tonight gets too intense for you, let me know, okay?"

As he expected, her gaze narrowed at the implied challenge.

"I mean it, Chloe. This isn't a competition. You don't have to do anything you don't want to. Got it?"

She murmured something vaguely resembling agreement. He supposed it was the best he could hope for in her current frame of mind. She looked girded for Spanish Inquisition-style torture. Oh, he planned to torture her, all right, but not like that.

He reached around behind her, his gaze locked with

hers, to unhook her bra. For just a moment, he thought he glimpsed a flash of fear. His hands froze and he waited until it faded from her gaze. He murmured, "Where's that brave, adventurous girl from Denver who ravished me within an inch of my life? I know she can do this."

Gratitude flickered in her azure eyes as her expression steadied and gained confidence. She nodded and whispered, "Continue."

Her bra fell away from her beautiful, delicate breasts. He could look at them forever and never get tired of their elegant shape or the way they fit in his hands.

"Do you have to stare at me like that?" she asked a little grumpily. "It makes me self-conscious."

He laughed darkly. "I'm going to look all I want. And then I'm going to do all I want with you."

A fine shiver rippled across her skin. "I could really use a couple of shots of whiskey."

He replied sympathetically, "Looking for a little liquid courage? You might lose a few inhibitions in a glass of whiskey, baby, but you'd still be the same person. Most people don't change as much as they'd like to think when they drink, and they certainly don't get cooler. They just get dumber."

She smiled in spite of herself.

"Remember what I told you in Denver? Don't overthink it."

"Right. Don't overthink." She reached for his belt buckle, and he let her. In a hurry to get it over with, was she? Well, she was in for a surprise, then. He planned to take most of the night doing this.

As she reached hurriedly for his shirt buttons, he captured her hands. "Easy, baby. Slow down. Relax and enjoy the moment."

She rolled her eyes. "I can't say as I've ever found sex relaxing."

He responded, "Note to self—end the night with slow, lazy sex. To show Chloe how relaxing sex can be."

Her eyes widened and darkened. She liked that idea, did she? He grinned to himself. Good to know. There was hope for her, yet. "So, Chloe. We still have a whole lot on your list of fantasies from Denver to get through. Any preferences?"

Her cheeks bloomed scarlet. "You choose," she mumbled.

Perfect. What he had planned for tonight wasn't on her list at all. "Into the bathroom, then," he announced matter-of-factly.

She frowned, obviously going through her list and trying to figure out which one involved the restroom. Her frown deepened and alarm bloomed in her gaze. Excellent. She was already outside her comfort zone.

"Why the bathroom?" she asked cautiously.

He merely took her hand and led her, half-resisting, into the small, subway-tiled space. Without releasing her hand, he plugged the big, claw-foot tub and turned on the hot water full blast. He poured in a generous dollop of bubble bath the B and B had thoughtfully provided, and the room filled with the smell of raspberries and vanilla. Mounds of fluffy bubbles formed, and the water steamed. Tendrils of fine hair curled around Chloe's face, framing it sweetly. He added just enough cold water to make the bath bearable.

"In you go," he announced cheerfully as he rolled up his sleeves.

"Are you coming in with me?" she asked doubtfully.

"Nope. I'm designated back scrubber, tonight. Besides, I'd take up the whole tub. This treat's just for you." He perched a hip on the edge of the tub, which put her lovely breasts at eye level for him. He drank in the view eagerly as her nipples abruptly tightened into tense little peaks. Good. He wanted her hyperaware of her body before this was all said and done. It was high time she got out of her head and acknowledged her most basic bodily urges.

He leaned over to the shelf above the sink and grabbed the big, plastic hair clip she'd put there. Reaching around behind her, which brought his mouth into entirely pleasing proximity with her chest, he twisted her hair up and off her neck, securing it with the clawed clip.

She would have stepped back, but he kept his hands behind her neck, trapping her in place. Leisurely, he took a rosy peak into his mouth, rolling his tongue around the little bud and scraping his teeth lightly across it until she exhaled on a light moan. Only then did his hands fall away from the back of her neck. She didn't step back. *Chalk up a win in the first skirmish to him.*

He gestured for her to climb into her bath, but she hesitated. He reached for her thong, using it to tug her between his knees. Hooking his thumbs under the hip straps, he whisked it off her body. She curled in on herself, embarrassed by her nakedness.

"You're so damned beautiful," he breathed. "Someday, I'll have you painted in the nude."

She stared, dismayed. "And where would you hang the resulting painting?"

"In my bedroom, of course. In a place of honor by the bed you sleep in."

Her eyes popped wide open in shock. Frankly, he was a little shocked himself to realize he was thinking in terms of years down the road with her. At least his comment had the effect of distracting her from her lack of clothing. That was, until he leaned forward and kissed her belly. An urge to plant his child within her, to watch this part of her swell with the miracle of life about knocked him off the edge of the tub. Whoa. *Not ready for kids, yet.* Hell, he didn't even know if their genetics were compatible enough to have kids. He had to give her credit. Chloe did a hell of a number on his head. Damn. Skirmish number two to her.

"Into the tub, darlin'," he directed. He held her hand as she climbed over the high edge and her leg disappeared into the bubbles.

She sank down into the steaming water by slow degrees. He'd made it as hot as he thought she could stand because she needed the tension relief badly. Eventually, she sat immersed to her neck in bubbles. He folded a towel and she leaned her head back against it.

"Close your eyes," he instructed.

"Mmm. With pleasure," she murmured.

He went out into the main room to prepare for the next part of his assault while she soaked her bones to the consistency of cooked spaghetti and her muscles to gelatin. When he was satisfied with his work, he returned to the bathroom. The mirror was fogged over, and the tropical humidity plastered his shirt to him in a matter of seconds. He solved that problem by shedding it and dumping it on the floor.

Chloe's eyes remained closed as he moved to the head of the tub and reached through the diminishing suds for her shoulders. Gently, he kneaded the slender muscles. If she'd been boneless before, she melted now. He moved around to the other end of the tub and reached into the hot water for her left leg. Starting at her knee, he massaged his way down her slim calf to her toes and back up again. He gave the same treatment to her other leg. She groaned in lazy pleasure and he reveled in the sound.

The bubbles were breaking into little white islands on

the surface of the water that afforded him glimpses of her rosy body here and there. He would never forget her in this moment, his own private sea nymph.

"I think my fingers have turned into prunes," she murmured.

He plunged his forearm into the water and pulled the drain plug out of the water. She stood up and he reached for the shower head on its flexible hose. He rinsed the remaining bubbles off her and reveled in how she looked, standing there. Quickly, so she wouldn't chill and lose the languid relaxation of her bath, he wrapped her in a fluffy bath sheet that enveloped her entire body. When she was cocooned in soft terry cloth, he scooped her up in his arms and carried her into the other room.

"Oh, Trent," she breathed.

He glanced around at the dozens of candles casting a soft glow through the space. The B and B owner's wife had even provided an armful of roses from her garden for the occasion. A dozen of the most stunning roses stood in a vase on the table. He had scattered the petals from the rest across the bed and floor in a splash of reds, pinks and whites. The heady perfume filled his nose, nearly as intoxicating as the woman in his arms.

He put her on her feet and slowly unwrapped her like his own personal gift. He smudged off the remaining moisture from her skin and released her hair from its clip. It fell in a glorious shimmer of silk across her breasts. The candlelight kissed her skin with gold. This was exactly how he wanted her painted.

He picked up his nymph and laid her down gently on the bed of roses. As he stepped back to admire the effect of her sleek limbs and pale skin against the brilliant shades of the rose petals, he revised his opinion. *This* was how he wanted her painted.

Her hands drifted up to cover her private places, and he stepped forward to capture them with his hands. Holding both of her slender wrists in one fist, he lifted her arms over her head, which had the most excellent side effect of thrusting her breasts up toward him. He leaned down to feather kisses across the tempting mounds until she arched up into his mouth of her own volition.

"Are you going to tie me up?" she whispered breathily.

He lifted his head to stare down at her. "I have a better idea. Take hold of the headboard here." He guided her fingers around two of the turned spindles. "If you let go, I'll stop whatever I'm doing. But as long as you hold on, I'll keep going."

Confusion flickered in her gaze, but she nodded her agreement readily enough. Mentally, he smiled darkly. She had no idea how that promise was going to come back to bite her. He would use her own passion against her. It would restrain her a hundred times more effectively than any rope.

He trailed his fingertips down her arms, and she wriggled as he approached her ticklish ribs. She let go of the spindles and he yanked his hands away from her. Immediately, she grabbed the headboard again. He took up where he'd left off, stroking his fingertips beneath her breasts, circling the mounds lightly. Without warning, he flicked his thumbnails across both of her nipples and she arched up sharply on a gasp of startled pleasure.

He resumed his leisurely trailing of fingertips across her skin. And so it went. He touched her lightly, interspersing the lightest of massages with occasional reminders of just how sensually charged her body was becoming. The rosy glow of the bath on her skin was replaced by a rosier glow of desire.

She sang him a veritable symphony of sighs, moans

and groans of wordless pleasure as he explored her body. In Denver, they'd been driven so hard by their desire that they'd never really slowed down for him to learn her body thoroughly. But tonight, he rectified that oversight. He found her ticklish places, the sensitive spots, the areas that made her fists flex on the spindles in frustration.

And when he finished exploring with his hands, he started all over again with his mouth. As soon as she figured out what he was about, she groaned aloud. "I can't take this, Trent. You're killing me."

He replied against her hip, "Then let go of the headboard."

Her only answer was a thick groan. He smiled against her satin flesh. Ahh, she was beginning to learn the nature of the warfare he waged against her. Time to scale the next wall: her self-consciousness.

He rose up over her and reached for her ankles. Until now, her legs had been pressed tightly together, and he'd let her have her modesty. She made a sound of protest as he pushed her knees apart far enough for him to kneel between them. But when his mouth closed over her big toe and his tongue darted between her toes, the sound of protest turned into a groan of approval. He nipped the pad of her toe and scraped his teeth across the arch of her foot until she squirmed, giggling. But, he noted with approval, she didn't let go of the headboard.

He gave the same treatment to her other foot. Her breathing became short and fast as she discovered the erogenous connection between her feet and her nether regions. He had a sneaking suspicion his nymph was going to develop a bit of a foot fetish before this night was over.

When she was panting hard, he nipped his way up to the back of her knee and laved the soft flesh there with his tongue. She twisted and turned beneath him as the sensations in other parts of her built to a fever pitch.

By the time he finished with her other knee, she started to beg. "Enough, Trent. No more. It's too much. I can't…"

And yet, she continued to grip the headboard as if her life depended on it. Granting her no quarter, he nipped and licked his way up the inside of her thigh. She was openly thrashing now, flinging her limbs wide and unintentionally giving him ready access to his ultimate target.

His mouth closed on her swollen, hot flesh and she all but came off the bed. Careful not to touch any part of her except the heaving, trembling flesh beneath his tongue, he launched a full-scale assault.

She cried out his name, and he maintained contact as she bucked and shuddered beneath him. He was far from done, however. He pressed his offensive, driving onward as she climaxed again, her entire body stretching into a taut bow.

"Trent!" she cried out, her voice begging for relief.

Oh, no. He would accept nothing less than her complete surrender. This was war. He sucked and licked and circled her flesh with tongue and lips, and when fatigue began to set into her limbs, he plunged his fingers into her tight heat.

She responded instantly, her entire body tensing for an endless, suspended moment around his invasion. He felt the mother of all orgasms rip through her, and she keened in complete and violent surrender as she literally came apart for him.

Finally taking pity on her, he lifted his head to gaze down at her. Slowly, her eyes blinked open and they were glazed with such pleasure that he doubted she knew her own name at the moment. Okay, this was definitely how he wanted her painted.

Obviously, he would have to do the painting himself. This was not a sight he ever planned to share with anyone else. Chloe was his. Her pleasure and her passion were his. Why she'd chosen him to share this intensely private part of herself with, he had no idea. But he treasured the gift beyond all else.

When she'd caught her breath and a small measure of awareness had flickered back into her eyes, he murmured, "Ready for more?"

"More?" she repeated blankly.

He smiled darkly. "The night is young, my dear."

Chloe stared up at Trent in complete disbelief. There was more than *that*? He just given her the most epic, shattering pleasure of her life. What more could there be? Her fingers ached from squeezing the headboard so tightly and her palms were all but cramping from the pleasure he'd given her. But as long as she was hanging on to the wooden spindles, she was in control. She had the power to call this thing off any time she wanted. Except she emphatically didn't want.

"More, huh?" she murmured. He'd already put his hands—and mouth—on every square inch of her. No man had ever touched most of the places he'd been tonight. But it was Trent. In spite of his infuriating secrets, in spite of his casual disdain for the order she craved, and especially in spite of his ease with floating in and out of relationships, she trusted him.

He might talk about her sleeping in his bed years from now, but she knew it for the insincere pickup line it was. She knew from her research that he had never allowed any woman to pin him down. She *knew* he would leave her someday, probably sooner rather than later. But none of it mattered. Not with the echoes of orgasm after orgasm reverberating through her entire being. He made her feel like a whole woman. He made her feel…loved.

Shock rocked her to her core. Wait a minute. Tonight was about her staying in control. Of proving that no man could touch her or her world. She could impose order on her life no matter what he made her feel!

But then his fingers started to move, dancing upon her most sensitive flesh, caressing and flicking at the epicenter of her earlier detonations. Her body responded eagerly, the terrible, exhilarating tension already building deep within her once more. He knew her better than she knew herself. He stroked and teased, drawing reactions from her flesh she didn't even know she was capable of.

Her eyes drifted closed, and the lure of pure, molten pleasure called to her. She felt the volcano deep in her soul and strained toward it, sinking ever deeper toward her most primal core. When she reached the heart of this indescribable feeling, she would gladly hurl herself into it, no matter that she would be incinerated by it, entirely consumed by it.

A warning hummed vaguely in her mind. She was losing herself in the pleasures of the flesh. Her mind was being subsumed by lust. But, ahh, it felt *so* good. Still, as incredible as what he'd done to her had felt, she had to let go of that headboard.

His finger slipped into her slick heat and muscles she didn't know she had gripped the invader tightly as it slid in and out with delicious languor. The volcano surged forward, threatening to blow at any second. *Must. Fight. This. Pleasure.*

A second finger joined the first, stretching her and filling her. And then Trent started doing the most clever things, rubbing and teasing internal nerves that roared to life and pushed the volcano right to the very edge.

She would let go of the headboard any second. Just a tiny bit more of this insane pleasure. Just a tiny bit more...

When the explosion came, it made everything that had come before pale by comparison. It erupted from the depths of her soul, ripping away the very walls of her existence, throwing the scattered bits of her to the heavens in a spectacular display that lit the night. It went on and on until she didn't know if it would ever end. And somewhere along the way, she ceased to care. She gave herself over to it, emptying her entire soul into this endless moment.

It was as if her whole life had built up inside an enclosed magma chamber, deep, deep underground. The stored up pressure had been unbelievable, beyond even her wildest imagining. Only when it completely blew like this did she finally understand the enormity of what she'd been carrying around inside her.

It all came out at once. Tears of pain and joy, longing and loneliness. Ambition and fear, dreams and loss, laughter and rage. Everything she was and wanted to be poured out of her in that apocalyptic release.

And finally, when it was all too much for her, the orgasm completely overwhelmed her and everything went black.

She blinked her eyes open—it could have been a second or an hour later—and Trent was there, his body warm and solid against the length of hers. He was propped up on one elbow, staring down at her. Even now, he gave her no quarter, his gaze capturing hers in no uncertain terms, allowing her no place to hide.

"How do you feel?" he asked.

She considered. "Empty."

His brows drew together in the beginning of a frown and she elaborated hastily. "Good empty."

"How so?"

"It's as if I've been carrying around this massive burden of…stuff…inside me for so long I didn't even know it was there. And now it's just…gone. I feel light. Empty."

"Got it."

"Do you?" she murmured. "I'm not sure I do."

He merely smiled down at her and offered no explanation. "You're still hanging on to the headboard."

She blinked up at him, not making the connection to his meaning for a moment. "Oh." She started to let go and was surprised to discover that her fingers were cramped into tight fists.

He reached up with his free hand to still her hands. "I wasn't suggesting that you had to let go. I was merely making an observation. Do you want to let go? Or will you let me fill that empty place within you?"

She gazed up at him, not quite understanding his meaning. Comprehension hovered just beyond the edges of her consciousness. That, and a compulsion to hang on to that headboard just a little bit longer and find out what he meant.

Her mouth curved into a slow smile. "I'm game if you are."

Trent laughed quietly. "Ahh, sweet Chloe. You are a brave woman. Let's see what we can do about that empty feeling."

He shifted until he rested between her thighs, supporting his weight on his elbows. He didn't move. He just lay there, staring down at her. And the strangest thing happened. Her body started, unbelievably, to respond to him once more. He didn't touch her, or kiss her, or even move against her. He just continued to stare deep into her eyes. It was if he'd stripped her soul bare and gained some sort of magical power over it. All she had to do was remember the pleasure and lust he'd brought forth from her and it was all right there. The building heat, the jangling need, the wild rush toward completion.

"How do you do that?" she whispered, amazed.

He merely smiled, his gaze enigmatic. And when she thought she was going to explode yet again, he thankfully shifted. Male flesh pressed impatiently against her and she shifted to bring their bodies into perfect alignment. And then he filled her, indeed. The stretching sensation was extraordinary, her ultrasensitized flesh weeping its pleasure.

She unraveled in a matter of seconds, crying out against his shoulder as he began to move within her. The exquisite pleasure went on forever, growing in force and power as he surged toward some unseen destination, drawing her with him. She hung on to him with legs and internal muscles wrapping herself around him body and soul and clinging tightly as he took her to the stars one last time.

As her now hoarse cries built in the back of her throat and the volcano gathered itself to explode one last time and incinerate them both, he froze, tensing against her.

"Do you surrender?" he demanded, his voice rasping with desperate control tenuously maintained.

"What?" she gasped.

"Do you surrender? Unconditionally and completely?"

"Yes," she groaned as he slammed into her, shoving her over the edge and into the heart of the beast. They burned up together, hanging on to one another for dear life as the volcano took them both. Her flesh and his fused into one. They had no beginning and end, just this moment of scorching perfection they'd made together.

Consumed and reborn in the same instant, she lost herself in Trent's eyes and found herself staring back.

They must have stayed that way for a long time, but she'd lost all sense of time passing in the wonder and discovery of it all. She'd had no idea…never guessed…but then, what they'd just done went a lot deeper than mere sex....

And then it dawned on her. *This* was what love felt like.

She let go of the headboard then and wrapped her arms around the man who'd finally had the courage to break down her stupid walls and silly misconceptions to truly and unconditionally love her. And then she cried.

Trent was deeply alarmed when Chloe burst into tears without warning. He'd meant to knock her off her rocker with great sex, not make her sob uncontrollably in his arms. He rolled onto his side and gathered her against him, completely flummoxed.

"What's wrong, baby?" he murmured into her tangled hair.

"Nothing," she mumbled wetly against his chest.

Huh? Women were the damnedest creatures, sometimes. He tried again. "What's upsetting you? Tell me."

"I'm happy." She hiccupped in punctuation to her declaration.

"You want me to fix that? Am I supposed to return you to your previously unhappy state?" God, he was confused.

"No, silly." A sobbing breath. "I'm crying because I'm happy and there's nothing to fix."

"Oh." Well okay, then. He'd never made a woman cry because the sex had been so great. He relaxed and drew her across his chest as he rolled over onto his back. She was warm and silken and boneless against him, just the way a satisfied woman should be. He was feeling pretty damned boneless himself, at the moment.

They relaxed like that for a long time. Long enough that he was just on the verge of slipping into unconsciousness before it dawned on him that he was actually falling asleep without drug assistance. Go figure. Epic sex apparently cured his insomnia. He drifted once more, reveling in the feeling of going to sleep with this gradual, natural ease.

Chloe murmured against his chest, "I know you'll leave me someday, and I'll probably be too mad to tell you then, but thank you for this night."

His eyes popped open and his body abruptly tensed. So much for sleep. "What do you mean I'll leave you?" he demanded.

She rolled off his chest and laid on her back, staring up at the ceiling. She answered matter-of-factly, "It's not like you've ever made any secret of your lifestyle. You're a playboy. You travel the world, and lord knows, the beaches you hang out on are full of girls all too eager to jump in the sack with you. Why would a hot guy like you settle down with a girl like me?"

He pushed up onto an elbow to glare down at her.

She continued, not looking over at him, "Denver was a casual hookup for you, and had someone not tried to kill me, we would never have seen each other again."

He'd been plotting ways to see her again before he'd ever climbed out of her bed that night in Denver. "Yes, we damned well would have seen each other again," he burst out.

That made her look his way. She recoiled, and he realized he was probably glaring daggers at her. Tough. She was really pissing him off. "News flash, Chloe. What we shared tonight was damned special. Once-in-a-lifetime stuff."

"Well sure, it was the best sex I've ever had, but I'm not like you. I don't have a ton of experience."

"That was not sex! That was making love, dammit!" He probably shouldn't be yelling at her like this, but he couldn't seem to help it. She seriously thought tonight had been some casual thing for him?

"I bared my soul to you, Chloe, and I thought you'd done the same to me." He exploded out of bed, too agitated to lie still another instant. He moved around the room fast, grabbing up bits and pieces of his clothes. He yanked a fresh shirt out of his bag and pulled it over his head.

Chloe was sitting up in bed, the sheets pooled around her waist, a red rose petal clinging to her left breast just over her heart. "How in the *hell* do you do that, Trent?"

He whirled to glare at her. "Do what?" he snapped.

"You move so fast my eye can barely follow the movement. No human being moves like that. What have they *done* to you?"

"They," he spit out the word angrily, "saved my life. They gave me stem cell transplants that restored my muscle tone and then some. Jeff Winston saved my life, but to do so he had to turn me into a superhero. Have you got a problem with that?"

She just stared, apparently struck speechless.

On that note, he stormed out the door and slammed it shut with an entirely satisfying reverberation of angry sound behind him.

The streets were dark and deserted. He stretched his legs into a ground-devouring run and flew into the darkness, losing himself in the night.

Chloe stood in the shadows of the room, peering around the edge of the curtains, using the rough cloth to hide her nakedness. And as Trent raced away from her at the speed of sound, a tear slid down her cheek.

What *had* they done to him? Jeff Winston and his doctors had turned Trent into some kind of freak. The inability to sleep, the incredible metabolism, and the speed. God, his speed. She'd never seen a human being even begin to move that fast as he'd raced away from her. Was it a fair trade-off? Life in return for being a circus sideshow? He'd been gone so quickly she'd barely had time to register what she'd seen.

And now she was alone. Again. Just like always, anyone she'd dared to love had run screaming from her at the first available opportunity. This time, it hadn't been enough for the guy to run away at normal speed. No, this one had run from her at superhuman speed.

She slid down the wall beside the window and curled into a little ball, hugging her knees and burying her forehead on them. This time, she wasn't going to recover. Trent had shown her just how magnificent love could truly be, and she had no illusions that she would ever find another man who could take her to the places he had. How could she ever settle for anything less?

No doubt about it. He'd ruined her heart. For good.

Chapter 11

Sometime during the night, Chloe dragged herself back to bed and pulled the covers up over her head. When she awoke, the morning outside was foggy and gray, totally appropriate to her mood. There was no sign of Trent having returned to the room during the night.

Heart heavy, she sat down at her computer and listlessly opened up Barry's files to poke at them. The entire list of files took a while to load, and she stared at the blinking cursor, blank-eyed. Idly, she wondered how he'd managed to get access to all of these files. She didn't come close to having the security codes to get half of these files....

And then it hit her. How *did* Barry get access to all of these files? God, it had been right in front of her all along! Paradeo was a highly compartmentalized company. *No one* had access to all the financial information sitting before her. Barry had to have broken into multiple servers to retrieve all this information. But how?

He had managed to get passwords and access codes for at least three different systems within the company. And if he could break into the servers, he could also break into every single account on those servers. Was *he* the thief?

Immediate guilt for suspecting a dead man swamped her and she pushed away the notion. But her brain kept circling back to it. There truly was no one else at Paradeo who could be the thief. Even the Chief Financial Officer had to have other members of his staff open locked servers for him when he wanted access to them. It was the one cardinal rule of the firm. Nobody could touch everything.

Except Barry had managed to do it. Had he been working alone? Or did he have a cadre of accomplices? Lord knew, enough money was missing for several people to live comfortably on it for a long time. Her calculations showed the missing funds to be on the order of twenty million dollars.

This must be why he'd been murdered. But then Chloe frowned. Why had Miguel Herrera accused her of stealing money from Paradeo if the big bosses had already identified and eliminated the thief? They must think she was one of the accomplices.

She picked up her cell phone and called Don Fratello but was passed immediately to his voice mail. "Don. It's Chloe. I've found something big at Paradeo. This isn't just a money laundering problem at all. It's an embezzlement case, too. Barry Lind—that bookkeeper who was murdered a few days ago—was stealing money from Paradeo. Lots of it. We're talking millions. I think he had help, though. If you look at his bank records, I'll bet he's been passing money to one or more people who've been helping him. The FBI should be able to track down his accomplices easily. Call me when you get this message."

Satisfied, she hung up the phone. A quick double-check

of the last time money had been skimmed off an account made her jaw drop. Yesterday. Even after Barry had been brutally murdered, his accomplice had continued to steal. She had to give the unknown person credit for having nerves of steel. No way would she have kept taking money right from under Paradeo's nose if she thought violent drug lords were on to her.

There was still plenty of work left to be done tracking down where Paradeo's money came from in the first place. The original money laundering case was still open. But it was time to hand that over to the FBI. It would take their resources and access to privileged banking information to track the transactions back to their various sources. She had all the starting points identified, though, and it would be an easy matter for the FBI to finish the investigation.

Which left her at loose ends with not much work to do. And that meant she had plenty of time to ponder her own mess of a life. She glanced at the time. Nearly 8:00 a.m. Where was Trent? Was he ever coming back?

Reluctantly, she picked up her cell phone again and stared at it doubtfully. She was too chicken to dial him directly after last night. He'd been so furious when she confronted him with the truth. But there was no way he would stick around for the long haul with any woman. It was written all over him. She'd merely read the obvious signs and called him on it.

He was right about one thing, though. She had a knack for pushing men away from her. Slowly, she dialed the Winston Ops phone number.

"Winston Ops. Good morning, Miss Jordan. What can we do for you today? Did you lose Trent again?"

It was the duty controller, Novak. She steadied her voice as it started to tremble. "Actually, I did. He left last night a little after midnight and he's still not back." Her voice dropped to a tearful half whisper in spite of her best efforts as she confessed, "I don't know what to do."

"Trent ordered up a full security team for you sometime last night. I can look up the time if you want. It was before I came on duty. At any rate, they're inbound to you now. Should be there in a couple of hours."

Oh, God. He'd washed his hands of her. Trent was handing her off to a bunch of strangers rather than look out for her himself. The pain of his departure cut right through her, eviscerating her soul. Her legs collapsed and she found herself sitting on the floor again, leaning against the bed this time.

"Just a moment, ma'am. I'll get Jeff." God, did Novak have to sound so sympathetic? She was so pathetic.

Jeff Winston's voice came on the line in a matter of seconds. "What's wrong, Chloe?"

It was the last straw. He was so gentle and sounded so concerned. She slapped her hand over her phone's microphone jack as a sob escaped her.

"Chloe? Where's Trent? What's going on? Are you okay?"

She dragged in another sobbing breath and then steadied herself. She had to get through this conversation. "I don't know where he's gone, Jeff. He left last night." She added reluctantly, "We had a fight."

Give the man credit for not asking what about. Instead he went for the safer but obvious question. "Are you in a secure location right now?"

"Yes. I'm in the hotel room Trent was using to do surveillance on my apartment."

"Stay there. We've got a team on a jet. They'll land in San Francisco in about—" he paused while somebody no doubt supplied the answer "—two hours. They should be with you by noon."

"I don't need your team," she replied wearily. "I solved my case a little while ago. Or at least the part that was going to get me killed."

"Really?" Jeff responded with interest.

She filled him in briefly, ending with an assurance that the FBI could take the case from here. The big dogs at Paradeo should find out the identity of Barry's actual accomplice(s) just in time to call their dogs off her before they went to jail themselves for money laundering. "And so," she concluded, "I'm pretty much off the hook."

Jeff made a noncommittal noise. "Still, I'd like to keep a few guys on you until the FBI's investigation is wrapped up and Paradeo's senior managers are behind bars. Just for your sister's peace of mind."

"Why does everyone keeping using Sunny to guilt me into cooperating? She's a grown woman and can take care of herself. She's got Aiden and doesn't need me anymore."

Jeff answered quietly, "We always need our family, Chloe. Sunny loves you wholeheartedly. She'd die if something happened to you. Why do you think she asked me to keep an eye on you in the first place? She was worried about your new line of work getting you into trouble. Frankly, if not for her concern, you could be dead right now."

"How's that?" Chloe asked, startled.

"It was because of her that I asked Trent to keep an eye on you at the wedding. Had he not been there to knock you out of the way, that SUV would have hit you."

Oh. My. God. *Trent had spent the night with her in Denver because he was under orders to?* He hadn't even wanted to hook up with her in the first place! Her humiliation was complete. And then she'd asked him to do all those things… God, what he must think of her. Poor, desperate, spinster sister of his buddy's hot bride. Where was a rock for her to crawl under and never come out?

She mumbled something incoherent and all but hung up on Jeff Winston. No way was she sticking around for another team of his guys to come and take pity on her. Gee whiz, maybe they'd give her a group orgy if she acted pitiful enough. Her skin crawled at what Jeff and his men must think of her.

Oh, God…what must Trent think of her? Not that it had kept him from having sex with her whenever he wanted it, of course. In the wake of her gut-squirming humiliation, anger took root, growing like Jack's beanstalk until it reached the sky and beyond. How dare he?

Literally shaking with fury, she punched out Winston Ops's phone number once more.

"Hi, Chloe, what can I do for you, now?" Novak asked cautiously.

"Where's Trent?"

"Excuse me?"

"I know you can track his cell phone. You did it before. Where is he right this second?" Her tone of voice brooked no refusal.

"Uhh, just a sec," Novak muttered. "He's in Malibu. Or rather, off the coast of Malibu."

"Like in the ocean?" Chloe asked in surprise.

"Yes. I'd imagine he's surfing. He's pretty good at it, you know. World champ two years ago—"

She hung up on Trent's accomplishments. Whatever. World champion surfer, world champion jerk. Same diff. Eyes narrowed, she considered how to find him and give him a serious piece of her mind. Her car. It was in the parking garage underneath her building across the street. She had to get to it without Herrera or whoever might be staking out her place spotting her.

She headed downstairs to ask the owner of the B and B for a favor. If the guy could buy Trent a laptop, he could certainly fetch her car for her. Sure enough, the fellow was more than happy to trot across the street and get her car for his best customer's girlfriend.

Right. Girlfriend. What the guy didn't know wouldn't hurt him. In a matter of minutes, she was seated behind the wheel of her car and on her way south out of San Francisco. It was nearly four hundred miles to Malibu, but traffic was moving fast on I-5 and she made outstanding time, killing the trip in a little under seven furious hours. Plenty of time to work up a really good head of steam.

It was late afternoon when she parked beside the Malibu Pier. If Trent was surfing, he was no doubt doing so at Surfrider Beach, just north of the pier. It was a blustery day and she secured her hair in a ponytail as it whipped in her face. She grabbed a sweater out of the trunk of her car and held it tightly around her body as she slogged out onto the sand.

The ocean roared its anger and only a few people sat or strolled on the beach. The water was dotted with dozens of surfers, however. And she could see why. The waves were easily twenty feet tall, and the occasional big wave topped thirty feet. These waves were not for amateurs. But then Trent was a world champion.

A half-dozen Jet Skis hauled wet-suit-clad surfers up and down the swells, depositing them just beyond where the breakers started. Which one of the neon-colored specks was Trent? Shielding her eyes from the wind and flying sand, she squinted out to sea.

"Looking for someone?" A grizzled beachcomber startled her by asking from right beside her.

"Uhh, yes. Trent Hollings."

"Hollings. Let's see. Big, good-looking guy. Dark hair.

Light eyes. Prefers a left-hand curl...big wave rider. Uses a long board. That the one?"

"Yes. That's him." She didn't know what kind of waves Trent preferred or what kind of board he used, but the physical description certainly fit.

The long-board thing narrowed down the possibilities of which surfer he was since the majority of them were using short boards. But there were still at least a dozen long-board surfers on the waves. At the end of the day, she supposed it didn't matter which surfer he was. It wasn't like she could march out into the ocean and demand that he come in to shore and explain himself.

Actually, she didn't give a darn what he had to say for himself. She did have a few things to say to him, however. She'd had the entire drive down from San Francisco to plan her scathing speech, in fact.

Realizing the beachcomber was still standing there, she asked him, "Any idea when the surfers will call it a day?"

"Not till sunset. That's in about an hour-and-a-half."

Impatient to give Trent a piece of her mind, she had no intention of leaving and letting him slip away from her unscathed. She would wait. But it was cold out here. She slogged back to her car to dump her shoes in the trunk and fetch her emergency blanket. Plopped down on a corner of the blanket on the sand, she wrapped the remainder of the wool-plaid throw around her shoulders.

The surfers were mesmerizing. They flew across the waves like ballet dancers with wings beneath their feet. And they looked as fragile as brightly colored butterflies against the towering walls of water crashing down around them. Although the occasional surfer was overtaken by a break and swallowed up for a heart-stopping minute in the frothing surf, most of these guys were really, really good. They safely dropped off the back side of the crests or rode the waves in until they petered out. Then they'd paddle over to the nearest Jet Ski, ride back out and do it all again.

Which one was Trent? She narrowed it down to three or four of the tallest, most powerful surfers. But beyond that, she couldn't tell. The sun expanded into a giant, pulsing ball of red as it slipped below the cloud deck to briefly show itself and then slide behind the sea.

No big surprise, teen girls started filtering onto the beach as sunset approached. Chloe was a bit shocked by the sheer number of groupies and the scantiness of their bikinis in this chilly weather.

The temperature dropped precipitously with the sun, and the last of the surfers grabbed quick waves and rode them all the way in to shore. She thought several of them actually eyed her appreciatively as she searched for Trent. But in light of the nubile, half-naked phalanx of hot chicks swarming the surfers, she probably was mistaken. At thirty years old, she was a senior citizen on this beach.

Trent was one of the last to jog ashore, a bright yellow-and-orange surfboard tucked under his arm. Her heart raced at the sight of him. Or maybe it was anticipation of the confrontation to come making it pound like that. Either way, she hurried to where he bent over his board, unhooking it from its ankle tether.

He glanced up as she drew near. The lanyard slipped out of his hand and fell to the sand as he straightened abruptly.

"What the hell are you doing here?" he demanded, his voice rough like he'd been shouting over the surf and swallowing saltwater all day.

"You and I need to talk," she shouted back over the crashing-ocean noise.

"I've got nothing to say," he growled. "You're convinced that I'm incapable of real feelings or sustaining a relationship. That basically says it all."

Dammit, he'd stolen her line! "And it's over?" she demanded. "Just like that?"

"Yup. Just like that." He picked up his board and commenced hiking up the beach toward a crowded surf shack. Warm, yellow light poured out onto the sand as twilight fell quickly.

She followed him, not about to let him get away with an exit line like that. Although she wasn't at all sure what there was left to say between them. If he could walk away from her without a backward glance like this, then she'd been right about him, after all. He wasn't capable of real feelings or any remotely resembling commitment.

"I loved you, dammit!" she shouted over the roar of the ocean.

Trent stopped a dozen yards short of the surf shack and its raucous crowd of surfers stripping out of wet suits and hoisting cans of beer, staring like she'd just spoken to him in Martian. "You love—" He broke off, looking past her first, and then all around the beach. "Where are your bodyguards?" he demanded.

"I told Jeff I don't need any."

"And he went along with that?" Trent exclaimed. He shoved a distracted hand through his wet hair, standing it up in every direction. "We've got to get you off this beach and under cover!"

"I'm fine. I figured out who was stealing the money from Paradeo. It was Barry. The FBI will find his accomplice or accomplices and the drug cartel will get off my back."

"And until the FBI finds these alleged accomplices? You're still in danger until then," he snapped.

She shrugged. After the pain of the past day, she didn't especially care about being in danger. It was such a small thing in the face of loving and losing Trent. The prospect of decades of gray, lonely years unfolding one after another until she died, bitter and alone, frankly wasn't all that appealing.

"Don't give me that I-don't-care-about-danger look," he growled. Dropping his board, he stepped forward aggressively, took her upper arm in his big hand and steered her bodily toward the parking lot.

"Stop! You're hurting me!"

"I am not, and you know it. Be quiet and let me get you out of here. And then you're telling me what you just said again."

She planted both heels in the sand and managed to bring him to a halt after he dragged her a half-dozen feet. "You can drop the fake-concern act, Trent. I don't buy it anymore. Jeff told me he ordered you to keep an eye on me in Denver as a favor to Sunny. You took that order a wee bit literally, didn't you? I highly doubt he meant for you to sleep with me."

"He didn't order me to watch you until after—" He broke off. "Not now. Get your cute little tush in gear before I toss you over my shoulder and carry you off this damned beach."

He sounded genuinely furious. Reluctantly, she had to admit he probably had reason to be mad at her. Still, his high-handed attitude irritated the daylights out of her. She stomped along beside him rather than give him the satisfaction of bodily hauling her out of here. As they reached the asphalt parking area, a streetlamp flickered to life with a loud buzz, and Trent started violently. Wow. He really was tense. Although, she failed to see why. The threat to her was all but over.

He stopped in front of a sporty SUV. "Get in the car."

"I've got my own car, thank you very much," she retorted.

"I don't care. Get in."

"No! You can't just order me around, Trent. I'm not one of your floozy fan girls."

"Clearly not," he retorted dryly. "I will pick you up and toss you in my car if you continue to be obstinate."

That was it. She'd had it with him. She turned on her bare heel, grinding sand into it painfully, and marched to her car. She grabbed her door handle and Trent's hand closed over hers. It was cold—probably from the ocean, but it still sent heat whipping through her.

"I'll drive," he said quietly.

At least he wasn't yelling at her anymore. She nodded stiffly and slipped her hand out from under his. He took the keys from her and slid behind the wheel as she walked around to the rear and opened the trunk. She slipped on shoes and stowed the blanket and sweater…and never saw the guy coming. One minute she was bent over the trunk, and the next, a large, fast-moving shadow swooped in on her. A powerful arm went around her waist as a hand slapped over her mouth. She was spun and thrown all in one movement. She landed on the floor of a van, slamming to the ribbed metal hard enough to knock the breath out of her.

Tires squealed beneath her and the sliding door slammed shut, enclosing her in darkness. She scrambled upright, hands up in fists.

"Easy, Miss Jordan. I have a gun on you."

Miguel Herrera. Where was Trent? Why hadn't he come roaring to the rescue? "What did you do to my… boyfriend?" She hoped Herrera didn't hear her hesitation.

"One of my boys is keeping him company. He isn't going anywhere until I say so, or until he fancies a gut full of bullet holes."

Oh, God. She was on her own. And as her eyes adjusted

to the van's dim interior, Herrera was, indeed, pointing a gun at her. Along with another man sitting on a crate in the back near the rear doors.

She'd learned very young never to show fear unless she wanted to get eaten alive. The more terrified she was, the more belligerent she knew to act. Right now, she scooted backward until she was leaning against the wall and propped her forearm on an upbent knee as casually as she could muster, even though she felt like throwing up. *Where are you, Trent?* "You keep kidnapping me, Miguel. Why don't you just call me and ask whatever you want to know? It would save us both so much trouble."

"Cool customer," he commented under his breath. Then, louder, "Shut up. When I want you to talk, I'll ask the questions."

Uhh, okay. She was in no hurry to spill her guts to this man. Death was probably in her very near future, but the decision wasn't in her hands at this point. She visually searched the floor of the van for a weapon or something to help her escape, but the vehicle was bare.

Somehow, she didn't believe that Trent would be kept off her trail for very long. For once, she was glad for his freakish speed. He would figure out a way to use it to his advantage and follow her. If nothing else, he would get word to Winston Ops and they would use their scary powers to track this vehicle and send help.

The key now was not to panic and to keep her captors relaxed. Happy even. Hence, she would be as cooperative as she possibly could be until the cavalry arrived. It was a plan, at any rate, and held the encroaching panic at bay.

Chapter 12

Trent saw a flurry of activity in the side mirror, and instinct had him ripping open his door and rolling out of his seat before his brain even registered what was happening. Panic and rage erupted in his skull and his body coiled to spring. Except when his feet landed on the pavement, he registered guns—several of them—trained on him. Even he wasn't proof against that many flying bullets.

He froze, snarling in fury as a man threw Chloe in the back of a van and jumped in after her. The thug in the parking lot in front of him didn't worry Trent. He could take that bastard. But the guy in the passenger window of the van pointing an automatic assault weapon at him with cool precision was another story. Even a bare instant's observation told Trent this guy was a pro who would neither miss nor hesitate to empty a full clip of lead into Trent's gut.

The van peeled out as Trent stared on in impotent fury. The vehicle moved far enough away that the guy in the passenger window no longer had a shot at him, and Trent turned his attention to the single shooter who had been left behind, no doubt to make sure Trent didn't follow the van.

He gauged his chances of reaching the thug's weapon before Herrera's man could pull the trigger. He figured about fifty-fifty. Good enough for him. Chloe was in that van and its taillights were diminishing to specks in the distance. Fast.

Trent leaped, keeping his trajectory extremely low and using every bit of speed his body possessed to close the gap. The guy got off one shot and Trent vaguely registered searing heat in a long line along the back of his right shoulder.

But then he was on the guy, wrenching the pistol out of the man's shocked grasp and putting all his momentum behind the elbow he swung at the guy's face. He was too close to use his fist, but the sharp point of his elbow caught Herrera's man in the right temple and dropped him like a rock.

Trent spun and leaped for Chloe's car. He backed up, running over the downed thug's legs, and effectively ensuring the bastard wouldn't give chase. As the man screamed invectively, Trent stepped on the gas, and Chloe's car peeled out of the parking lot exactly the same way the van had.

Last he'd seen the van, it had been heading west toward the Pacific Coast Highway. As he sped after it, he searched the glove compartment and door pockets for Chloe's cell phone. No sign of it. He had no time to stop and call Winston Ops for backup or he'd lose the van, and Chloe, for good. He was on his own. Swearing, he floored the accelerator and used his reflexes to maximum advantage as he swerved in and out of traffic.

A white van came into sight well ahead of him. *Hang on, Chloe. I'm coming, baby.*

Chloe was tipped over on her side as the van turned abruptly. It felt like they were going uphill. Heading inland, huh? If only she knew this area better she might have some idea where they were taking her. The hard rectangle of her cell phone was comforting in her pants pocket. As soon as the bad guys left her alone, she'd call for help. Funny, but her first thought was to call Trent and not the police. Had she really come to depend on him that much? Did she trust him with her life over anyone else she might call? Like Don and the FBI? Or even the local police?

Shocked, she righted herself and tried to catch a glimpse of something out the windshield that would identify where she was. But sitting low on the floor like this, all she could see was the rapidly darkening sky.

She comforted herself with imagining Trent overpowering the guy Herrera had left behind. Poor schmuck probably hadn't even known what had hit him when Trent jumped him at superhuman speed. She envisioned Trent jumping into her car to give chase and calling in every law enforcement agency on the west coast and Winston Ops to come rescue her—

Wait a minute. What was he going to call with? She had her cell phone with her, and he was wearing a wet suit that didn't have anywhere to store a phone in its form-fitting neoprene. Her heart sank. Trent was on his own, and even he couldn't take out three armed kidnappers all alone, assuming he even made it past the first guy back in the parking lot.

The van drove for maybe an hour. The car noises from outside diminished and the roads got bumpier. They must be taking her someplace nice and isolated to torture her and kill her. Were it not for her complete panic at the notion of never seeing Trent again, never getting a chance to thank him for all he'd done for her, never working up the courage to tell him how she felt about him, she might have dozed off in the darkness and monotony of the ride. But as it was, she started working on the hypothetical speech she was going to give him when he hypothetically over-came the massive odds against him and rescued her from this mess. It was better that screaming in terror.

She was still working on how to properly apologize to him for putting herself in this danger in the first place when the van slowed, stopped, and its ignition turned off.

The guy in the back of the van opened the double doors and jumped out. All she could see were trees behind him.

"Out," Herrera barked at her.

She rose to her feet, bent over, and made her way to the back. Her legs were so wobbly they barely held her weight. They did collapse when she jumped down to the ground. The first thug grabbed her roughly by the arm and yanked her upright. And then, as if thinking better of having helped her, he gave her a hard shove that nearly knocked her over again.

She drew up short when a gun barrel appeared under her nose. "Move," Herrera growled.

Glancing around frantically, she saw they were sur-rounded by pine trees and a small cabin was in front of her. Wasn't there some kind of national forest not too far from Malibu up in the hills? That must be where they'd taken her. Not that knowing where she was would do her any good if Herrera shot her before she could call Trent.

She stumbled toward the cabin, hoping it had a working restroom. She sneezed when she stepped into the dusty, dark interior. Someone switched on a light behind her and illuminated the filthy room. No one had been in this place for months or maybe years. A thick layer of gray dust cov-ered everything. The furniture was decrepit and broken chairs were stacked in one corner of the main room.

Herrera spoke in rapid Spanish, ordering both his men

to sweep the area outside and then stand guard. Chloe was left alone with him.

"I'm almost afraid to see it, but is there a working restroom in this place?" she asked her captor.

He didn't answer her, but rather moved to a closed door and poked his head inside. He flipped a switch inside the space, and she glimpsed an old-fashioned stand sink below a mirror that had lost much of its chrome finish.

"In there," Herrera grunted. "One minute. After that, I come in and kill you."

Nodding, she closed the door and breathed a huge sigh of relief not to have a gun pointed at her for a few seconds. The toilet was rusty and filthy and the water in it had a green, goopy biology experiment growing in it. Knowing Herrera, he was listening at the door and she was going to have to actually use it. She maneuvered herself in the tight space so she didn't actually have to sit down on the disgusting toilet. She checked the tiny window high on the wall to make sure none of her captors were peering in the window, and she whipped out her cell phone.

She turned the volume all the way down and dialed the Winston Ops number from memory. She stuck the phone in her armpit and pressed down on it frantically lest Herrera hear someone talking from the other end. As it was, she wouldn't be able to speak into the device, but hopefully someone would figure out she was in trouble, triangulate the phone's position, and come to rescue her.

She relieved herself quickly and at least found a few tissues from the moldy box on the back of the toilet. And then she had a sudden inspiration. Herrera was no dummy, and at some point he was likely to search her. Her minute was almost up so, working fast, she burrowed her fingers deep into the tissue box and stashed her cell phone under the pile of tissues.

She flushed the toilet, skipped washing her hands in a sink that was even more disgusting than the toilet and opened the door. Sure enough, Herrera loomed inches from her and she lurched backward, startled.

He grabbed her arm and yanked her out of the bathroom, all but throwing her down onto a wooden chair he'd placed in the middle of the room. As for him, he perched a hip on the corner of the kitchen table.

"All right, Chloe. Enough games. Where's Paradeo's money?"

"I don't have it, Miguel." As he took an aggressive step forward, no doubt to backhand her or worse, she added quickly, "But I know who took it."

He subsided back on the edge of the table. "Oh, yeah? I can't wait to hear this."

In line with her scheme of keeping this guy as happy as possible for as long as possible while rescue came, she explained, "Barry Lind was embezzling the money."

Herrera shook his head sharply. "He didn't have access to all the accounts money was going missing from. But you did."

"You're right," she replied. "He either had more than one accomplice inside the company, or he had a top-notch hacker outside the company working with him."

Herrera looked surprised at the admission, but then snapped, "So where's the money now?"

"I have no idea. But if you give me a computer and a few days, I can probably track where it went." That, of course, was a lie. She had no way of getting banks to surrender transaction records to her, and goodness knew, she wasn't a good enough hacker to break into any bank's computer system and steal the records. It would take the FBI's clout to do what she had promised.

Herrera snorted. "You may have been clever enough to steal some money, but you're not that good."

Dang. He'd seen through the lie.

He took an aggressive step forward. "You seem to have no idea exactly who you're dealing with, Chloe. But you've made a terrible mistake stealing from my employer. They kill without a second thought."

"I know exactly who they are, thank you very much," she snapped. "Well, I don't know exactly which cartel it is, but I know I've been laundering drug money for the past six months." As soon as the words were out of her mouth, she knew them for the monumental mistake they were. This was not a man to be that honest with. Particularly not with that pistol in the holster under his left arm.

Herrera reeled back at that. "You knew? And you didn't turn them in?" he demanded incredulously.

Must backtrack hard and fast if she didn't want to get shot in the next sixty seconds. She shrugged. "I think it's insane that drugs aren't legal. At least some drugs. It's not my job to wonder where Paradeo's money comes from. I'm just a bean counter collecting a paycheck and trying to get by." God, she hoped he bought it. She delivered the explanation with as much sincerity as she could pack into her voice.

One of the thugs opened the door and told Herrera in Spanish that the area was clear. Miguel snapped back that they should split up and guard each side of the house. From outside. The thug nodded and left.

"How did you discover that Mr. Lind was stealing money?" Miguel asked, his voice dangerously quiet.

She briefly considered how to answer him. Sticking to the truth as much as possible was her best bet.

"Answer me!" Herrera barked so sharply she about fell off the chair. Lord, that man scared her. The violent look in his eye promised worlds of pain beyond anything she'd ever imagined.

She stammered, "Barry called me when I got back into town after my sister's wedding. He wanted to talk with me." She described in detail her meeting and conversation with Barry, including every detail she could recall. Now it was all about stalling until help came. But finally, she was down to the meat of the matter. She took a deep breath and admitted, "And then he gave me a flash drive. He told me he'd copied every financial record he could lay his hands on, and he wanted me to take a look at them and see what I could find."

Herrera stared. "How did he get every record the company has? He didn't have that kind of access across the board."

She nodded. "You're smarter than I am. It took me until yesterday to ask myself that very same question."

"And?" Herrera sounded genuinely interested.

"Like I said, the only way for Barry to have obtained the records he did was to have help. I have to say I don't think Barry was good enough with computers to have broken into the various compartments of the company's records by himself."

"Neither do I," Miguel answered thoughtfully.

How did he know Barry well enough to have an opinion about the guy? Lind had been murdered within a few days of Herrera arriving at the company. Weird.

"It's not nice to throw a dead man under the bus," he commented lightly.

"Excuse me?"

"Obviously, you were one of Mr. Lind's accomplices. And now that the guy's dead, you're trying to throw all the blame onto him."

"I am not! I was *not* one of his accomplices!"

Herrera's arms were crossed in a posture of patent disbelief, but all he said was, "Convince me."

How on earth was she supposed to do that? She opened her mouth to ask for a computer so she could show him the trail of transactions Barry had used, and how she'd figured out the accounting entries led back to an ISP address that turned out to belong to one Barry Lind. But before sound could come out of her throat, the door burst open.

It was the van driver. He announced in rapid Spanish that a pickup truck had been spotted on the main road headed this way with its headlights off.

Herrera surged up off the edge of the table and strode over to her, grabbing a handful of her hair and yanking her head back painfully. "Who knows where you are?" he demanded harshly.

Her scalp felt like it was about to detach from her skull and tears ran down her cheeks from the sharpness of the pain. "Nobody!" she cried out.

He flung her head forward in disgust, snapping her neck hard enough that it ached. Miguel moved over to the driver. She had to strain to hear him tell the guy in Spanish to guard the driveway and scare off any trespassers.

A pickup truck? Trent would be either be in her car or the small SUV he'd been driving. Had Winston Ops already sent someone out to investigate her open cell phone line? It had only been a few minutes. No way could they have responded already. Who was it, then? She desperately hoped it wasn't some innocent bystander about to be in the wrong place at the wrong time.

The driver left and Herrera turned to her. He looked violent. Angry. But in a few seconds, it was almost as if he…deflated. It was the strangest thing. He pulled the only other chair from the kitchen table over and sat down in it directly in front of her, knee to knee.

"Tell me exactly how you figured out Barry Lind was the thief," he ordered quietly.

His demeanor was so strikingly different from a few moments before she had no idea what to make of it. If he was playing some sort of interrogation head game with her, it was working.

In all the detail she could muster, she described her search of Paradeo's financial records, of spotting the first discrepancies, of tracking the pattern that emerged. "It looked for all the world like I took the money," she confessed. "It was almost like I was being framed."

"By Barry?" Miguel scoffed. "He wasn't that smart."

"Maybe his accomplice is the brains behind the scheme," she replied.

Herrera stared at her hard for a long time, like he was thinking hard. Abruptly he asked, "Who hired you to work at Paradeo?"

Her gaze slid away from his before she realized what she'd done, and she looked back at him hastily. She named the woman in the HR department who had interviewed her, adding, "I don't know who made the final decision. But she must have been the one to recommend me."

Herrera leaned in aggressively. "You're lying. Don't do it again, or you'll regret it. If you want to live past tonight, you'll tell me the whole truth and nothing but the truth."

An ironic choice of words, this hardened criminal quoting the U.S. Court system's oath for witnesses.

"I'll ask you one more time," he snarled. "Who hired you?"

She'd never been any good at lying, and there was no reason to believe she'd get away with it now. But admitting to be an FBI plant was as good as signing her own death warrant. "An interested party asked me to try and get hired at Paradeo and take a look at its books."

"Who?"

"I can't tell you."

"Why not?"

She took a deep breath and told the God's honest truth. "Because you'll kill me if I do."

His brow lowered thunderously and he leaned back hard, staring at her. "Which is it, Chloe? The Feds or a rival of my employer's?"

Wow. He'd drawn the logical conclusion darned fast. It was easy to forget how smart this man was beneath all that brawn and threatening swagger.

Time for one last bit of honesty. "So here's the thing, Miguel. If I tell you, you'll kill me. At this point, I'm better off refusing to talk and enduring whatever torture you have planned for me than I am answering any more of your questions. I think it's safe to say we're done talking."

For an instant, she thought she saw admiration flash in his black gaze. But then he stood abruptly, dumping his chair over behind him with a crash. "So be it," he growled.

Trent was grateful for the pickup truck that had swung in between him and the van. It provided great cover for his smaller vehicle from the van's driver. But as the miles passed and the roads became more and more deserted, worry began to set in. How was it this truck was going in the exact same direction and making all the exact same turns as the van? Was its driver an accomplice of the kidnappers? His suspicion became certainty that the truck was following the van as the miles rolled by. He was looking at four or more kidnappers—no doubt all armed and dangerous—that he was up against. Alone. This night just continued to get worse.

Caution dictated that he drop much farther back than he'd like to, trailing both truck and van from far enough behind that they couldn't make him as a tail. It was dicey, keeping visual contact and not losing the two vehicles. They wound higher and higher into the hills and the road deteriorated to a rutted and poorly maintained dirt road.

The van's brake lights went on and he made out the white blob ahead turning left. The truck continued on. He swore. Where was it going? Why had the kidnappers split their forces? Was the truck heading around back to set a trap for anyone who might try to rescue Chloe?

It wasn't like he had any choice. He'd walk right into their trap if he had to. He'd die before he allowed harm to come to her. The mental declaration shocked him to his core. Not because he wasn't prepared to do his duty and lay down his life—he surely was. He knew he loved her, but was stunned to realize he was willing to die for her.

In spite of her unwillingness to open up or maybe because of it, he loved her. In spite of her prickly exterior, he couldn't get enough of the woman beneath. In spite of her cussed independence, in spite of her lousy self-esteem, in spite of her difficult past.

No, he corrected himself. It was because of all of that that he loved her. She'd survived everything life had thrown at her. She'd raised her sister, kept her little family together as a child herself, managed to scrape together a decent education and to make something of herself. He loved her protectiveness, her fierce loyalty, her determination and drive. She was a hell of a woman. And all those qualities would stand her in good stead now. She just had to hang on a little while longer.

He turned where the van had, squinting ahead into the darkness. He'd turned off his headlights miles ago, and in spite of his eyes being fully adjusted to the night, he could barely see a thing ahead. His progress up the twin tracks of what looked like an overgrown driveway was maddeningly slow.

He paused yet again, window down to listen for the van ahead. This time he heard nothing. Immediately, he eased the car off the track and into the brush. Picking up the pistol he'd lifted off the guy in the parking lot, he slipped out of the car and into the woods.

It didn't take long for him to see a clearing ahead nor to spot an armed man slouching at the end of the driveway. Trent hunkered down to watch for a few minutes and get the lay of the land, even though a terrible need to hurry pressed in upon him. God only knew what was happening to Chloe inside that cabin.

Based on where this guy was deployed, he guessed there was another man on the other side of the cabin as well. He moved off to his right to check it out. Just as he moved out of sight of the first guard, he spotted a second man. But this one was moving stealthily through the trees.

He crept after the guy, his entire body screaming for action. This sneaking around stuff was the complete opposite of how he was designed to function and it took an extreme act of discipline not to explode into motion. It was for Chloe, he reminded himself. His nerves calmed slightly.

The man he was following made his way carefully toward…a third man! This one was armed and leaning against a tree just beyond the clearing that contained the cabin. Trent frowned. What was the sneaking man he was following doing? Playing a practical joke on his buddy? Or had the pickup truck's driver not been an accomplice in the kidnapping after all?

Confused, he followed along. The sneaking man eased a knife out of an ankle sheath and closed in on the third man. There was a flurry of movement. The sneaking man jumped, slashed the guy leaning against the tree across the throat with the knife, and blood erupted everywhere. The guy with the slit throat didn't go down quietly, however. He let out a hoarse cry and grappled with his attacker.

Who in the hell was the guy with the knife?

The first guard came sprinting around the corner of the cabin, and the guy with the knife was about to be outnumbered. The guard with the slit throat wasn't bleeding out fast enough to die before guard number one joined him.

Trent made a fast decision. He didn't know who knife guy was, but he'd taken out one of Chloe's kidnappers, and the enemy of Trent's enemy had just been promoted to the status of friend. He scooped up a fist-sized rock and glided forward, his muscles weeping with relief at finally getting to move quickly. The first guard, focused entirely on the fight in front of him didn't even look to his right as Trent swung in behind him.

It was child's play to race the last half-dozen strides forward and clack the first guard across the back of the head with the rock as hard as he could. The first guard tumbled to the ground, rolled over once, and sprawled unconscious.

The kidnapper with the slit throat was finally collapsing in knife guy's arms, and their struggle was moments from over. Knife guy's back was turned, and Trent took advantage of his unknown friend's distraction to slip back into the woods and out of sight. No sense revealing himself if he didn't have to. For all knife guy would know, the unconscious kidnapper could have tripped on a tree root and knocked himself out.

Trent winced as knife guy knelt down to check the guy he'd hit with the rock and efficiently slit the man's throat. What the hell? The kidnapper was unconscious and out of the fight. There was no need to kill him. Who *was* this violent enemy of the kidnappers? Glad he hadn't identified himself to the man, Trent crouched, still and silent and waited to see what the bastard would do next.

Apparently convinced no more guards lurked out here, knife guy strode across the clearing to the cabin's front porch. Wincing, Trent left the cover of the trees, and the moment the man slipped inside the cabin, he raced at full speed across the clearing to the porch. Heart pounding, he plastered himself beside a window and eased the safety off his stolen pistol.

Miguel advanced menacingly toward Chloe, and for all the world, death glittered in his gaze. So terrified she could only sit there and stare she watched him stalk her. If only Trent were here. What would he do? He'd move really fast—he'd *move*. In a flash of clarity, she realized she wasn't tied down to this chair. She leaped to her feet and picked the chair up, brandishing it like a lion trainer in a cage with a raging lion.

The front door slammed open, and Herrera whirled to face this new threat. A man in dark clothes with mud smeared all over his face leaped through the door and came to a halt, a gun at the ready in his right hand. "Perfect," he purred.

"Thank God. Don!" she cried as he locked the door behind himself.

"You know this guy?" Herrera asked over his shoulder without ever taking his eyes off Don Fratello.

She almost blurted that he was an FBI agent and her boss, but remembered at the last second that Herrera would kill Don if he knew it. "Yes. He's a friend."

"Damn good friend to come in here guns blazing to rescue you," Herrera grunted.

"You've got it all wrong," Don chortled. "I'm not here to rescue Chloe. I'm here to kill her."

Chloe stared, shocked to the core of her being. "What?" she gasped.

Herrera seemed likewise stunned. "What have you got against her?"

"Stupid bitch almost outed me. Thankfully, she left her little message explaining how she'd figured out old Barry's scheme on my personal voice mail and not my work number. As soon as I shut her up, I can put some other dimwit accountant fresh out of school in her place and keep my little operation running."

Revelations were exploding one after another in her head like fireworks on Fourth of July. Don was Barry's accomplice in robbing Paradeo. Of course. With his FBI resources, he'd been able to crack Paradeo's various security codes and pass them to Barry. Poor Barry must've figured out that Don considered him expendable, or maybe Barry just got scared and wanted out of the scheme.

"You killed Barry, didn't you?" she demanded.

"Piss ant chickened out on me. He figured out who really owns Paradeo and freaked out. Got all holier than thou about stopping the damned drug cartels."

More revelations exploded in her brain. Don had hired her because he thought she was so inexperienced that she would never figure out what he was doing. He'd used her as a cover in case he got found out by the FBI. And that meant he'd probably—

"You framed me!" she exclaimed.

His scornful gaze slid off Herrera for an instant to mock her. "Of course I did. No way am I going down for this. Not after I finally got the nice little nest egg I deserve for all my years of hard work."

"Nest egg? You and Barry stole almost twenty million dollars!" she blurted.

Herrera lurched and Don's weapon jerked. "Easy there,

buddy. I'd hate to have to shoot you before I'm done with you."

"What do you want from me?" Herrera snarled. "My bosses are going to chew you up and spit you out when they find out you stole that kind of money from them. You better offer me a hell of a deal to keep my mouth shut."

"I'll do you one better than that," Don replied. "You kill the girl. And then I'll kill you. I'm a hero with the FBI for killing a high-level drug cartel hit man. I'm a hero with the drug cartel for killing the bitch who was stealing from them. Nobody wants me dead, I walk away with my millions and I live out my life sipping Mai Tais on a tropical beach while some hot babe sucks my—"

Herrera reached for his gun and dived for the cover of the table simultaneously, but Don was too fast and too well trained. Two gunshots rang out in quick succession deafening Chloe. Herrera rolled onto his back, arms splayed, still and silent, while a pool of blood slowly formed beneath him. Chloe stared at the downed man in sheer, frozen terror.

Don's pistol swung at her. She braced herself for the impact. "Don't worry, Chloe. You've got a few more seconds to say your prayers. Gotta get Miguel's gun first. Wouldn't do to have rounds from my weapon found buried in your gut. The Mexican shot you, after all. I was tragically a few seconds too late to stop him. But, hey, I gunned him down for you."

Don moved past her to where Herrera lay, and she pivoted to face them, holding the chair in front of her like a shield. Realizing he was no longer between her and the door, she took a step backward. Another.

"One more step and I shoot you where you stand," Don snarled. "And I won't kill you with the shot. I'll let you suffer for a while first. Stray bullet accidentally hit you in the cross fire, you know."

He had all the answers, didn't he? He was supposed to be one of the good guys! Rage and horror roiled in her gut as Don placed Miguel's pistol in the downed man's fingers, wrapping them around the butt and slipping a flaccid index finger into the trigger guard. The weapon lifted toward her.

The window behind her exploded in a fury of flying glass and wood splinters. A large, familiar body arced through the gap, hit the floor, rolled, and came upright between her and Don.

Trent heaved something hard and fast, baseball-pitcher-fashion, at Don. A handful of dirt smashed into the FBI agent's face and he screamed in pain and fury, dropping Miguel's hand to claw at his sandblasted eyes. Miguel's pistol fired, and Chloe instinctively ducked, although the shot had already sailed over her head and into the ceiling.

Trent's gun was against the FBI man's head in a flash. "You so much as twitch, and I'll kill you," Trent snarled.

Chloe took a sobbing breath, her first since Trent had burst through the window, it had all happened so fast. But Don Fratello wasn't an FBI field agent for nothing. He surged up and into Trent, his hands wrapped around the butt of Trent's pistol. The two men grappled, and it looked like about an even fight.

She dived in with the chair, swinging it at Don's back so hard she broke off both back legs. He grunted and heaved, arching Trent backward until she feared Trent was going to break in half. *Ohgodohgod.* Don was winning. She had to do something, but what? Don's hand reached down toward his ankle. He had a hidden weapon there. He was going to kill Trent!

She wasn't close enough to stop the FBI man. She

opened her mouth to scream a warning, but a hand lifted off the floor, yanked the knife out of Don's ankle sheath, and buried it in the FBI agent's calf. Don crashed to the floor screaming profanities. Trent slammed his fist in Don's temple, and the crooked FBI agent went still.

Miguel groaned and dropped the knife with a clatter. Trent darted over to the sofa, tore off a couple strips of the upholstery and brought them back to tie up Don.

Chloe ran forward to kick the knife out of reach and dropped to her knees beside Miguel. She put her hand on his chest to check for a heartbeat and was startled to feel something heavy and padded covering his chest. The gunshot wound in his shoulder was bleeding profusely, and she pressed the heel of her palm against it. Herrera groaned faintly. She stared down at him, grateful he'd helped Trent but mightily confused as to what had just happened.

And then Trent's hands pushed hers aside, and he peeled back Herrera's shredded shirt to look at the bullet wound. "Nasty, but he'll live. Good thing he had on a vest to catch that other bullet. Saved his hide."

Don shifted slightly behind them and Trent moved fast to the FBI man's side and slugged him, hard, in the jaw. The FBI man went limp once more. Trent moved back to her and drew her to her feet.

"Are you all right, baby? Are you hurt?"

"Miguel never laid a hand on me. Are you okay? Don didn't hurt you, did he?"

Trent chuckled. "Never laid a finger on me. I'm too fast for that. Have you got your phone on you? We could use a little backup, here."

"It's hidden in the bathroom." She fished it out of the tissue box and passed it to Trent. He made two phone calls, one to the local police and another to Winston Ops. In under ten minutes, the property was swarming with flashing lights, police, park rangers and even firefighters. Their paramedics declared the two guards whose throats Don had slit dead. Don himself regained consciousness and was securely strapped down to an ambulance gurney while a medic stitched up the gash in his lower leg. He was refusing to say anything to anybody.

It was chaos, and Trent had disappeared somewhere in the fracas to brief someone. He'd promised to return soon, but she didn't see how he'd be back for hours. Chloe sat on the porch steps with a blanket around her shoulders. She wasn't cold, but she desperately needed a hug—a hug from Trent to be more precise—and the blanket was better than nothing.

And once again, she'd managed to end up alone. She must have some sort of special talent for this, and, she had to say, it sucked. She couldn't believe Don Fratello had used her like that. She'd trusted him and he'd set her up. He'd put her square in the sights of a dangerous drug cartel and had planned to kill her all along. What a bastard. Thank God Trent had come along when he had or Don's plan would have worked.

She dropped her forehead onto her knees. Why did men treat her like this? What was it about her that shouted, take advantage of me?

At least the whole mess was over—

Oh, God. *It was over.* There was nothing to hold Trent to her anymore. It truly was over. When he left, he would take her heart with him, and she was pretty sure she would never get it back. Tears came then. And racking sobs that shook her whole body. Cops stomped up and down the steps past her, and none of them gave a darn that her life had just ended.

But then hands stroked her hair gently, and drew her

off the steps and to her feet, into a warm, strong, familiar embrace. "Aww, baby, what is it?"

"You're going to leave me now…and my heart's breaking…and I'm always going to be alone…" Her words were punctuated by great, heaving sobs.

A gentle kiss landed in her hair. "Hold that thought for a minute. There's someone who wants to talk to you, but he has to leave soon. Come with me."

Frowning, she let him lead her across the crowded clearing to the back of an ambulance.

Trent said, "Sweetie, I'd like you to meet undercover DEA agent Miguel Herrera. That's not his real name, of course, but it's good enough for now."

Chloe stared down at Paradeo's security chief, a man who had scared her silly from the first moment she met him. "DEA?" she repeated in shock.

Miguel grinned up at her from the gurney. "Hell of a time I had keeping you alive and unharmed, while convincing the cartel men that I was still a badass. Sorry I had to scare you like that. Couldn't blow my cover."

Snippets of her encounters with him flashed through her head. He never had really hurt her the first time he'd kidnapped her, other than ripping off a few pieces of duct tape. Those momentary flashes of admiration in his eyes. And he'd fallen and knocked out the other thugs chasing her and Trent when they'd fled the Paradeo offices. And tonight. He'd actually been pretty calm with her. He'd let her use the toilet and never searched her. He must have known she'd have a phone and use it somehow to call in help. And most importantly, he'd helped Trent against Don.

She clasped Miguel's icy cold hand gratefully in both of hers. "Thank you," she choked out. "I owe you my life. I'll never forget that you saved Trent's, as well."

He grinned and mumbled, "You're welcome, ma'am. All in a day's work."

Trent told Herrera to take care of himself, and then a pair of medics pushed the DEA agent into the ambulance.

As its flashing lights retreated down the driveway, Chloe murmured to Trent, "He scared me worse than anyone I've ever met, except you."

"I scared you?" he asked in quiet dismay.

She looked down at her feet, embarrassed. A finger hooked under her chin, forcing her reluctant gaze up to his silver one. "Why?"

"You completely messed up my world. I had everything worked out and you came along and screwed up every plan I had, every notion of how my life was going to be." She shook her head and confessed sadly, "I'm never going to be the same. My life is ruined." She looked up hastily. "It's not your fault. I let it happen. I don't blame you."

"Actually, it is my fault."

Her jaw dropped open. "How's that?"

"I knew from the moment you told me there were some things you wanted to try that you were the one woman for me. I did everything in my power to rock your world and blow apart all your silly ideas about order and control and never letting yourself get hurt."

She stared up at him, not sure whether to be annoyed or intensely grateful. She chose to concentrate on the first part. "The one woman for you?" she repeated in disbelief.

Trent spoke in a rush. "Look. I know we haven't known each other that long. And I'm not even remotely close to the normal, boring, safe guy you've always pictured yourself with. But is there a chance you might consider seeing if we could make a go of it?"

Her heart leaped and jumped in her chest like an excited puppy, but she still asked cautiously, "What do you have in mind?"

"I'm thinking marriage and kids and old age and a bunch of grandkids."

Was it true that all her need for structure and order and normalcy had been wiped away by this man? She could hardly believe it herself, but she said, "That all sounds so…normal." She wrinkled her nose at him.

"Well then, how about we travel the world, I teach you how to surf and we have wild, unplanned adventures in between plenty of smoking-hot sex?"

"That's more like it, Mr. Hollings."

"Then we have a deal, Miss Jordan?"

"Really? You and me?" she said in a small voice. Was it possible that all her dreams hadn't been even a pale shadow of the reality that awaited her?

"You and me, baby. Together forever." He kissed his way to her earlobe, and in between nibbles on it, he whispered, "As soon I get you in bed, I'm going to tie you up and make love to you until you agree to marry me."

Her heart full to bursting with joy, she replied, laughing, "Where's my car? Suddenly, I'm terribly, terribly tired and need to lie down in the worst way."

Yup, this man was a whole lot more than a dream. He was the real deal. "I love you, Trent."

"I love you more, Chloe."

Hah. That remained to be seen. She still had a few more things on that list of hers to get through.…

* * * * *

"Once he found out what I knew or decided I didn't know anything at all, he still would have tried to kill me. And he'll try again, because he didn't get the answer he was looking for."

Max clenched his hands, not willing to think about another attempt on Colette's life. "He'll have to come through me to do it. We didn't know how far he'd carry things before. We know now and we'll be more prepared."

"But how? We're sitting ducks. He can just sit in the swamp and wait for us to leave."

"I'm working on that. Just try not to worry about it. When I've worked everything out in my head, I'll let you know."

She nodded, but didn't look convinced.

Lightning flashed, and he peered into the darkness, trying to ferret out any sign of movement. Any sign that the shooter had returned. He couldn't see anything.

But he knew something was out there.

THE VANISHING

BY
JANA DeLEON

First published in Great Britain 2013
by Mills & Boon, an imprint of Harlequin (UK) Limited,
Eton House, 18-24 Paradise Road, Richmond, Surrey TW9 1SR

© Jana DeLeon 2012

ISBN: 978 0 263 90345 4
ebook ISBN: 978 1 472 00695 0

46-0213

Harlequin (UK) policy is to use papers that are natural, renewable and recyclable products and made from wood grown in sustainable forests. The logging and manufacturing processes conform to the legal environmental regulations of the country of origin.

Printed and bound in Spain
by Blackprint CPI, Barcelona

Jana DeLeon grew up among the bayous and small towns of southwest Louisiana. She's never actually found a dead body or seen a ghost, but she's still hoping. Jana started writing in 2001 and focuses on murderous plots set deep in the Louisiana bayous. By day, she writes very boring technical manuals for a software company in Dallas. Visit Jana on her website, www.janadeleon.com.

To my recently married friend, Leigh Zaykoski.
May you and Phil have your own happily ever after…

Prologue

November 1833

The young Creole man pushed open the door on the shack and sat on a chair next to the bed. The fifty-seven-year-old Frenchman lying there wasn't much longer for this world. The only thing keeping him alive was the news the Creole would bring.

"Have you found my son?" the Frenchman asked, then began coughing.

The young Creole winced as the dying man doubled over, his body wracked with pain. "Wi."

The dying man straightened up, struggling to catch his breath. "Where is he?"

The Creole looked down at the dirt floor. He'd hoped the man would be dead before he returned to the village. Hoped he'd never have to speak the words he was about to say. Finally, he looked back up at the man and said, "He's dead."

"Nonsense! They've said I'm dead now for over a decade. Bring me my son!"

"Somethin' bad went through New Orleans last year that the doctors couldn't fix. A lot of people died."

The anguish on the dying man's face was almost more than the Creole could bear to see. "You couldna done nuttin'," he said, trying to make the dying man's last moments easier.

"I shouldn't have left him there, but there was nothing here for him—hiding in the swamp for the rest of his life."

"You did what you shoulda. You couldna known."

The dying man struggled to sit upright. "I need for you to do something else. Something even more important."

The Creole frowned. "What?"

"Under this bed is a chest. Pull it out, but be careful. It's heavy."

The Creole knelt down next to the bed and peered underneath. He spotted the chest in a corner and pulled the handle on the side, but it barely budged. Doubling his efforts, he pulled as hard as he could and, inch by inch, worked the chest out from under the bed.

"Open it," the dying man said.

The Creole lifted the lid on the chest, and the last rays from the evening sun caught on the glittering pile of gold inside. He gasped and stared at the gold, marveling at its beauty. All this time, the Frenchman had been sleeping over a fortune. The Creole stared up at the man, confused.

"It's cursed," the dying man said. "I stole it, and now it's taken my son and my life from me." The dying man leaned down, looking the Creole directly in the eyes. "Promise me you'll never let the gold leave that chest. It will bring sorrow to anyone who spends it. You must keep it hidden forever. I'm entrusting you and your family with this task. Do you understand?"

The Creole felt a chill run through him at the word *curse*. He didn't want to be entrusted with guarding cursed objects, nor did he want that burden transferred down his family line.

"Promise me!" the dying man demanded.

But the Creole knew he was the only one in the village who could be trusted to keep the gold hidden. The only one who could be trusted to train those who came after him to respect the old ways. To respect vows made.

"I promise."

Chapter One

The fall sun was already beginning to set above the cypress trees on Tuesday evening, when Colette Guidry parked her car in front of the quaint home in Vodoun, Louisiana. An attractive wooden sign that read Second Chance Detective Agency was already placed in front of a beautifully landscaped flower bed, but the sounds of hammering and stacks of lumber on the front lawn let her know that the office conversion wasn't exactly complete.

She reached for the door handle and paused. Maybe this was a bad idea. She'd worked with Alexandria Bastin-Chamberlain, one of the partners at the detective agency, at the hospital in New Orleans before Alex resigned to open the agency with her husband. She shouldn't feel self-conscious about asking for her help.

But what if Alex thinks you're crazy, too?

And that was at the crux of it. The rest of the hospital staff and the New Orleans Police Department had already informed her that her concern over her missing employee was misplaced. Anna Huval had a history of skipping town with undesirable men and usually surfaced when the disastrous relationship had run its short course. Colette had intimate understanding of choosing the wrong man, although her choices hadn't been near as wild or frequent as Anna's. But her two disappointing whirls with noncommittal men had given her enough sorrow to be sympathetic to Anna's heartbreak, even if it was self-induced.

But all that was in the past. With Colette's guidance, Anna had turned her life around, and for the past six months, she had been on a path that guaranteed her a healthy, successful future. The only problem was no one believed it would last, and Anna's disappearance was a signal to many that she'd relapsed into the behavior that was so familiar to her.

Colette understood exactly why people felt that way. Logically, it was the best explanation, and if Colette hadn't gotten to know Anna so well, she would have bought completely into it, also. But despite the lack of evidence of something dire, and a seemingly logical explanation for what had happened given Anna's past, Colette knew something terrible had happened to the young nurse's aide.

She pushed the car door open and stepped out. The detective agency specialized in situations the police wouldn't handle—giving concerned friends and family a second chance for answers. Anna's disappearance fit that description. If Alex and her husband, Holt, didn't think her case had merit, then they'd tell her, and that would be that.

The door to the agency was partially open, so she pushed it a bit farther and stuck her head inside. Alex stood talking to a contractor in the middle of what was probably going to be a reception area once it had paint, flooring and furniture. As the sunlight crept in through the open door, her former coworker looked over and waved when she saw Colette.

"Did you come to take my temperature?" Alex asked as Colette stepped inside.

"Why? Are you sick?"

"I must be to think I could handle the construction management myself."

Colette laughed. "Well, I'm hardly going to accuse a psychiatrist of being crazy, so sick it is. Perhaps a mind-altering flu."

"Sounds lovely," Alex said and pointed to the only portion of the house away from the loud saws and other construction equipment. "My office is this way. It's the only place with decent flooring and chairs." She leaned over and whispered, "Plus, I have the gourmet single-serve coffeemaker hidden in my filing cabinet."

Colette felt her spirits rise as she followed Alex into a pretty office with blue walls and white trim located in a corner of the building. In addition to being intelligent, attractive and empathetic, Alex was the most intuitive person she'd ever met. If there was help to be found, she'd find it here.

She took a seat in front of the desk and made small talk while Alex made them coffee, catching her up on all the hospital gossip since she'd resigned the month before. Then Alex slid into the chair behind her desk and gave her a shrewd look.

"While I am very happy to see you, I doubt you drove all the way to Vodoun to bring me up to speed on the latest inner workings of New Orleans General."

"No. I have a problem…one I'm hoping you can help me with."

Alex pulled a pad of paper and pen out of her desk drawer. "Tell me."

"Anna Huval didn't report to work on Friday. She was scheduled for the evening shift, but was a no-show/no-call."

"You tried to reach her, of course."

"Yes. I called her apartment and her cell. When I didn't

get an answer, I checked with the emergency room of all area hospitals, then when I came up empty there, I called the police. Fortunately, they had no Jane Does in the morgue that matched Anna's description, and they let me file a report but said they probably wouldn't look into it until Monday. Yesterday."

Alex nodded. "Because most adults turn up within twenty-four to forty-eight hours and haven't been victims of a crime."

"Exactly."

"So did they investigate on Monday?"

"I pestered them and they finally agreed to check her apartment. I'd already tried to get in but the landlord has gotten in trouble for letting unauthorized people into apartments before and wasn't budging."

"Did you find anything inside?"

"No sign of forced entry or a struggle, and her backpack was missing. Since she started nursing school, she carries it with her everywhere, sneaking in study time whenever she can." Colette frowned. "But the thing is, her books were on her bed. Scattered like they'd been tossed there in a hurry. The bed itself was still made."

"Could you tell if any clothes were missing?"

Colette shook her head. "I don't know. There were no large gaps in her closet, so if she intended to leave, she didn't take much, but then, she didn't have much to begin with."

"Tell me more about her cell phone."

"She has a prepaid one that I've been calling every couple of hours, but it goes straight to voice mail. The police called the cell-phone company to track it, but they said it's either turned off or not in range."

"Did the police find any other reason to suspect she'd taken off on her own volition?"

Colette struggled with her own frustration and disappointment. Now that she was repeating the facts out loud, she could see exactly why the New Orleans police weren't taking her seriously, and the next bit of information was not going to make the situation any better.

"Colette?"

She sighed. "Her bank said she withdrew four hundred dollars on Friday evening, a couple of hours before her shift was due to start."

Alex raised her eyebrows and tapped her pen on the desk.

"I know how this looks," Colette said. "If you take the facts and couple them with Anna's reputation for hooking up with the wrong men, then you have a foolish girl adding one more wild weekend to a very colorful past. But I promise you, that is not the young woman Anna is now."

"How can you be sure?"

"Well, I suppose no one can be one hundred percent sure, but I've worked with her every week for the last year. When she told me she wanted to turn her life around, I got her counseling with hospital staff as a start. After three months of therapy, she told me she wanted to be a nurse, and I helped her get grants for nursing school. She comes to me with questions on her courses, and I can see her interest and focus clear as day."

"Maybe a family emergency…"

"She's always claimed she has no family left, and I've never seen evidence of any since I've known her. Besides, if it was an emergency, why wouldn't she call me? She trusts me. She knows I would help."

"Perhaps it's not the sort of emergency you would help with."

"What do you mean?"

Alex sighed. "I know a little about Anna—some from

the rumor mill at the hospital, some from Anna herself. If she's involved in something she knows you wouldn't approve of, she wouldn't tell you. It's clear from what you've told me that she respects you, and I got the impression that with Anna, respect doesn't come lightly. If she thought telling you would damage that, she may choose to handle it alone."

Colette slumped back in her chair. Everything Alex said made so much sense. "But that doesn't mean she's not in trouble, whether or not she chose to walk into it."

"That's true."

"So will you take the case? I have the money, and Anna's become…well, like a little sister to me. I have to do something."

"Of course you do," Alex said, and Colette could tell by her expression that Alex truly did understand.

Alex was the only person at New Orleans General whom Colette had ever confided in about the boating accident that killed her parents when she was young and being raised by her only living relative, a spinster aunt who never wanted children and who'd died years ago. More than anyone else, Alex knew the loss she felt at having no family and would understand why Anna had become so important to her.

"I have no problem with our taking the case," Alex said.

Relief swept over Colette like a wave. "Thank you. I can't even tell you how much this means that someone is actually listening."

Alex leaned forward in her chair and looked directly at Colette. "But you have to be prepared for whatever we find—even if it's not the answer you wanted."

Colette nodded. "I can handle that. I just can't handle doing nothing."

"Good. As it happens, Holt's half brother Max is starting at the agency this week. I'll get all the information from you and bring him up to speed at dinner tonight."

"Holt's half brother?" Colette struggled to control her disappointment. "I was hoping you and Holt would do the investigation."

"We're busy on two other cases as the moment, but I promise you Max is an expert. He's got ten years with the Baton Rouge Police Department and was the youngest detective in the department's history. If anyone can find out what happened to Anna, Max can."

"Okay. If you have that much confidence in him, then he must be worthy of it."

Alex smiled. "He'll probably want to talk to you tomorrow. Since you knew Anna better than anyone else, you'll be a big help."

"Anything I can do," Colette said, hoping between now and tomorrow she could think of something—anything—that would help find Anna. If Alex's assessment was correct and Anna was in some sort of trouble, then she needed Colette's help now more than ever before.

MAX DUHON HANDED A BOARD to his brother Holt, who was up on a ladder replacing a rotted section of roof trim on his little cabin on the bayou. "It doesn't sound like much of a case," Max said.

Holt held the board in place with one hand and secured it with his nail gun with the other. "It's not sensational or meaty, no, but Alex agreed to take the case, and you're the only one available at the moment to handle it. She'll bring you a folder tonight, but what I told you is the gist of it."

"But the entire case is based on Alex's opinion of someone else's opinion. That's hearsay in court. Why in the world is it good enough for you to launch an investigation?"

"The client meets our criteria. She suspects something has happened, and the police won't open an investigation. The client is credible, even if the missing person is questionable."

"And if it turns out to be nothing but a loose woman taking an unscheduled weekend with her latest passing fancy?"

Holt climbed down the ladder and placed his nail gun in its case. "Then we've still solved the case and earned our fee. We find answers here, Max, and the answers don't always have to be criminal in nature. Turning her away would be going against the very reason we opened the agency in the first place."

Max sighed. "I get it. I just don't know how much more I can do than what the police have already done."

"Talk to the client and try to find a new line of investigation. Poke around into things the police wouldn't have bothered with—question classmates, see if she had a favorite hangout." Holt clapped him on the shoulder. "Do what you do best. If anyone can ferret out an answer on this, it's you."

Max picked up the ladder and followed Holt to the storage shed. He wished he had as much confidence in his abilities as his brother did. Maybe that was why Alex had assigned him a relatively straightforward, boring and safe case. Maybe they didn't really believe he could handle the work, either. Not now.

The old Max was invincible…indestructible. At least that's what he'd thought.

The bullet wound ached in his shoulder as he lifted the

ladder onto the rack in the back of the shed—a constant
reminder of what had happened.

Of his failure.

Chapter Two

The knock on Colette's apartment door sent her into a nervous flurry. Holt's brother was right on time, but despite a sleepless night, she still didn't have a single thing to add to the information she'd already given Alex. She smoothed the wrinkles out of the bottom of her T-shirt and took a deep breath, blowing it out slowly, before opening the door.

Then sucked it back in when she saw Max.

She shouldn't have been surprised by the prime male specimen in front of her. After all, Holt was an attractive man, but his brother was a work of art. The dark hair, finely toned body and beautifully tanned skin were an equal match for Holt, but the chiseled facial features and turquoise eyes belied a Nordic mother. It was a masterful combination of DNA.

"Colette Guidry?" he asked, his voice as smooth and sexy as his appearance.

"Yes."

He stared at her for a couple of seconds. "Can I come in?"

"Oh, yes, of course." Colette opened the door and allowed him to pass, flustered that she'd completely lost her sense and her manners. "I'm sorry. I just feel so scattered."

He stepped inside her apartment and glanced around

the open living room, kitchen and dining area. Colette got the impression that he was sizing her up, both by her own appearance and by that of her home. For a moment, she bristled, but then remembered he was a career cop. His mind probably automatically shifted to such things if he was working, and she could hardly fault him for assessing her when she was paying for his natural ability to do just that in the first place.

"Can I get you something to drink?" she asked. "I just made a fresh pot of coffee."

"That would be great."

"Have a seat," she said and waved a hand at the kitchen table. "How do you take your coffee?"

"Black."

He slid into a chair at the table, and she poured two black coffees and carried them to the table. "I guess Alex filled you in on everything?" she asked as she took a seat across from him.

He nodded.

"I know it's not much, and given Anna's past, it's probably less than anything, but I can't help but think something has happened."

"You care about her, so you're worried," he said simply. "I'm here to get you answers."

His words were meant to be comforting, and Colette didn't doubt their sincerity, but something in the tone of his voice made her think Max considered this entire case a waste of his time, which only strengthened her resolve. Regardless of Max's opinion, she'd paid for his services and she was going to get her money's worth.

"I've thought about it all night," she said, "but haven't been able to come up with anything I didn't tell Alex."

"It's hard to know what may be important. Likely, you'll think of things as I move through the investigation."

"Where would you like to start?"

"At her apartment. I know the police went through it, but they would only have looked for signs of a crime. Since we have to assume at this point that she left of her own accord, I want to look for things that might tip me off as to where she may have gone and for what reason."

Colette nodded. "Now that I've had the police out, I don't think the landlord would have a problem letting us back in."

"Us?"

"Yes. The landlord isn't likely to let you in without me. She's very particular about the rules."

He frowned. "I suppose it's all right for you to accompany me to her apartment."

"Actually, I've taken some long-overdue vacation time. I intend to accompany you everywhere."

His jaw dropped then clamped shut and set in a hard line. "I can't allow that."

"I wasn't aware that I had to have permission when I'm footing the bill."

"It's a matter of safety," he said, not bothering any longer to hide his frustration. "If Anna is in some kind of trouble, then the investigation could be dangerous."

"Then I guess it's good you'll have a medical professional with you."

MAX CLIMBED INTO HIS JEEP, completely frustrated and with no outlet for expressing it, as the main source of his frustration was perched in the passenger seat. If he'd known he was going to be playing escort to an untrained civilian, he may have told Alex he couldn't take the case. The young, shapely Cajun woman with miles of wavy dark hair and green eyes was the last thing in the world he'd been expecting.

When Alex had described Colette as one of the head nurses where she used to work, he'd immediately formed a picture in his mind of an old, blue-haired woman with ugly white shoes and a perpetual frown. But there wasn't a single thing about Colette that was old, blue-haired or ugly. Even in jeans, T-shirt and tennis shoes, and with her hair in a ponytail, she was still one of the sexiest women Max had ever seen, and he couldn't help but wonder how those long legs would look without the jeans encasing them.

She's a hard-core, hardheaded career woman, just like Mother.

And that was really where all train of thought came to a screeching halt, which was just as well. Max knew better than anyone that combining pleasure with work was a huge mistake.

He shook his head to change his train of thought and get back to the business at hand. They'd talked to all of Anna's neighbors at her apartment building but gotten only the same story: Anna was a quiet, polite woman whom they rarely saw. The search of her apartment had yielded nothing but more questions. Max hadn't located a single thread of information that might give a clue as to why the young woman had left. She kept no diary, no notes and, oddly enough, nothing related to her past.

It was as if she'd materialized out of thin air two years ago on the streets of New Orleans. And that, in itself, was very suspicious.

He could tell by Colette's expression that she was also bothered by the lack of personal items in Anna's apartment, but she wasn't about to admit it to him. And apparently, it hadn't changed her mind about accompanying him to the bank to see if they'd part with information on Anna's bank transactions.

"Don't you need a warrant or something to get information from the bank?" Colette asked.

"Usually."

Colette raised one eyebrow, clearly waiting for an explanation, but he didn't feel like giving one. He may have to let her along for the ride, but that didn't mean he had to consult with her on his actions or explain the way he worked. She was paying for an expert to handle the situation, and that's what she'd get. Teaching wasn't part of the job description.

She was smart enough not to press the issue, but she still followed right behind him as he parked in front of the bank and went inside. A young woman in a glass office at the front of the lobby jumped up from her chair and beamed as he walked in the door.

"Max," she said and rushed to give him a kiss on the cheek.

"Brandy," he said, both embarrassed and flattered by the attention.

"To what do I owe the pleasure?"

Max glanced around the lobby and was happy to see all the other employees and customers were out of hearing range. "I need your help," he said and explained the situation to her.

Brandy's eyes widened and her mouth formed a small O. When he finished, she nodded and gestured toward the office she'd come out of earlier. Colette and Max stepped inside and took seats across the desk from Brandy, who sat down and immediately started typing.

"There's been no other activity on the account since the withdrawal last Friday, but there's only thirty dollars left in the account."

"What about the month before that?" Max asked. "Is there anything unusual that you can see?"

Brandy scanned the screen, shaking her head. "It all looks like normal stuff—a check for rent, automatic draft for utilities and Netflix, and a couple of small cash withdrawals—never more than twenty dollars at a time."

"Can you tell where she made the withdrawal on Friday?"

Brandy nodded. "Let me look up the branch number associated with the transaction." She typed in some numbers and then said, "It's located on Highway 90 close to Old Spanish Trail, northeast of New Orleans."

Colette sucked in a breath. "That's on the way to the village where Anna's from. But she said she had no family left there."

"Maybe she lied."

Colette frowned, and Max knew she wasn't happy with the thought that the girl she'd invested so much in had been lying to her all along. "Maybe so," she said finally.

"Can I get a printout of the transactions and the address of that branch?" Max asked.

"Of course," Brandy said.

Max felt his cell phone vibrating in his pocket and pulled it out to check the display. "It's Holt," he said. "Excuse me for a moment."

He left the office and stepped outside onto the sidewalk in front of the bank. "What's up?" he asked.

"Alex got a call this morning from the morgue at West Side Hospital outside of New Orleans. They have a body that matches Anna's description."

Max's heart sank.

He'd known there was a possibility that Anna had met with foul play, but he'd really been hoping for a happy ending for Anna and Colette.

Unfortunately, it seemed that the worst-case scenario was visiting the investigation before he really got started.

COLETTE WATCHED AS BRANDY stapled the printouts together. The girl was certainly attractive and apparently knew Max well enough to risk being fired for what she was doing, but Colette couldn't help but think she was a little too young for him. She couldn't be over twenty at the most.

Whatever the status of Max's relationship with Brandy, it was none of her business, but that didn't prevent her from wanting to know. "You're not really supposed to give out that information, are you?" Colette asked, figuring she couldn't be faulted for the mostly innocent question, even if Max found out she'd asked.

"No, but you want it for a good reason. Besides, I owe Max."

Colette wasn't sure she really wanted to know the answer, but she couldn't help asking. "Owe him for what?"

"I wasn't the most respectable teen," Brandy said, looking a bit sheepish. "Max busted me with the wrong crowd three years ago in Baton Rouge but agreed to let me go if I would go back to school and ditch my troublemaking friends. He lied to his captain and told him I got away while they were rounding up the others. If anyone had found out, he probably would have been fired."

"Wow. That was really nice of him." And totally not the answer Colette had expected. So far, she'd seen only the hard-nosed-cop side of him.

Brandy smiled. "You know how he is."

"No...actually, I just met him this morning."

"Oh. I'm sorry. It's just that you two looked nice together. I guess I figured you were together."

"No, we—"

Before she could explain, Max stepped back into the office.

"We have to leave," he said.

Brandy handed him the printouts. "Let me know if there's anything else I can do."

"I will. Thanks."

"I hope you find her soon."

Max nodded and left the office, but not before Colette saw something dark pass over his expression.

"It was nice meeting you," Colette said to Brandy and hurried out of the office behind Max.

"What's wrong?" Colette asked as soon as he pulled the car away from the bank.

His jaw flexed and a wave of fear washed over her. Whatever he was about to say, Colette knew it wasn't going to be something she wanted to hear.

"Alex got a call from the morgue at West Side Hospital."

Colette felt the blood rush from her face. "Oh, no!"

"I need to take you over there. You're the only one…"

"Yes, of course." She stared out the windshield as he made the twenty-minute drive to the hospital, unable to believe it may all be over. That Anna could be inside the morgue on a cold slab of metal.

Somewhere in the back of her mind, she'd known that if things went horribly wrong, she'd have to be the one to identify her friend, but she was completely unprepared for it to happen in a matter of minutes.

She felt as if she was almost out of her body as she walked into the morgue, Max close behind. Feeling numb, she waited while Max spoke with the clerk, who gave her a sad glance, then buzzed them through a secure door. A medical technician met them on the other side. He spoke to them, but Colette didn't hear his words or Max's reply.

Anna's gone. Anna's gone. The cry repeated in her head.

Finally, they stopped in front of a window with closed

blinds, and the tech looked at Colette. "Let me know when you're ready."

A chill washed over her and she crossed her arms over her chest. She felt Max's arm encircle her shoulders. The warmth should have been comforting, but she was too numb to feel it. She took a deep breath and let it out slowly, then nodded to the tech.

Every muscle in her body tightened as the tech opened the blinds. She took one look at the girl on the table and almost collapsed.

Chapter Three

"That's not her," Colette gasped. "Oh, thank God."

Everything hit her at once, and she began to cry. Max pulled her close to him and stroked her back. She buried her head in the crook of his shoulder and struggled to get herself together.

"I'm sorry," she said, as she broke free of the hug and took a step away from him, embarrassed that she'd fallen apart.

"It's okay," he said.

"I'm so relieved, and at the same time, it feels wrong to be relieved, because there's another family that won't be."

Max nodded. "Every time I had to bring bad news to a family, there was a tiny voice in the back of my mind giving thanks that it wasn't my own. That's not wrong. That's human."

"Thank you. I thought I'd prepared myself that things may end this way, but I guess I was fooling myself."

"There is no preparation for someone close to you dying. If they're younger than life expectancy and it's not from natural causes, then that makes it a hundred times harder."

Colette studied him for a minute, struggling to hide her surprise. The empathy and understanding he shared with her was the last thing she'd expected from the hard-nosed, closed-off cop who had entered her apartment that morning. But then, Brandy's story about Max had already alerted her to the fact that Max ran a lot deeper than what showed on the surface.

Unfortunately for her, every layer she uncovered made him even more attractive than before, and falling for emotionally unavailable men was her Achilles' heel. She needed to shut down her overly active imagination and focus on finding Anna. She couldn't afford to be personally invested in the situation any more than she already was.

"So what's next?"

"A visit to the bank where Anna made the withdrawal. I'm hoping I can charm them into letting us review the tape of the ATM, maybe see if she was with anyone when she withdrew the money."

"You don't have a Brandy tucked away at every branch?"

He grinned. "Unfortunately, no. I'll have to wing this one."

"Then we better get going."

She started to move toward the exit, but he placed one hand on her shoulder. "Hey," he said, "are you sure you want to continue this? Working with me, I mean? This isn't really what you're trained to do, and as much as I'm hoping for a good outcome, things could get more unpleasant."

"I know, but I have to see it through. I'd understand if you don't want me along, though, especially after this. If that's the case, then just say the word and I'll get out of your way."

He studied her for a minute, and she knew he was weighing the pros of having the only person who knew Anna on a personal level against being saddled with a rank amateur. Using every advantage available must have finally won out because he shook his head.

"If you're willing, I can probably use your help," he said grudgingly. "If she's on the run from something, she may run even faster with only me pursuing her. With you there, she'll believe I'm an ally."

"Good," she said, despite his lack of enthusiasm.

"But if things get too intense, I reserve the right to sideline you."

"Okay." *And I reserve the right to ignore you if you do.*

He gave her a nod and walked out of the building. She watched him for a minute, unable to stop herself from admiring the way his muscular back rippled beneath his T-shirt. He was one hundred percent alpha male—strong, direct and physically capable of handling his adversaries.

And Colette couldn't help but think that the biggest risk for intensity was in her attraction to Max.

THE BRANCH MANAGER AT the location where Anna made the withdrawal turned out to be a man, so Max couldn't try the charm route to get an inroad. But Max figured with his stiffly starched shirt, perfect hair and neat-as-a-pin office, the man would probably bend the rules to avoid anything remotely messy or unattractive for him or the bank.

As soon as he explained that the woman was missing and a crime may have been committed, the manager was more than willing to pull the tapes for them. They waited impatiently as the manager sifted through a box of tapes and finally pulled the right one out and placed it in the ancient VCR.

"We really should upgrade to digital," the manager said, clearly nervous about the entire situation. "I keep asking, but corporate claims there's no funding. I hope this thing was working properly that day. It has its moments."

Max frowned. A "moment" from a VCR was the last thing he needed when he already had almost nothing to go on.

"Thank goodness," the manager said when the tape fired up a fuzzy display of the ATM on the outside of the bank. "What was the time of the withdrawal?"

"Three thirty-two p.m."

The manager forwarded the tape to just before three-thirty, and they all leaned in to watch. An older gentleman was using the ATM, but in the background, at the edge of the parking lot, stood a young woman.

"That's Anna!" Colette said.

The gentleman finished his transaction and left the ATM. Anna glanced around then hurried across the parking lot to the ATM. She fumbled with her wallet, dropping it, but finally retrieved her card and withdrew the money. Her expression told Max everything he needed to know.

This wasn't a woman out for a weekend fling. This woman was terrified.

They watched as she withdrew the cash and shoved it into her wallet. She looked nervously up and down the parking lot before hurrying back across to her car and driving away. Max leaned in toward the monitor to get a closer look at her car. A second later, she was gone.

"I didn't see anyone coercing her," the manager said, although his voice lacked conviction, probably based on Anna's clearly nervous disposition.

"Don't worry," Max assured the man. "There's nothing here that the bank can be faulted for. Do you mind if I take this tape?"

"No, of course not," the manager said, his relief apparent. "Don't worry about returning it. I need to change out the old tapes, anyway."

"I really appreciate the help," Max said and took the tape and motioned to Colette to leave.

After identifying Anna on the tape, Colette hadn't said another word, but Max didn't think for a minute that she hadn't formed an opinion. As soon as the climbed into his Jeep, she let it out.

"She looked scared," Colette said.

"Yes, but we have no reason to assume she's scared because she's in danger. Maybe there's a sick friend or family member she never told you about."

"She would tell me about a sick friend. I'm a nurse, for goodness' sake. That's enough of a reason for me to assume she's in danger. If the problem was benign or anyone else's to bear, why wouldn't she tell me?"

He blew out a breath. As much as he hated it, the fact that Anna hadn't contacted the only person she'd become close to didn't add up, unless Anna herself was the one in trouble.

"You said she didn't have family," he said.

"*She* said she didn't have family." Colette shook her head. "Look, clearly I don't know Anna as well as I thought I did. Maybe I don't know her at all, but the woman on that tape didn't know anyone was watching her, so she had no reason to fake being scared."

"I agree, but we need a starting point. Her past is the most likely choice."

"Okay."

"You said her hometown was on this highway, right?"

"Not exactly. I said it was on the way to her hometown."

Something in her tone let him know he was in for more

answers he didn't want. He looked over at her. "Where is Anna from?"

"Cache."

He stared at her. "You've got to be kidding me."

"I wish I were."

"The entire village is the Louisiana swamp version of a unicorn. The name itself means 'hidden.' Even if it really exists, which I'm not certain of, how in the world are we supposed to find it? Every teenager I know, including me, tried to find Cache. No one ever came close."

"It's there…somewhere in the swamp. It has to be."

Max shook his head. "Even if it is, there are other things to consider. You grew up in New Orleans, right? You know the stories."

"What—that the entire village materializes at the will of the village people and can disappear just the same? That no one's ever seen it and lived to tell about it? That if an outsider sets foot in the village, a curse will descend on ten generations of their family?"

She blew out a breath. "It's all just stories made up by parents to keep their kids from wandering in the swamp. Maybe even made up by the villagers to keep people from looking for the village. A bunch of old Creole lore can't possibly concern you."

"It's more than a bunch of lore. Mystere Parish is different."

"Different how? The Louisiana mystique extends beyond that one parish."

"Things happen here," he said. "Things that aren't possible. When we went into the swamp as boys, sometimes I'd feel a presence, something watching our every move."

"Well, of course, there are animals out in the swamp and probably hunters—"

"It wasn't anything like that. Look, I don't know how to

explain it to you without sounding crazy. I just know that you can't take things in Mystere Parish at surface value."

Colette bit her lower lip. "You think they're practicing voodoo in Cache?"

"Maybe, *if* the village even exists. But regardless of whether or not they're practicing the old ways, they will not take kindly to intruders. Finding the village could be enough to put us at risk to the same thing that happened to Anna."

Just going into the swamp will expose us to whatever's out there watching. He thought it, but didn't say it.

"Are you telling me you won't try?" she asked.

"No, I'm telling you why we shouldn't try. But if you still want to move forward, then I will."

"Of course I want to continue," she said, but Max could see the uncertainty in her expression. "You saw her on the tape. She needs our help."

He pulled out of the bank parking lot and merged onto the highway, directing his Jeep down the lonely stretch of road. "Pirate's Cove is the closest town to where Cache is supposed to be. We'll see if we can get some help locating the village there, and we need access to a boat."

"I do know one thing about Cache," Colette said, her voice wavering. "Until Anna Huval, no one's ever left the village and talked about it. And they made her promise never to return."

ANNA STUMBLED THROUGH the wall of decaying moss, the thick brush scratching her bare arms as she ran. Her leg muscles burned from the exertion of an hour-long race through the swamp, and her head throbbed above her right eye, where the creature had struck her. She paused for a couple of seconds and looked up, trying to ascertain that she was still running in the direction of the highway, but the thick canopy of cypress trees and moss choked out any view of the moonlight.

If she could get to the highway, she might be able to get help. The only town anywhere near was Pirate's Cove, where she'd left her car, but she had no idea which direction it was anymore. Besides, the residents of Pirate's Cove had to know about the curse. Someone was shielding the creature…either by helping it remain hidden all these years or by calling it up from the darkness if it hadn't been there before. Either way, it was likely that person was in Pirate's Cove.

The highway was her safest bet. There wasn't much traffic, but truck drivers often used that stretch of road because it was wide open and not cluttered with regular traffic.

Taking a deep breath, she pushed forward again, knowing that the creature was behind her somewhere…tracking her as it would an animal. And if it found her, it would kill her like one.

As soon as she told him her secret.

Chapter Four

It was almost one o'clock when Max pulled into Pirate's Cove. The town consisted of six buildings, scattered on both sides of the highway. The swamp stretched behind the buildings and went on for thousands of acres. Max pulled up to a café and parked.

"I figure we can get a bite to eat and use the time to feel out the locals. See if we can get some information on the location of Cache."

Colette nodded. Her stomach had started rumbling after leaving the bank. With all the stress of the morning, she was a bit surprised that food even entered into her thoughts, but apparently, biology prevailed.

They exited the car and walked to the café entrance.

Max paused outside the front door and said, "Don't tell anyone about Anna."

"Then what do we say?"

"I'll think of something. Let me get a read on the people first, and then follow my lead."

She nodded and followed him inside, reminding herself of Alex's confidence in Max's abilities. No matter how much she wished the investigation could progress faster, she had to take a step back and let Max do the work she'd hired him to do. He'd struck just the right note with the bank manager in getting access to the video footage.

Hopefully, he could find a way to do it again with the citizens of Pirate's Cove.

The lunch rush was either over or there wasn't much of one to begin with. Two men with sparse gray hair were the only patrons in the café, along with one cook and a waitress. All four stared as they took seats at the counter.

"Can I get you something to drink?" the waitress asked.

"Iced tea," Colette said.

"Same for me," Max chimed in.

The waitress filled the glasses and placed them on the counter. "You want something to eat?"

"I'll take the special," Max said.

Colette looked up at the board and saw the special was a BLT with chips. "I'll take the special, too."

The cook pulled some bacon from a fryer and began preparing the two sandwiches. "You folks passing through?"

"No," Max said. "Actually, we're looking for Cache."

The waitress dropped a plastic bottle of ketchup on the floor and some of it squirted out onto her shoe. The cook glared at her, and she snatched the bottle up and hurried through a door to the back of the café. The two old men leaned toward each other and started whispering.

The cook slid the plates in front of them and wiped his hands on a dish towel. "You a little old to be chasing after fairy tales, ain't you?"

"I don't think it is a fairy tale," Max said.

The cook laughed. "You and about a hundred new high-school seniors every year. All tromping through town and into the swamp, looking for something that ain't there. But hell, I can't complain. Brings me business."

"We're looking for a young woman, a friend of my fiancée's," Max said.

Colette struggled to keep her expression neutral at

Max's comment, but a moment later, she understood his tactic. He didn't want to reveal himself as a detective. That might make them close up even more. If she and Max had a personal relationship, it gave him a good reason to be involved.

"She told my fiancée she had an emergency back home, but when she didn't return, we started to worry. We know she's from Cache, so we figure that's where the emergency was. We want to help her if she's in some kind of trouble. If you know anything about the town, I'd really appreciate the help."

"Can't tell you what I don't know. Far as I know, there ain't no Cache and never has been."

The cook dropped his gaze to the sink behind the counter, then picked up a glass and started washing it. Colette was certain he was lying.

"Are you from this area?" Max asked.

"Yep. Name's Tom. I've owned this café for over thirty years."

"You mean to tell me that no one lives in the swamp outside of this town?" Max asked. "I find that hard to believe."

Tom rinsed the glass and started drying it with a dish towel. "Plenty of people live in the swamp," he said. "But that don't mean they all living in some legendary community, and certainly not one running everything with black arts, like all the rumors say. If something like that was going on around here, don't you think we'd have heard about it by now?"

"I guess so. So where did my fiancée's friend come from, you think?"

Tom shrugged. "I got no idea. I guess when you find her, you can ask?"

"*If* we find her. Even if she's from this area, a young woman has no business roaming the swamp alone."

"That is a fact." Tom cocked his head to one side and studied them for a moment. Then he narrowed his gaze on Colette. "How come you know the girl if she's from the swamp?"

"She works for me at a hospital in New Orleans," Colette said. "She's studying for her nursing degree. I've been helping her, so we've become close."

"And she said she was from Cache?"

"Yes."

"You must not be from around here if you didn't think that was odd."

"I grew up in New Orleans, and I've heard all the stories about Cache. I don't believe half of them, but that doesn't mean the village doesn't exist."

"You hadn't heard all the stories about Cache, because even if you believed only half of 'em, you wouldn't want to be finding it."

"I'm not a coward. I want to help my friend."

Tom shook his head. "You ever stopped to think that it's far more likely your friend has told you a story because she's got trouble with the law or a man? Some women always got problems with a man."

"You could be right, but I won't be able to live with myself if I don't at least try to find her and help if she's in trouble."

He sighed. "You seem to be a nice woman, looking out for someone that ain't even kin. I wish I could help."

"Do you recall anyone with a daughter, about twenty or so, that lives out in the swamp?" Max asked.

"The swamp people's got very little cash, and what they have they don't spend on food service, so I don't see them much. When they come into town, it's for gas and minimal supplies. Talk to Danny over at the gas station. He may be able to help you."

"Thanks," Max said. "I'll check with him when we leave."

Tom glanced at the two old men in the corner and they rose to leave. They nodded to Tom and left the restaurant without so much as a backward glance. Colette looked out the plate-glass window and saw them cross the street and go into the gas station. She looked over at Max, who barely shook his head.

Colette tackled what was left of her lunch, anxious to leave. She felt more uncomfortable in this café than she ever had anywhere else. The undercurrents were almost palpable.

The waitress returned from the back and removed their empty plates from the counter. Colette noticed her movements were jerky and she barely looked at them. "Do you know where to find any of the swamp people?" Colette asked the waitress.

She stiffened and glanced over at Tom before replying. "I don't ever go into the swamp. It's too dangerous."

"Have you ever met any of the people when they come here?" Colette asked. "A young Creole woman, about twenty?"

The waitress grabbed a dish towel and started wiping down the coffeepot behind the counter. "I don't know any girl. Don't know any swamp people."

Max pulled out his wallet and left some money on the counter. "Thanks for the information and the food," he said.

Tom nodded, but the waitress didn't even look up. As soon as they got outside the café, Colette said, "The old men went to warn the gas-station guy we were coming, didn't they?"

"Probably, which is interesting."

"Tom was lying. What are they hiding?"

"I don't know. Maybe they don't believe our reason for wanting to find Cache." Max pointed to the gas station and they started across the street.

"Then what else could we possibly want?"

"Maybe reporters writing a story. Maybe someone looking for the ability to do black arts. If Cache really exists somewhere in the swamp near this town, they've managed to keep its location a secret for a long time. There must be something in it for the locals to keep the town protected."

A chill passed over Colette, even though it was a warm fall afternoon. "What could be so important or so dangerous that generations of people made sure it stayed a secret all these years, and what would the villagers have to give to the townspeople to gain such a collective silence?"

Max shook his head. "I don't know, but I have to tell you, I don't get a good feeling about this."

As they approached the gas station, the two old men who'd left the café walked out the front door and hurried down the sidewalk, careful to avoid making eye contact. Colette looked beyond the gas station to the dense swamp behind it.

She didn't get a good feeling, either.

Max held open the door and they walked inside the station. A man, probably in his thirties, with unkempt brown hair and wearing a greasy shirt and jeans was stocking a beer cooler and looked up when the bell above the door jangled on their entry.

"You folks need gas?" he asked.

"No, we were hoping for some information."

The man straightened and walked over to them. "My

name's Danny Pitre. I own this station." He extended his hand to Max, who shook it, and then nodded at Colette.

"What kind of information you looking for?" Danny asked.

"We're looking for Cache," Max said.

Danny narrowed his eyes. "You the people from the café?"

"Yes."

"Old Joe told me you was looking for a missing girl that claimed she was from Cache."

"That's right. She's my fiancée's friend and coworker. She hasn't reported to work for several days and we can't reach her by cell."

Danny rubbed his chin and studied them for several seconds. "Truth is, I had a boat stolen last week. One of the old-timers said he saw a young girl with dark hair in it but figured I'd rented it to some city fool, which is why he didn't tell me about seeing it till I mentioned it was missing."

Colette felt her pulse spike. It must have been Anna who stole the boat, trying to get to the village.

Danny looked over at her. "Your friend a thief?"

"Not usually," Colette said, "but her message said it was an emergency. I suppose she may have borrowed your boat intending to return it."

"Did you ever find the boat?" Max asked.

"Yeah. A fisherman towed it in yesterday. He found it floating loose out in the swamp."

Colette felt her back tighten. Surely Anna would have known the proper way to secure a boat. Had something happened to her while she was on it? Had she fallen off somewhere in the swamp and met with one of the many deadly predators? Colette didn't want to think about the many unpleasant possibilities.

"Tom over at the café said you may know where some of the swamp people live," Max said. "I figure if we could find some of them, even if they aren't the girl's family, word may get back to them."

"Ain't no way to get back to the swamp people but by boat. You got one?"

"No. I was hoping to rent one, but if that's not possible here, I guess I'll head back to New Orleans and rustle one up."

Danny shook his head. "Well, I sure do give you dedication to your word. I can loan you the boat that was stolen, no charge. It's small but you can't fit much where you'll be going. I'll have to charge you for the gas, though. It's been a slow month."

"That's no problem. I appreciate the loan."

"You may not be so grateful once you get out into the swamp. It's no place for the untrained. Did you grow up around these parts?"

"Vodoun. I did plenty of tromping through the swamp as a boy."

"I thought your accent was local," Danny said. "Well, then you might be all right, but I'll loan you my shotgun, just in case." He waved to the back door and started walking toward it. "Boat's out back. Let's get it in the water and then I'll tell you where to start looking."

Colette struggled with feelings of relief, anticipation and fear that they were already too late to help Anna. If everything turned out badly, she had to be ready to accept that at least she had an answer. Living without one would be something she never could have accepted.

Max helped Danny push the tiny, flat-bottom, aluminum boat into the bayou, and Danny tied it off at the dock. Then he pointed west down the bayou.

"You're going to want to head that way about a mile,"

Danny said. "When you come to the cypress tree that's been split by lightning, take a right into that channel. Follow it for another two miles or so into the swamp. When you see a line of crab pots, look east and you'll see a dock almost hidden in the undergrowth. There's a cabin about fifty yards back from the dock. You got that?"

"Yeah, it seems straightforward enough."

"Finding a cabin isn't the problem. The real danger comes if you find the people. They don't take kindly to strangers, and they're just as apt to shoot you as talk to you. Make sure you tell them straight out that you're not the police. They probably don't even know the rules, much less follow them, so it causes them some problems with the law on occasion. There's no love lost there."

"I'll make sure I yell it loudly."

"Just a minute," Danny said and walked back inside the gas station and came back a few minutes later with a shotgun that he handed to Max.

Max checked the gun and took the handful of spare bullets that Danny offered. "Thanks. I hope I won't need to use this."

"Me, too," Danny said. "The walk from the dock to the cabin is probably the most dangerous part. Be sure to watch for snakes and alligators, and of course, any unhappy swamp people. You don't stand much of a chance against any of them in a one-on-one fight, except maybe a snake, and I guess I don't have to tell you how far off the hospital is."

Danny looked over at Colette. "Ma'am, are you sure you want to go? You're welcome to wait here if you'd like."

"No, thank you," Colette replied. "I'm the one who made the promise. I can't let someone else take all the risk for keeping my word."

Danny grinned. "You got spunk. I like that." He walked

toward the gas station and gave them a wave. "I'll be here when you get back."

"You know, he's right," Max said. "You don't have to come. In fact, it would probably be safer if you didn't."

"I don't know that I agree." Colette glanced back at the town. "I don't get a good feeling about this place."

Max nodded. "There's definitely an undercurrent of something unpleasant. More than just resenting nosy strangers."

"Do you think they know something about Anna that they're not telling us?"

"Maybe, or they may be hiding something completely unrelated that they don't want us to stumble onto. It's impossible to say."

"Well, despite the many dangers of the swamp, I'd rather be out there with you. Besides, if we find people who know Anna, you won't be able to answer questions they may have about her. I can. And the reality is, you'll probably look less threatening to them with a woman tagging along."

"That's true enough."

"There's something that bothers me," Colette said. "Anna took money out of her account before coming here. Why would she steal the boat when she could have rented it?"

"You said she wasn't supposed to return, right? Maybe she didn't want anyone knowing she was coming. If she'd rented the boat, word would have spread. A young girl traipsing around the swamp alone would raise some eyebrows."

"I guess so."

Max pulled his cell phone from his pocket and frowned. "No service. I figured as much, but it means we have no backup. You still sure?"

She should have known that cell phones would be useless this deep in bayou country, but it hadn't even crossed her mind. Still, it didn't change what they had to do.

"I'm sure."

"Okay," he said and motioned to the boat. "Hop in and I'll push us off."

Colette stepped into the boat and took a seat on the narrow bench in the middle. Max untied the boat and pushed it from the dock, stepping into the boat as it backed away. He took a seat at the back and started the outboard motor, then powered the boat down the bayou in the direction Danny had indicated.

As soon as they were out of sight of the town, he slowed down to a crawl. "Do you know how to fire a shotgun?" he asked.

"Doesn't everyone in Louisiana? The natives, anyway."

Max smiled. "Probably." He handed her the rifle. "I have my pistol, but I didn't want to turn down the offer of the rifle. If you're comfortable handling it, then I think it's better if we're both armed."

Colette took the rifle and laid it across her legs. "I can handle it."

The weight of the rifle across her legs provided a bit more feeling of security. She trusted Max to protect her to the best of his abilities, but sometimes the swamp offered up more than any one man could handle. If the legends were to be believed, the swamps of Mystere Parish could offer up more than a team of men could handle.

Max increased the boat's speed and they continued down the bayou. The farther they progressed, the narrower the channel became until the trees from each bank met each other at the tops, creating a dark tunnel.

Colette blinked a couple of times, trying to hurry her eyes to adjust to the dim light. She scanned the bank as they went. She told herself she was looking for a sign of habitation, but Colette knew that deep down, she was hoping to spot Anna standing on the bank, alive and well and ready to go back to New Orleans and resume her new life again.

Ready to escape this dank tomb of moss and dead vegetation.

Max slowed the boat's speed even more as the waterway became narrower and more clogged with debris. Decaying water lilies spread out in front of them, a cover of death over the still water. The smell of salt water, mud and rot filled the silent air. Only the hum of the boat motor echoed around them.

Even for the middle of the day, which was traditionally nap time in the swamp, it was too quiet. It was as if all living things had gone still in order to watch them as they moved deeper into the abyss. For a practical woman like Colette, it bothered her how unnerved she felt. One look at the grim expression on Max's face let her know he wasn't any happier with the situation than she was.

"Over there," he said finally, breaking the silence.

She looked toward the shore where he pointed, and could barely make out a dock, hidden in the tall marsh grass. Max guided the boat over to the dock and inched it onto the bank.

"The dock doesn't look too sturdy," Max said. "We're going to get our feet wet, but I don't think stepping out on that relic is a good idea."

"I agree," Colette said and handed Max the rifle while she stepped out onto the muddy bank. She sank several inches in the soupy, black mud and felt mud and water ooze into her tennis shoes.

She took the rifle back from Max and plodded up the

bank until she hit firm ground. "I hope we don't have to run. I just added ten pounds of weight directly on my feet."

"Yeah," Max said as he stepped carefully out of the boat. "You can move slowly to minimize impact, but Louisiana mud is still going to claim a portion of your legs. We really weren't prepared for this. We need boots."

"Do you think we should have gone back for equipment?"

"No. We were already here, and the longer Anna is missing, the more likely something bad will happen. We can take a look around, and if we don't find anything, we'll come back tomorrow better prepared."

"I guess we tipped our hand by coming here, right? If we'd left earlier, it would have given them all the time in the world to design stories and hide things. Assuming the locals are part of whatever Anna got into."

"Yeah, but sending us on a wild-goose chase would give them the same opportunity."

"I hadn't thought about that. Danny could easily have sent us off in the wrong direction." She sighed. "I would make a horrible criminal."

"Fortunately for law enforcement, most people do." Max scanned the brush and pointed just to the left of where they stood. "I think I see the trail there."

He walked about ten feet into the undergrowth and paused, scanning the area again. "It's definitely not well traveled, but I don't see signs of another trail. This must be the one."

Colette peered down the tiny path, but within a matter of feet, the dense undergrowth had swallowed up the tiny trail. She took a deep breath, trying not to think about all the things that could go wrong following this tiny trail into the unknown.

"You ready?" he asked.

"As ready as I'm getting."

"Make sure you keep the shotgun handy, but stay close to me. The last thing we need is an accident with that gun."

He pushed some brush aside and started down the trail at a steady pace. She swallowed, then clutched the shotgun and fell in step a foot behind Max. Far enough away not to bump into him but close enough that she couldn't lift the shotgun and fire on him if panicked. He set a slow, deliberate pace, scanning the brush in front of them as well as the sides. The cypress trees clustered closer and closer together, reducing visibility to the equivalent of twilight.

She clutched the gun, tucking her arms as close to her body as possible. The dying bushes and brambles scratched her bare arms as they passed down the trail. When tiny rays of sunlight managed to slip through the canopy of trees, huge spiderwebs glittered.

"Watch overhead, will you?" he asked. "I'm casing the ground and scanning ahead and to the sides, but snakes may still be in the trees."

Colette said a silent prayer as she looked up into the branches ahead of them. If a snake fell out of a tree onto her, the investigation would be over. She was certain she'd have a heart attack on the spot.

"If someone lives back here, why isn't this path more worn?" she asked.

"Given that the dock was also falling apart, my guess is they have another way to get to the living quarters and have abandoned the old one."

"Assuming anyone still lives out here."

"Yep, which is questionable given that we don't know if the source of the information is trustworthy."

"How did you do this every day?"

"Ha. In all my years of police work, I never once

tromped through a snake-infested swamp, but I assume that's not what you're asking."

"No. I meant questioning people and trying to figure out what was the truth. Considering that everyone is probably lying about something, and trying to figure out whether it's about something important."

"I don't know that it's much different from what doctors do when diagnosing a patient. Basically, the symptoms are the answers, but some of the answers may be inaccurate or related to something else completely. Sometimes you have to track a symptom back to the root to determine it's benign or unrelated to the bigger problem. It's the same with answers."

"Yes, I guess you're right." Colette appreciated his take on her line of work. It was a perspective she hadn't considered before.

The light dimmed suddenly, and Colette looked up through the narrow slit between the trees to see a dark cloud covering the sun. "Is it supposed to storm today?" she asked.

He glanced up at the sky and frowned. "No, but that doesn't mean it won't."

The last thing Colette wanted was to get caught out in the swamp in a thunderstorm. "How much farther, do you think?"

"I'm just guessing at distance, but we should be close."

"Too close!" A burly man wearing overalls stepped out from the brush with a shotgun leveled directly at Max's chest.

Chapter Five

"You're trespassing on private property," the man with the shotgun said.

An involuntary cry escaped from Colette before she could stop it. Max drew up short and put his hands in the air. Figuring it was a good idea, she followed suit, lifting the shotgun above her head. The man studied them, his finger never leaving the trigger.

"I'm sorry, sir," Max said. "We didn't mean to disturb you. Danny, the gas station owner in Pirate's Cove, thought you might be able to help us."

The man narrowed his eyes. "You got the stench of big city all over you, and the swamp ain't no place for a woman lessin' she was born here. What do you want?"

"We're looking for Cache."

The man's jaw set in a hard line. "Wrong answer."

"Please," Colette said. "My friend is missing. She told me she was from Cache. I just want to make sure she's safe."

The man lowered his gaze to Colette and she reminded herself to breathe. She could feel her heart pounding in her chest under his scrutiny and hoped that her worry and sincerity showed in her expression.

"No one leaves Cache," the man said.

"She told me she did. I'm not lying to you. I just want to find my friend. I'm afraid she's in trouble."

"If she's from Cache, how do you know her?"

"She works for me at a hospital in New Orleans."

"You a doctor?"

"No, sir. I'm a nurse. My friend is a nurse's aide."

"What does she look like?" he asked.

"She's twenty years old and Creole. Tall, thin and has long dark brown hair. She usually wears it in a ponytail. Her favorite color is blue and she usually wore blue T-shirts when she wasn't working."

The man studied her a bit longer then nodded. "I seen a girl the other day that looked like that. It was a ways back in the swamp. There was a boat pulled up on the bank and she was walking into the trees. She wasn't dressed right to be back here—no rubber boots—and I didn't see a firearm."

Colette's pulse quickened. "Do you remember what day it was that you saw her?"

"Don't have much use for time out here, but I reckon I've slept five nights since then."

Friday.

Colette looked over at Max, not sure which direction to take their conversation next, especially as the man had yet to remove his finger from the trigger of the shotgun, much less lower it.

"Sir," Max said. "The girl never returned home, and we're afraid she ran into trouble. If you could just tell us where you saw her, we'll be happy to get off your property and go look for her there."

Finally, the man lowered his shotgun. "This swamp is a dangerous place for people that don't know their way around."

"I know," Max said, "but we have to take the risk."

"If the girl you're looking for left Cache then tried to return, the risk may be a lot higher than you think."

The man looked up at the darkening sky. "A storm's coming. Maybe it will hold off until tonight or tomorrow, maybe not. But if you're determined…" He pulled a knife from his pocket and cleared some brush away from the ground until only dirt was exposed. Then he began to draw a crude map and explain how to reach the area of the swamp where he'd seen Anna.

Colette watched as he drew one turn after another, and listened as he explained all the channels in the bayou that they had to navigate, and she grew more nervous by the second. Max studied the drawing, asking the occasional question, until finally, the man drew an X.

Max took a picture of the drawing with his cell phone. "Thank you for your help. My name is Max and this is Colette."

The man nodded. "People call me 'Gator. Ain't got no given name that I know of. You run into trouble, tell them 'Gator gave you directions. Most of the swamp people know me. It might buy you enough time to ask about your friend fore someone shoots you."

Colette sucked in a breath and felt Max squeeze her arm.

"We appreciate the help, 'Gator."

"Good luck," the man said, but his skeptical look told Colette that he didn't expect them to succeed.

Before she could thank him, he spun around and disappeared completely into the brush. Colette stared into the undergrowth where he'd left the trail, but couldn't see any sign of him. Nor could she hear him. No wonder he'd been on top of them before they knew it. It was as if he'd vaporized into the swamp.

"How did he do that?" she asked.

Max stared into the undergrowth and frowned. "Experience." He started back down the trail to the dock and she fell in step behind him.

"The same experience the people of Cache will have," she said.

"Yeah. They'll know we're coming long before we arrive."

"Should we continue? Maybe we should go back for supplies or help or both—maybe an entire branch of the Marine Corps."

He smiled. "That might appear a bit confrontational."

"Okay, I'll admit, I'm scared to death of getting lost out here."

"I have a plan for that," he said as they stepped out of the undergrowth onto the muddy embankment at the boat dock.

He looked down the bayou in the direction 'Gator had indicated. The foliage was even denser, the light fading as you progressed deeper into the swamp. "It's everything else I'm worried about."

Colette stared at the dimly lit bayou and bit her lip. She looked back at Max. "I didn't pay you to risk your life. If you don't want to do it, I'd completely understand. I don't consider this part of the job."

"No. You paid us to find Anna. This is where the trail leads. As much as I'd prefer to have equipment and a better boat, I don't want to waste time returning to New Orleans to get it. I think we should take a look around. If we haven't found anything in a couple of hours, we'll return the boat and come back tomorrow better equipped."

She looked up, studying the tufts of dark clouds that littered the sky. "And if it storms?"

Max glanced up and shook his head. "We'll just hope that it doesn't."

She watched the clouds swirl across the sun. A chill came over her, and she hurried down the muddy bank to climb into the boat. The temperature must have dropped as the shadow covered her body. That was why she felt a chill.

That's what she told herself, anyway.

MAX PUSHED THE BOAT away from the bank and hopped inside. He started the engine and backed the boat away from the shoreline before turning it deeper into the bayou. The nagging feeling that he was missing something festered in the back of his mind, taunting him for his lack of clarity.

He'd ignored that feeling once before, and it had cost him his self-respect and almost his life.

This entire situation had been sketchy from the beginning, but his sexy sidekick had been the only bother he'd felt when he left New Orleans that morning. The further into the investigation he progressed, the more uneasy he became. He'd have rather Anna's trail lead them to Alaska than the swamps of Mystere Parish.

He slowed the boat at the first corner and took a shot of the turn with his cell phone. Then he made a note to make a right turn when returning.

"That's a smart idea," Colette said. "As long as the battery holds."

She tried to make the sentence light, as if she was making a joke, but the strained smile and the anxiety in her voice were a dead giveaway to Max. This had become much more than she'd bargained for when she'd strong-armed him into taking her along. But then, it had become more than he'd bargained for as well, so he couldn't really blame her for her unease. As a nurse, she was trained to handle trauma, but not the kind of stress they were under now.

Still, most women would have already buckled under the pressure. None of the women he knew, except his sister-in-law, Alex, would be sitting in the boat with him, attempting to make a joke. Even his mother, for all her brass in the corporate boardroom, wouldn't have managed five comfortable minutes in the swamp.

"It was fully charged this morning," he said, hoping to reassure her, if only a tiny bit. "And I keep it plugged in while I'm driving. As long as it stays dry, we're in good shape."

"Then I'll leave off praying for the cell-phone battery and just pray for no rain."

He waved one hand out toward the bayou. "It's going to be slow going. With all the water lilies, I can hardly see the surface at all. I'm afraid to move too fast in case something is submerged."

"I understand."

She faced straight forward on her seat, scanning the banks on each side of them. She was saying all the right things, but Max could see the tension in her back and neck as she looked for any sign of Anna or the village.

He'd been surprised that 'Gator had given them information so easily. Granted, he'd held a gun on them long enough to form an opinion, but usually swampers were very protective of each other. Maybe seeing the girl was so odd that 'Gator knew something was wrong, too.

Or maybe he was sending them right into a trap.

'Gator had made it clear that no one left Cache, and Anna had told Colette that she'd been directed never to return. If Anna had dared to leave and now dared to return, the people of Cache wouldn't be happy to see her. And that sentiment would extend to anyone looking for her.

He checked the picture of the map on his cell phone and steered the boat left into a tiny cut. The cypress trees were so thick with moss that they blocked all but the tiniest ray of light from entering. Max squinted in the dim light, trying to keep the boat in the middle of the narrow channel, where he'd be less likely to hit the knotty roots of the trees that grew underwater and claimed many propellers.

"Colette, check in that bench you're sitting on and see if there's a flashlight."

She rose from the bench and lifted the lid. She dug around in it for a minute or so and emerged with a weather-beaten flashlight.

"It doesn't look like much," she said and pressed the button. It flickered then went out. She tapped the side of it with the palm of her hand and it flickered back on.

"Better than nothing as long as it holds," she said.

He nodded. "Go ahead and turn it off for now to conserve what's left of the battery. We'll need it more once we're onshore."

She clicked off the light and closed the bench storage, but no sooner had she sat down than she popped back up.

"I saw something out there." She pointed to the left bank.

Max cut the motor and looked where she pointed. "Something moving?"

"I'm not sure. It was a flash of light color—one that didn't belong."

Max removed an oar from the bottom of the boat and paddled them slowly backward, scanning the swamp. The bank here didn't slope up from the bayou. Instead, the roots of cypress trees made up the embankment, creating a swirled, knotted patchwork of wood that lifted the ground two feet above the water.

Max scanned the ground past the cypress roots and located what had caught Colette's eye. It was a patch of light color on the ground in the dense undergrowth. One of the few thin rays of sunlight that managed to breach the cypress trees was shining right on it. Otherwise, he doubted it would have been visible at all.

He paddled the boat up to the bank and removed his pistol from his waistband. "Stay here and have the shot-gun ready. Remember, the shot will scatter. If you have to, shoot as far away from me as possible."

Colette's eyes widened and she lifted the shotgun into her lap, holding it with both hands, ready to fire if necessary.

Max scanned the bank for predators then climbed up the roots and onto the ground above the bayou. He inched slowly toward the object, watching and listening for any sign of life, of movement. About ten feet from the object, he realized it was light blue cloth.

...*she usually wore blue T-shirts*.

His heart caught in his throat as he recalled Colette's description. Abandoning all caution, he rushed through the brush, his heart dropping when he saw the motionless body of Anna Huval.

She was slumped over on her side, her back to Max. Her clothes were torn and dirty, her shoes caked with mud. Scratches ran up her arm, dried blood still clinging to her skin. He squatted down next to her and placed his fingers on her neck, Colette's certain devastation the only thing on his mind.

He felt a pulse!

Faint, but she was still alive. Gently, he rolled her over and immediately locked in on the purple lump on her forehead. There were no obvious breaks or gashes, so he gently lifted her up and slowly made his way back to the bank.

"Max," Colette called out. "Is everything okay?"

"I found Anna," Max said as he stepped onto the bank

above the boat and looked down at Colette. "She's hurt but still alive."

"Oh!" Colette's hand flew up to cover her mouth and her eyes filled with unshed tears. "I can't believe it."

Max looked up and down the embankment, trying to find a lower place to climb into the boat. "Lift the motor," he instructed Colette, "and use the cypress roots to pull the boat down the bayou to that low spot."

Colette almost leaped into the back of the boat and then lifted the motor so that it hovered above the roots that could damage it beyond functionality. Then she grabbed the cypress roots and pulled the boat to the low spot in the bank that he'd indicated. Carefully, he stepped into the boat with Anna and gently placed her in the bottom, where Colette had already placed a life jacket to support her head.

Any doubts he'd had about Colette's ability to handle the situation were erased in a moment. With the injured girl safely in the boat, she immediately shifted into professional mode, checking Anna for injury, looking at her eyes, taking her pulse, inspecting her mouth.

"Is that knot on her head why she's unconscious?" he asked.

"I don't know exactly. The bruising on her scalp is probably a day old, but she hardly ran through the swamp unconscious. Still, that much exertion could have exacerbated the head injury, causing her to black out." She looked up at him. "Her breathing is too shallow, her pulse too weak. We have to get her to the hospital soon."

He nodded and pushed the boat away from the bank. "I'll go as fast as safely possible." He lowered the motor and proceeded down the bayou as quickly as he dared.

Colette looked down the bayou then back at Anna, her face taut with worry. Max wished he could go faster, but the incoming tide combined with a northern wind was creating ripples across the usually smooth water. If he went faster, the boat would bang on top of the waves, jarring the already injured girl even more.

As they crept down the bayou, he scanned the banks. He didn't want to say anything to Colette until they were out of Pirate's Cove, but he doubted that lump on Anna's head was accidental. The location he'd found Anna in contained no path leading to it, so he had to assume she'd arrived there by randomly traversing the swamp. The most logical explanation was that she was being pursued. Anna, of all people, knew the dangers of this swamp and would not have left the trail except by necessity.

Whoever was pursuing Anna hadn't found her, which meant that he was probably still looking. The sooner they were safely out of Pirate's Cove, the better.

It took an excruciatingly slow hour to reach Pirate's Cove. As they pulled up to the dock, Danny Pitre stepped outside the back door of the gas station, carrying a bag of trash. As he lifted one hand to wave, Max jumped out of the boat and dashed up to the startled gas-station owner.

"I need help!" Max shouted as he ran. "Where's your phone?"

Danny dropped the bag of trash and hurried inside the station. He pointed to the phone behind the counter and watched, wide-eyed, as Max called 911 and asked for Care Flight.

Danny jerked his head around to look out the back window of the station. "Is your lady hurt?"

"No," Max managed before he rushed back outside and back to the boat.

Carefully he lifted Anna from the bottom of the boat and placed her on the dock at the feet of a dumbfounded Danny.

"I thought…heck, I don't know, maybe that you guys was fooling," he said, his eyes wide. "Is she…"

"No," Colette said and stepped onto the dock. "But she needs care."

"What happened to her?"

"I don't know," Max said, "but I'm going to find out."

The sound of a helicopter echoed in the distant sky, and Max pulled out his wallet. "What do I owe you for the gas?"

Danny held a hand up in protest. "No charge, man. I hope she's all right."

"That was fast," Colette said.

Max nodded. "They already had a chopper out this way on another call, but it wasn't needed."

He carefully lifted Anna from the dock and hurried as fast as he dared to the service road, the best landing place for the helicopter.

Colette insisted on riding with Anna, but they had room for only one. She yelled to Max that she'd call him as soon as she knew anything, and hopped into the helicopter. A couple of minutes later, they were above the swamp and off to the hospital.

Max pulled his keys from his pocket as he ran to his Jeep, but he drew up short when he saw something hanging from the driver's side mirror. He knew immediately what the small pouch made of burlap was that hung there, even before he got close enough to see the markings drawn onto the coarse material.

A gris-gris.

It meant different things in different countries and cultures, but in this area, in this culture, it was a warning. Someone was letting him know that black magic was at play and he should quietly disappear.

He glanced up the street, where all the business owners

and customers had stepped outside to see the helicopter. They were all looking back at him, their expressions full of curiosity. Had they seen the gris-gris? One of them must have placed it here, but which one?

He yanked it off the mirror and fought the overwhelming urge to toss it into the street. It was evidence in an investigation, so despite the distasteful feeling it gave him, he tossed it on the floorboard in the back of his Jeep before jumping into the driver's seat and leaving Pirate's Cove as fast as possible.

Chapter Six

Colette looked at the monitors the Care Flight paramedics had hooked to Anna and frowned. Her blood pressure was dangerously low and dropping more every minute. Her normally tanned skin was so pale that the black-and-purple bruise on her forehead almost seemed to glow.

The paramedics kept the hospital alerted to Anna's condition, and the emergency room was prepared for her arrival. Colette hoped it wasn't too late. She had no idea how long Anna had been unconscious, but from the ragged appearance of her clothes and the dried blood crusted around the scratches on her bare skin, it looked as if she'd been in the swamp for a while.

Why was she in that spot, with no sign of life around her? Had she lost her way and tripped, hitting her head on the way down? Max had asked only about her condition but hadn't commented on how it might have happened. If he had any ideas, he'd kept them to himself.

An emergency-room crew was waiting for them at the landing site on top of the hospital. They transferred Anna to a gurney and rushed her down to the emergency room. Colette insisted on accompanying them, explaining on the way that she was a trauma nurse at another hospital and Anna's supervisor.

In the emergency room, she found a place where she

wouldn't be in the way and let the doctors and nurses do their job. As much as it pained her to stand by while other people did her job, she knew that staff who worked together every day were more efficient and knew each other's rhythm. Her trying to help would only hinder.

So she stood to the side, hands clenched, and prayed for good news as the trauma team worked.

Twenty minutes later, the doctor nodded to his team and stepped over to where Colette stood. "She's stable for now, and I can't find any sign of injury other than the blow to her head," the doctor said.

Relief coursed through her. "Thank goodness."

"I know I don't have to tell you the risks associated with her condition or that we're not out of the woods."

She nodded. "I know you've done everything you can."

"We'll keep her in ICU until she awakens, but you're welcome to stay, if you'd like. I can have one of my staff bring you a recliner. Not the most comfortable chair in the world, but it will do in a pinch."

"I'd love to stay, and I would appreciate even an uncomfortable chair."

"Well, she could do worse than a trauma nurse watching over her while she sleeps. I'll check back in before my shift is over," he said then left the room.

The nurses finished up their work and left as well, but one returned a couple of minutes later pushing a lopsided recliner. "It's a bit beaten up," the nurse said.

"It's fine. Thank you."

Colette pulled the chair close to Anna's bed, where she had a clear view of her friend's face and the monitors, then collapsed on it, the worn-out cushions sinking around her like a beanbag. Stress and exhaustion had worn her body and mind to a frazzle. She'd been running on adrenaline for so long that she could feel it leaving her body.

Anna's condition wasn't great, but it wasn't life-and-death. Within the next twenty-four hours, Anna should awaken. When they could question her and test her motor skills and physical control, they'd know better the extent of the injury and could make a better estimate of what the short- and long-term effects might be.

The most important thing was that she was alive and safe.

Colette's mind raced with all the activity of the day. That morning, she'd wondered if anything would ever be accomplished with Max, who clearly didn't think her case was worth the time spent. But he'd pursued every avenue like the professional Alex had assured her he was and had found Anna in one day. Granted, there were a million unanswered questions about why Anna had left and what had happened to her, but Max had finished the job he'd been hired to do.

A wave of disappointment washed over her as she realized exactly what finding Anna meant—that she had no reason to see Max again. Perhaps once to wrap up the finer points, but then, Alex may handle that along with the billing.

It was hard for Colette to wrap her mind around the fact that she'd grown so used to leaning on him in such a short time, even though it felt as if they'd lived a lifetime in a single day. He was so guarded, so private, that it had been hard to learn anything much about him, but when she'd been able to peek through the veneer into the man himself, she always liked what she saw.

Max Duhon was a strong, capable man with a good heart. He was also the most gorgeous man she'd ever seen, and she'd be lying to herself if she didn't admit that she was hugely attracted to him on a physical level. Maybe it had just been too long since she'd enjoyed the company of an attractive man, the feel of a man's bare skin pressed against hers.

She sighed. Whom was she kidding? It wasn't a drought causing her attraction to Max. It was Max causing her attraction to Max. She'd have to be blind not to be attracted to him.

It was just as well that the investigation had wrapped up so quickly. The last thing she needed was to get tangled up with another emotionally unavailable man, and Max showed all the signs of being exactly that. If only she could find a nice, balding accountant with a potbelly attractive, all her relationship problems would be solved.

She rose and checked Anna's charts and the machine readouts again, just to break her mind off from thinking about the unattainable Max. A couple of minutes later, she sat back down and closed her eyes, just to rest them.

She didn't even remember falling asleep.

HOLT CHAMBERLAIN STEPPED through the front door of his cabin and gave his wife a big smile. Alex stood in the kitchen, a place he thankfully didn't find her often. She frowned over a pot of something red and bubbly.

"I see you're trying to cook again."

Alex tasted a bit of the red stuff and shook her head. "It's just spaghetti sauce. It comes out of a jar, for goodness' sake. How do I manage to mess that up?"

Holt laughed and stepped up behind her, then wrapped his arms around her and nuzzled her neck. "You have talents that far outweigh cooking."

She turned around to kiss him and then smiled. "I don't want Max to think I'm slacking, letting you prepare all the meals."

"I see. This isn't about wanting to pull your weight or

some burning desire to be a better cook. It's about impressing my brother. Should I be jealous?"

"Probably. He's gorgeous."

Holt grinned. "All the girls always thought so."

"He did break a lot of hearts in Vodoun." Alex inclined her head toward the kitchen window. "He's outside. Said he was going out to the dock to think. That was over an hour ago."

"Hmm, you thinking something's up?"

"I think he's at odd ends, trying to figure out what he wants to do with his life."

"I don't understand. He's here working with us."

Alex sighed. "You men are all the same. I don't think it's his profession that's troubling him. Correction—I don't think it's his profession that's troubling him the most. There's far more to life than what you do to make a living, which is often the easy part."

Holt looked out the window to the dock. He could just make out the top of Max's head in the fading sunlight. "I guess I should talk to him, huh?"

She kissed him again. "That's why I love you so much. You always know the right thing to say."

He opened a cabinet and pulled out a bottle of Tums. "I'll get him ready for dinner while I'm there."

She flicked a dish towel at him and he hurried out the back door, laughing.

If anyone had told Holt when he planned his brief return to Vodoun that he'd not only end up staying and opening a business but settling down in marital bliss with his high-school sweetheart, he would have told them they were crazy. But now he couldn't imagine any other life. He had rewarding work, a beautiful place to live, and the most incredible woman in the world working beside him every day and, even better, lying beside him each night.

A little indigestion now and then was a small price to pay for such a good life.

He walked down the path to the dock, thinking about Max as he walked. If only he could convince his brother that change could be the thing that made his life complete. That the need to distance himself from everyone would only hurt him in the end. But Holt knew he needed to tread lightly with his advice. Max was a grown man and definitely his own man. He respected Holt and had always looked up to him, but he wouldn't appreciate Holt poking into his personal life uninvited.

The worn wooden slats of the dock creaked as Holt stepped on them, and Max turned slightly to see who was approaching. He gave Holt a wave but didn't seem overly enthusiastic to see him.

Holt sat on a pylon diagonal to Max and tossed him the antacids, hoping to lighten the strain he could see on his brother's face. "Alex is cooking tonight."

Max looked down at the bottle and smiled. "Did she see you leave the house with these?"

"Yeah."

"And she didn't shoot you?"

"She's a very honest woman and admits her weaknesses, but she may have hit me with a dish towel on my way out."

Max opened the bottle and shook a couple of the tablets onto his palm. "I hate to agree with both of you, as it doesn't seem polite since you're giving me a place to stay, but my stomach lining appreciates your looking out."

"No problem. I hear congratulations are in order. You keep solving cases in one day, you're going to make the agency look good or my own work look really bad."

Max shrugged. "It wasn't any big deal. I did everything you would have done. We just lucked out finding

Anna in the swamp. I don't think she would have made it much longer."

"Alex said she's in ICU and Colette's staying with her."

"Yeah. She's stable, but they won't know if that blow to her head caused damage until she wakes up and they can run some more tests."

Holt studied his brother, wondering what he was leaving unsaid. He'd expected Max to be satisfied with the work he'd done, maybe even a bit happy that they'd found the girl alive. Instead, he had that brooding look he always got when he was thinking hard on something he didn't like.

"You don't seem all that satisfied with the outcome," Holt said. "Any particular reason why?"

Max blew out a breath. "The whole situation doesn't make sense. Colette said that head injury was about a day old because of the color of the bruising. If she was already injured, why was she unconscious in a completely uninhabited area of the swamp? I checked the area where I found her and there wasn't a trail anywhere nearby."

Holt frowned. What Max said didn't sit well with him, either. "You think she was running from someone?"

"That's the best explanation, isn't it? That someone attacked her, maybe even held her somewhere, and she got away. Running from her attacker would explain why she seemed to have no designated course. As exhaustion set in, that head injury might have worsened until she finally collapsed."

"That's sounds plausible, even likely." Holt sighed. "So what do you think we should do about it?"

"Until Anna wakes up and tells us what happened, there's nothing much we can do. Technically, our job is over as soon as I finish up the paperwork."

"And that bothers you."

"Doesn't it bother you?"

"Yeah, it does."

"There's something else. Something I didn't tell Colette when I talked to her on the phone or Alex when I briefed her earlier."

"What is it?"

Max told him about finding the gris-gris on his jeep. "I don't like anonymous threats from someone who attacks young girls. Pisses me off."

"Pisses me off, too."

"Good. So if I wanted to spend some time checking up on a couple of things—hours that we wouldn't bill Colette for—that would be okay with you?"

"Of course," Holt said, surprised at the question. "You know I trust your judgment. If you think there's something there to find, then you should do it."

"Even if it's not official agency business?"

"Max, we all have personal things that need tending to. I wasn't exactly following the rules of my temporary sheriff's position when I helped Alex search for her missing niece. If this is weighing on your conscience, you have to do something about it."

Max nodded and stared down at the dock. Holt studied his brother, wondering how much more he'd left unsaid. Wondering if his personal interest in this case was only because of the injuries Anna Huval had sustained and the mysterious way in which they'd found her or if his interest was because of Colette.

Holt would have to be blind to have missed how attractive his wife's former coworker was, and no one would ever accuse him of being blind. Before he could change his mind, Holt asked. "Your personal interest in this wouldn't have anything to do with Colette, would it?"

"Why do you ask?"

"Because I have eyes. She's an attractive woman—smart and capable. Reminds me of someone else."

Max smirked. "Yeah, she reminds me of someone else, too, and I'm not referring to Alex."

Holt frowned. As far as he knew, Max had never been in a serious relationship. At least, they had never been serious for Max. He'd always figured his brother was concentrating on his career and didn't want to get side-tracked with a relationship, but maybe he'd been wrong. Maybe Alex was right about his brother trying to figure out his life.

"You going to fill in the blanks?" Holt asked. "Or do you just plan on leaving me hanging?"

"Come on, Holt. We both know I spent more time with you and your mother growing up than I did with my own. She was always at a board meeting or a client meeting—this state, that country. She could have rented a hotel room for cheaper than what our house cost given the amount of time she was home."

Holt stared at Max for a couple of seconds, surprised at his words and trying to connect them with their childhood. "I guess I never thought about it," he said finally. "You and your mother always seemed to get along fine, and it wasn't like having you stay with me was any hardship. The best times I had were with you and Tanner."

"They were great times," Max agreed, "but it just wasn't very often. I spent a lot more time with nannies and housekeepers than you were ever aware of. Even when my mother was around we were more roommates than parent and child."

Max rose from the bench and paced the pier. "She got pregnant on purpose," he said, "thinking our dad would leave your mom. I heard her telling a friend. She never wanted kids. All she ever wanted was her career and our dad."

Max blew out a breath. "When Dad was killed, I told everyone she was on a business trip and couldn't be reached, but it was a lie. She was at the airport in New Orleans."

"Why didn't she cancel her trip?"

"She did and then hopped a plane to Bermuda so she could figure out a way to 'deal' with his death. The housekeeper stayed with me, sat up nights with me, cried with me. Even after she came home, she never mentioned Dad even once and never has since."

Holt tried to imagine what Max must have felt, must still feel, but he couldn't stretch his mind that far. His own mother had made a bad choice in trusting their father over and over again, but Holt had never once doubted how much she loved him and his two half brothers, even though they weren't hers. "I'm sorry, man. I had no idea."

"You were a kid, too. It wasn't your job to know those things or fix them."

Holt knew Max was right, but it still bothered him to know that Max had been alone so much when they were boys. Their father had fidelity issues, producing three sons with three different women, all born within a two-year span. He'd been married to Holt's mother at the time, and she'd tried to stick it out after Max was born, but when another mistress turned up pregnant, she filed for divorce.

Unfortunately, their father hadn't been overly interested in being a good parent, either. He spent more time making money than he did making men out of his boys, which left most of the child-rearing responsibilities to their mothers.

Holt's mother and Tanner's mother had never been able to resist their father's charm, and he bounced in and out of their houses and lives for years. If he hadn't been murdered, Holt had no doubt he'd still be playing them against each other. Only Max's mother had cut him off completely, and now Holt realized that had left Max with even less parenting than he and Tanner had.

"So what does any of that have to do with Colette?" Holt asked.

"Colette's a career woman. She's dedicated to her job, and it's not the sort of job you can be less dedicated to just because you feel like it that day. She's got to be one hundred percent all the time or not do it at all." Max shook his head. "Don't get me wrong—I admire and respect that. I just don't want it for myself. I especially don't want it for my kids."

"So what…you want to put women back in the fifties? I have to tell you that may get you shot."

"Not at all. I just don't want a woman in my life who's chosen a career that has to come before everything else. I'm not going to do it, and I expect my spouse not to do it, either. I quit police work for that reason. It can swallow you up."

Holt rose from the pylon and clapped his brother on the shoulder. "Only if you let it." He left the dock and walked back into the cabin.

"You were right," Holt said as he walked inside.

"Of course, I was right," Alex said. "About what this time?"

"He's got things on his mind." Holt recounted their conversation. "I feel guilty that I never realized…"

"If it makes you feel any better, I've never thought about it, either. Looking back with a different perspective, everything he says is clear as day, but it wouldn't have been when we were kids."

Holt sighed. "He's carrying a lot of anger around over

his mother, not that I blame him after hearing all that. His views on careers and parenting are totally skewed, but I don't think he's ready to hear that things don't have to be that way."

"No. In his mind, his mother made a choice between her job and him because she couldn't do both. You and I know she could have chosen both, but she didn't. That's the part he doesn't want to come to grips with—that she chose to cut him out of her life."

"Who the hell would want to come to grips with that?" Holt blew out a breath. "Given all that, I can't even imagine what he thinks about our father."

"You're going to have to ask. You'll need help from him and Tanner if you ever want to solve your dad's murder."

"I know, but the time's not right just yet. Maybe when all this business with Colette is settled, I'll pull out the files and go over everything with him."

Alex nodded. "You know him best."

Holt stared out the kitchen window, barely able to make out Max's silhouette in the fading sunlight. "I used to think so," he said.

He turned to face Alex. "There's something he's not telling me. I could see it racing through his mind, on the tip of his tongue, but he wouldn't let it out."

"Be patient. He's trying to find balance in his own life. Right now, everything is either-or. When he gets to the middle himself, he'll be able to understand that in others, then I imagine he'll talk to you."

"Hmm." Holt glanced back outside before turning on the sink water to wash up for dinner. He hoped whatever Max was hiding didn't cause him more trouble before he decided to talk.

Chapter Seven

A gasping sound yanked Colette out of a deep sleep and sent her bolting out of the recliner and to her feet. When she managed to get her sleepy eyes into focus in the dim light of the ICU, she screamed.

Someone was holding a pillow over Anna's face, trying to smother her.

Her scream caused the attacker to drop the pillow, and he grabbed the IV stand. Before she could even register what was happening, he swung it around and struck her in the head. Her temple exploded in pain and the entire room blurred as she stumbled, trying to remain standing. Unable to maintain her balance, she crashed to the floor.

A second later, the IV stand clanged on the floor next to her. By the time her vision cleared, he was gone. She heard yelling down the hallway and the sound of running.

Anna!

She struggled to rise from the floor, still dizzy from the blow, and staggered over to the bed. Pressing her fingers against Anna's neck, she let out a huge burst of air she hadn't even realized she'd been holding. Her pulse was steady. Anna was still with them.

A second later, a nurse burst into the room. "What happened?"

"Someone was attacking her. He hit me with the IV stand and ran."

"Is she all right?"

"She's fine for now. Please call security and try to catch him before he gets out of the building."

The nurse nodded and ran back out of the room. Colette picked up the IV stand and reconnected the tubes that had come loose in the fray. When she stepped next to the bed, Anna grabbed her wrist.

Her nerves were so shot, she almost screamed again before she realized it was Anna. She looked down, surprised to see the girl looking back up at her.

"Anna, are you all right? Can you hear me? Can you talk?"

Her eyes were wide-open, her gaze wild. She stared at Colette for a couple of seconds, as if trying to figure out who she was, then she clenched Colette's wrist tighter.

"He'll kill them all," she said, her voice raspy. "My fault. Shouldn't have taken the coins. Have to find them. Have to save them."

"Save who? What coins? I want to help, Anna. Please tell me more."

"Cache... Please save my mother...." Anna's voice trailed off and her eyes closed again.

Colette shook her gently but couldn't awaken her again.

Who had attacked Anna and why? Was he going to kill all the residents of Cache, including Anna's mother? Had Anna gone there to warn them and then run into the killer herself? Had he tracked her to the hospital to finish off what he'd started in the swamp?

The nurse rushed back into the room. "I alerted security. They're searching the building now. I've also called the police."

"Thank you."

The panicked nurse scanned the monitors. "Is she okay?"

"She woke up for a very short time and spoke, but then slipped back into unconsciousness. I'd like for the doctor to check her again given everything that happened."

"Of course. I'll page him now. Is there anything else I can do for you?"

"Just keep an eye on the doors and make sure that no one gets in here without the appropriate credentials."

The nurse nodded and hurried out of the room, probably wishing she worked any shift but this one. Attempted murder in the ICU wasn't exactly something she was trained to handle. Colette, either, for that matter.

But she knew someone who was.

Before she could change her mind, she pulled her cell phone out and dialed the number of the one person she knew could get her answers.

MAX RAN DOWN THE HOSPITAL hall, completely ignoring the nurse at the ICU desk who yelled at him to stop. Holt and Alex were only minutes behind him. They could explain. He didn't slow until he reached the room Colette had given him during her phone call.

Colette stood at the end of the bed, speaking softly to a police officer. He felt a rush of anger when he saw the knot on her head. "Are you all right?" he asked.

"Yes. The doctor checked me out. It's just a bump."

"And Anna?"

"Stable but unconscious again."

"What do you mean 'again'?"

"She woke up for just a bit after the attack and talked to me."

"Wow," Max said, trying to process that bit of information. "Did they catch the guy who attacked you?"

Colette frowned. "No. Security couldn't find him in the building. He must have gotten out before the nurse sounded the alarm."

Max looked at the cop. "Are you reviewing security tapes?"

The officer nodded. "Are you the detective who found Anna Huval?"

"Yes, Max Duhon." He extended his hand to shake with the officer.

"Ms. Guidry has been explaining to me the particulars of the case she hired you for. When you finish your paperwork on it, I'd like a copy."

"Sure. I typed up my notes last night. I can email you everything."

The officer pulled a business card from his wallet and handed it to Max. "My email's on that card."

"What do you plan on doing as far as protection goes?"

"We'll put a guard on the room."

"And the investigation?"

The officer shook his head. "I have to be honest with you. There's probably not going to be a lot we can do. The man wore gloves, and so far, my guys have found one person on the security tapes exiting the hospital that might be our guy, but he was wearing a hooded sweatshirt and there's no clear view of his face."

"My friend was attacked," Colette said, "likely twice. The first time was in the swamp near her hometown. Surely you could start there."

"And if it was on a map, we'd probably try." The officer blew out a breath of frustration. "Look, right now I've got five murders and two sexual assaults on my desk—all happened this week. We'll look into it, but we're short-staffed and overworked already."

"I understand," Max said. In fact, he understood all

too well what the officer was describing because it was one of the big reasons he'd left police work himself. Too many victims. Not enough resources. Not enough time.

The officer looked at Colette. "If that's everything, ma'am, I'm going to get going. You have my card. Please call me if you think of anything else or discover anything else."

"Thank you," Colette said, but Max could tell she was less than pleased.

The officer had barely exited the room when she let loose. "He's not going to do a single thing, is he? Tell me the truth."

"He'll do the basics but unless a solid lead comes up that he can follow, he's not likely to have time for more."

"And that doesn't make you angry?"

"At a system that's underfunded and mismanaged, absolutely. That's one of the main reasons I got out. But it doesn't make me angry at the men and women who are doing their best with limited resources."

Colette sighed. "You're right. I know you're right. But I still want to be angry."

"I don't blame you."

Max wanted to reach out and gather her in his arms, comfort her. The woman had been through hell the past twenty-four hours, and given that her normal day consisted of nothing but emergency-room trauma, that was saying a lot. He knew it wasn't a good idea to take things to a personal level, but at the moment, he didn't care.

But before he could make his move, Holt and Alex entered the room. Alex rushed over to Colette and did the exact thing he'd started to do.

"Are you all right?" Alex asked once she broke off the hug. She studied the knot on Colette's forehead as she replied.

"The doctor cleared me," Colette said. "I just have a headache and I'll have to wear bangs for a bit." She gave them a brave smile.

Alex's relief was apparent. "Scared me half to death. I'm sleeping like the dead one minute and then Max comes tearing through the cabin, yelling that you'd been attacked. He was already in his Jeep and gone before Holt and I even managed to throw on shoes. I bet he broke fifty major laws getting over here."

"Only forty-nine," Max said.

Holt clapped his back. "Good man."

Now Colette smiled for real. "I don't know what I'd do without you guys. This whole thing is surreal and I'm so out of my element."

"I felt the same way when I was trying to find my missing niece with Holt," Alex said. "But don't worry. You've got the full support of all of us. Max is going to figure this out."

Max felt his pride swell just a bit at the conviction in Alex's words. They really did believe in him, and that meant a lot. Holt and Alex were the two people he respected the most in this world. If they thought him capable, then maybe it was time to let the past go and move forward.

Colette looked at him, her expression hopeful. "So you'll continue to investigate?"

"I will continue until you're satisfied," Max said.

Alex pointed to the recliner. "Why don't you have a seat and rest? Then if you're up to it, tell us everything that happened tonight."

Colette took a seat as Alex pulled a recorder out of her purse. "If you don't mind?"

"Not at all," Colette said and recounted the night's events.

Max tried to keep a damper on his emotions, but he couldn't help the anger that rose as Colette described the attack on Anna and herself. Just as he thought he'd have to comment, Colette launched into Anna's burst of consciousness and they all went completely quiet and still, focusing on every word that Colette relayed.

"Coins?" Max repeated when Colette finished. "Do you have any idea what she was talking about?"

"No," Colette said. "Anna never mentioned coins to me before, and I don't recall seeing any in her apartment, although I guess that's not what we were looking for."

"Maybe we need to take another look with that in mind."

Colette nodded. "What about Cache and Anna's mother?"

Max blew out a breath. "Are you sure she was sane… or whatever you call it?"

"Lucid? Yeah, I'm pretty sure. Why?"

"I wondered if there was a chance she was confused about her mother being alive, given what she told you before about her family."

"I see. You wonder if her mind has slipped to some point in the past, but that her mother isn't alive today." Colette shrugged. "It's possible, of course, but wouldn't it make more sense that Anna risked returning to Cache to protect her mother?"

"It's possible. I suppose for now we'll work on the premise that her mother is alive, which means we'll have to make another try at finding Cache."

Colette bit her bottom lip and stared at him for a couple of seconds. "Do you really think he's going to kill them all?"

Max looked over at Holt, who wore a grim expression. "I don't know," Max said. "There's a lot of assumptions we're having to make already. The guy had no trouble walking into a hospital and attacking Anna and you. That smacks of desperation, which is dangerous, regardless of anything else."

Colette's lip quivered just a bit. "You're not going to tell me I can't help any longer, are you?"

Max hesitated for a second before shaking his head. On one hand, he'd love to have Colette completely and totally out of the situation and safe, but on the other hand, she'd already been attacked once, and if the attacker thought she knew anything, he probably wouldn't hesitate to return. If Colette was with him, he could keep her safe.

At least, he hoped he could. And that he wasn't making a big mistake.

Like last time.

EVEN WITH A POLICEMAN sitting in a chair outside Anna's room, Colette couldn't bring herself to leave until morning. It was childish superstition, she supposed. Just as many bad things happened during daylight hours as they did at night, but despite offers from Alex to bunk at their cottage and Max to stay with her at her apartment, she didn't feel right leaving. With every offer of a comfortable bed and clean sheets, her mind flashed back to the swamp, and that same feeling of unrest came over her that she'd felt when they were there.

She was beginning to wonder if maybe there was more to Mystere Parish than just rumors and tales to scare children.

Despite her many protests, Max insisted on staying with her. The harried ICU nurse scrounged up another chair for him, relieved that she would have so many reinforcements of the male persuasion for the remainder of her shift. Colette didn't think she'd be able to sleep a wink after everything that had happened, but exhaustion must have won out and she drifted off, safe in the knowledge that Max was only five feet from her.

COLETTE AWAKENED WITH a sore neck, probably due to the odd way she'd slept slumped in the chair. Visions of a hot shower ran through her mind, and she decided it was the first order of business before any more investigating could happen. She'd already been in the same clothes for twenty-four hours, and considering what they'd been through, it was definitely time for a refresher.

She turned to the spot next to the door where Max had placed his chair the night before, but it was empty. For a split second, she felt a twinge of disappointment, then chided herself. His chair had been even older and quite possibly more uncomfortable than hers. He was probably pacing the halls, waiting for her to wake up.

Besides, wanting Max to be the first person she saw in the morning was very dangerous ground. He saw protecting her as doing his job, whether he was on the clock or not. Whatever he felt for her was about the case or his sense of duty, not personal.

Sighing, she rose from the chair and stretched, then gave Anna a thorough check, relieved to find the girl was still stable despite the night's events. Voices drifted from the hallway and into the room, and she recognized one of them as Max. She stepped into the hall and found him talking to the policeman who was stationed outside Anna's room.

Max flashed a look of concern at her as soon as he saw her in the doorway. "Is Anna all right?"

"She's fine. Still unconscious but her vitals are good, especially given the night she had."

The police officer extended his hand to her. "I'm

Officer Monroe, ma'am. I came on shift at six this morning. I'll make sure she's safe."

She shook the young man's hand. "Thank you, Officer Monroe. You don't know how much better it makes me feel having you here."

Officer Monroe blushed just a bit. "Just doing my job, ma'am." He motioned down the hall to the reception desk. "I'm going to introduce myself to the morning shift."

Max smiled at her as Officer Monroe walked away. "I think he has a crush on you."

"Don't be silly."

"Blushed when you thanked him."

"He probably blushes at all compliments. I'm sure it wasn't personal."

He stared at her for a couple of seconds. "You're an attractive woman giving him positive attention. He'd be a fool not to be flattered."

She felt the heat rise on her neck and silently wished it away.

"I see Officer Monroe is not the only one who blushes at flattery," he teased.

"Maybe neither of us hear it often enough to be comfortable with it."

"That's a shame—in your case, anyway. Officer Monroe isn't exactly my type." He smiled at her. "Are you ready to leave, or were you waiting to talk to the doctor?"

Colette tried to process Max's words. Was he saying *she* was his type? Or maybe she was reading entirely too much into simple banter. "I left Alex's number with the doctor. She'll understand everything and relay it to me. I don't want to hold up the investigation any more than it already has been. If those villagers are in danger, we have to find them before Anna's attacker does."

He nodded. "I've already arranged to rent a boat at a marina on the way to Pirate's Cove."

"I want to stop by my apartment first. Take a shower and get some more suitable clothes and gear for the swamp. What about you?"

"Holt already brought me a change of clothes and my boots this morning. If you don't mind my using your shower, then we can be on our way shortly."

"Of course," she replied, judiciously preventing her thoughts from sliding into a vision of Max in her shower. There were some things that weren't safe even only in your mind.

Twenty minutes later, she was safely ensconced in the passenger seat of Max's Jeep and they were headed across town to her apartment. The events of the past day ran through her mind over and over as she tried to make sense of it all.

"You haven't moved an inch or spoken in ten minutes," Max said. "You all right?"

His words brought her out of her thoughts. "I've been running everything through my mind, hoping to clue in to something new." She sighed. "But I can't come up with anything. I don't know how you do this kind of work all the time without staying frustrated."

"A lot of detective work is tedious, and sometimes you have to catch a break because there's not enough facts to put you in the right direction. Sometimes you never solve a case. But the worst is having to give up on a case that you think you could have solved if you'd been given more time."

"Last night, that police officer said they didn't have the resources to investigate properly.... That's what you mean, right?"

"Yeah, I spent a good bit of time being angry about it

before I finally realized the only person it was hurting was me. All my righteous indignation wasn't going to change anything."

"So you went to work with Holt."

He nodded. "I knew Holt wouldn't tell me to let something go just because there was no evidence. I knew he had respect for the intuition you develop on the job and would back me if I wanted to follow what others would consider a whim."

"Holt was never a cop, was he?"

"Except for his temporary stint as sheriff, no. But he fought in Iraq. He doesn't talk about it much and I don't ask, but he came back different. I imagine he learned plenty about trusting his instincts."

"He's a good man. I know that for sure because otherwise Alex wouldn't be with him. She's the smartest, most together woman I know."

"She's kinda scary. I haven't found a flaw in that armor yet, except her cooking, which can be deadly. For the record, she was just as scary as a kid—her self-control and practicality are unmatched. Holt is either very brave or in big trouble."

She smiled. "No, he's just in love. You have a great family."

A momentary look of surprise crossed Max's face, but he immediately masked it. "Yeah, I guess I do," he said, almost as if the thought hadn't occurred to him until she'd said it.

Colette studied him for a couple of seconds, but the determined look was back in place. *Still waters run deep.* It was a favorite expression of the night nurse she'd exchanged shifts with for years. She'd never really given it much thought until now. With Max, she understood exactly what the nurse meant.

None of it is your concern.

And that was the crux of it. Max was a temporary employee—bought and paid for. And as soon as he solved the case and Anna was out of danger, he'd be gone from her life so cleanly, it would be as if he never entered it.

"I think we ought to look through Anna's apartment again before we head out to the swamp," Max said.

"To look for the coins?"

"The coins or any reference to them. I can't help but think the coins might be the key to all of this."

"Is this one of those whims you referred to?"

"Not really. I guess I figure if an injured woman briefly comes out of a coma and the coins are one of the only things she mentions, then it must be important."

She stared out the car window. Another variable was the last thing they needed. This situation was already full of them, and unless Anna woke up and filled in the gaps, Colette feared they were always going to be one step behind.

She hoped that one step didn't get Anna's mother killed.

Chapter Eight

Max paced Colette's apartment as she showered. It was pleasant, he decided, with its blend of blues and browns. Comfortable and not overly girly. Most of the women he'd dated had rooms filled with floral patterns with pink and yellow. His mother had an affinity for floral print and lace, and his childhood home had been riddled with it. Only his bedroom had attested to the fact that a male presence existed in the house. His mother had given him free rein in that one small space, but then, she'd also never set foot in it.

He stepped to the window and glanced outside at the street below, unable to shake the feeling that someone was watching. An elderly couple walked hand in hand on the sidewalk across the street as a hot-dog vendor began his morning setup. People in business clothes rushed by, cell phones pressed to their ears. Nothing looked out of place.

He looked down at the table in front of the window and picked up a picture frame. The photo was of Colette and Anna, both in their hospital uniforms and smiling for the camera. He placed the picture back on the table and glanced around at the other photos scattered around the room. They were all of Colette and other women, most of them either doctors or nurses.

He frowned. Where were the pictures of her family?

There were no aging grandparents or parents, no pictures with siblings all sharing a common facial feature, no pictures of a beloved pet.

Perhaps Colette had even more in common with Anna than she'd let on. It seemed that both of them had erased their family from their past. He glanced into Colette's bedroom at the closed bathroom door. She showed every sign of being a loving and caring person, risking her time, money and life for an employee. What had happened to her to cause her to block out her family?

The bathroom door opened and Colette stepped out clad in her jeans and a T-shirt. Her eyes locked on his, and she hesitated ever so slightly before waving her hand toward the bathroom.

"It's all yours. Towels are in the linen closet behind the door."

Her voice sounded normal, but Max knew he hadn't imagined her reaction to seeing him standing there staring at her. He made her nervous, but she was careful to keep it hidden behind that polished veneer she wore. Only occasionally did he see the veneer slip.

Max grabbed the spare set of clothes Holt had brought for him and headed into her bedroom. Colette stood in front of the dresser, pulling her hair up into a ponytail. As he stepped past her, his arms jostled hers and she dropped a barrette. They both bent down to reach for it at the same time and his hand closed over hers, their shoulders touching, heads not even an inch apart.

They rose slowly, still just inches apart, and Max suddenly realized why he made her nervous. He knew it was a really bad idea—the worst idea in the world, really—but he closed the small gap between them and lowered his lips to hers.

Her eyes widened, but she didn't move away. Instead,

as their lips touched, she leaned into him, her body barely brushing against his. As her breasts pressed gently against his chest, he deepened the kiss, parting her lips and slipping his tongue inside. He placed one hand on her cheek, wishing she'd left her hair down and he could run his fingers through the wavy, dark mass of it.

She placed a hand on his chest and he felt himself start to stiffen. The instant tightness of his jeans brought him back to reality and he broke off the kiss. She stared at him, clearly confused, as he took a step back.

"I'm sorry," he said. "I shouldn't have done that. With everything that's happened to you lately, it's not fair. It won't happen again."

She opened her mouth to speak, but before she could utter a word, he stepped past her and into the bathroom, closing the door behind him. He turned the cold water on full blast, shed his clothes and stepped underneath the icy stream. The shock to his system would bring him back to reality, and right now he needed a double dose.

What in the world were you thinking?

He stuck his head under the freezing water. Scratch that question. He already knew the answer, and those kind of thoughts had no place in the middle of an investigation. Of all people, he knew that too well.

Granted, he couldn't help his attraction to her. She was a beautiful woman with the kind of curves you saw on the old-fashioned pinup girls. She was smart, motivated, courageous and had a huge heart for others. Colette was definitely the type of woman who was impossible to ignore.

But he was going to find a way.

COLETTE STARED AT THE closed bathroom door and brushed one finger across her lips. They still tingled from their contact with Max, along with other body parts that hadn't seen that kind of stimulation in a long time. All efforts to convince herself that she was attracted to him only because he was helping her had become permanently and utterly useless.

The simple truth was that Max Duhon moved her in ways that no other man ever had. With a single kiss, he'd left her body begging for more.

And then he left you hanging.

She sighed as reality came crashing into her very brief fantasy. Clearly, Max was attracted to her, but for whatever reason, he was determined to keep his distance. Colette knew he'd view this momentary slip as weakness and probably work even harder to keep her from getting through the wall he'd erected around himself.

Turning her attention back to her hair, she saw her flushed neck and face in the dresser mirror. It was just as well that Max had stopped things. When this was over, she'd have no cause to see him again. He'd be back in Vodoun working with Holt and Alex, and she'd be back in the E.R. working with Anna.

She couldn't afford to become any more invested than she already had.

When her hair was in place, she went into the kitchen and popped a couple of croissants with ham slices into the microwave. It wasn't the best breakfast, but she was hungry and figured Max was, too. Neither of them would want to stop to eat, but they could eat the croissants on the way to Anna's apartment.

She stiffened just a bit when she heard the bathroom door open, but focused on wrapping their breakfast in paper towels for easy transport. When Max stepped into the kitchen, she could feel the tension coming off of him, and he avoided looking directly at her.

"I didn't make coffee," she said, trying to get things

back to a comfortable business relationship, "but I have some canned sodas and I did a makeshift breakfast to take with us." She lifted one of the croissants.

He relaxed and nodded. "That's good thinking. It shouldn't take long to search Anna's apartment. She didn't have much and the place was small. But I want to spend as much daylight as possible in the swamp."

A tiny shiver passed through Colette's body and she crossed her arms across her chest. The swamp was dark enough even in the daylight, but it wasn't just the lack of light that bothered her. It was something else. Something she couldn't quite put her finger on. Something dark and unsettling.

She shook her head. Those were fanciful thoughts for a woman who was supposed to be grounded in reality.

"You don't have to go with me," he said quietly.

She stared at him. "I didn't—"

"There's something…off…in the Mystere Parish swamps."

She felt a chill run down her back. If Max thought there was something to all the old tales and superstitions, maybe she shouldn't be trying to dismiss them. "I'm just jittery," she said, determined to keep her cool. "With everything that's happened."

He took a step toward her and placed his hand on her arm. "Don't ignore feelings of unease, especially in the swamp. That intuition may be what keeps you safe."

He dropped his hand and scooped up the other croissant from the kitchen counter, then he pulled a couple of sodas from the refrigerator.

"You ready?"

She nodded, afraid to speak. Her emotions were at war with her logical mind. All of this was so far-fetched, so much to absorb in a minimal amount of time. She grabbed her purse from the counter and followed Max out to his Jeep. She'd get her head straight on the way to Pirate's Cove.

Anna's mother's life may depend on it.

It was a short and silent drive to Anna's apartment. Colette stood silently as Max updated Anna's apartment manager on the situation. The woman was suitably horrified with what had happened to her tenant and promised to keep an extra watch. But when she let them into Anna's apartment, it took only a second to realize that the warning had come too late.

Every drawer was open and dumped onto counters and the floor. The cabinets looked as if they'd spit their contents out. Not a single item remained on the shelves. The fabric of the couch had been slit open, spilling the stuffing.

"Call the police," Max told the shocked apartment manager.

The woman nodded and hurried down the stairs.

Cursing, Max scanned the mess. "I should have come here last night after the attack."

"I don't understand," Colette said. "Why do this now? Why didn't he come here before, when Anna was missing?"

"Maybe he didn't know who she was or where she lived before last night. Her name would have been on her chart in the ICU, right? If by leaving Cache she put others in danger, she was probably using a fake name."

"Oh, no! I didn't even think about that. I guess I assumed whoever attacked her knew her already. I never even considered that she might be using a false name."

Max clenched his teeth. "I should have thought of this. I should have been better prepared."

"You couldn't have known—"

"It's my job to know. To anticipate. It's my fault for not assessing the threat level better."

One look at Max's jaw, set in a hard line, let Colette know it was useless to argue. She didn't agree with him in the least. No one could have known what they were walking into, especially now that Colette realized exactly how little she really knew about Anna. But she understood that feeling of responsibility from a professional standpoint and knew that no matter what she said, Max would still blame himself.

"Do you think they found what they were looking for?" she asked. "The coins, maybe?"

"I don't know. If they did, it took a while. They really tore the place up."

"If they found the coins, wouldn't they leave Anna alone now?"

He frowned and looked past over her shoulder and out the window. "I don't think so. Anna said her mother was in danger. If all it took to protect her was giving him the coins, she would have done that in the first place. Instead, she made an almost deadly trip into the swamp."

Colette's emotions shifted from hopeful to resigned. "Maybe she doesn't have them anymore."

"Maybe." He blew out a breath. "Whatever is going on with Anna is centered in Cache. We've got to find that village."

THE MAN SAT IN A coffee shop down the street from Anna's apartment building. He'd seen the woman from the hospital and the man enter earlier, and now a squad car was pulling up in front. Twice now he'd had Anna in his grasp, and twice she'd escaped death. More important, without telling him what he wanted to know.

He worried that Anna had gotten a good look at him

when she'd pulled up his mask during their struggle in the swamp, but if she had, either she didn't recognize him or she was still unconscious and hadn't been able to tell the police. Either way, the clock was ticking, and with more people getting involved, the risks were higher.

He shook his head. All those years, a veritable fortune had lain somewhere in the swamp. If it hadn't been for Anna, he would never have known about the lifetime of financial security waiting to be plucked.

The nurse was a problem. It looked as if she had no intention of leaving the situation alone, and unless she did, the man would probably stay involved, as well. The police wouldn't have the time, inclination or knowledge needed to find the village or track anything back to him, but if the woman and man kept looking, they might be able to do so.

He took a sip of coffee and thought about all the dangers that could befall someone in the swamp. If the man and woman went back there, he would make sure they didn't return.

It took three long hours for Max and Colette to provide their statements and fingerprints to the police, collect the boat Max rented and get on the highway to Pirate's Cove. Colette was frustrated all over again by the bureaucracy of paperwork and apologies about staffing shortages. Once more, she found herself grateful that she'd saved more than spent and had the means to hire someone dedicated to the case.

Alex and Holt were good people, and they'd been right in assigning Max to work with her. Despite his initial apprehension about Anna's character, he'd launched himself one hundred percent into the job and had found her protégé on the first day. She couldn't have asked more of him, but yet, here he was, still by her side, willing to ride it out until the end.

He was an admirable man, which only made her wish she could get to know him better. Unfortunately, he seemed to guard his feelings as much as he did his pistol. When he'd kissed her, she'd thought for just a moment that he was finally going to let her take a peek inside. But then he'd broken it off and closed up even more than before.

She sighed and stared down the empty highway that stretched in front of them.

"Are you okay?" Max asked.

She glanced over at him, just realizing her sigh had been loud enough to hear. "Yes. I'm frustrated and tired, but neither of those is going to keep me from pressing forward."

"You're an accomplished woman. I wouldn't expect any less."

She stared at him, a bit surprised at his words. "I guess so. I've never really thought about it."

"I don't know why not. Alex says the job you do is one of the toughest and most demanding at the hospital."

She felt a blush creep up her neck. "That's nice of her to say."

"She wasn't being nice. You know Alex. If she didn't mean it, she wouldn't say it."

"Yes, that's true enough."

"Is that what you always wanted to do—work in the emergency room?"

"Heavens, no. I sorta fell into it."

Max looked over at her, one eyebrow raised. "How exactly does one 'fall into' being a trauma nurse?"

"My first year out of school, I was working a night shift in the pediatric ward. There was a chemical fire at a warehouse nearby. It exploded and ten firefighters were injured in the blast. There was a huge thunderstorm going at the time and the on-call staff couldn't get here as fast as usual, so they asked me to assist."

"And you did a terrific job."

"I guess. We were far too busy for anyone to stop and hand out compliments, but two days later, the hospital administrator called me in and offered me a lead position in the E.R., at double my current salary."

"Wow. I guess that was compliment enough. You're cool under pressure, even with this investigation, and that's far outside of your norm. They were smart to promote you."

Her cheeks burned as the blush crept up from her neck. "Thank you. If anyone would have told me during nursing school that this is what I'd be doing today, I would have laughed. I wasn't always this capable. Being a nurse gave me confidence in myself that I'd always lacked." She frowned. "It was doing the same thing for Anna."

Max placed his hand on hers and gave it a squeeze before releasing it. "And it will again. Soon, you'll both be back to saving lives."

Colette nodded as she studied Max's face. The words had been delivered almost with hesitation. It was very slight, but she had become very adept at picking up even the most obscure indication from people. Was Max more worried about the situation than he'd let on?

Or had his words pricked a personal sore spot within herself? Lately, she'd been restless with her job, her satisfaction with her work diminished from what it used to be. She'd thought it was just a slump and it would go away, but over the months, it had festered, there in the back of her mind despite all attempts to push it back. Maybe when all this was over, she'd feel differently, and if she didn't, then it was time to admit she was ready for a change.

They rode in silence the remainder of the way to Pirate's Cove, her mind racing with the events of the past twenty-four hours. The facts alone were a lot to absorb, but her emotions were the part she struggled with the most. This situation had brought to the surface issues she'd pushed back in her mind, not wanting to deal with them. Now it seemed they were all catapulted to the forefront.

"Where will you launch the boat?" Colette asked as they pulled into Pirate's Cove.

"I figured I'd ask the gas-station owner, Danny. His boat launch was good enough for small craft, and he was helpful before."

He parked in front of the gas station and Colette climbed out of the Jeep. She'd taken only one step toward the gas station when bony fingers grabbed her shoulder. She spun around to find an old Creole woman looking at her.

The woman's hair was silver with only a few streaks of black remaining. It fell to her waist, like a wiry shawl. Her skin showed the years spent on the bayou with no protection from the sun. Black eyes stared at Colette as if they could see inside of her.

"Don't go into the swamp," the woman said, her voice low and raspy. "Only death awaits you."

A wave of panic spiked through Colette's body. Her chest tightened and her pulse leaped. Before she could formulate a response, Tom rushed out of the café and placed his arm around the old woman, pulling her away from Colette.

"Now, Marie," he said, "you shouldn't try to scare people with your nonsense."

The woman pushed his arm off her shoulder and pointed one bony finger at Colette. Her dead eyes stared. "Mark my words, if you enter the swamp, you'll kill us all. The curse will descend on this swamp and all its inhabitants."

She began to back away as if she were afraid to turn her back to them. "He's one of them. He knows," she said and cast her gaze at Tom.

Then with more speed than Colette would have imagined she was capable of, the old woman hurried down the embankment and into the line of cypress trees that marked the edge of the swamp.

Max stepped beside her as Tom gave her an apologetic look.

"I'm sorry about Marie," Tom said. "She's not all there anymore."

"She said something about a curse?" Colette asked.

Tom shrugged. "Marie's always talking about curses and omens and such. She was raised in the swamp with the old ways. Everyone around here knows not to pay her ramblings any mind." He gave them a nod and walked back across the street and into the café.

"Well," Colette said and looked at Max, who stared at the line of trees where Marie had entered the swamp. "What do you make of that?"

Max shook his head. "I don't know. Maybe nothing."

"But maybe something."

"If she lives in the swamp, she may have an idea what's going on out there. I wish she hadn't run off so quickly."

"Do you think she would have talked to us?"

"Probably not. At least, not in front of other people. But if I knew where to find her…"

Colette gazed into the swamp where Marie had disappeared. She wasn't sure finding Marie was something she wanted to do. The conviction in the woman's voice had unnerved her, as had her black eyes.

"Well," she said, trying to shake off the feeling of doom surrounding her, "daylight's wasting. We best get going."

Max studied her, and she knew he didn't buy her attempt to brush off the incident. For a moment, he looked as if he was going to say something, but he only nodded and motioned to the gas station.

Danny was stocking cigarettes behind the counter and looked over as the bells above the front door jangled when they entered the store. He brightened when he saw them and walked around the counter.

"I was just wondering about that girl, but didn't know any way to contact you. Is she all right?"

"Her condition is stable, but she's still unconscious," Colette said.

Danny frowned. "That's rough. Do the doctors think she'll be all right?"

"They can't know for sure, but the medical trauma appears minimal. They'll know more as the swelling leaves her brain."

Danny nodded. "You know, when you showed me the picture of her the other day, I didn't recognize her. But when I saw her in the bottom of the boat, without being all fixed up, she looked familiar."

"You've seen her before yesterday?" Colette asked.

"Not her, but a picture of her. Took me half the night to place it." He pulled off his ball cap and scratched the top of his head. "There was a guy in here a couple of weeks ago looking for her. Showed me a photo that looked like it came from a security camera."

"You're sure it was a security photo?" Max asked.

"Not positive, but it was taken from above and it was black-and-white. Real grainy, like what they show on the news when they're looking for someone."

Max nodded. "Did the man say what he wanted with her?"

"He was some kind of antiques collector. Said the girl had something he wanted to buy."

The coins.

Colette sucked in a breath.

"Did he give you his name?" Max asked.

"No, but he did ask for directions to Cache, just like you. Don't get me wrong. We get high-school kids and the occasional reporter here looking to find Cache, but we usually don't get anything outside of that. First that guy and now you…well, it's just odd, ya know?"

"Yeah," Max agreed. "What did he look like?"

"Maybe fifty, tall but stocky. Had black-and-silver hair and wore a suit. Sorry, but I wasn't looking all that close."

Max nodded. "Did he talk to anyone else?"

Danny shrugged. "Maybe. People usually either stop here or the café or both. Tom's almost always at the café. You may want to ask him."

"Thanks. I will. Hey, do you mind if we use your dock?"

Danny's eyes widened. "You going back into the swamp? I thought with the girl found and all…"

"We need to find her mother," Colette said.

Danny looked back and forth from Max to Colette. "Oh, I get it. In case things go bad for her. Sorry, I wasn't thinking. Of course you can use my dock."

"Thanks," Colette said, not bothering to correct Danny's take on the matter. Better that the locals thought they were looking for Anna's mother because of her medical condition.

"Should we talk to Tom first?" Colette asked.

Max shook his head. "No. We've already lost too much

daylight, and the news said a storm's moving in this evening."

Colette glanced out the window at the clear sky that could go from blue to black in a minute's time.

Danny nodded. "You don't want to get caught out there in a storm."

"We'll talk to him when we get back," Max said. "Are you ready?"

"Yes," Colette said, hoping her voice sounded steady. She didn't want Max to know how uneasy she was about going back into the swamp. The whole drive from New Orleans, she'd thought she was okay with it, but now that they were about to launch the boat, she could no longer ignore the feeling of foreboding deep inside of her.

She could pretend that the old woman had caused her current unease, but she'd be lying to herself. The old woman had only reinforced a feeling that was already there and had been growing with each mile they drew closer to Pirate's Cove.

Chapter Nine

Max jumped into the boat after Colette and started the outboard motor. The engine purred to life, and he slowly backed away from the dock, lifting a hand to wave at Danny, who'd helped them launch.

This entire day was disintegrating rapidly, creating more questions faster than they had found a single answer. His frustration with the case was growing, as was the overwhelming feeling that he was being led around by his nose. Something was moving below the surface. Something that had been in motion long before Anna Huval went missing. He could feel it, but he couldn't put his finger on it.

He was certain the answers were out in the swamp.

Colette glanced back at him as he increased speed and directed the boat down the bayou. She had put on a brave face, but he knew the old woman's words were weighing on her. Max was certain it was the old woman who'd left the gris-gris on his Jeep the day they'd pulled Anna out of the swamp, but she'd left before he could question her.

Now he sat there wrestling with whether or not he should tell Colette about the gris-gris. He'd thought finding Anna was the end of it and was quite happy to let the entire subject go unmentioned, but apparently finding Anna was only the beginning. The reality of the situation was that he'd promised Colette he wouldn't lie to her and he was doing just that—lying by omission.

After they rounded the corner of the bayou away from the view of Pirate's Cove, he slowed the boat to a crawl. Colette turned to look at him.

"I need to tell you something," he said and told her about finding the gris-gris on his Jeep.

Colette's eyes grew wide and she sucked in a breath. "You think the old woman put it there?"

"That's my first guess."

"But why? What does it mean?"

"In Mystere Parish, it's usually seen as a warning."

The apprehension was clear in Colette's expression. "Like today. She doesn't want us to go into the swamp."

Max nodded. "It seems that way. I wish I could have talked to her, without any of the townspeople around, but she shot out of there so quickly…"

"Do you think she's from Cache?"

"No. Tom knew her by name, and I doubt the Cache villagers would be that well-known in town. If they really have been hiding in the swamp for almost two hundred years, they're good at it. They wouldn't make strong connections with outsiders."

"She said Tom was 'one of them.' What do you think she meant?"

"I don't know. Maybe just the rambling of an old woman who's not that clear on reality any longer. Maybe she meant he's one who doesn't believe in curses. It's impossible to say."

Colette's jaw flexed. "Some creepy old woman is not going to keep me from finding Anna's mother."

"Then we better get a move on."

He increased the speed on the boat as much as possible in the narrow channel and headed back to the area where they'd found Anna the day before. It was the most logical place to start the search. Unfortunately, Max figured Anna had traveled quite a ways before her collapse; otherwise, her attacker would have caught her. But with no other option presenting itself, the search would start there.

The light dimmed as he moved deeper into the swamp. He glanced overhead and frowned when he saw gray clouds already beginning to form. The storm was still a ways off, but it was coming. And when it did, any tracks that Anna left would be erased. The window of opportunity was quickly closing.

It only took thirty minutes to reach the bank where he'd found Anna. He'd probably progressed more quickly than was safe, but the sense of urgency he felt kept driving him to twist the handle on the engine just a bit more. It took him a minute to locate the place where he'd climbed the bank, then he eased the boat alongside the cypress roots and tied it off.

"So what's the plan?" Colette asked, casting an uneasy glance into the dense foliage above the cypress roots.

"I want to go back to the place where I found Anna and see if I can figure out which direction she came from. Track her steps backward."

She nodded.

"I would suggest you wait here for me, but if the trail leads me deeper into the swamp, I think you're safer with me than in the boat."

She glanced back down the bayou and then scanned the swamp surrounding them. "Yeah. I want to come with you."

He heard the words, but he also heard the sliver of fear that she was trying to hide. He could hardly blame her. Revisiting the swamps of Mystere Parish was the second-to-last thing he wanted to do. The first was protecting a woman he was attracted to. So far, he was batting a thousand with his return to Vodoun.

"Let me make sure it's clear," he said and peered over the bank of cypress roots and into the swamp. Nothing dangerous was immediately visible, so he motioned for Colette to climb up.

She hesitated only a moment before grabbing the thick cypress roots and pulling herself up and onto the embankment above the boat. Max lifted his backpack of supplies up to her and she pulled it over the ledge. Then he climbed up beside her and pulled on the pack.

"She wasn't very far from here. This way." He pointed south of where they stood. "Follow closely behind me and keep an eye above us, same as last time."

Colette nodded and he started through the brush, the damaged foliage indicating his path from the day before. It took only a minute to reach the location where he'd found Anna. He scoured the surrounding area, looking for any sign of the path she'd traveled before collapsing here, but aside from the damage he'd caused, he saw no entry or exit from the location.

He'd thought as much the day before but knew he needed a more thorough look when he wasn't pressed for time. Unfortunately, a closer look hadn't revealed anything new. He ran one hand through his hair and blew out a breath.

"What's wrong?" Colette asked.

"There's no indication of her path to this location."

"How can that be? She couldn't have dropped here from the sky."

"No, but I think she may have done what we did—entered this area of the swamp from the water."

Her eyes widened. "But if she was running from her attacker, she was on foot. Why in the world would she get in the water, knowing full well all the dangers that presented?"

"It might have been the best choice at the time. Assuming her attacker was tracking her, the only way to lose him would be to travel some ways in the water. The cypress roots are the perfect place to get back on land."

"Because there wouldn't be tracks," Colette said. "That makes sense, but it leaves us with nothing to go on."

"Not necessarily. When I found Anna, her clothes were dry, so she'd been out of the water for a couple of hours, at least. The tide was just starting to come in when we found her, so assuming she arrived here hours before, the tide would have been going out when she entered the bayou. It would be smarter to get into the water and float downstream rather than swim, which might attract the attention of her attacker and any number of other predators."

"You think she floated from somewhere upstream."

"Yes. I think we should head up the bayou, keeping a close look out for the location where she entered the water."

"So you think she came up at the same place we did?"

"It certainly looks that way."

Colette turned and headed back down the trail to the embankment. Max followed closely behind, hoping they could find the needle in the haystack, or in this case, a footprint in the swamp. Given the shifting of the tide and the water level, it was a real long shot that any evidence of her passage remained close enough to the bank for them to see. At the moment, it was the only chance they had.

Once they were back in the boat, Max checked the tide. It was going out, which meant he might be able to make an educated guess at the floating path Anna would have taken in the current. He looked upstream about a half mile until the bayou curved out of sight, watching the swirling water as it pushed its way back out toward the Gulf of Mexico, concentrating on the most likely flow of a large object.

"If she entered the bayou anywhere in the stretch that we can see," he said, "I think it was from the opposite bank. That would have allowed her to drift right by the cypress roots with minimal swimming involved."

"At least that's a place to start," Colette said and sat on the bench in the middle of the boat.

He started the engine and eased across the bayou to the other side. The bank was lower there and the foliage less dense right near the bank. As he drew the boat up alongside the bank, he cut the engine and lifted a long pole from the bottom of the boat. They both stood balanced in the center of the boat as he used the pole to push them slowly up the bayou.

Although the incoming tide would likely have washed footprints away, he scanned the muddy bank for any, then turned his attention to the brush at the edge of the muddy bank. If Anna had walked through the brush, he'd be able to see signs of her passage.

He moved the boat at an agonizingly slow pace, but a glance was not enough to catch a single broken leaf or a partial imprint of a shoe on the worn ground. Colette concentrated on the bank, her brow wrinkled as she squinted into the brush. It almost made him smile. She probably couldn't track an elephant through the swamp but darn if she wasn't going to give it a hundred percent effort. He had to admire her dedication.

They'd progressed almost to the end of the channel when he caught sight of a single broken branch on a bush near the bank. The bayou tide was halfway up the bank now and had likely covered the dirt completely when the tide was in, erasing any footprints.

He dug the pole into the thick bayou mud to stop the boat. Colette looked over at him, her expression hopeful.

"Do you see something?"

"A broken branch. It may be nothing," he warned.

She nodded as he stepped out of the boat and onto the bank. His boots sank into the soft black mud that made a sucking noise each time he lifted his foot out of it. When he reached the broken branch, he knelt down to get a closer look. The ground was littered with weeds and marsh grass so no prints were visible, but it was clear to Max that something had passed this way recently.

"Did you find something?" Colette asked.

"Something came through here and into the bayou, but I can't be certain it was human. I'm only certain it wasn't an alligator."

"Ha, well, good. Um, exactly how do you know it wasn't an alligator?"

"Something walked through the marsh grass. It's pretty hardy, so it mostly recovered, which is why I can't tell you the size or shape of the print, but if an alligator had passed through here, all of the grass would have been pressed down by his body. There would be no evidence of individual steps."

Colette looked anxiously into the brush. "I'm going to store that information just in case I ever have an alligator in my yard. When I buy a house, of course. Or if I ever go into the swamp again, which after today is looking like less and less of a possibility."

"I can't say that I blame you." Max looked past the line of marsh grass and into the trees. "The trail leads into the trees. I think we ought to check it out."

Colette nodded and he stepped back down the bank to extend a hand to her.

He heard rustling in the brush behind him just as he

clasped his fingers around hers, but he was barely able to turn to look before the alligator lunged out of the brush to his right.

Chapter Ten

Colette emitted a strangled cry as she clenched his fingers and yanked him toward the boat. He launched at an angle toward the side of the boat, praying that the mud would turn his feet loose in time to get away. He felt the tug on his legs and for a moment thought it was all going to end, then he felt his boots break free and tumbled over the side of the boat, knocking Colette down into the bottom beneath him.

A giant splash of water showered them and Max peeked over the side of the boat just in time to see the twelve-foot monster glide silently away. He looked down at Colette, who stared up at him, her eyes wide. The entire weight of his body was pressed against hers and he suddenly realized that his current position was no less dangerous than being on the bank with the alligator.

"I'm sorry," he said as he pushed himself up from the bottom of the boat. "Did I hurt you?"

"No," Colette assured him as she sat up. "Except for the heart attack, I'm fine." She glanced out at the bayou. "Is he gone?"

"Yeah. Probably off in search of easier prey."

Colette looked at the bank. "Do you think there are any more in there?"

"Not likely. They're not the most sociable of creatures."

"Thank goodness."

Max extended his hand to help her rise from the bottom of the boat. She stood and took one nervous step back from him.

"If you don't want to go into the swamp," he said, "I completely understand. This is not what you signed up for."

Colette shook her head. "I want to find the village and Anna's mother, but if you think I'll get in the way of your progress, I can stay here with the boat."

"No, I don't want you out here alone. You'd be a sitting duck for predators of the two-legged variety."

Her hand flew up to cover her mouth for a moment. "I'm sorry. That was a silly thing to suggest."

"It wasn't silly. I don't expect you to think like a criminal. That's what you've got me for."

She gave him a small smile. "I guess so."

"Are you ready?" he asked.

She glanced once more across the bayou and then back at the brush where the alligator had been hiding. "As ready as I'm getting."

"Then that will have to do."

COLETTE CLASPED MAX'S extended hand and stepped out of the boat and into the mud. She struggled to walk up the bank to solid ground while he tied the boat off to a piece of driftwood on the bank. She peered into the cypress trees in the direction Max had indicated they needed to proceed, but she couldn't see anything but a dimly lit wall of decaying foliage.

Max reached into the boat and pulled out the backpack and the shotgun, then handed the shotgun to her. "It's pumped and ready to shoot, so be careful with the trigger."

She took the shotgun, trying to keep her hands steady,

and she grasped it at the barrel and the stock. It felt good to have the weight of the weapon in her hands, and she knew how to use it. It was all the reasons why she might have to that had her nerves shot.

That alligator had seemed to come out of nowhere—a harsh reminder of the deadly things the swamp contained and her complete lack of knowledge about any of them. Max knew the swamp and its creatures, but even he seemed to be extra cautious, extra alert.

"Ready?" he asked.

Colette nodded and followed him into darkness.

They started at a good pace at first, Max able to discern the faint tracks in the bent marsh grass, but as they moved farther away from the bayou, the marsh grass disappeared and gave way to vines and moss. Signs of Anna's passage, if that's even what they were following, became more sparse and harder to locate—a bent branch, a broken vine. The pace slowed to a crawl.

Max stopped to tie a strip of white cloth around a branch each time they changed direction. It was something Colette would never have thought of given her lack of knowledge of the swamp or tracking, but it made perfect sense. It also gave her comfort as they moved deeper into the swamp that they'd be able to find their way out with ease.

Despite the fact that it was October, it was still warm, and the humidity made the air thick and made it hard to breathe. Sweat formed on her brow and she wiped the beads away with the back of her hand. The only sound was their footsteps on the dying vines that seemed to echo in the dead silence.

"Shouldn't there be more noise?" she finally asked, unable to stand the silence any longer.

"In other swamps, there is. You can hear insects and

birds all around you. But the swamps in Mystere Parish are always silent."

Like a giant tomb.

Her hands tightened on the shotgun. "How is that possible? Surely there are insects and birds here."

"There are, but they don't make noise very often."

"Is it something genetic—a mutation in the swamps of Mystere?"

"That's one theory."

"What's the other?"

"That they're scared."

Despite the warmth of the swamp, a chill ran down Colette's spine. No wonder Anna had fled from this place, this cocoon of fear and death. The bigger question was, why did people remain?

"How do people live with this? Vodoun is surrounded by the swamp."

"It's a nice small town with mostly nice people. Those who make a living on the water get their job done and get off the water before nightfall. No one much messes with the swamp unless they are fishing, hunting or earning a living."

"Not even kids?"

"We tromped around the swamp a lot when we were kids, but there was always that feeling that you were somehow intruding. We never went into the swamp at night. No one ever talked about it. It was just something we all knew."

Intruding. That single word so accurately described what Colette had been feeling since they'd entered the swamp. As if she were somehow walking on hallowed ground without permission. That every step she made was against the desire of something much larger than herself.

All of a sudden, Max stopped and Colette bumped into

his back. He held up his hand, signaling her for silence. Every muscle in her body strained to keep her absolutely still, and she held her breath, afraid that even the tiny sound of exhaling would echo in the silence.

Max turned to look at her and whispered, "I see something ahead about fifty feet. It looks like the top of a building. Stick close to me and tread as quietly as possible, but don't be surprised if they already know we're here."

"Do you think it's Cache?"

"Maybe."

They crept through the brush, each being careful to deliberately choose every step for stealth. Colette kept both hands on the shotgun, ready to swing it around and fire in an instant. She mimicked every step Max took, keeping her body only inches from his. Over his shoulder, she could see the tops of buildings begin to appear, the old wood barely visible against the wooded backdrop.

When they reached the edge of the clearing where the building stood, Max drew up short. She eased up beside him and peered through the brush. Before she could stop it, she sucked in a breath. It wasn't just a couple of buildings. It was an entire village.

Cache.

Her heart fluttered as she scanned the rows of shacks that lined makeshift dirt paths. She pointed at a steeple, visible above the roofs of the row of shacks. A church.

Max glanced at the church and continued to scan the village. His worried expression made Colette stiffen slightly and she looked back at the village, trying to determine what it was that was bothering him. And that's when it hit her.

The village was empty.

It was the middle of the afternoon and the weather was reasonably clear, but not a single person stirred in the streets of Cache. Not a single noise wafted through the dead air.

"We're too late," she whispered.

"We don't know that," Max replied and stepped out of the brush and into the clearing.

He paused for several seconds, probably waiting for the alarm that would never sound, then motioned to Colette and started walking toward the first shack. He stopped before they reached the doorway, and sniffed the air. She felt a sliver of horror run over her as she realized he was smelling for decomposition.

She sniffed the air as well, but could detect only the scent of bayou mud, dying brush and dust. Max must have been satisfied because he stepped into the shack. She followed close behind, with no idea what to expect, but bracing herself for the worst.

But all they found was an empty cabin.

Clothes hung on nails along one wall. A tiny table and chairs sat opposite a wood-burning stove. The table was set, as if the occupants were about to eat. Max walked over to the stove and lifted the lid of the pot.

"Oh," he said and covered his nose with his hand as he quickly replaced the lid.

The smell of spoiled meat hit Colette and she felt her stomach roll.

"Let's check the others," he said and left the cabin.

It took only a matter of minutes to determine that the entire row of shacks revealed the same thing—meals left untouched, laundry left unfolded—but not a single sign of a human being.

She looked back down the row of abandoned cabins. "It's as if they…"

"Vanished?"

"Just like the legend says."

Max gazed around the village and shook his head. "It's not possible. No matter how strange these swamps are, they do not swallow up an entire village of people and leave no trace of what happened."

He started walking toward the center of the village and entered the church. Rows of handmade pews lined the assembly, and a pulpit carved from driftwood stood at the front. Colette reached down to pick up a book from one of the pews and was surprised to find it was a traditional hymnal that she'd seen before.

"I don't understand," she said, "If they observed the old ways, why have a church? This is a Christian hymnal."

"I've known people who practiced both."

"How do they reconcile the two?"

"I never asked." He walked to the front of the church and opened a cabinet behind the pulpit. "Look at this."

She joined him at the front of the church and peered into the cabinet, then gasped. It was filled with candles and jars of crushed herbs. A wooden bowl and pestle stood on a shelf just below a black mask that looked as if it were carved from wood.

"What is that?" she asked, pointing at the mask.

"A ceremonial mask."

"What kind of ceremony?"

"I don't know, and I don't think I want to." He slammed the cabinet door. "These people did not disappear into thin air. They must have left. Maybe they knew the threat Anna spoke of was coming, and fled the village."

"But if they're in the swamp, how can we find them?"

"I'm not sure we can."

"You can't track them, like you did Anna?"

"Anna was running from her attacker. She didn't take the time to cover her tracks, but the villagers probably did. My guess is that we'll find no sign of their passage."

"But we have to help them. They're in danger."

Max blew out a breath, clearly frustrated. "I don't know that we can. We have nothing to go on."

"Surely somewhere in one of these cabins there has to be a clue…something that gives us a starting point."

Max didn't look convinced, but he nodded. "We can try."

As they stepped outside the church, the light dimmed. Colette looked up to see a dark cloud passing in front of the sun with more surrounding it.

"We need to work fast," Max said. "You take the row of shacks to the left that we've already given a cursory look. I'll check the next row. I wish I could tell you what to look for, but at this point, I honestly have no idea."

"Hopefully, we'll know it if we see it."

She glanced once more at the dark sky overhead and hurried into the first shack. She was afraid for the villagers, but she was afraid of being caught in the swamp in the storm even more. Even if they found something, they wouldn't be able to act on it today.

It took very little time for her to dig through the villagers' meager belongings. The shacks contained only the most basic of necessities—food, dishes and clothes. In one of the shacks toward the end of the row, nearer to the tree line, she found a handmade sock doll that made her pause and sigh. She hadn't thought about the villagers in terms of families, but of course, there must be children. What must they be thinking—fleeing their homes at a moment's notice? Hiding in the swamp from an unknown enemy?

Unless they knew him.

Maybe he'd tried to kill Anna in the hospital because she could identify him. If Anna knew him, other villagers might, as well. Or maybe she was completely wrong about everything.

She tossed the doll on a cot in the corner in disgust. Her throw was a bit too hard and the doll slipped off the side of the bed and fell between the cot and the wall. Then, feeling guilty that a little girl would come home and be unable to find her doll, she sat on the cot and reached down the side to retrieve the doll, hoping nothing else was dwelling on the floor with it.

Her fingers grazed the top of the doll and she leaned farther over. As she wrapped her hand around the doll, her fingers brushed something hard. She pulled the doll out and peered in the space to see what else was down there. It was dark, but she could barely make out the straight edges of a book. She reached back down and drew the book out.

It wasn't dusty, which meant it hadn't been down there very long. *Grimms' Fairy Tales*. Figures. Cache was weird enough to belong in a Grimm fairy tale. She flipped through the first couple of pages, and a sheet of paper slid out. Her breath caught in her throat.

It was a pencil drawing of a young woman who looked exactly like Anna.

She turned the pages of the book, removing sheet after sheet of drawings. The quality was amazing. Whoever the artist was had captured the personalities of the people as well as their features. She studied each portrait to see if any others looked familiar, thinking if others had left Cache, they might be living in Pirate's Cove, and they might know where the villagers would hide.

The last drawing made her pause. The face was somewhat familiar, but she couldn't put her finger on where she'd seen the man. He was old with heavy lines across his troubled face. He had a scraggly mustache and beard and his hair was down to his shoulders. None of his hair showed any sign of recent grooming. Where had she seen him, and was it during their investigation?

Maybe Max would know.

She placed the book and the drawings on the table and hurried out of the shack to find him. As she stepped out the doorway, a shadow appeared across her path, but before she could spin around, something hard hit her across the back of the head, sending her down to the ground.

Colette's vision blurred and she struggled to maintain consciousness. Turning around, she tried to get a look at her attacker, but all she saw through blurred vision was a black mask. She felt herself slipping away as her attacker grabbed her under the arms and started dragging her into the swamp. She tried to yell, but the strangled cry probably wasn't loud enough to attract Max's attention.

Think! She concentrated, trying to focus her fuzzy mind on her options. Even if he hadn't hit her, she probably couldn't outmatch him physically. She reached out, trying to grab on to something, if only to slow his progress, but he yanked her even harder, ripping the branches from her fingers.

She felt the flesh on her hands tear as the sharp branches sliced across them, and she cried out. Her attacker dropped her and a second later struck her head again. Then she sank into darkness.

Chapter Eleven

Max stepped out of the last cabin in the row he was searching and immediately checked the sky. The light had dimmed even more and the accumulation of dark, swirling clouds was the answer. It was time for them to leave even though they hadn't found the answers they were looking for.

He walked around the corner and down the row of shacks that Colette was searching. "Colette?" he called as he walked.

Only silence greeted him.

A spike of panic hit him full force. Something was wrong. He ran down the row of shacks, ducking in and out of every doorway, but found nothing.

"Colette!"

She wouldn't have wandered off, of that he was certain. He walked the line of shacks again, this time studying the dirt path that ran down the middle. At a shack close to the edge of the clearing, he saw two lines in the dirt that ran straight into the swamp. Like the lines the heels of rubber boots would make if they were being dragged.

He pulled out his pistol and hurried into the swamp where the line trailed off. Brush was flattened by the passage of something large. Tracking as fast as he could, he hoped he wasn't already too late.

And that's when he heard a faint cry.

It took him only a second to zero in on the direction of the sound and he was off like a shot, running directly through the brush, not even bothering to try to follow the trail. It had to be Colette, which meant she was still alive.

He burst through a clump of bushes and almost tripped over Colette before sliding to a stop just inches from her body. A patch of blood glistened in her hair above her ear and he felt his heart skip a beat as he felt for a pulse.

A wave of relief washed over him as he placed his fingers on her wrist to check her pulse. He scanned the swamp surrounding him for sign of her attacker and heard the crack of gunfire. He dropped to his knees and pulled Colette behind the bushes he'd charged through earlier. Then he peered through the foliage, trying to locate the shooter.

The shot sounded as if it came from the right, but sound direction wasn't always easy to interpret in the swamp. Still, right was a better guess than nothing. Aiming his pistol toward a thick grouping of brush to the right of him, he squeezed off a couple of rounds.

A yelp sounded from some distance away, and Max knew he'd gotten off a good shot. A second later, he heard someone running through the brush, the sound growing fainter with every passing second.

Max scooped Colette up and hurried back to the village. There was no way he could risk carrying her to the boat with the shooter in the swamp. And for all he knew, the shooter may have found the boat and set it adrift. The village was hardly secure, but it offered a lot more safety than the swamp.

Thunder clapped overhead and he cursed as he picked up his pace. He'd forgotten about the storm, but it was coming. Whether they were ready for it or not.

He ran to the center of the village and paused for a moment to consider the options. The church offered a good view of everything and the advantage of a loft with windows. The disadvantage was all the windows downstairs, but he could grab blankets from the cabins and cover them. Mind made up, he dashed into the church and gently placed Colette on one of the pews.

She was still unconscious, but the cut on her head was no longer bleeding and her pulse was still strong. He needed to find blankets, medical supplies, and food and water, but he hated the thought of leaving her here alone. Still, the windows were solid glass and there was no back door, so if he kept his cabin search to areas where he had a clear view of the church's front door, he should be able to protect her.

He ran out of the church and into the nearest shack. Once the storm hit, gathering supplies would become only more difficult. He needed to locate as much as possible before it began to rain.

The first shack yielded two blankets but no medical supplies. All the food was spoiled, so he tossed the blankets through the front door of the church and sped into the next shack. In this one, he found a bag of potato chips, probably from trading at Danny's gas station.

He managed to scour ten more shacks before the rain began to plummet, reducing visibility to almost nil. Dripping wet, he burst into the church and dropped the last of the spoils on the floor beside the others. He'd managed a decent haul in a short amount of time. Plenty of blankets for the windows and to cover Colette, a hammer and nails, bandages and peroxide, aspirin, chips and canned food, a couple of canned sodas and some jugs of distilled water. It wasn't the Ritz, but it was enough to outlast the storm and the night, if necessary.

He went to check on Colette and was relieved to see her starting to stir. Her eyelids fluttered and her hand moved.

He placed his hand on hers and said softly, "Colette."

Her eyes flew open and she tried to bolt up, but she barely lifted herself from the pew before clutching her head with both hands. She stared at Max, clearly frantic at first, but then the panic left her eyes as she focused in on him.

"Max! Thank goodness." She lowered her hands from her head and glanced around. "What happened?"

"I was hoping you could tell me."

"I was searching the shacks..." She frowned, her brow scrunched in an effort to remember. Suddenly her expression cleared. "I found drawings and wanted to show them to you. I left the shack and someone hit me on the head."

"Did you get a look at him?"

"No. He was wearing a mask, like the one we found here."

Max hurried to the front of the church and opened the cabinet. The black mask was still hanging in place. "He must have brought his own."

"He started dragging me into the swamp. I tried to fight but I was so dizzy. He hit me again, and I don't remember anything after that."

Max took a seat next to her and filled in the gaps.

"Oh!" She covered her mouth with her hand as he described dragging her through the brush as the attacker fired on them. He went on to tell her about his return fire.

"Do you think you hit him?"

"Yeah, but he ran away at a good pace. He may be injured, but I have no way of knowing how badly. I might only have nicked him."

"You made him leave. That's all that matters."

Her bottom lip quivered and a single tear fell out of the

corner of her eye and down her cheek. "I thought I was going to die," she whispered. "If you hadn't found me…"

Max wrapped his arms around her and held her close, the memory of his own fear slamming back into him. They'd both been very lucky. "But I did find you. Don't even think about anything else. You're safe and we're going to keep you that way."

She clung to him a little longer then leaned back, wiping the tears from her face with her hand. "I don't understand—if he had a gun, why didn't he shoot me?"

He frowned. She'd narrowed in on the one thing that had been bothering him, too. "I can only guess that he wanted something from you."

"But I don't know anything."

"He doesn't know that. You're friends with Anna and you spent the night in her hospital room. Maybe he thinks she woke up and told you something, or maybe he thinks she told you something before she left."

"About the coins?"

"If we assume that's what he's after, then yeah."

"He still would have killed me," she said, her voice shaky. "Once he found out what I knew or decided I didn't know anything at all."

He struggled for the right answer, because the honest one wasn't very pleasant. But ultimately, all he could do was nod in agreement.

"And he'll try again," she said, "because he didn't get the answer he was looking for."

Max clenched his hands, not willing to think about another attempt on Colette's life. "He'll have to come through me to do it. We didn't know how far he'd carry things before. Now we know and we'll be more prepared."

"But how? We're sitting ducks. He can just stay in the swamp and wait for us to leave."

"I'm working on that. Just try not to worry about it. When I've worked everything out in my head, I'll let you know."

She nodded but didn't look convinced. "In the meantime, we're staying here?"

"Yeah. I scouted some supplies before the storm hit." He rose from the pew and dug through the supplies. "I haven't had time to get them sorted, but I found some aspirin, and we need to clean those cuts on your hands."

He retrieved the bottle of aspirin and a can of soda from the pile and brought them to Colette. "It's not much, but it should help your headache."

He went back to the pile and dug out a jug of water and some cloth. "Use these to clean your hands. I want to get the blankets up as soon as possible."

"I can help," she said and started to rise.

He placed a hand on her shoulder, preventing her from standing. "Stay here and rest. I need you in top shape for when we run."

She wanted to argue, but with her medical training, he knew she wouldn't. He was right and she knew it. Finally, she nodded and started cleaning her hands.

He grabbed a blanket, the hammer and some nails from the supply stack and began covering the first window. Lightning flashed, illuminating the village, and he peered into the darkness, trying to ferret out any sign of movement. Any sign that the shooter had returned. He couldn't see anything.

But he knew something was out there.

COLETTE SHOOK A COUPLE of aspirin out of the bottle and downed them with a swig of the soda. Her hands throbbed a bit from the cuts, but they were mostly superficial and should heal quickly. It was already dim inside the church with the storm raging, but as Max covered the windows, the light was reduced to only what filtered through the windows of the loft at the front of the church.

Watching Max move quickly from window to window with blankets and a hammer, she tried to come to grips with the fact that she'd almost been killed. She flipped the aspirin bottle over and over between her fingers, staring down at it as her pulse beat its rhythm in her temples. It could have been over. That easily. Despite all the things she'd never done. Despite all the goals she had that would have gone unaccomplished. Despite having never found that one person to share her life with.

"It will take a while to process it." Max's voice sounded quietly behind her.

"Oh." She hadn't even realized he'd stopped working, much less that he'd walked up behind her. He handed her a blanket then climbed over the pew and sat down beside her.

"At first, it's like you dreamed it all," he said. "Then when it hits you that it's real, you either get upset or mad or both. Then you figure out how to deal with it. And the more time that passes, the less you think about it, so the less you have to deal."

"Have you ever been close…"

"I've been as close as I was today several times. It was the nature of my job."

"But it doesn't seem to bother you as much."

"I got used to it, I guess. I go straight to pissed off and skip the dream state. But I wasn't talking about the possibility of dying, exactly. I just meant when something happens that stretches the boundaries of even our wildest imagination, it takes some time to absorb."

He sounded so certain that she wondered what had happened that was so bad it knocked him into a surreal state. What was worse than the fear of dying? She looked over at him, but he was staring up at the cross at the front of the church. Had he sought answers in religion before? Had he gotten any?

Before she could change her mind, she asked, "So what happened to you that took time to process?"

He continued to stare at the cross for several seconds, and she thought he wasn't going to respond. Finally, he said quietly, "My father was murdered."

Her breath caught in her throat and she placed her hand on his. "I'm so sorry. I didn't know."

"I was only ten when it happened. It's not something I talk about much."

"I understand."

He looked at her and nodded. "People say that a lot, but do they really?"

"I can't speak for other people, but I think I do. My parents were both killed in a boating accident when I was six. I was raised by my aunt, a stern, humorless woman who tolerated children but never liked them."

Max shook his head. "That's tough." He turned his hand over to clasp hers and gave it a squeeze. "I guess you do understand."

"Did they ever catch him? The man who murdered your father?"

"No."

The answer was so brief, given the huge revelation, that Colette knew he was leaving something out. Something big. Perhaps something that he still hadn't processed, even all these years later.

He released her hand and rose from the pew. "Are you hungry? I have some cans of chili and potato chips. It's not exactly five-star fare—"

"Sounds wonderful to me, and yes, I'm starved."

She watched as he dug through his bounty and was surprised to see a glow of light. He turned around and she saw the candle he carried on a plate. As he approached the pew, she got a better look at the candle and felt an irrational spike of fear run through her body.

The candle was black.

It doesn't mean anything. The words sounded logical as they echoed in her mind, but all the logic in the world wasn't enough to eliminate the creepiness of that black candle, its flame burning brightly in the still, silent air of the church.

He placed the plate with the candle on a table just behind the pew where she sat, then turned and went back to retrieve the food. Colette was glad he hadn't clued in on her unease. He had enough to worry about already without having an irrational female on his hands.

She looked back at the candle and watched the flame flicker, swaying to an unheard beat on its black dance floor. Despite the small flame, the candle put off quite a bit of light, illuminating a ten-foot area with its glow.

"It's not much," Max said as he walked back over to her, his arms loaded with supper fixings. "But it gives us enough light to see in here."

"Do you think if he's out there…"

"That he can see the light? Probably, but there was no place in the village we could hide that he couldn't find us. The church was the best choice out of a lot of bad choices."

He handed her the chips, can of chili, can opener and a spoon, but didn't sit back down next to her. Maybe it had been easier to bare his soul in the dark. Disappointed, Colette opened the can of chili and tasted a bit. It would have been better hot and loaded with onions and cheese, but it wasn't bad.

Max walked from window to window, pulling each

blanket to the side and peering out into the darkness. Then he climbed the stairs to the loft of the church and looked out the windows on all three sides. Apparently satisfied, he climbed back down and grabbed another can of chili, then sat in the pew in front of her, stretching his legs out on the pew, turned so that he was facing her.

She handed him the can opener and he opened his supper. "You said you found some drawings you wanted to show me?"

"Yes. They were tucked between the sheets of a book— *Grimms' Fairy Tales.*"

"How appropriate," he muttered.

Colette smiled at their shared thought. "They were very detailed pencil drawings. One of them was of Anna."

"You're sure?"

"Positive. It's a perfect rendition of her, even down to the mole on her left cheek."

"Then this must be Cache."

"Oh." She stared at him for a moment. "I guess I have assumed all along it was. I probably shouldn't have. There must be more villages like this in the swamp."

"That's it!" He jumped up from the pew. "They must have another village."

"Another village?"

"The legend was that the village disappears, but what if the truth is that it's not the village that disappears but the villagers?"

Colette nodded, cluing in to his line of thought. "And over the years, the story got skewed and eventually became a campfire tale."

"Exactly. And that's why they didn't need to take supplies. All these years, the villagers have managed to live in the swamp without issue, and maybe now we know why."

"But why all the secrecy? What danger were they in

that would prompt them to build entire alternate communities?"

"Something to do with the coins, perhaps? As soon as we get back to New Orleans, I want to look harder into this coin angle."

Colette felt a trickle of warmth run through her at his confidence. He wasn't saying "if" they got back to New Orleans. He was assuming it would happen, and that gave her own slagging confidence a boost it dreadfully needed.

"Maybe Anna will be awake when we return."

"That sure would be the most direct route to information. Do you think it's possible?"

"Yes. There's really nothing about her medical condition that would keep her unconscious. At this point, it's simply her body's way of speeding up the healing process."

"Then we'll hope for the best on that end." He walked over to a back window and peered outside. "Did you recognize anyone else in the drawings?"

"Not straight off, but there was one drawing that looked familiar. It was an old man, wrinkled and unkempt, but there was something about him that I know I've seen before. I just can't place it."

"Maybe a descendant? Someone in Pirate's Cove who shares the same features, but younger?"

She shook her head. "I did a mental comparison between the drawing and everyone I've met in Pirate's Cove, but none of them resemble the man in the drawing. I wish I had the book. You might be able to recognize someone."

He glanced outside once more and frowned. "What cabin did you say the book was in?"

"The second one from the end nearest the edge of the clearing."

"Where the attacker hit you?"

"Yes, that's it exactly."

"I wonder..." He stared outside for several seconds, then looked back at her. "That cabin is only twenty yards away, if I cut through the next row. Do you think you'd be okay—"

The apprehension must have shown clearly on her face because he cut off his sentence entirely. "I'll be fine," she said, trying to sound tough and calm.

He didn't look convinced.

"I promise. My headache is almost gone and you've recovered the shotgun. Quite frankly, between the storm and the shooter, I'm safer in here than you are out there."

"That's true," he said, but she could tell he still didn't like it.

"I'll take the shotgun and move up to the loft. If he comes in, I'll have a clear shot at him from up there."

He nodded. "You're right. I'd planned on moving us up there for the night. Go ahead, then."

She put down what was left of her chili, food completely erased from her thoughts, and hurried to the front of the church. She grasped the first rung of the ladder as Max slid behind it to hold it as she climbed. She pulled herself onto the loft then reached back down to grab the shotgun, which Max handed up to her.

"You're sure you're okay with this?" he asked.

"Positive. Just go, and hurry."

"I promise," he said as he hurried to the entrance. "I'm only going for the book. It should take a couple of minutes."

He opened the door a crack and looked outside, then slipped out the door and eased it shut behind him. Colette watched as the door closed and tried not to think of what she would do if he didn't return.

She glanced around the loft, trying to figure out the

best vantage point among the boxes strewn around. A wooden crate sat in a corner back a bit from one of the loft windows and would offer her a clear view of the church entrance. A row of boxes sat two feet in front of the crate, given her the perfect cover. If anyone but Max walked through the front door, she'd drop down behind the boxes and start firing.

Taking a seat on the crate, she peered out the window and into the storm, but she couldn't see a thing in the inky black and pouring rain. It was dark in the loft, and for a moment she wished she'd brought a candle with her, but with the loft windows uncovered, it would have been a dead giveaway of her hiding place. Better the candle was left at the back of the church, where it would illuminate whoever walked in the door.

She placed the shotgun on the boxes, where it was in easy reach, and leaned forward to look out the window again. The rain pounded down on the tin roof of the church, creating a loud echo in the otherwise silent chamber. It blew in sheets past the window, the occasional flicker of lightning illuminating the village surrounding the church.

It looked almost like a painting, the rows of shacks and their straight-lined roofs, surrounded by the swamp. Granted, it wasn't a particularly comforting picture. More likely, one you'd find in a horror story. Certainly, Colette felt she'd landed smack in the middle of one.

She saw a speck of light past the last shack, just at the edge of the swamp, and strained trying to make out what was causing it. It was such a small glow, and it flickered like the candle in the church, completely unlike the steady, round light that a flashlight would emit.

Certainly, no one was standing at the edge of the swamp with a candle. It wouldn't even be possible to keep a candle lit in the wind and rain. Then what was it? A lantern, maybe? But the flame was so small, that idea didn't fit, either.

Suddenly, the light disappeared and, a second later, reappeared a good ten yards away right at the edge of the village. She sucked in a breath. No way had someone moved that distance so quickly. Were there two people out in the storm? Only one person attacked her, but could he have gone for reinforcements after Max shot him?

The light disappeared again and she scanned the village, frantically looking for the reappearance of the light. Two seconds later, it appeared again directly across the dirt path from the church.

Her heart pounded so hard that her chest ached from the strain. Slowly, she reached for the shotgun, certain that any second, the person with the light would realize she was inside the church. A huge bolt of lightning flashed across the sky and she stared at the location of the light.

It was empty!

She jumped up from the crate and pressed her face to the glass. The glow from the lightning faded away and the flicker was back, exactly where it had been before. Somewhere that no human had been standing. A cold sweat broke across her forehead and she felt a chill run up her back and into her neck.

There was something out there, watching. She could feel it. Even though nothing could possibly see her through the window, tucked away in the dark shadows of the loft, she could feel the eyes on her…studying her. For the first time in her life, she wondered if humans and animals weren't the only things to be afraid of.

The light disappeared again.

And reappeared, hovering right outside the window.

Chapter Twelve

Alex hung up the phone and shook her head at a very worried Holt. "He hasn't returned the boat to the rental company," she said. "He only rented it for the day and didn't call to extend. The owner is fluctuating between being mad his boat's not back and worried that something happened."

"Something did happen," Holt said. "Max would never worry us this way. If he had a change of plans, he would have checked in."

"No luck with his cell?"

"It goes straight to voice mail."

"Can we send the sheriff's department to look for Max's Jeep in Pirate's Cove? At least narrow down where we need to start the search?"

Holt nodded. "I've already called. They sent someone out about twenty minutes ago."

His cell phone rang and he checked the display. "This is them."

He answered the phone, and Alex could tell by his expression that the news wasn't good. He disconnected the call and looked over at her.

"His Jeep's still parked there in front of the gas station. The boat's nowhere in sight. The gas station is closed for the night, but the sheriff asked around in the café across the street. No one's seen them since they drove into town this morning."

Alex opened the closet behind her and pulled out rain slickers and rubber boots. Holt gave her an appreciative look.

"I'll grab the spotlight from the garage and hook up the boat. Bring the rifle as well as our pistols."

Ten minutes later, they were speeding down the highway to Pirate's Cove. Although Alex knew Max was a very capable tracker and knew the dangers of the swamp well, worry wracked every square inch of her body. The swamps of Mystere Parish were no place for people after dark. Truth be told, she avoided them day or night. She could only imagine how scared Colette must be.

All she could do was hope something simple had happened, like boat trouble. Maybe they were rowing their way back to shore. She didn't want to think about other possibilities.

Holt's cell phone rang, and he glanced at the display and frowned. "It's the New Orleans police."

Alex stiffened as he answered and grew more worried as he barked out the words "when," "any evidence" and "sign of forced entry." A chill ran through her as she imaged the worst had happened with Anna, despite the police guard on her hospital room.

Holt disconnected the call and cursed. "Someone broke into Colette's apartment."

Alex's entire body relaxed a bit. "Thank God. I was afraid something had happened to Anna."

"No, she's still safe. They checked as soon as they found out the apartment belonged to Colette."

"What do they know?"

"Not much. The manager was trying to track down a plumbing leak and thought it might be coming from

Colette's apartment. She left Colette a message this morning, but when she hadn't heard from her by this evening, she finally let herself in to check the plumbing. She found the place ransacked and left immediately to call the police."

"Why go through Colette's place? I don't understand."

Holt shook his head. "Maybe they thought Colette had what they were looking for—that Anna gave it to her or told her about it at the hospital. Nothing valuable was taken, so we can't assume it was routine theft."

"But Colette doesn't have anything. She doesn't even know what they're looking for. I mean, Anna mentioned coins, but that's the first Colette had heard of them."

"You and I and Max know that, but that doesn't mean the bad guy does. Colette went looking for Anna and was at the hospital when she was attacked. They're probably assuming she's close enough to know Anna's personal business."

Alex took a deep breath and blew it out slowly, processing all the ramifications of Holt's words. "So that means Colette is in danger, as well. Assuming they think she has what they want or knows where to find it."

Holt looked over at her and gave her a single nod.

The grim look on his face said it all.

MAX FOUND THE BOOK of fairy tales on the bed in the shack, exactly where Colette had described leaving it. He'd wondered at first if it would still be there or if her attacker had noticed her interest and had taken it with him. He placed the drawings back in the book to keep them from getting bent then wrapped the book in a blanket to protect it from the downpour.

It was a short run back to the church. The blanket should prevent the book from getting wet for that distance. He peered out of the shack into the darkness, scanning both directions, but couldn't see more than a couple of feet in front of the shack in the downpour. The lightning had dwindled down to a burst only every couple of minutes, but the rain continued to come down in buckets.

He was just about to make his dash for the church when a scream ripped through the village.

Colette!

Clutching the bundled book to his side and his pistol in his other hand, he sprinted into the storm and across the village toward the church. Although it probably would have been a good idea to case the church before approaching, he didn't even slow as he burst from between the last row of shacks and ran across the open area to the front doors of the church.

He burst through the doors and flung the book to the ground. Clutching his pistol with both hands, he frantically scanned the church, looking for the attacker.

"Max!"

Colette's voice sounded from the loft above and relief coursed through him. The terror in her voice was unmistakable, but she was safe. He hurried up the ladder and rushed over to her.

"What happened?"

Both her body and her voice trembled as she spoke, telling him about the light that she'd watched outside the church window. He leaned over to peer outside the window she'd indicated, but all he could see was rain.

"There's nothing out there," he said.

She crossed her arms across her chest. "I didn't imagine it."

"I believe you. But whatever it was that you saw isn't out there anymore."

"It was a mass of light, about the size of my hand. It

waved like candlelight in the wind and it pulsed smaller to bigger, brighter to less bright. It floated there, right in front of me."

"Maybe it was a bug."

"A bug the size of my hand with no facial features, no wings and whose body changes shape?"

"Okay, that was a dumb idea." He looked outside once more. "I was trying to come up with something that would make you feel better."

"The truth would make me feel better."

Max shrugged, feeling helpless. "How can I tell you what I don't know?"

Colette slumped down onto a crate. "You've never heard of this? I guess I thought with you growing up in Vodoun…"

Max sat on the crate next to her, his mind searching the archives of his childhood in Vodoun. "I heard a story once, but I guess I never wanted to consider if it was true."

"What was it?"

"There was an old woman in Vodoun who claimed to be a psychic. She may still be there, for all I know, although she'd be ancient by now. Anyway, she caught me and Holt catching fireflies at the edge of the swamp late one evening."

"Catching fireflies?"

"It was something for young boys to do in a small town that didn't offer much by way of night entertainment. If you collected enough of them in a Mason jar, they created enough light to see by. We had a good bit in both our jars, but we'd seen brighter, bigger lights in the swamp and we were standing there debating going after them."

"And the psychic stopped you?"

He nodded. "She told us that what we'd seen wasn't fireflies, that it was the wandering spirits of those the swamp had claimed. They were unable to rest and roamed the swamp until they could make peace with their death and ascend."

"That's horrible."

"Then she said if we were to catch one of the souls in our jar, we may extinguish its life force before it could cross over and the soul would be stranded in limbo forever."

Colette's eyes widened. "What an awful thought. What an awful story."

"It definitely kept us from venturing into the swamp after those lights."

"Did you ever see them again?"

"I don't know. The swamp made up the back property line of our home. My bedroom faced it, and I spent a lot of time looking out that second-story window. I saw lights often, but I can't be certain it wasn't fireflies or flashlights or some other completely explainable thing."

"But the lights from the swamp never entered your yard?"

"No. Fireflies were all I ever saw in the yard."

"Maybe they can't leave the swamp."

"If you believe the old woman's story, then that might be true."

She pursed her lips and looked directly at him. "Do you believe it?"

"I don't know if I believe they're wandering souls, and I definitely don't know that trapping them in a jar would condemn them to haunting the swamps of Mystere Parish forever…"

"But?"

He sighed. "But I've never seen anything like them except in the Mystere Parish swamps, and despite spending a good bit of time researching the subject, I haven't been able to come up with anything more plausible than what the old woman said."

"Lost souls." She crossed her arms across her chest and shuddered. "Did the old woman say if they could hurt you?"

"She didn't say, but I don't see how they could."

"I felt something watching me. It wasn't just the light that caused me to panic. It was an overwhelming sense of being watched. It kept moving closer and closer, and then when it floated right outside the window, I lost it."

He put his arm around her. "I don't blame you. What you describe would have frightened anyone."

"Even you?"

"Especially me."

She looked up at him and gave him a small smile, but he could tell she was losing her grip. With everything that had happened, he could hardly blame her.

Suddenly, she stiffened and pointed at the window. "The lights," she whispered.

He rose from the crate and edged up to the window. The rain had slowed to a drizzle but the moon was still hidden behind the clouds. Across the village and into the swamp he saw them, individual spots of light, pulsing and flickering, seeming to float.

Colette stepped beside him and clutched his arm. "There're hundreds of them."

He stared out at the balls of light, strewn as far as he could see, not wanting to accept what he saw as reality, but having no other explanation.

Then he said a silent prayer that he'd been right when he told Colette they couldn't hurt them.

ALEX SAT IN THE BOW of the boat and directed the spot-light according to Holt's instructions. Despite her hooded slicker, she was already soaked as the rain blew across the bayou, drenching her face and dripping down her neck.

It had been three hours since they'd launched their boat at the gas-station dock, but the storm had limited their pace to a crawl. She was relieved that Max had left a detailed description of where he intended to start his search for Cache, but even with details, navigating the swamp at night was risky business, especially in a storm. One wrong turn and they'd be just as missing as Max and Colette.

"On the end of that bank there." Holt pointed to their left. "Are those cypress trees twisted at the bottom?"

She directed the light right at the trunk of the trees, exposing the two trunks wrapped around each other like twine. "Yes."

He directed the boat into the channel in front of the twisted trees. "He was starting his search here."

She shone the spotlight down the tiny inlet, but the light couldn't reach the end. "Did he give you any other indication as to where?"

"He found Anna on the left side, not too far from where the cypress roots take over the bank, but he wasn't sure he'd pick up her trail there."

"Why not?"

"He scanned the area when he found her and didn't see tracks leading into or away from that area."

"But if he just scanned the area…"

"He would double-check to make sure, but I have no doubt that he saw what was there to be seen. When it comes to tracking, the only person better than Max is Tanner."

"Okay, so where would he go after he double-checked?"

"He'd search the bank on each side, trying to find signs that Anna had entered the water to dodge her attacker."

Alex sucked in a breath at the thought of sticking even

a foot in this channel, but if she was running for her life, she supposed she would manage it. She directed the spotlight to the bank on the left, scanning the mass of cypress roots, then swung around to the right.

A glint of metal reflected in the light of the spotlight and she jumped up, causing the boat to rock. "There!" She pointed to a pile of brush caught in the tide next to the bank. The bow of the boat peeked out, wedged between the brush and the bank. Maybe it was intentional. Maybe they'd had engine trouble and were doing their best to camouflage the boat until morning.

Holt threw the motor in Reverse and backed up a little, then changed direction and eased their boat alongside the other. Alex shone the spotlight into the other boat and felt her heart sink when she found it empty.

She stepped carefully from Holt's boat into the empty one and lifted the storage compartment at the front of the boat. The life jackets were clearly stamped with the name of the rental company. She lifted a jacket up and shone the light on it for Holt to see.

"There's no sign of a struggle," she said. "No blood. Thank goodness."

Holt leaned over and reached for the tie line dangling off the bow of the boat and into the water. He pulled it out of the water and held the end up. "It's been cut."

Alex stepped back onto Holt's boat, feeling her anxiety kicking up about ten notches. "He intentionally stranded them out here in this storm. What would Max have done?"

"Attempted to find cover. Cover with a clear line of sight so that no one could sneak up on them."

She brushed her eyes with the back of her hand, trying to stop the rising panic she felt. "The killer could be out there hunting them. What do we do?"

"We try to figure out where they went onshore, and then I try to track them."

"Is that even possible in this storm?"

"It's going to have to be."

MAX LOOKED OUT THE CHURCH loft window, scanning the village and surrounding swamp for any sign of movement. The storm had finally pushed past them and the clouds had thinned. A dim glow of moonlight filtered through the village, creating areas of faint illumination and dark shadows.

He looked back over at Colette, curled in a blanket on the floor, dozing. Seeing the lights had seriously frightened her, and it had taken him sitting with her for almost an hour before she calmed down enough to drift off into sleep. Exhaustion, he figured, had finally taken over, which was just as well. Once he was ready to move, she'd need her strength.

And what he needed was a plan.

Waiting for morning to travel through the swamp made them an easy target, especially as the attacker knew where they were. But trying to traverse the swamp at night came with its own set of dangers. What worried Max the most was that if they managed to arrive safely back at the bank, there was no guarantee the boat would be there. In fact, he seriously doubted it would be.

Which then led to enormous problem number two—getting back to town. Returning to Pirate's Cove on foot was a huge risk that would require swimming across several channels. Anna had been very fortunate when she'd taken her dip. There was no guarantee that he and Colette would be as lucky.

He rose from the crate with a sigh. Before he could do anything, he needed to put together some supplies. With no way of knowing how long it would take for them to get out of the swamp, it was best to travel with as much food and water as they could manage.

As he took one step away from the window, he caught sight of a light out of the corner of his eye. Whipping his head around, he stared into the swamp, watching as the light bobbed up and down, moving through the trees. Moving directly toward Cache.

He hurried over to Colette and shook her gently. She stirred a little at first then bolted upright, her eyes wide.

"What's wrong?" she asked.

"There's a light out in the swamp. It's moving this way."

"Is it a lost soul?"

"No. It's a spotlight."

He could tell by her frightened expression that the implications of what he relayed weren't lost on her. "I need you to get behind that first row of crates and cover me."

"Where are you going?"

"Downstairs. If I can take him alive, I want to."

"Max, I never thought I'd say this, but if you kill him, all this is over."

"Not necessarily. We don't know that he's working alone. Killing him wouldn't give us answers, and I want those answers."

He picked up the shotgun from the crates and handed it to Colette. "Get behind those crates on the right-hand side. Aim at the door, but do not shoot unless I tell you to. I don't want to risk you shooting me by accident."

She nodded and slid onto the floor behind the crates. Her hands shook as she leveled the gun across the top of the crates and pointed it at the church door. Before he could change his mind, Max climbed down from the loft and hurried to the church entrance. At one of the back windows, he pulled the blanket to the side and peered out into the village. The beam from the spotlight shone down the path in front of the church.

The attacker was close.

Max pressed himself against the back wall, as close as possible to the church door, then pulled out his pistol. When the attacker walked in, he was going to press the gun to his head and hope the man didn't decide to take a risk.

He heard the footsteps as the attacker approached. Then they stopped right in front of the church. The beam of the spotlight hit the front door full force, its powerful light streaming in through the cracks between the door and the frame. The footsteps picked up again and Max's heart dropped.

There were two men coming.

It was too late to rethink it. In a matter of seconds, they'd both be inside the church. He'd just have to grab the first man and hope that the sight of a gun shoved to his partner's head would cause the second man to put down his weapon.

The creak of the wooden steps echoed through the stillness in the church. Max glanced up at the loft, but he could make out only the outline of Colette's head. He gripped his pistol and said a silent prayer as the church door inched silently open.

As the first slicker-suited figure stepped through the door, he placed his pistol to the side of the man's head. "Don't move or I blow you away."

Chapter Thirteen

"Max?"

Holt! Max dropped his gun as Holt pulled back the hood of his slicker suit and stepped aside to allow Alex to enter. He heard Colette cry out from the loft, and seconds later she hurried down the ladder and rushed to the front of the church to hug Alex.

Holt gave his brother a hug, his relief apparent. "Man, are we glad to see you."

"That goes both ways. How did you find us?"

Alex stepped over to give Max a hug and then released him, smiling. "We used your map to get to the channel. We found your boat downstream stuck in some brush. The line had been cut."

"Oh!" Colette cried out. "I hadn't even thought about the boat." She looked over at Max. "But I bet you had." She shook her head. "I never thought I'd say this, but thank you for keeping things from me. I don't think I could have processed one more piece of bad news."

Max smiled at her. "You did great. Give yourself some credit."

In the bright light of the spotlight, it was easy to see the blush that crept up her neck. "Thanks," she said and smiled.

"So you found the boat…" Max prompted.

"Yes," Alex continued, "then Holt found the end of the tie line where you'd secured it to that piece of driftwood, and that's where he began his magical tracking." She elbowed Max in the ribs. "You've got some competition. I don't know how he managed to find a single sign of your passage in that storm."

"Well," Holt said, "I don't think I would have gotten very far without your markers. The white fabric reflected right off the spotlight, so all I really had to do was figure out which direction you went from each marker."

"You didn't encounter anyone else in the swamp?" Max asked.

"Not even a sign of another person," Holt said. "What happened to you?"

Max gave them a quick rundown of what he and Colette had experienced. Holt and Alex were suitably dismayed and enraged over the situation.

"The lost souls," Alex said as Max described the lights they saw from the church window.

"You say you shot the guy?" Holt asked.

"I think so," Max replied. "He screamed like I did, but I have no way of knowing how serious the injury is. It may only be a nick."

"Even a nick may be enough to zero in on him if he's favoring it tomorrow. Assuming he lives in Pirate's Cove."

"Assuming."

"Well," Holt said, "you'll have plenty of time tomorrow to check all that out. But what do you say we get the hell out of here for now?"

Colette sighed in relief. "I thought you'd never ask."

ALEX TOSSED SOME BLANKETS onto the couch next to Max. She'd already settled Colette in the guest bedroom that Max had been using, and that left the couch for him.

Not that he minded. He was glad that Colette had agreed to stay at Holt's cabin for the night, especially as Holt had pulled him aside and told him about the break-in at Colette's apartment. The night had already been stressful enough. Best to wait until morning to spring yet one more issue on her.

"I'm going to hop in the shower and then turn in," Alex said. "Colette fell asleep as soon as she hit the pillow. Let's all try to get some rest. Morning will come soon enough."

Max glanced at his watch and sighed. Three a.m.

He had a week's worth of work to shove into a single day. So many things to look into. So many loose ends that needed to be tied up.

COLETTE PULLED THE COVERS straight on the bed and fluffed the pillows before leaning them against the headrest. She'd had a long, hot shower and a change of clothes and felt remarkably refreshed despite the short amount of sleep.

Voices carried through the bedroom door, and she hoped her shower hadn't awakened the rest of the cabin's occupants. She reached for Max's backpack and pulled out the book of fairy tales with the drawings. They'd almost left the church without it, but Max remembered it before they entered the swamp, and ran back to get it. She was glad he'd made the effort. Something told her the drawings were important. They'd been too exhausted to review them last night, but she planned to look over them with Max at the first opportunity.

She heard a faint knock on the bedroom door and then Alex poked her head inside.

"How are you feeling?" Alex asked.

"Surprisingly good," she replied as Alex stepped into the bedroom.

"I understand. It wasn't that long ago that I was in your

shoes—desperate for answers and putting myself in danger with every step."

"I'm glad your answers turned out to be happy ones and that you found your niece. And now you do this full-time with Holt." Colette shook her head. "It's hard to imagine volunteering for this."

"It's worth it to help people like you. People who couldn't get help otherwise."

"Well, I certainly appreciate it."

Alex smiled. "Then you'll also appreciate that I am not making the breakfast, but Holt makes a mean pancake." She turned to leave the room.

"Hey, Alex."

Alex stopped and turned to look at her. "Yes?"

Colette twisted the hem on the T-shirt Alex had loaned her, trying to figure out how to phrase what she wanted to ask. "Last night, when Max was telling you about the lights, you said they were lost souls."

Alex nodded.

"Max told me the story he'd heard from the psychic woman when he was a kid, but I wanted to ask…have you ever seen them?"

"Many times. Our house backed up to the swamp. Sometimes my cousin, Sarah, and I would sneak out in the middle of the night and sit at the edge of the swamp and watch them. They were especially active in the clear night after a storm."

"It doesn't bother you?" Colette asked. "I mean, you're a doctor. You studied science."

Alex frowned. "I used to tell myself that there was a logical explanation for all the things I'd seen growing up in Vodoun, and I found that logical explanation for some of them. But the others…well, let's just say I've stopped denying the things I've seen just because I can't explain them."

"And you're okay with that?"

"I have to be if I want to live here and remain sane. There are a lot of unanswered questions in Mystere Parish." She smiled. "Don't be too long or Max will eat all the pancakes," she said before she left the bedroom.

Colette slipped the book with the drawings into her backpack and zipped it closed. She would ask Max about them later, and as soon as she got to her apartment, she was going to do a little computer research. Surely they could spare a few minutes for her to check out some possible leads.

The tiny breakfast nook should have felt crowded with all four of them crammed around the four-top table, but to Colette, it felt cozy and happy. She watched as Holt shooed Alex away from the stove and smiled at her playful pout as Max laughed and handed her a stack of dishes to place on the table. Despite everything that had happened and everything they had to face that day, they were so normal.

Family.

Colette sighed. That summed it up, really. They were a family—able to tease each other about their shortcomings, able to share the good things and the hard things, always there for each other when support was needed, even if that meant taking risks.

The old feelings of longing crashed into her, and she struggled to keep from tearing up. She hadn't felt the loss this strongly since she was a child, watching other children play with their siblings and parents, watching them get ice cream at the corner store, watching them in their frilly dresses and suits going to church on Sunday.

All the things she'd never had.

Alex slid a plate in front of her. "You all right?"

"Yeah," she said, trying to collect herself. "Just wandering."

Alex placed her hand on Colette's arm. "Take a break from thinking. We have a rule here—no shoptalk over meals. When we're done eating, we'll all lay our ideas on the table. We're going to get through this. I promise you."

Colette nodded. Alex's words and the tone of her voice held so much conviction that it was impossible not to believe them.

"I hope everyone's hungry," Holt said as he placed a huge plate of pancakes and bacon on the table, "because I have outdone myself."

"You say that every time," Max teased as he slid into a chair next to Colette.

Holt grinned and sat across from Colette. "I'm right every time."

Alex handed each of them silverware and napkins and slid into her chair. "Before we dig in, I just want to say that I'm grateful that Max and Colette are safe with us this morning."

"I second that," Holt said and held up his coffee cup in salute. "Now, dig in."

It was hard not to relax while they ate. The horseplay between Alex and the two brothers and the macho one-upping between Holt and Max were lighthearted and fun. It was so obvious how much they cared for each other and how comfortable they were. Part of that was likely because they'd all grown up together and shared so much history, but the rest of it was because of the great respect they had for each other.

She ate way too much, but with Holt insisting on seconds and Max slipping extra pieces of bacon on her plate, it was hard to resist. Alex, always the hostess, was ready with fresh coffee each time a cup emptied.

Finally, when everyone was stuffed and the last of the dishes was cleared from the table, Holt put on his serious look and Colette knew it was time for business.

"Colette, we didn't want to worry you with this last night," Holt said, "but someone broke into your apartment yesterday. That's why we insisted you come home with us last night."

"Oh, no!" Of all the things she'd expected Holt to say, this one wasn't even on the list.

Holt explained how the manager became aware of the break-in and called the police. "It doesn't look like anything was taken, but they need you to say that for sure."

"I'll take you to your apartment first," Max said, "to take care of things there before I head back to Pirate's Cove."

"Actually," Holt said, "Alex and I wanted to poke around Pirate's Cove ourselves."

Max shook his head. "I can't let you do my job."

"It's the agency's job," Alex pointed out, "and while we appreciate your dedication, we also think it might be time to change tactics."

"What do you mean?" Max asked.

"When you first went to Pirate's Cove looking for Anna," Alex said, "you introduced yourselves as a couple, so no one knows you're a detective. If Holt and I show up there with credentials and asking about Anna and the attack on you yesterday, it might change the attacker's point of view."

Max frowned. "You think if he knows professionals are working on the case, he'll back off of Colette?"

"I can't know for sure, because I have no idea how much the attacker has invested in the information he thinks Colette can give him. If he's an opportunist only, then I do think there's a chance he'll back off."

Max blew out a breath and Colette could tell he was struggling between wanting to keep her safe and wanting to be in the middle of things. "So what am I supposed to do here?"

"Take care of things at Colette's apartment," Holt said, "then do some background work on the people in Pirate's Cove. Maybe try to run down some leads on the coins. I know it doesn't sound like much, but you can't go back into the swamp until we have a better grip on what we're dealing with, and I don't want to leave Colette exposed."

"I don't, either," Max agreed.

Colette was torn between wanting Max with her and wanting him to do what he clearly preferred to be doing. "If Max wants to go with you, I'm sure I'd be fine by myself—"

"Not an option."

"No way."

"Not going to happen."

All three of them spoke at once, and Colette gave them a shaky laugh. "I guess I'm outvoted."

"We just want you safe," Alex said. "He's targeted you twice already."

"And my home," Colette said. "I can't even be safe there."

"Don't worry about that right now," Alex said. "Holt and I have to testify tomorrow in a case in Lafayette. We're leaving this evening as soon as we get back from Pirate's Cove. That will leave plenty of room here, so you'll stay with Max."

Colette looked over at Max but couldn't get a read on what he was thinking. His expression was serious and he had a far-off look in his eyes, as if his thoughts were far beyond what was being said in that room. Probably he was thinking that if she hadn't gotten in the way to begin with, he'd be the one going to Pirate's Cove to investigate.

Instead, he was stuck playing babysitter.

COLETTE STARED AT HER formerly tidy apartment and wanted to cry. It wasn't the mess but the violation she felt at the intrusion into her personal space. She picked pieces of a broken vase up from the floor and placed them in the trash can, not knowing what to do or where to start. The smell of spoiled milk and rotting food assailed her senses, forcing her to place her hand in front of her nostrils.

Max picked up the torn milk carton from the floor and poured what was left of the milk into the sink. He turned on the hot water and grabbed a roll of paper towels from the counter. "Based on the decomposition of the food and milk, the police estimated the break-in happened sometime yesterday morning. I'm guessing it was while we were at Anna's apartment."

Colette scooped up broken eggs with what was left of the carton. "What makes you say that?"

"If we assume it's only one man, then he had to have done this early enough to get back to Pirate's Cove and follow us into the swamp."

"If it's one man."

"So far, my gut is telling me that it is."

Colette tossed the eggs and carton into the garage and blew out a breath. "Well, what does your gut tell you he's going to do next?"

"He thinks you know something, and it's important enough to him that he risked trying to kidnap you in the middle of the swamp. I think he's going to continue to come after you until he gets what he wants or gets caught. I'm planning for the latter."

"Ha. Me, too." She glanced around at the mess once

more. "I guess I should start picking up the worst of this, at least so that the stench doesn't get any worse."

"Let me take some pictures first."

"For your investigative files?"

"Yes, and for your insurance company."

Colette sighed. Filing an insurance claim hadn't even crossed her mind. If Max hadn't been here, she probably would have cleaned it all up and moved past it without even thinking about her insurance coverage. A week ago, something like that would never have skated past her, but since she'd been looking for Anna, her mind seemed unable to focus on anything besides the mystery surrounding her friend.

If only Anna would wake up, but the nurse had confirmed that Anna was still unconscious when she'd called earlier.

As Max snapped pictures, she dug out cleaning supplies and trash bags from the cabinets. When Max finished snapping photos in the living room, she took a trash bag in there and started picking up broken items, then moved back into the kitchen and started clearing the mess from the refrigerator off the floor. A couple of minutes later, Max joined her with paper towels and cleaner.

"This is just so silly," she said as she picked up a broken jar of jelly. "What in the world would I have hidden in milk or eggs or jelly?"

"Nothing. My guess is he was mad because he didn't find what he was looking for and had a bit of a fit."

"That doesn't sound much like a professional."

"No, which makes him harder to predict."

"I wish he would have spared that jelly," she grumbled as she pulled out her mop and bucket. "It was homemade."

It took another hour before she was willing to call the apartment in habitable condition. The worst of the mess was cleaned up, broken items were thrown away, and scattered items were collected and sorted into stacks to be dealt with later. Now that she had a reasonable grip on her home, Colette wanted to pull out her laptop and do some research.

She pulled the book of fairy tales out of Max's backpack and placed it on the breakfast table next to her laptop. Max grabbed two of the few undamaged sodas out of the refrigerator and took a seat across from her.

She pulled the drawings out and flipped through them until she reached the one of the old man. "This is the one," she said and slid the drawing across the table. "The man looks familiar, but I think in the picture he's older, which is why I can't place him exactly."

He picked up the drawing and studied it, his brow scrunched as he analyzed every inch of the paper. Finally, he frowned and handed it back to her. "You're right. There's something vaguely familiar about him, but I can't place him, either."

Colette stared at him. "That's interesting, because the odds of us knowing the same person but when he was younger can't be very high."

"Maybe we're both thinking of different people but he resembles both of them."

"Maybe, but what if we both think he's familiar because he's someone famous? Not A-list-actor famous, but maybe a local politician or television news reporter."

His eyes widened and he nodded. "That's a great thought. So we have to think younger and someone we probably saw on television or in print, like a newspaper."

"Yeah, but that's when I run out of steam. And somehow, it feels to me like I haven't seen the face in a long time. I mean years and years." She frowned. "The first time I saw it, I had the fleeting image of elementary school in my mind, but it passed so quickly, I didn't think anything of it. Do you think it could be that old? Something we saw in schoolbooks?"

"Maybe." He got out of his chair and moved behind her, then leaned over to study the drawing again.

She could feel the heat from his body on her back and was dismayed to find her skin starting to tingle from such minimal contact. Before she could stop herself, a mental picture of her and Max at the cabin flashed through her mind—the two of them preparing a meal, as Alex and Holt had done that morning.

As fast as it came, she forced it out of her mind, but still her heart ached just a bit at the vision that could never be. She knew Max was attracted to her, but the walls he'd erected around himself were too high for her to scale. She wouldn't even know where to start.

"It's not a president," he said.

"No," she agreed, forcing her mind back on the drawing. "I don't think it would be anyone that important, or the answer would be obvious."

"Maybe Louisiana history?"

She narrowed her eyes at the drawing, tilting her head first one direction, then another, and suddenly it hit her. She pulled the laptop toward her and began typing.

"What is it?" Max asked.

"An idea. A far-fetched, really crazy idea that happens to fit."

She clicked on the first link that her search returned and cried out, "Look!"

Max leaned over her shoulder to look at the laptop screen. "Jean Lafitte?"

"Yes." She fairly bounced in her chair, unable to contain her excitement.

Max frowned. "I guess the drawing does look a bit like him, but I don't see—"

"Jean Lafitte disappeared and no one knows what happened to him or his treasure. There's a ton of speculation, but one of the theories is that he died right here in Mystere Parish and took his treasure with him to the grave."

Max's eyes widened and he stood upright. "You think he died in Cache? And the coins that Anna spoke of belonged to him? Wow. You're right. That is far-fetched."

"But it fits. They even named the town outside of Cache Pirate's Cove, but I'll bet no one knows why."

Max stared at the computer screen again and then back at the drawing, slowly shaking his head. "I guess it's no more ludicrous than anything else we've encountered."

"Do you realize what this could mean?"

"Yeah, it could mean that Anna knows the location of the most sought-after treasure in the state. And someone thinks that she told you."

Colette let out her breath in a whoosh as his words registered. She felt the blood drain from her face and clutched the table as a wave of dizziness came unbidden.

"Hey." Max pulled a chair close to her to sit and placed his hand on her arm. "Nothing is going to happen to you. Not on my watch."

She took a deep breath and slowly let it out. Looking him straight in the eyes, she could see the determination and conviction. "I believe you," she said, not even a bit surprised that she meant it.

He gazed at her, not moving, and for the first time, she saw a glimpse of the man who hid behind the wall. The man she knew was there.

"Colette...I..." He started to lean toward her, and her heart began to pound. Never in her life had she wanted someone to kiss her more than she wanted Max to kiss her now.

The inches between them disappeared, and just as their lips were to come together, her cell phone blasted through the silence of the apartment. Max jumped up from the chair and walked into the kitchen, as if that was always his plan. Colette looked at his retreating back and sighed as she answered her phone without even bothering to check the display.

"Ms. Guidry, this is Nurse Agnes in the ICU."

Colette jumped up from her chair and gripped the phone, praying that something hadn't happened to Anna. "Yes, Nurse Agnes. Is something wrong?"

Max whirled around as she took a breath to steady herself for the worst.

"No, ma'am. It's good news," the nurse said. "Anna's awake and she's asking for you."

Chapter Fourteen

Holt pushed open the door to the gas station in Pirate's Cove and let Alex enter in front of him. As he approached the counter, a tall, thin man who fit the description of Danny smiled at them.

"You're out early," Danny said. "How can I help you folks?"

Holt took out his business card and handed it to Danny.

Danny's eyes widened as he read the card. "Private investigator? What in the world do you want with me?"

"My brother is Max Duhon."

Danny nodded. "The guy that's been looking for Cache with the nurse lady. He used my dock yesterday."

"Yeah. Someone also left them stranded in the swamp, tried to kidnap the lady and took some shots at them both. My wife and I found them late last night and brought them out."

Holt studied Danny's face as he delivered those words, but his shocked expression appeared genuine. "Oh, man! Are they all right?"

"They're fine, but a little concerned."

"Yeah, I'm sure. Your brother's Jeep was still here when I closed for the day, but I just thought maybe they found what they were looking for and got delayed."

"What time did you close?"

"About four-thirty. Business is slow this time of year so I'm repainting the inside of my house. I try to get a little done every evening."

"And you didn't notice anyone else on the bayou yesterday?"

"Yeah, there were people on the bayou. Most of the people in this town make a living off of that bayou."

Which was exactly what Holt figured he'd say. "But you only saw locals?"

Danny frowned and was silent for several seconds. "I guess. I mean, I didn't really look at them, but I don't recall seeing someone I didn't know."

"You told Max that an antiques dealer came looking for Anna?"

"That's what he said he was. He didn't leave me no card or nothing."

"Can you describe him?"

"Yeah, he was maybe fifty, about as tall as me, but a bit more sturdy. He had black hair that was starting to turn silver and he was wearing a suit." Danny shrugged. "Sorry, but that's about all I remember. I don't spend too much time thinking about how guys look, ya know?" He grinned at Alex, who just raised her eyebrows and sighed.

"I can appreciate that sentiment," Holt said and winked at Alex, who rolled her eyes. "Do you think that antiques dealer asked about Anna over at the café?"

"Maybe. Tom's usually there most days. He would know."

"Thanks. If you think of anything else, give me a call."

Danny opened the cash register and stuck Holt's card inside. "You bet, man."

Holt and Alex exited the gas station and started across the street to the café.

"I didn't see a bullet wound," Holt said.

"He was wearing long sleeves and jeans, and if it was only a nick, he might not show any signs of injury."

"Or could disguise them well enough when needed."

"That, too," she agreed. "I notice you pulled the P.I. card."

"Yeah. I figured it wouldn't hurt to put them on alert that someone else with a license to carry concealed is involved."

"Might not help if they're desperate, but you're right, it doesn't hurt. How come you didn't mention finding the village?"

"I figured we'd keep that quiet for the moment. That way, the only ones who know are us, Max, Colette and whoever shot at them."

She paused in front of the door to the café. "How are you playing this one?"

"The same. They'll be talking to each other before we even reach the highway, so it's in our best interests to stay consistent."

Alex nodded and pulled open the door to enter the café.

Four older men occupied a table in the corner. From their dark skin and rugged look, Holt guessed they were fishermen. They stared as he and Alex entered the café and took a seat at the counter, but they didn't say a word. As soon as they sat down, he heard the low rumblings of whispering from behind.

A man wearing a white apron stepped out of the back of the café and gave them a nod. Holt assumed this was Tom, the owner.

"You want coffee?" the man asked.

"Yes, two please," Holt said.

He filled two cups of coffee and placed them on the counter in front of them. "You folks visiting?"

"Not exactly," Holt said. He pulled his card from his

wallet and handed it to the man. "Are you Tom, the owner of the café?"

The man read the card and frowned. "Yeah, that's me. What's this about?"

"My brother was in here a couple of days ago with a lady, looking for information on Cache."

Tom nodded. "I remember. He and the nurse lady were looking for a girl that claimed she was from Cache. But I thought they lifted her out of here by helicopter that same day?"

"They did. She's alive but still unconscious."

"That's too bad, but I don't see what I can do for you. I didn't know her then and still don't. Don't know anything about Cache."

"Danny said that a man came in here a couple of weeks before my brother. He thinks the man was also looking for Anna. Claimed to be an antiques dealer."

"Yeah, there was a guy that came in a while back. I'm not sure how long. Had a black-and-white photo of a girl. I suppose it could have been the same one. The quality wasn't too good."

"Do you remember the guy's name?"

Tom shook his head. "Don't know that he gave it."

"What about a description? Danny was only able to remember the basics."

Tom narrowed his eyes at them. "You think that man's the one who hurt the girl?"

"That's what we're looking into."

He stared at Holt for a couple of seconds longer then nodded. "I can do you one better."

He pulled a pad of paper and pencil out from under the counter and began to draw. Holt and Alex leaned forward to watch his quick strokes across the paper.

"You're really good," Alex said. "Did you take lessons?"

"No," Tom said and handed them the paper. "My grandfather taught me."

"He doesn't look familiar," Holt said as he studied the drawing, "but this is a much bigger help than Danny's general description. I appreciate it."

"Oh," Alex said and pointed to Tom's sleeve. "It looks like you're bleeding."

Tom glanced down at his sleeve and frowned at the dark spot that was slowly growing. "Cut it yesterday working on my boat. If you folks are done, I best get this bandage changed before it bothers the customers."

"Sure," Holt said. "Thanks for your help."

He placed some money on the counter and they left the café. He knew Alex was just itching to talk, but as soon as they stepped outside, he said, "Wait until we're in the car."

Alex jumped in the car and slammed the door then gave him an exasperated look for taking longer than her.

"He had an injured arm," she said as soon as Holt closed the car door. "Recent, too, if it's still bleeding."

"Yeah."

"So?"

"So what?" he asked, teasing his wife.

"So what do you think? Is he telling the truth about the antiques dealer?"

"I think so." He frowned.

"What? I know that look."

"Nothing I can put my finger on. I just get the feeling that he's lying about something."

"So do I. Damn." She sighed. "I don't think I'm ever going to get used to fieldwork. When I was a therapist, people told me everything—lots of times, things I didn't even want to hear. Now it's like pulling teeth."

He grinned. "Welcome to my world."

"Your world stinks. So now what?"

He handed Alex the drawing of the man who'd alleg-edly come to Pirate's Cove looking for Anna. "We head back to New Orleans and see if we can locate this antiques dealer before we have to leave for Lafayette."

COLETTE RUSHED INTO ANNA'S room and drew up short. Anna was sitting up in bed, drinking apple juice and pick-ing at the food on a hospital breakfast tray. She smiled at Colette, who hurried over to the bed to give her a hug.

"I've been so worried," Colette said as she released Anna and sat on the edge of her bed. Max hovered in the doorway, and she waved him over. "This is Max Duhon. He's the detective who found you."

As he stepped up to the bed, Anna gave him a shy smile. "Thank you," she said then looked at Colette. "I didn't know you were keeping company with a detective."

"Oh, I'm not… We're not… That is, Max is Alex's brother-in-law."

"The psychiatrist lady?"

"Yes. Well, she used to be. She resigned a couple of months ago to open a detective agency with her husband. Max was a police officer in Baton Rouge and now he's working with the agency, too. You were his first case."

Anna looked at Max. "So you've got a one hundred percent success rate at the moment?"

Max shook his head. "Not until all the questions are answered."

"Can you tell us what happened?" Colette asked.

"The last thing I remember was studying for the anat-omy exam, and then I woke up here."

"You studied for that exam on a Thursday. That was over a week ago."

Anna stared at them, clearly horrified. "That's not possible."

"I'm afraid it is," Colette said.

"Maybe you better tell me what you know," Anna said. "Maybe then I'll remember."

Colette looked over at Max, who nodded, then she began with Anna not showing up for work the previous Friday. When she described how she and Max found Anna in the swamps around Pirate's Cove, Anna gasped.

"Cache," she whispered. "I was going home."

She gripped Colette's hand, staring past her at the wall. Her breathing was shallow and her brow was scrunched in concentration. Suddenly, she bolted completely upright in bed.

"My mother! He'll kill my mother!"

Colette could barely control her excitement. "You remember?"

Anna nodded. "As soon as I got my cell phone after leaving Cache, I went back to the swamp near Pirate's Cove and left the number under a rock where my mother would know to find it. I knew she'd never use it unless it was bad because I'd broken the rules by leaving. The others wouldn't have liked her to contact me out here."

"But she did?" Max asked.

"Yes." Anna dropped her gaze down and twisted the edge of the blanket over and over in her hands. "I took something that I shouldn't have, and it put them all in danger."

"Coins?" Colette asked.

Anna jerked her head up and stared at Colette. "How did you know?"

"After we brought you to the hospital, someone attacked you. After the attack, you were lucid for a couple of seconds. You mentioned your mother being in danger and coins. Were the coins in Cache?"

"Yes. My family has been protecting them for over a hundred years. The legends say the Frenchman brought them into the swamp to hide. He sent people to look for his son, but when he found out the child had died, he blamed the coins, saying they were cursed. He said that anyone who used the coins for personal gain would bring down death and despair on the entire village."

Colette pulled the drawing from her purse. "Is this the Frenchman?"

Anna nodded and Colette's pulse spiked. Her theory may have been right.

"So Cache has been protecting the coins ever since?" Colette asked.

"Yes."

"Until you took some."

"I shouldn't have. I knew it was wrong, but I wanted to leave there so desperately and we had no money. I got by at first without using them—mostly living off the wrong kind of men." She looked at Colette. "You know how things were before."

Colette nodded. "But you changed all that."

"I needed money for a decent apartment and for the registration fees for school. I'd been gone for over a year and nothing bad had happened…"

"So you sold them?"

"To a pawnshop dealer who traded in antiques." A single tear fell from her eye and slid down her cheek. "I thought everything was fine, that the legend was all a bunch of nonsense, and then my mother called."

Anna's hands began to shake. "She said the bokor came and told them to turn over all the coins or he'd bring a plague of death over them and then resurrect them and leave them to wander the swamp forever."

"What's a bokor?" Colette asked.

"A sorcerer," Max said. "Capable of white or dark magic, according to legend."

"The bokor is real," Anna said. "That night the goats came down with sickness and collapsed. They died the next day. Then the children of the village started to take ill. My mother is guardian of the coins. She counted them and realized what I'd done."

Anna started to cry and Colette handed her a tissue. "I took out all the money I could from my bank account. I thought if I returned the money to the village, it would make everything all right with the bokor."

"But, Anna," Max said gently, "the bokor didn't ask for the coins to be returned. He told the villagers to give him the coins. Don't you see? He's not real. He's just a thief who figured out the coins were hidden in Cache. He's trying to scare the villagers into turning them over to him."

Anna looked at Max, a glimmer of hope in her expression. "Do you really believe that?"

"Yes, and let me tell you why." Max told Anna about the antiques dealer who'd looked for her in Pirate's Cove just weeks before her mother's call, and then told her about the attacks on Colette and the break-ins at both their homes. "He's looking for the coins. That's all he wants."

"But the sickness…"

"Could have been anything. One of the adults who visited Pirate's Cove could have brought something back and the children caught it."

"And the goats?"

"He probably poisoned them to scare the villagers. All of this is very serious, but I promise you, it's all the doings of a very real, very alive man. One I'm going to catch."

"But my mother and the others—"

"Are safe," Colette assured her. "We found the village and it's empty."

Anna relaxed back onto the bed. "Thank goodness. I told my mother to get them into hiding. The villagers can sustain themselves at several other locations in the swamp for months without leaving. Those safeguards have been in place as long as anyone can remember."

"That's good," Max said, "and smart. And it buys us time to catch the man doing this."

"So you never reached the village when you went into the swamp?" Colette asked.

"No. I was almost there when the bokor caught me. He must have been waiting for me, because I never heard him approach."

"Did you get a look at him?"

"No. He grabbed me from behind and threw a bag over my head. He held me in a shack somewhere in the swamp for days. He returned every night to bring food and try to convince me to tell him where the coins were, but he was always wearing a mask."

"How did you get away?" Colette asked.

"One night, he decided to move me. He had to untie my legs so that I could walk, and I'd managed to loosen the ropes on my hands a little. I waited until we reached thick brush and swung around, knocking the gun from his hands. He grabbed me and I fought with him. As we fell, I pulled on the mask, but I was twisted around and couldn't get a glimpse of his face. Then he hit me in the head with something, maybe a rock. I kicked him in the gut to knock his wind out then I ran."

"You are very brave," Colette said, unable to imagine everything her friend had been through.

"Did you notice anything familiar about the bokor?"

Max asked. "Maybe he is one of the men from Pirate's Cove."

Anna shook her head. "I don't really know the people in the Cove. Only selected people from the village went into Pirate's Cove to trade, and it was usually the elders."

"But the people in Pirate's Cove are aware that Cache exists?" Max asked.

"I guess. I'm sure they know people live out in the swamp, but there's other villages out there besides Cache."

"We're going to figure all this out," Max assured her.

Anna nodded, a determined look on her face. "What do you need from me?"

"The name of the pawnshop, for starters. That shop is where it all started."

"Do you think the man who bought the coins is the bokor?" Anna asked.

"Possibly. It's also possible that when he went to Pirate's Cove looking for you, he tipped off someone locally and they decided to try their hand at collecting a fortune."

"No one in Pirate's Cove said that the dealer asked about coins," Colette pointed out.

"Exactly," Max said. "If someone in Pirate's Cove is the bokor, he'd be careful not to mention the coins at all. We need to track who knew about the coins, and that starts with the pawnshop. Where did you sell the coins?"

"Landry's Pawn on Canal Street."

Colette gave Anna a hug. "You're safe here. There's a policeman right outside your room. I'll call you as soon as we know something."

Anna squeezed her tightly. "Please keep my mother safe."

Colette released her and looked her straight in the eyes. "I promise."

Chapter Fifteen

Max's cell phone began ringing as soon as they walked out of the hospital, and he was relieved to see it was Holt. He'd been worried about them going to Pirate's Cove and stirring things up. Not that he didn't trust Holt. His brother was the shrewdest person he'd ever met and it was Alex's profession to size people up, but whoever was behind this had already shown how far he was willing to go. If he'd moved from determined to desperate, then things could go from bad to worse in a millisecond.

"Boy, do I have news for you," Max said.

"I've got some for you, too," Holt said. "You first."

Max filled in his brother on Anna's awakening and her story.

"I have a drawing for you of the antiques dealer," Holt said when he finished.

"How did you manage that?"

"The café owner drew it. I let him think he was the guy who'd hurt Anna."

Max could feel his excitement growing. They were closing in. He could feel it.

"There's something else, though," Holt said then told him about the café owner's injured arm. "It could be co-incidence."

"But?"

"But he's hiding something. I just have no idea what."

"So how do you want to handle this?"

"Unfortunately, I have some bad news, too. I'm going to have to meet you somewhere in New Orleans and give you the drawing. The attorney for the case we're testifying on wants to meet with us tonight, and we haven't even packed a bag. We're going to have to head home and organize our notes for the trial and get on the road by early evening."

"That's fine. We're leaving the hospital now. There's a gas station at the first exit off the highway to New Orleans. We'll meet you there, then you're not going much out of your way."

"We'll be there in about fifteen minutes."

Max closed his phone and relayed everything to Colette.

"Do you think Tom could be the bokor?"

"Anything's possible at this point."

"Then why would he draw the picture of the antiques dealer?"

"To send us on a wild-goose chase, maybe?"

Colette frowned. "I see. So what do we do now?"

"We get the drawing and pay a visit to the pawnshop guy to see if he resembles it."

"And if he sold the coins?"

"Then we find the buyer."

IT TOOK ONLY twenty minutes to meet Holt and Alex and obtain the drawing and then another fifteen minutes to locate the pawnshop on Canal Street. One glance was all Max needed to know that the bald, overweight man behind the counter at the pawnshop and the man in the drawing were not the same.

Max introduced himself and gave the man his card.

"You bought some gold coins from a woman named Anna Huval a couple of months ago. I need to know what happened to them."

The man's jaw set in a hard line. "I don't give out information about my customers. Not even to detectives."

"The woman who sold you the coins is being stalked by someone who believes she has more. She's in the hospital right now because of it. You can tell me or I can get the police to come down here. But if they have to get a warrant, you know they're going to look at everything. All I want is this one piece of information."

The man's eyes widened. "Someone attacked her, you say? That pretty young blonde girl?"

"Yes. And he's threatened her family. I need to know who else knew about those coins besides you."

The man held up both hands. "I ain't looking to do business with people that attack girls. I'll get you the name of the buyer."

He pulled a notebook from under the counter and flipped back through the pages. "He's a coin collector and the first prospective buyer I called. Turned out to be the only one I needed to. He paid top dollar for the coins, no questions asked." He sighed. "I guess that should have tipped me off that something was up."

"How much did he pay, if you don't mind my asking?"

"A thousand each. I'm guessing they were worth a lot more based on the girl being stalked, but he was smart about it—if he'd have offered more, I would have put them up for bid."

"He probably knew that."

"Yeah." Clearly disgusted, the man grabbed a business card from the holder on the desk and wrote the coin buyer's information on it.

"Good luck," he said as he handed the card to Max. "If

you need me to testify or something, that's no problem. This kind of thing is bad for business, for all of us pawn-shop owners, not just me."

"Thanks for your help," Max said and they left the shop.

"Marshall Lambert." He read the name and address on the card as soon as they climbed into the Jeep. "I know this area of St. Charles Avenue. Mr. Lambert is doing very well."

"Do you think he'll talk to us?" Colette asked.

He put the Jeep in gear and pulled away. "We're about to see."

Colette whistled as they pulled up in front of the massive iron gate that separated the long, curved drive of Lambert's mansion from the general population. Thick, enormous hedges grew along the gate, preventing a view of the house from the street. Max pulled up to a speaker and pressed the button to call the main house.

"Can I help you?" A very proper voice sounded over the intercom.

"My name is Max Duhon. I'd like to speak to Mr. Lambert."

"Do you have an appointment?"

"No, but I think Mr. Lambert will be interested in speaking to me. It's in reference to some gold coins he purchased a couple of months ago."

"I'll check with Mr. Lambert. Please give me a minute."

Max looked over at Colette, who held up crossed fingers.

A minute later, the intercom crackled and the same proper voice returned. "Mr. Lambert will speak with you. Please proceed through the gate to the main house."

The gate creaked slowly open and Max drove through, following the drive as it curved around. He could see the rooflines of the house, but a thick grove of trees blocked a clear view. As he pulled through the trees and into the courtyard, he heard Colette gasp.

The house rose up in front of them like something out of an old gothic movie. Dark stone walls towered above them with stained-glass windows flickering in the sunlight like blinking eyes. Dying vines clung to the walls, the brown, decaying tendrils clutching at the stone like bony fingers.

"How can he live in there?" Colette whispered.

"Maybe he's as creepy as the house."

"I'm not sure that's possible."

Max opened the Jeep door. "Let's find out."

They walked slowly up to the front door, and before he even knocked, it swung open and a white-haired butler, in a black suit and dress shirt, motioned to them to enter.

"This way, sir," he said and Max recognized the proper voice from the intercom.

He led them down a dimly lit hallway so cluttered with tables, vases and objets d'art that only a narrow walkway remained. At the end of the hallway, he opened a door. Only the light from flickering candles could be seen from where Max stood.

The butler stepped back and motioned for them to enter. Colette reached for Max's hand, and he took her hand in his and gave it a squeeze before stepping through the doorway and into the room.

Candles lined tables along every wall, creating a dim glow in the room. Colette's grip on his hand tightened as she scanned the walls along with him. They were covered with artifacts, mostly Haitian. Ceremonial masks, similar to the ones found in the church, statues and weapons hung on every available area of wall space. Tables with statues, jewelry and hand-carved tools littered the room, leaving only a small area to stand.

Something moved in the corner and Max stiffened, automatically beginning to reach for his weapon, but Colette's hand kept him in check.

"Good evening." The man in the corner stepped closer to them and the candlelight illuminated his face.

It was him. The man in the drawing.

Colette sucked in a breath and took an involuntary step back. He released her hand and extended his hand to the man. "My name is Max Duhon."

"Marshall Lambert," the man said. He barely clasped Max's hand then released it as if offended by the very touch. "You're here about some coins I purchased?"

"Yes. You bought them from Landry's Pawnshop on Canal Street."

"I remember them well. Very unique. In fact, I have been unable to trace their origin or to find a match to the ones I acquired."

"But you tried to find the seller. You went to Pirate's Cove looking for the woman who sold them to the pawnshop."

"Yes. I hoped to get some background on the coins and see if the woman had any other coins I might be interested in."

"How did you know to look in Pirate's Cove?"

"The pawnshop owner told me where the woman came from, but apparently, he was wrong. No one in the town had ever seen her before."

"The townspeople said you showed them a photo of the woman. Where did you get that photo?"

"From the pawnshop owner, of course. It came off his security camera."

"Funny, I just came from the pawnshop, and the owner

didn't mention telling you the woman's hometown or providing you with a picture from his security cameras."

Lambert laughed. "I'm sure he didn't. He could hardly afford for word to get out that he reveals detailed information about his sellers. It took a bit of convincing to get the information myself, but everyone has their price."

"The woman was attacked last week and injured so badly that she's still in the hospital."

Lambert shook his head, but looked neither surprised nor dismayed at Max's words. "That's unfortunate."

"I don't suppose you know anything about it."

"Me? I think you misunderstand what I do, Mr. Duhon. I purchase artifacts and collectibles from willing sellers. I don't manhandle people for their property. You've seen my house. I'm hardly a ruffian."

"Sorry, Mr. Lambert, but I've been hired to protect the woman. I have to ask."

"Of course. If you have no other questions for me, I'd like to return to my cataloging. I have quite a bit of work to do before bedtime."

What Max would prefer to do was turn on the lights and take a good, hard look at Marshall Lambert and see if he could remove that smug sound from his voice, but he couldn't afford to get arrested. Not to mention that physically harassing the man would probably weaken the district attorney's case against him if things got that far.

"I appreciate your time," Max said as Lambert retreated back into the shadows.

Max heard a door open and close at the far end of the room. "Let's get out of here," he said, keeping his voice low.

"I thought you'd never ask." She hurried ahead of him, pushing her way out of the room and down the hall as quickly as she could skirt Lambert's collectibles. Max hurried behind, giving the butler a quick thanks before exiting the house.

They jumped into his Jeep and drove back to the gate that seemed to magically open as they approached. No doubt, somewhere in the little mansion of horrors, Marshall Lambert was watching them on a security camera.

"That was weird," Max said as soon as they pulled onto the street.

"That's putting it mildly," Colette said. "Do you think he's that strange all the time or was that show supposed to scare us?"

"He didn't decorate that room in the time that it took us to drive up from the gate, and based on the liquid wax in the tops of the candles, they'd been burning a while before we got there."

"He's definitely the guy in the drawing. Do you think he was telling the truth about the pawnshop guy giving him all the information on Anna?"

"I don't know. Something about him was entirely off, and I don't mean his decorating choices, but what he told us is plausible enough. Most people's ethics have a price tag, and it looks like Lambert could afford to breach a lot of them."

"That's depressing."

"Yeah…hey, what do you make of that junkyard museum he's got going on in there?"

"I'd never hire on as a housekeeper. It would take an eternity to dust it all. What are you getting at?"

"I was thinking more from a mental perspective. I know people who have a tough time getting rid of stuff, but all that stuff cluttered in the hallway was over-the-top."

Colette frowned. "I see. You're thinking some sort of

mental illness? It's entirely possible. Alex would be the best person to ask."

"I have a couple of things I want to run by them before they leave. Let's make a stop by your apartment to pick you up some clothes and then head to Holt's cabin. I also want to do some research on our friends the pawnshop owner and Lambert. I have a buddy back at the Baton Rouge Police Department who'll be willing to break a few rules and give me the lowdown."

"You're sure you don't mind my staying with you at Holt's cabin? I feel a little strange about it."

"Don't. They want you to be safe and so do I. Staying at Holt's is the best way to accomplish that."

Colette nodded but didn't look convinced. Surely her unease didn't come from trusting him with her safety. Clearly, she did. Was it because he'd almost kissed her earlier? He would have gone through with it if that well-timed phone call about Anna hadn't come through. The reality was, the more time he spent with Colette, the more time he wanted to spend with her. He was drawn to her in a way he never had been to another woman. Not even the last one—his ultimate failure.

He stared out the windshield down the busy street. It was going to be a long night in very cozy surroundings.

Colette wasn't the only one uneasy about that.

Chapter Sixteen

"I don't like it," Holt said as he frowned down at the laptop sitting on the kitchen table in his cabin.

"I don't, either," Max agreed.

"So this Lambert is in hock up past his eyeballs?"

"Yeah. My buddy at the Baten Rouge P.D. called his sister-in-law at the tax assessor's office and got the whole story. Unless he pays his back taxes, his house will be foreclosed on. His credit cards and every line of credit he's been extended are maxed out."

"Probably from buying all that stuff he's hoarding," Colette said. "The place had more artifacts than any museum I've ever been in."

"That combined with the state of his house," Alex said, "makes me think something psychological is going on there."

"Like he has an overwhelming compulsion to be surrounded by stuff?" Max asked.

"It's far more complex than that, but yes, that's the bottom line."

"So he'd be willing to do anything to obtain what he wanted, right?" Max asked.

Alex nodded. "That's a very real possibility."

"The room we saw was full of masks," Colette said.

"If he found Cache, he could have easily played the part of the bokor."

"What about our friends Danny and Tom?" Holt asked.

"Danny is straightforward. He grew up in Pirate's Cove and did eight years in the Marine Corps after high school. His dad owned the gas station and passed away when Danny was doing his last tour. He came home after that to take over the place. Mother's been dead for years. He has no debt, no big assets and a DUI conviction from a couple of years back."

"Typical small-town boy. And Tom?"

Max shook his head. "Not a thing on him in the system, but the interesting thing is that he inherited the café in Pirate's Cove from the previous owner when he was eighteen. Before that, there was no record of a Thomas Pierre Fredericks anywhere in the public school system in Louisiana."

"You think the name's a fake?"

"I think he's hiding something. He's consistently denied the existence of Cache, but we all know it exists. Why keep insisting on that line of argument?"

"That's a good question." Holt rubbed his chin. "Any ideas on what to do about him?"

"Not much we can do. No one could shadow him in a place that small."

"True. What about Lambert?"

"I've got a buddy watching his house. If Lambert leaves, he'll follow him." Max leaned back in the chair and blew out a breath. "But I still don't have any idea what to do about Cache or the coins. As long as those coins are in the swamp, the villagers will always be in danger. Even if we catch the guy this time, the press is going to have a field day with it, and then everyone will know their secret."

Holt clapped him on the shoulder. "You'll figure something out. You always do."

Max watched as Holt and Alex left the kitchen to finish packing for their trip. He hoped his brother was right, because at the moment, he didn't have a single idea.

Which meant Colette, Anna and the villagers would remain in danger.

THE SUN WAS STARTING to set as Colette watched Alex rushing from room to room in the cabin, each dash taking only a dozen steps in the small space.

"There's extra blankets in the hall closet," she told Colette, "and there's a casserole in the refrigerator that Holt made last weekend. It's enchiladas, and you have my word that it's fantastic."

"Sounds great," Colette said.

"If you need to use it, please remember that the hot and cold water faucets are reversed in the master bath." Alex shot an aggrieved look at Holt, who stood in the kitchen in deep conversation with Max. "So I suggest you get the water to the right temperature before stepping into the shower. Otherwise, you'll scald or freeze yourself. Neither is good first thing in the morning."

Colette laughed. "The guest bath is fine. Stop worrying."

Alex put a stack of clean towels in the second bathroom and stepped back into the living room. "I can't help it. Worrying is what I do best, especially if I can't fix it."

"I understand."

Alex smiled. "I know you do. Sometimes I wonder if our professions make us want to fix things or us wanting to fix things drove us to our professions. Ah, well, that's one to ponder sometime when I have nothing to do."

Holt and Max walked into the living room, and Holt

pulled out his car keys while giving Max last-minute instructions.

"There's no storm in the forecast for tonight, but if you lose power for any reason, the generator is gassed up and ready to go. If you have to leave the cabin tonight for any reason, turn on the alarm."

"I know," Max said, guiding his brother to the door. "You've already told me twice."

Holt paused in the doorway and cast one last anxious glance around the cabin then at both of them. "You're sure there's nothing we've forgotten?"

"I'm certain. Go take care of that trial." Max gave Holt one final push and closed the door behind him. Then he leaned against the door and sighed.

Colette smiled. "Holt certainly takes his older-brother role seriously. How much older is he?"

"Four months."

"Oh." She stared at him, all the implications of what he'd said running through her mind. "I'm so sorry. I didn't realize…"

"That our father was a serial cheater? That my mother was sleeping with a married man, trying to get him to leave his wife?" He crossed the room and sank down in the recliner next to her.

All the anger and misery were so clear in his expression, and she struggled to understand what kind of woman deliberately sought to tear down another's family. And what kind of man pitted his mistress against his wife?

"I don't even know what to say," she said. "I guess I assumed since you had different last names that you shared the same mother and different fathers. I can't even imagine how difficult that situation was for your mothers and mostly for you and Holt."

"Oh, my mother was just fine. She treated getting pregnant with me like the calculated risk of any other business decision. When our father refused to leave Holt's mother, she hired nannies and babysitters and domestic help, gave up men completely and moved on to conquer the business world instead."

"But surely…I mean, she was your mother."

"She gave birth to me, but she didn't care for me. I'm not certain she likes me even now. I look like our father. I was a constant reminder of the one thing she truly wanted and couldn't have."

The heartbreak in his voice was buried under so many years of explaining things away and making excuses to himself, but she heard it—that unmistakable voice of an unloved child. She knew it all too well. All of a sudden, it was so clear why he'd erected such an impenetrable wall around himself and why she'd sought relationships with the wrong men, looking for the family she'd never had.

They'd taken entirely opposite approaches to fix their wounded inner children, and yet both of them were still broken.

"I don't even know what to say," she said. "Your mother's actions are something I can't wrap my mind around on so many levels. Having a family is something I dream of, a happy, intact family. I can't imagine taking such a risk to start one, but even more so, I can't fathom emotionally abandoning my child."

He shrugged. "I got used to it. The only time it really bothered me was when I'd stay with Holt. His mom was great. She invited me to stay over all the time, and when I was there, she treated me the same as Holt. I had rules to follow and chores to do and even punishment when I did things wrong."

"She sounds like a wonderful woman."

"She was. Still is. She stayed in Vodoun to raise Holt

after our father was murdered, but part of her died that day. No matter all the grief he'd put her through. No matter that he cheated again every time she took him back, she still loved him. Right until the bitter end."

"So she's no longer in Vodoun?"

"She moved to Florida as soon as Holt went into the service. I've visited her there. In Vodoun, there was always a dark cloud over her. Even when she was smiling, it was there like a thin veil of sadness. It's not there anymore."

"I'm glad she found happiness. She was a strong woman to have endured all that and still keep her heart open."

"She was a saint. You know we have another brother, right? Tanner's only a year younger than Holt and me. When my mom pulled up stakes, dear old Dad just moved right on to the next willing woman."

Colette stared at him for a moment. "It boggles the mind. So what happened to Tanner's mother?"

"Our dad played her and Holt's mother against each other right up to the day he died. He moved her out of town when she came up pregnant, but he didn't stay with her. He bounced back and forth from woman to woman, ignoring all of his children and pretty much only caring about himself. She moved around a lot and passed away a while back. I'm not clear on the details."

"And where is Tanner?"

"He's a game warden in the Atchafalaya Basin."

"Really? That sounds like an interesting job."

Max shrugged. "It's okay, I guess. Holt's talked to him some about coming in with us on the detective agency. Our father made plenty of money and left it all to his sons. We all have the flexibility to do whatever we want. It's the one thing I'm grateful for."

"So do you think Tanner will join forces with you?"

"I hope so. I'm a good tracker, but Tanner makes me look like an amateur. We could have used him on your case."

"Seems like you did fine to me."

Max gave her a small smile. "Thanks."

He rose from the chair. "It's getting dark. I better check on the boat and lock up the shed. I'll be back in a bit."

"Okay. I'll put that casserole in the oven." She followed him into the kitchen and watched as he walked out the back door and down the path to the dock. So much hurt at such a young age. She'd give anything to have Max's mother and father right here in front of her.

She'd probably throttle them both with dish towels.

MAX WALKED DOWN THE PATH to the dock, a million thoughts running through his head. He hadn't meant to dump his miserable childhood and his poor excuse for a father onto Colette that way. The horrified look on her face had said it all.

Not that he blamed her. It was a fairly gruesome tale.

She'd surprised him a bit with her disapproval of his mother's actions. He'd have thought a successful woman like Colette would have understood better his mother's desire to be at the top of her profession, but then, maybe the loss of her parents as a child had given her all the more reason to want something different for her own children.

Maybe he'd misjudged her.

Maybe his own mistakes and prejudices were causing him to make incorrect assumptions about other people's beliefs and desires. Holt had said as much that day when he'd talked to him out on the dock. His older brother had known his thinking was flawed, but he hadn't pressed the issue. He'd simply put some thoughts out there and left

Max to roll them around in his mind as he always had. Holt always believed a man should make up his own mind.

Maybe it was time for him to man up and do it.

He checked to make sure the boat was securely tied and then locked the storage shed. He could see Colette through the kitchen window as he walked back toward the cabin. She was taking dishes down from the cabinets. Her long dark hair was up in a ponytail held in place with a blue ribbon that matched her T-shirt.

She was the most gorgeous thing he'd ever seen.

He walked in the back door to a wonderful smell coming out of the oven. "That smells incredible."

Colette grinned. "It does, doesn't it? If that tastes half as good as it smells, I'm giving Holt an award for best husband ever."

Max laughed. "It's self-defense. Have you ever eaten Alex's cooking?"

"No, but I've heard the stories." She opened the oven and pulled out the steaming pan of enchiladas. "I put chips and salsa on the table already."

He nodded and opened the refrigerator. "We have diet soda and beer. What would you like?"

"Beer and enchiladas? Sounds like a good bet to me."

He grabbed a couple of beers as Colette set the pan of enchiladas on a trivet in the middle of the table. She stuck a serving spoon in the pan and slid into a chair.

"I cannot wait to dig into this," she said.

Max placed the beers on the table and sat in the chair next to her. "Me, either."

The food was every bit as good as Max had imagined it would be, but altogether the dinner was nice and relaxing. They carefully avoided talk of childhood disappointments and instead shared stories about attending college and pursuing their careers.

He was surprised to find how easy it was to talk to her and how much he enjoyed hearing her more outrageous emergency-room stories. It was like talking to an old friend.

When he couldn't eat another bite, Max rose from the table and picked up his and Colette's dishes. "Since you did most of the work, I'll do the dishes."

"Well, technically, Holt did most of the work, but if you wash, I'll rinse."

She grabbed a dishrag and stepped up next to him at the sink, their elbows touching. He began washing dishes and passing them over to her so that she could rinse them and place them in a rack next to the sink.

They worked in silence, and Max was surprised to realize how natural it felt doing such a domestic chore with a woman he'd met only days ago. For a moment, he flashed back to helping Holt's mother with the dishes when he was a boy. That same feeling of comfort and caring was always present in Holt's home. That feeling was why he spent so much time there.

"Last one," he said and passed her the final dish.

She rinsed the dish, gave it a swipe with the dish towel and placed it in the drying rack with the other dishes.

"So what's on the agenda for tonight?" she asked, turning to face him.

She didn't move away from the sink and her body was only inches from his. It would be so easy to kiss her, to wrap his arms around her and press every inch of his body against hers as he'd longed to since he first laid eyes on her.

Before he could rationalize all the reasons why it wasn't a good idea, he decided it was time to take a risk. Life held no guarantees, but if you stopped living, you were guaranteed to have a less fulfilling life than if you took a risk that paid off.

It was time to take that risk.

He lowered his lips to hers and slid his arms around her. As she leaned into him and wrapped her arms around him, he deepened the kiss, parting her lips gently with his tongue. She pressed her body tightly against his and he felt himself harden.

He moved from her lips and kissed her neck, trailing kisses down to her exposed breastbone. She sighed and he lifted her up from the floor in a sweeping move and carried her into the bedroom.

"I've wanted you since the first day I saw you," he whispered as he put her down to stand facing him. "You're the most beautiful woman I've ever met, inside and out."

She pulled the bottom of his T-shirt up and over his head and ran her hands down his chest. "Then don't make me wait any longer."

He wrapped his arms around her and kissed her again, then released her so that he could undress her. As he slipped her shirt over her head and tossed it onto the floor, she unfastened her jeans and pushed them over her curvy hips and to the floor. As she removed her lacy pink bra and underwear, he took in every inch of her and decided he was the luckiest man in the world.

He kicked off his shoes and removed the rest of his clothes, tossing them on the floor. Unable to wait another second without having his hands on her, he lay on the bed and pulled her down beside him. He explored every inch of her with his hands, his mouth, and she moaned until his own need could wait no longer.

He moved over her and entered her in one fluid motion. For a moment, he was perfectly still, relishing the way her body felt wrapped around him. Then he began to move. She matched his rhythm, and in no time they both fell over the edge.

Chapter Seventeen

He pulled her close to him, and she rested her head on his chest. She was sated as she'd never been before, as if every ounce of flesh on her body had been given the most relaxing and satisfying massage in the world. If required to stand and walk, she wasn't sure she'd be able to manage it.

As she ran one hand up his bare chest, she felt the scar tissue from the injury she'd seen when he'd undressed. It was small and so perfectly round, and she would bet anything a bullet had made it. So close to his lungs, but in a place on the body where a millimeter could be the difference between life and death.

She felt him stiffen slightly as she ran her fingers across the scar, and she wondered how he'd gotten it. Was he scared when it happened? Was this scar part of the reason he'd left police work?

"I got shot two years ago," he said quietly.

"How bad was it?" she asked, surprised that he'd said anything when she could tell it made him uncomfortable.

"It missed everything that keeps me alive, but my shoulder aches a bit from time to time."

"You were lucky."

"That's what they say."

"How did it happen?"

He was silent for a long time, and she was afraid he'd

throw the wall around him back in place. "I'm sorry," she said. "You don't have to talk about it if you don't want to. I imagine it's hard remembering such a frightening event. I know I wouldn't want to talk about the things that have happened to me this week at length. Not yet."

You're rambling.

She clamped her mouth shut, frustrated at herself for ruining such a pure moment between them.

"It's okay," he said. "It's only normal that you'd ask, and maybe it's time I told someone."

She leaned up on her elbow so that she could see his face. "Only if you want to."

"It's time to let certain things go," he said.

He ran one hand across his head and blew out a breath. "I guess I'll start at the beginning. I was guarding a woman who was being stalked. The stalker had already attempted to kill her by running her car off the road into a drainage ditch."

"That's horrible. That poor woman."

"I was impressed with how tough she was with her refusal to let the situation ruin her life or her son's. Her husband had died in Iraq when her son was still a baby, so she was facing all of it alone with an eight-year-old to care for."

"But she faced it all head-on. That's admirable."

"I thought so at the time, but as the days passed and we got no closer to catching her stalker, she grew impatient. She was an attorney with a big firm in Baton Rouge and was competing for a partner position. Every day she spent out of the office and the courtroom was one step further away from everything she'd been working for."

"But surely the partners understood, and even if they didn't, there would be other opportunities."

"Everyone told her that, but she was obsessed, determined not to let one man ruin her obtaining her goal."

"So what happened?"

"She got careless, then reckless. There was a case she'd been handling before all that happened, the case she thought was going to get her the partnership. The partners were about to reassign it to the other attorney vying for the position. So she sent me upstairs in her home on a wild-goose chase to investigate a noise and then snuck out."

"But her son?"

"I guess she figured he was safe in the house with me. She knew I wouldn't leave him there alone, not even to chase after her."

"That's awful, using her child to manipulate the situation."

"The whole thing backfired in the worst way possible. Her son saw her leaving the house and yelled up the stairs to me. When she started pulling down the driveway, he ran outside to stop her. I tore down the stairs and outside, but the stalker had already gotten off two rounds."

She gasped. "Oh, no!"

"The first shot took out one of her front tires. The second went through the radiator. The car rolled to a stop and she was a sitting duck in the middle of the driveway. She knew her only chance was to get back to the house, so she jumped out of the car and started running for the front door at the same time I ran outside."

He stopped for a couple of seconds and Colette could see how much it hurt to revisit it all. "The stalker fired again. I tried to gauge the direction of the shot and fired off a couple of rounds as I ran. I was almost to her when I saw the glint of metal in the hedges near the road. The barrel was leveled directly at her. I tackled her but it was too late. He'd already gotten off the shot."

She stared in surprise. She'd assumed he'd been shot in the chest, but his story didn't support that theory. "It went through your back and out your chest?"

"Yeah." He closed his eyes for a moment and then looked back at her. The anger and pain were so visible, and that's when it hit her.

"The bullet went through you and into her," she said.

"Directly into her heart. She was dead before I could even call the paramedics."

A tear ran down her cheek. "That poor little boy. He saw it all, didn't he?"

He nodded. "From the living-room window. The nanny had dragged him inside but he broke away from her and ran to the front window. Everything was over before she reached him."

She wiped the tears from her cheeks with her fingers. "That is the most awful story I've ever heard. I can't believe she took such a risk. How could something as stupid as a job promotion possibly have outweighed the safety of her and her son?"

"It was all such a waste. She was so impatient. So hardheaded. And in trying to have it all, she lost it all, even her own life. And her son has to live with her choice the rest of his life."

As he delivered those words, his expression was a mixture of sadness and anger and something else. Regret? Probably, but deep down, she knew it wasn't that simple. Then a thought sparked in the back of her mind, and the more she contemplated it, the more it made sense.

"Were you involved with her?" she asked. "I mean, on a personal level?"

He sighed and nodded. "She was beautiful, intelligent and driven. I crossed a line I never should have, especially when I was on the job. I invested part of myself in a woman who was just like my mother."

He gave her a rueful smile. "I bet Alex could make a lot out of that one."

She laid her hand on the side of his cheek. "Maybe you should let her try."

"Maybe I will," he said. "It feels good telling you everything. It's hard and sad, but I also feel almost relieved that someone else knows. That someone else understands."

"I'm so sorry you went through that. Sorry for you and her and most of all, for her son. You're right, it was a waste. Anytime you think talking will make you feel better, I'd be happy to listen."

He wrapped his arms around her and gave her a squeeze. "Who listens to you?"

"Oh, well…I don't have things that difficult to deal with."

"Hmm. Well, that offer runs both ways."

She closed her eyes and drank in his masculine scent as his words warmed her even more than the heat from his body had. If only this night could last forever.

Tomorrow would come too soon, and all their problems would be right back in front of them. And once those problems were solved, where did that leave them?

It was a question she wasn't ready to ask.

MAX AWAKENED BEFORE DAWN. Colette was still curled in a ball next to him, sleeping soundly. She was beautiful even when she was worried, but at rest and completely peaceful, she was even more gorgeous. Last night, when he'd been on top of her, inside her, she'd reached the heights of angelic.

He'd thought he was taking a big risk last night, letting down his guard, exposing his darkest secrets, but he felt better than he had in years. Even with his future completely up in the air and even if Colette wasn't part of it, he would never regret last night. It was a reawakening of his heart and soul. He was more energized, more determined, and his first priority was gaining the safety of Anna's mother and the other villagers.

He slipped quietly from the bed, not wanting to disturb Colette. An idea burned at the back of his mind. It was indecently early, but the woman at the museum he needed to talk to was an early bird. She'd probably already put in an hour of work. If anyone could offer a viable solution for the villagers, it would be her.

COLETTE CLUTCHED THE PIECE of paper with the notes she'd taken from Anna during their visit to the hospital that morning as they sped down the highway to Pirate's Cove. They'd had a hard time convincing Anna to give them directions to the place she thought the villagers were hiding, but she'd finally agreed that Max's idea was sound and a permanent solution to the problem of the coins.

Unfortunately, they were pushed to act on it immediately.

Max had received a phone call early that morning from his buddy who was watching Lambert. He'd tailed the man from his house to the highway that led to Pirate's Cove. Apparently, they'd spooked him with their visit the day before, and he was probably desperate to obtain the coins before they did. That desperation combined with his likely already unstable mind made him a complete wild card.

Colette was still asleep when Max awakened her and filled her in on the situation. She hadn't stopped worrying since, afraid of what the man might do to the villagers if he found them before they did.

Max tried to get her to stay behind at the hospital with

Anna, but she'd refused. No way was he going into the swamp alone. She may not be trained for combat, but she was an extra set of eyes and an extra finger on a trigger. Two against one sounded like much better odds to her.

His agreement had been reluctant, and she wondered if he was afraid she'd strike out after him, especially given the horrible story he'd told her the night before. She wasn't that brave or foolish, but saw no reason to elaborate on that as it might change his mind on taking her with him.

"Do you think Lambert is going to Cache?" she asked.

"I think he's going to try to find the villagers."

"But how? If he knew where to find them, he would have been there already."

"I know. I'm afraid he may try to force someone to talk."

"Oh!" Her back tensed up. "Like who?"

"Someone in Pirate's Cove. Someone he thinks knows where their hiding place is."

"And what if they don't know?"

He stared down the highway, a grim expression on his face. "I don't think that would be good."

Colette said a silent prayer that Lambert hadn't gone to extremes. From what she'd seen in his house the day before, he had the weapons to back himself up.

As Max pulled into Pirate's Cove, Danny ran out of the gas station and flagged them down. He hurried up to the Jeep as Max slammed on the brakes.

"I tried to call you a while ago but it went straight to voice mail. That dude, the collector dude, was here and he was all agitated. Kept insisting I tell him where Cache had disappeared to. I told him I didn't have any idea what he was talking about and he finally left."

"Did you see where he went?"

"Hell, yeah, I saw! He went right out back and stole my rental boat."

"How long ago?"

"Twenty minutes, maybe more."

"Can I use your dock?"

"Yeah, man! You going after him?"

"That's the plan." He threw the Jeep in Reverse and backed the boat trailer down the dock behind the gas station.

"There's something else, man!" Danny yelled as Max jumped in the boat. "Tom found the voodoo woman passed out behind his café. It looks like someone worked her over a bit. She's alive, but the waitress is taking her to the hospital in New Orleans."

"Thanks!" Max yelled and gunned the engine on the boat.

The boat barely skimmed the top of the water as they flew down the bayou. Colette gripped the front of the bench every time the boat twisted around a corner or bounced up and down on the choppy water. A north wind ripped across the bayou, the first signs of a front due to hit the parish that evening. The farther they traveled, the stronger the wind blew and the bigger the waves became.

Finally, he was forced to cut his speed down to half in order to keep them safely afloat. Her joints were happy at the reprieve of banging, even though she could see the stress on Max's face. It took another forty-five minutes of pounding before they reached the bank where they'd tied off the day they found Cache.

They were not the only boat there.

Danny's rental boat was pulled up on the bank, and even Colette could see the tracks leading up the bank and into the swamp.

"Do you think the voodoo woman told him where their hiding place is?"

"I hope not."

Max checked his pistol and the shotgun, then handed the shotgun to her. "Take this." He placed his hands over hers as she gripped the gun. "Do not hesitate to use this. If Lambert attacked that woman, he's desperate."

She nodded, the full weight of the situation crashing down upon her. She might be forced to kill another human being, which was in direct opposition to what she did every single day in the emergency room.

"Can you do that?" he asked.

"Yes," she said, momentarily surprised at how easily the word had left her lips and how much she meant it.

"I'm going to move as quickly as possible with as little noise as can be managed. Stick close to me and keep watch. If you see or hear anything, tug on my shirt, but don't speak. I want to keep any advantages we may have."

Max jumped out of the boat onto the bank and reached back to extend his hand to her. She climbed out next to him and followed him into the brush.

He seemed to be in stealth mode as he moved through the thick foliage, deliberately choosing avenues that provided them the most silent entry to Cache. She followed closely behind in silent admiration for his ability to instantly determine the best path without slowing.

When they drew close to Cache, he stopped and put one finger to his lips. He listened for several seconds, but she didn't hear a thing in the gloomy silence of the swamp. Finally, he motioned to her and continued another twenty yards until they reached the edge of the clearing that contained Cache.

He stopped once more and scanned the village. She

peered around him, looking down the rows of shacks, but didn't see anyone stirring.

"Looks empty," he whispered, "but I don't want to take any chances. We'll skirt the edge of the village in the brush until we get to the north side, where Anna's map starts."

She nodded. It was a good plan. That way if anyone was lurking in the village, they wouldn't see them pass through. The last thing they wanted was for someone to follow them to where the villagers were hiding. Max was good at tracking, but he couldn't match the villagers for passing without leaving a trace, nor did they have the time for him to even attempt it.

They made a wide circle around the village, staying about ten yards from the clearing. As the brush allowed, Colette checked the village for any sign of movement and noticed that Max did the same, but it was as still as the swamp surrounding it.

Despite her sweatshirt and the hunting jacket that she'd borrowed from Alex, Colette felt a chill. Something was wrong in this swamp. Something besides the man-eating alligators and rumors of voodoo curses.

Something evil.

She took a deep breath and blew it out slowly, saying a silent prayer that they found the villagers and brought an end to Lambert's reign of terror. Otherwise, she, Anna and the villagers would never be safe again.

MAX PAUSED FOR A MOMENT, listening to the swamp surrounding them. The silence was almost unbearable, making him want to whistle just to cut the tomblike feeling. It was almost as if the swamp needed reminding that living things existed. But such fanciful ideas weren't an option. He could hardly afford to announce their presence.

Checking Anna's map, he gauged their position and
started walking again. He hadn't heard anything when he
stopped, the same as all the other times, but he couldn't
shake the feeling that someone was watching. If the eyes
upon them were human, he hoped it was a villager watching their progress and not Lambert.

More than anything, he wanted the opportunity to take
Lambert down, but not with Colette exposed. No matter
how overwhelming the urge to pummel the guy for what
he'd done to Colette and Anna, once the villagers were
safe, he fully intended to expose Lambert and take him in
with the support and backup of the sheriff's department.

Max traversed the swamp as quickly as he could while
being careful not to misread Anna's directions. It would
be easy to get turned around and lost in the swamp. Anna
had estimated it would take them an hour to reach the
remote location, but a quick glance at his watch let him
know they were already fifteen minutes beyond that mark.

It was too soon to get concerned, but he paid very
close attention to the next marker, a pair of twisted cypress trees next to a stump. Praying that he'd found the
right marker and that things in the swamp hadn't changed
since Anna was last there, he pointed to the right and they
changed direction.

Minutes later, he knew they'd found the right place.

Four men stepped out of the brush, seeming to materi-
alize out of nowhere. They surrounded him and Colette,
shotguns leveled.

Chapter Eighteen

"Hand me the shotgun," one of them said to Colette then looked at Max. "And you, drop your pistol."

Colette flashed a glance at him and he nodded. She handed the shotgun to the man, her hands shaking as she passed it over. Max slowly pulled his pistol from his waistband and dropped it to the ground.

"This way," the man said and waved his shotgun in the direction they'd been walking.

One of the other men picked up the pistol as Max took Colette's hand and followed the first man through the brush.

The hiding place was a smaller version of Cache. There weren't as many shacks and no church at all, but Max figured for temporary housing, it worked fine for their purposes. The man led them to an open area in the center of the shacks. Villagers started easing out of the shacks toward the open area until they formed a circle around Max and Colette.

"What are you doing here?" the man asked.

"We were looking for you, the villagers of Cache. You're in danger."

The man shook his head. "Don't look like anyone's in danger but you."

"Please," Colette said. "My name is Colette Guidry. I

work with Anna and she's desperate to find her mother, Rose."

A woman burst through the circle and ran up to Colette. "You're the woman that my Anna works for at the hospital?"

"Yes."

"How is she? Is she all right? I expected her to come to us, but she didn't."

"She was kidnapped by the bokor on the way to the village. Max found her in the swamp and we took her to the hospital in New Orleans. She's going to be fine, but she's worried about you."

For a moment, the woman looked relieved, then the panicked look was back. "We can't do what the bokor wants, so we hid."

"We know about the coins," Colette said. "And the bokor is just a man in a mask. A really evil man who wants the coins for himself."

"No." Rose shook her head. "The bokor is real."

The man stepped closer to them. "You don't know nothing about our business."

"I know," Max said, "that the bokor is a man named Marshall Lambert. He bought the coins from the pawnshop where Anna sold them."

There was an intake of breath from the villagers, and Rose's hand flew up to cover her mouth. "She sold the coins?"

"To pay for her schooling," Colette explained. "She's very sorry, but I promise you the threat to you is from a very real, very human man."

The man who'd led them to Cache lifted his shotgun in the air. "So if we kill this one man, then we'll be safe again."

The villagers began to cheer.

"I don't think so," Max said. "Too many people know about the coins and Cache. Word will spread and you'll constantly be watching for the next bad guy. But I have an idea of how to solve the problem."

"We can't sell the coins," the man said. "Even if we didn't believe in the curse, we gave our word. That may mean nothing in your world, but it does in ours."

"You don't have to break your word or risk the curse if you do what I'm suggesting," Max said.

The man stared at him, his eyes narrowed, and Max held his breath that they'd actually listen to him.

"Tell us your idea," the man said finally, "and then we'll decide."

"I have a friend who runs a museum. She would like to display the coins at the museum for everyone to see with the agreement that they still belong to the villagers. That way they could never be sold, and no one would look for them in Cache any longer."

The man shook his head. "The coins can't leave Mystere Parish."

"And they won't. The museum is on the south tip of Mystere Parish. Barely in the parish lines, but there."

The man waved one hand in the air and several villagers huddled around him, including Rose. Max assumed they made the decisions for the village.

Colette leaned toward him. "Do you think they'll go for it?" she whispered.

"I hope so."

After several minutes, the man finally turned around and said, "We're interested in your idea. The villagers have had the burden of the coins for a long time. Some would like to leave the village and have different lives. Because of the coins, it's never been allowed, which is why Anna ran. We don't want our children and grandchildren to have no options. We'll talk to your museum lady."

Relief washed over Max for a moment, then he was right back in cop mode. "That's great, but we have a problem right now. The man who wants the coins is here somewhere in the swamp looking for you. He attacked the old woman, Marie, in Pirate's Cove, trying to get information on where to find you."

"Oh, no!" Rose cried out. Another woman stepped up next to her and placed her arm around her shoulders.

"Marie is Rose's mother," the man said. "When she started wandering off, we felt she'd be better off in Pirate's Cove with a friend."

"Does she know how to find this hiding place?"

"If her mind is working properly, yes."

"What can we do to protect ourselves?"

Max took a breath, knowing the villagers would find his suggestion rash and hurried. "By turning over the coins. Get them out of the swamp and allow me to make it known to everyone that they're somewhere safe."

The man turned to the small group he'd conferred with earlier and then all leaned in, their voices only a low rumble that Max couldn't make out. Finally, the man turned and said, "We will give you the coins if you will take them to the museum lady, but if you are lying, not even prayer would save you from the wrath of the pirate who left us to guard them."

"I'm telling the truth. I have nothing to fear from the pirate."

The man nodded. "Then I will take you to where the coins are hidden."

"Thank you," Max said. "You won't regret this."

Rose grabbed Colette's arm. "My daughter? You will tell her I love her?"

"Of course," Colette promised. "As soon as she gets out of the hospital, she can come visit."

Rose shook her head, a sad expression on her face. "Anna made her choice when she left the village. It is against the rules for her to return."

The man looked at the others then at Rose. "We will talk about that later."

He motioned to Max and Colette. "My name is Will. Come with me."

"Can I have my weapon?" Max asked. "In case we run into trouble."

Will handed Max his pistol and Colette the shotgun. "I hope we run into the man who's brought the plague down on this village. I hope I have the clearest shot."

Max stuck the pistol in his waistband, unable to argue with Will's sentiment. "Are we going far?"

"No, but only Rose and me know how to find the hiding place, and only one of us can go there. The other must remain behind so that if something happens, there is someone left who knows where the coins are hidden."

"Then let's get going. I want those coins out of the swamp before Lambert finds this place."

Will nodded and headed into the swamp. Max gave Colette's hand a squeeze and they fell into step behind him.

Max watched closely as Will picked his way through the swamp, but he could see no visible trail that the man was following. The foliage grew even denser the farther they traveled, to the point that it was brushing against them, scratching their arms and faces as they pushed through it. When he glanced back, he realized that the thick foliage had popped right back into place after they passed, creating a wall of branches and dying leaves behind them.

It was a smart move, hiding the coins in an area that

no man would elect to traverse, even to hunt. He glanced at Colette and gave her an encouraging smile. She had been so strong through all of this, despite the fact that she had no training for such things and was completely out of her element. He could tell she was ill at ease in the swamp, but she'd refused to stay behind, and he couldn't help but admire her for that.

He checked his watch and realized they were almost at the twenty-minute mark. He was about to ask Will if they were close when the man stopped walking and pointed to an enormous cypress tree that must have been in the swamp for hundreds of years. The roots of the tree had broken through the ground and swirled around it like tentacles.

Will stepped in between the tentacles and pushed a stone about the size of his head over on the ground. He motioned to Max. "If you don't mind. It's a bit heavy."

Max stepped in between the roots and looked down into the hole. Inside was a chest, about one foot in length and covered with tattered leather. The fake chests in toy stores were modeled after this chest, but this one was the real thing. The real thing with a real bounty of gold. He reached down for the handle on one side while Will grabbed the other and they lifted the chest from the hole.

Max was momentarily surprised at the weight of the chest, but then remembered the density of gold. The chest must be full of it. "How did you manage this alone?" he asked Will as they hefted the chest over the roots and onto the ground next to Colette.

"Well, it's a bit of effort, but I wasn't in a hurry then, either."

Colette reached down and tugged on one end of the chest. "Will I be able to help carry this out of the swamp?"

"You won't have to," Will said. "I'll help you get the chest to Pirate's Cove."

The brush directly behind Colette shook, but before Max could reach for his pistol, Danny Pitre stepped through it, his shotgun pointed directly at Colette.

"Help won't be necessary," Danny said. "I brought a backpack, and with all of you dead, I'll be able to take my time getting out of here."

Colette gasped and the blood drained from her face. Will put his hands up, looking at Max for an answer he didn't have.

"People will come looking for us," Max said. "People who already know what's going on here."

"Sure they will," Danny said. "And what they'll find is you dead and Lambert missing, along with the coins. I should thank you for finding him. He's a perfect cover."

"You called him and told him you knew where Cache was," Max said, everything becoming clear. "You lured him to Pirate's Cove and planted your boat in the swamp to support your story."

"Yep. He rushed right here, and the tail you put on him called you. If you thought Lambert knew where the gold was, I knew you'd try to beat him there. All I had to do was tie Lambert up, tell you he stole my boat and follow you to the gold."

Danny laughed. "All these years living in this town with nothing to offer and there was a fortune in my backyard. It boggles the mind. If that girl hadn't stolen those coins, I never would have known."

"I'll give her your thanks," Max said.

"No, you won't. What I want all of you to do is put down your weapons. One at a time and starting with the pretty girl."

Colette's hands shook as she dropped the shotgun on

the ground at her feet. Her face was pale and her lip quivered. Max wanted so badly to wrap his arms around her and comfort her, and at the same time, he was mentally cursing himself for how all of this had played out. Once again, he had failed the woman he was supposed to protect, and this time, it meant losing everything.

"Now you, pops," Danny said to Will, keeping his shotgun trained on Colette.

Will's jaw flexed and Max knew he was thinking about taking a shot at Danny, but with his shotgun pointed at the ground, there was no way he could get it up and get off a shot before Danny shot Colette. Max held his breath and waited, praying that Will didn't take that risk. Finally, Will tossed his shotgun on the ground in disgust.

"Last up is the lover boy," Danny said. "Slow and easy with that pistol, now, or girlfriend goes first."

Slowly, Max reached for his pistol, but he knew that dropping it was a certain death sentence. He didn't know that he could get a shot off before Danny did, but his chances were a lot better than Will's had been. What he knew for certain was that if he dropped his weapon, they had no chance.

Colette looked over at him and his heart broke in two. He wanted so badly to tell her he loved her, that his entire view on life had changed for the better since meeting her, but he knew he couldn't risk talking. Her eyes met his and the fear faded away from them. It was as if she understood everything he'd been thinking without his saying a word. She moved her head downward an almost imperceptible amount, but Max knew she was telling him to go for it—to take the chance even though it might come at her expense.

Overwhelmed with her trust in him, with her willingness to sacrifice her own life for the others, he tried to focus his mind and body on the split second that was to come. He said a silent prayer that he could make the perfect shot, and hoped that Will was ready to spring into action to back him up.

Chapter Nineteen

Max eased the pistol out of his waistband, trying to put his fingers in the perfect position to make his move. A bead of sweat ran down his forehead and onto his cheek. Every second felt like an eternity as he waited for the right moment, the right second. Danny's eyes were locked on him, his finger whitening on the trigger of the shotgun leveled at Colette.

He inched the pistol forward, waiting, waiting, waiting…and then Danny blinked.

He spun the pistol around in his hand and fired, then launched at Colette, dragging her over behind the cypress roots. Danny screamed and Max's heart dropped. The shot hadn't killed him.

They fell to the ground with a crash and he popped up, ready to take another shot, but Danny already had his shotgun pointed directly at him. He had no time to aim. The shot rang out and he waited for the moment where everything went black, but instead, Danny's mouth dropped and blood began to pour out of it.

A second later he crashed to the ground. Behind him stood Tom, holding a shotgun.

Max jumped up and aimed his pistol at Tom, but he lowered his shotgun and waved a hand at him.

"You won't be needing that," Tom said. "Tell 'em, Will."

Will, who'd been standing in what appeared to be a state of shock, jumped to life. "Thank God, Tom."

Max lowered his pistol as Colette rose from the ground to stand beside him. "You know him?" Max asked.

"Yeah. Tom's our first line of protection. The village has always had one person living in Pirate's Cove looking out for them, directing others away."

"The drawings I found in Cache," Colette said. "The style was similar to the one you did. I just realized."

"All my family was good at drawing," Tom said. "Each generation taught the next."

"You were the one in town keeping an eye on Rose's mother," Max said. "When she yelled that you were one that day, she meant you were one of the villagers."

Tom nodded. "I swear I didn't know it was Danny behind all this, or things wouldn't have gotten this out of hand. When one of the old-timers told me he saw Danny take off after you two, I figured there wasn't any good coming of it. I was hoping to be wrong."

A million thoughts rushed through Max's mind, but the one that kept repeating was *You're alive.* He turned to Colette and placed his hands on her cheeks.

"I love you," he said.

She sucked in a breath, her eyes wide.

"I thought I wouldn't get to say that," he continued, "so I'm saying it now when I know I have the chance. I don't expect you to feel the same and that's fine, but I need to start being honest with myself, and I'm starting now."

Colette threw her arms around him and kissed him softly on the lips. "Are you crazy? Of course I love you."

"I want a life with you, but I have to warn you that I have a lot of issues to address."

"So do I. Maybe Alex will give us a group discount."

Max laughed and wrapped his arms around her, feeling complete for the first time in his life.

MAX WAS TALKING TO THE ambulance driver in Pirate's Cove when Holt's truck screeched around the corner and onto Main Street. He and Alex jumped out and ran over to Max, the worry on their faces clear.

"Are you hurt?" Holt asked.

"No."

Alex threw her arms around him, hugging him tightly, then released him. "Where's Colette?"

Max pointed across the street to the café. "Talking to Tom. He's one of the villagers. A scout of sorts. Apparently, they have always had a lookout in Pirate's Cove."

Alex gave him a wave and hurried across the street to the café.

Holt glanced at the café then back at Max. "I have a feeling you've got a really interesting story to tell."

"Oh, yeah, and it ends with Danny Pitre."

"What about Lambert?"

"We found him in the walk-in cooler in the gas station, single bullet through his head. My guess is Danny intended to feed him to the gators at first opportunity. Then he would have effectively disappeared."

"And everyone would have thought he got away with the coins," Holt finished.

"Yep. Danny played his part well. I never took him for anything else but a gas-station owner."

"Sir," the ambulance driver interrupted. "If you wouldn't mind identifying Danny's body…"

"Sure," Max said, and he and Holt walked over to the gurney behind the ambulance.

The driver pulled the blanket back and Max nodded. "That's Danny Pitre."

He started to pull the blanket back up, but Holt caught the driver's arm.

"What's wrong?" Max asked.

The sleeve of Danny shirt was ripped, maybe during his trip through the swamp. Holt reached over and pulled the cloth aside up close to the shoulder, revealing a nick, likely made from a bullet, and a tattoo.

"I figured I nicked him when he kidnapped Colette."

There was no mistaking the surprised look on his brother's face, but Holt released the shirt and walked away from the gurney.

"Thanks," Max said to the driver, and hurried after Holt.

"You want to tell me what that was about?" Max asked.

Holt blew out a breath. "I didn't want to at this moment, but it's staring me straight in the face."

"That tattoo means something to you?"

Holt nodded. "And you, too."

"What?"

"It was the same tattoo I saw on the man who murdered our father."

It was the last possible thing Max ever expected his brother to say. He staggered backward a couple of steps to lean against the gas-station wall. "You're sure?"

"Yeah. The guy who kidnapped Alex's niece had it, as well. It means something. All of these men are part of something very, very wrong."

"But we're going to find out what?"

Holt clasped Max's hand, and Max could see the relief and hope in his brother's eyes.

"Count on it."

Epilogue

Colette helped Alex transport dishes of food to the picnic table they'd set up on the dock at Holt's cabin. It was sunny and seventy degrees, perfect weather for a Thanksgiving celebration outside. Holt and Max were on the bank frying a turkey and giving each other grief as only brothers could do.

She looked down at the glittering diamond on a platinum band and smiled at Alex. "It's hard to believe…all of this. Sometimes I have to pinch myself so that I'm sure I'm not dreaming."

Alex smiled. "Well, Holt and I couldn't be happier, and Max has been beaming ever since you said yes."

"Like there was any chance of a no. I still think it's sweet that he was worried." Colette looked over at him, unable to believe that so much had happened in a month.

"How did the hospital take you giving notice?" Alex asked.

"They were sad to see me leave, but excited for my new opportunity. I always wanted to pursue being a nurse-practitioner, and running the new Mystere Parish clinic not only gives me the time for school, but they've also agreed to pay for some of the tuition."

"That's great. I'm really happy for you, and even happier that you'll be moving to Vodoun. I was outnumbered here for a while."

"It's amazing how it all fell into place—the villagers giving the coins to the museum and voting to let Anna return to visit her mother. She finished the semester with straight A's, despite everything that happened."

"She's a fighter. Is she excited about coming to work for you at the clinic?"

"Absolutely. She'll be closer to her mother and she says she'll feel more comfortable in a smaller place. I think New Orleans was always a bit overwhelming for her. She can take some of her classes online and will take others at night or on weekends. I'll work her schedule around them."

"Did the sheriff ever find her car?"

"No. We figure Danny dumped it in the bayou somewhere, but she had insurance and it was enough to cover another used car."

Strong arms circled around her from behind, and Colette squealed as Max lifted her off the ground, kissing her neck. He put her back down and she spun around to face him, still in his arms.

He glanced at the table behind her, filled with food. "Looks like everything's perfect."

Colette kissed him softly. "It certainly is."

* * * * *

INTRIGUE...

BREATHTAKING ROMANTIC SUSPENSE

My wish list for next month's titles...

In stores from 15th February 2013:

☐ *Gage* – Delores Fossen

& *Mason* – Delores Fossen

☐ *Alpha One* – Cynthia Eden

& *Internal Affairs* – Alana Matthews

☐ *O'Halloran's Lady* – Fiona Brand

& *Seduction Under Fire* – Melissa Cutler

☐ *Colton's Deep Cover* – Elle Kennedy

Available at WHSmith, Tesco, Asda, Eason, Amazon and Apple

Just can't wait?

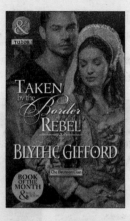

MILLS & BOON®
Book Club

2 Free Books!

Get your free books now at
www.millsandboon.co.uk/freebookoffer

Or fill in the form below and post it back to us

THE MILLS & BOON® BOOK CLUB™—HERE'S HOW IT WORKS: Accepting your free books places you under no obligation to buy anything. You may keep the books and return the despatch note marked 'Cancel'. If we do not hear from you, about a month later we'll send you 5 brand-new stories from the Intrigue series, including two 2-in-1 books priced at £5.49 each and a single book priced at £3.49*. There is no extra charge for post and packaging. You may cancel at any time, otherwise we will send you 5 stories a month which you may purchase or return to us—the choice is yours. *Terms and prices subject to change without notice. Offer valid in UK only. Applicants must be 18 or over. Offer expires 31st July 2013. **For full terms and conditions, please go to www.millsandboon.co.uk/freebookoffer**

Mrs/Miss/Ms/Mr (please circle) _____

First Name _____

Surname _____

Address _____

_____

Postcode _____

E-mail _____

Send this completed page to: Mills & Boon Book Club, Free Book Offer, FREEPOST NAT 10298, Richmond, Surrey, TW9 1BR

Find out more at
www.millsandboon.co.uk/freebookoffer

Visit us Online

0113/I3XEb